LORD *of* SCANDALS
ETHAN

GRACE
BURROWES

sourcebooks
casablanca

Copyright © 2013 by Grace Burrowes
Cover and internal design © 2017 by Sourcebooks, Inc.
Cover art by John Paul

Published by Sourcebooks Casablanca, an imprint of Sourcebooks, Inc.
P. O. Box 4410, Naperville, Illinois 60567-4410
(630) 961-3900
Fax: (630) 961-2168
sourcebooks.com

Printed and bound in Canada.
MBP 10 9 8 7 6 5 4 3 2 1

Also by Grace Burrowes

The Windhams
The Heir
The Soldier
The Virtuoso
Lady Sophie's Christmas Wish
Lady Maggie's Secret Scandal
Lady Louisa's Christmas Knight
Lady Eve's Indiscretion
Lady Jenny's Christmas Portrait
The Courtship (novella)
The Duke and His Duchess (novella)
Morgan and Archer (novella)
Jonathan and Amy (novella)

The MacGregors
The Bridegroom Wore Plaid
Once Upon a Tartan
Mary Fran and Matthew (novella)
The MacGregor's Lady
What a Lady Needs for Christmas

The Lonely Lords
Darius   *Gabriel*
Nicholas   *Gareth*
Beckman   *Andrew*

To those of us to whom Bad Things have happened.

One

"WHERE IN THE BLOODY, BENIGHTED, PERISHING *HELL* ARE my sons?"

Rage and fear drove the exhaustion from Ethan Grey's bones as he tore open closets and peered under beds in what had become the boys' dormitory at Belle Maison.

"Jeremiah! Joshua!" He tried to keep the panic from his voice, but he'd just ridden through a gale-force storm, and it was no kind of night for two little boys to be abroad alone. A long, deafening crack of thunder drowned out Ethan's bellows, and lightning illuminated the room.

All four little beds were empty, the sheets rumpled.

God in heaven, could his sons have taken off with John and Ford and decided to sleep in a tree house tonight of all nights? Ethan had seen a tree hit by lightning before his very eyes not an hour past, and the idea of his sons wandering around at this hour, in this weather...

"I thought I heard you," came a pleasant baritone from the doorway.

Ethan crossed the room in three strides and glared at his younger brother. "I leave my children here with you, Nicholas, so they can get to know their uncle, and I come back to find it's damned near midnight, they're nowhere to be found, and you've lost not one but four little boys. Well?"

More thickly muscled and even taller than Ethan, Nick yet managed to project a benevolence Ethan would never possess. "The children are safe. Come, I'll show you."

Safe... The word registered, but the empty beds had registered first.

"The storm has all the children awake," Nick went on easily, but he cast a curious glance over his shoulder at his older brother. "I'm surprised you decided to travel tonight."

"I told you I'd be here tonight." In truth, Ethan had told his sons he'd be back to Belle Maison on this specific date. At five and six, Joshua and Jeremiah were literalists with faultless memories. If Ethan expected them to keep their word—and he did—then he was hell-bent on keeping his word to them.

"You said you'd be back." Nick paused outside another door on the third floor. He signaled Ethan to wait, conferred momentarily with the footman at the end of the corridor, then returned to the door. "But unless I miss my guess, you've ruined a fine pair of boots, put yourself in a foul humor, and are likely courting lung fever as well."

Ethan's retort was cut off by Nick's motion for silence. Slowly, Nick opened the door then gestured for Ethan to peek through.

He saw a bedroom apparently used for nannies and

governesses, but a well-appointed room nonetheless. The fire had been built up, and there on the hearth rug were his two sons, one on each side of some governess-type female. She sported a gray dress, a book in her lap, glasses on her nose, and a bunned-up coiffure that did not countenance disorder from a single dark hair.

Two more little boys flanked Joshua and Jeremiah. Nick's wife sat across the rug from the governess, an arm around the Belmonts' daughter, Priscilla.

"And the big, nasty wolf," the governess said, "who had very malodorous breath from eating a deal of onions with his supper, said, 'I shall bite off your toes and bite off your noses...'"

"Wolves don't eat onions," Jeremiah interjected.

"On their steaks, they do, and this wolf liked them in his lamb and mutton sandwiches too."

"What was his name?" Joshua asked. "The wolf. He has to have a name."

"We shall call him..." The governess—a drab creature with an unaccountably pretty voice—glanced up from her book at Ethan and Nick in the doorway. "Mr. Grey. Good evening."

"Papa?" Joshua and Jeremiah were on their feet, and Joshua had even taken a few running steps toward Ethan when Jeremiah's hand shot out and grabbed his little brother's nightshirt.

"Hello, Papa," Jeremiah said, his voice quavering. "Uncle Nick said we might have more stories because of the storm. Priscilla was frightened."

"Of course you must have more stories tonight." Nick ambled into the room and lowered himself to sit beside his countess. "Your aunt Leah wasn't frightened, but I was a little nervous. She decided if she was going to read me stories, you children should have a few extra as well."

Ethan realized his sons were watching him warily, as were the other boys, and the girl; even Nick and Leah seemed to be regarding him with some caution. The governess, however, merely blinked at him through her spectacles and bent her head to the book.

She ran her finger down the page. "This wolf with the predilection for onions, he might like us to get on with the story. We were reaching the part he likes best."

"Papa?" Jeremiah stood before his father, back more militarily straight than any six-year-old should stand, his hand still clutching his brother's nightshirt.

Ethan tried for a smile, telling himself he was glad they were safe, glad there'd been an innocent explanation for his sons wandering the house at a late hour. "Of course you may finish the story. I'll see you both in the morning. My regards to the wolf." He nodded in the general direction of the women and children, then at Nick, and turned to leave.

"I'll walk with you," Nick said, rising in one smooth movement. "I am still afraid of the storm and require company on my way to my bed. Children, let Miss Portman get her rest; Leah, I *will* wait up for you, and I have sworn off onions for life."

He blew his wife a kiss, growled at the boys, bowed to Priscilla, and waved to the governess. Had there been a dog in the room, Nick would likely have scratched its cheerfully proffered belly before he took his leave.

"My apologies for interrupting the fairy-tale festival," Ethan said as they traversed the house to the second floor. His boots—a pair he'd just broken in to his satisfaction—were squishing. Walking the last two miles rather than riding a panicked horse was likely to ruin one's footwear.

"You reassured your sons you were safely home," Nick said, "and you would have been welcome to join us, you know. Miss Portman does the best job with the old standards. Makes me wish I were a little boy."

"You are a little boy. You're just the largest little boy in the realm." He eyed Nick's great golden length as they approached his bedroom, and got a complacent nod for his comment.

"Was there something you wanted, Nicholas?" Ethan asked, opening the door. He saw a footman setting up screens by the fire, indicating Nick had ordered him a bath.

"Some time with my brother, perhaps?" Nick suggested, following Ethan into the room uninvited. "There's food on the way up, too, and you don't need to tell me the roads were horrible."

"A tree was hit by lightning not fifty feet from the road." Ethan squished over to the fireplace and settled into a cushioned chair, which would no doubt bear stains from where his damp fundament came to rest. "Argus nearly tossed me in the ditch, and I walked him in hand from that point."

He started tugging on his boots, only to feel a stabbing ache in his back brought on by walking in the mud, being cold and wet for hours, and having gone without decent sleep for more nights than he could count.

"Allow me." Nick grasped the heel and toe of one boot and gave a stout tug. The boot barely moved, so Nick turned around, stepped over Ethan's calf, and tugged more firmly. By degrees, the wet boot gave up its hold on Ethan's equally soaked foot. The second boot was no easier, and in truth, Ethan wasn't sure he could have gotten them off himself.

"My thanks." Ethan rose—carefully—and hung his wet waistcoat over the back of a chair. "Shouldn't you be in bed with your wife?"

"We *were* in bed, then we heard the patter of little feet—even over the thunder. Leah thought she heard Priscilla get out of bed. When we went to investigate, we found the boys were all awake, two to a bed, so Miss Portman hailed them across the hall for a story."

None of which explained why a belted earl had troubled himself with the doings in the nursery.

"Doesn't Leah need her rest?" Ethan asked, tugging his shirt over his head and glancing around for somewhere dry to hang it.

"Give it to me." Nick hung the shirt over a bedpost, like a wet flag of surrender. "Your breeches too, and those stockings."

"The stockings are beyond repair." Ethan paused to yawn then stepped out of his remaining clothes and considered the tub. "I thought I was too tired to soak. I was wrong—you will note the occasion, it being a rarity." He crossed the room and lowered himself into the steaming water with a grateful sigh.

Now if only Nicholas would take himself off.

"When did you get so cynical?" Nick asked, going to the wardrobe and extracting towels and a bar of hard-milled soap.

"When I was fourteen."

Nick frowned but said nothing, passing Ethan the soap, which Ethan sniffed.

"Clove. This has to be expensive."

"Not particularly." Nick resumed his seat on the stool. "It lasts quite a while. So how is our dear brother Beckman?"

"This cannot wait until morning?" One very large male foot emerged from the water, was lathered, and subsided like a retreating sea monster.

"Morning." Nick crossed his arms over his chest. "At the breakfast table we have my houseguests, the Belmonts, all three delightful people, but Priscilla's voice when she's trying to get attention would cut frozen glass. Then we have the real entertainment, as our nephew Ford and Leah's brother John, both being five, still sport the peculiarly shrill voices of the very young. Your own two are models of decorum, of course, but often inspired by their confreres. Then we have Nita, Kirsten, and Suzannah, our sisters, whom we love to distraction even first thing in the morning, and let us not forget little sister Della, whose dramatics can be counted on to get the day off to a rollicking start."

Ethan regarded his brother with a slight smile, comforted to know not all the local miseries were born of wet boots and an aching back.

"Other than the assault to your ears at breakfast, does all go well for you?" With their father's death less than three months previous, Nick had inherited the earldom of Bellefonte. He'd married mere days before the old earl's passing, and had taken up residence at Belle Maison with his family only at the start of the summer.

"Well enough. There is a great deal to be done, of course, and Papa's affairs are not yet entirely settled. You saw Beckman?"

"I did." Ethan dunked and scrubbed his hair clean

to give himself time to fashion a report. "Our brother is as brown as a savage and roundly displeased with Lady Warne for letting Three Springs get into such a sorry condition, but he's doing a nice job with the place. He hasn't entirely gotten things sorted out with the housekeeper, though."

That should be enough of a hint without violating fraternal confidences.

"Oh?" Nick passed Ethan a glass of brandy, then rose to answer a knock at the bedroom door. When he returned, he was carrying a tray with meat, cheese, buttered bread, a bowl of strawberries, and a steaming bowl of soup.

Ethan regarded the tray and found the strength to dunk again and rise from the warmth and comfort of the tub. "Towel?"

"A moment." Nick set the tray down and picked up one of the two ewers of rinse water. "Eyes closed." With his superior height, Nick could pour the water directly over his brother's head, sluicing Ethan clean from the crown downward.

"Your towel." Nick passed Ethan a bath sheet and stepped back, taking both drinks and the tray over to the hearth while Ethan dried off. He stepped into the dressing gown Nick held for him and settled into a chair.

"You would make somebody a good wife, Nicholas."

"Valeting my brother is hardly a difficult skill." Nick passed Ethan the bowl of soup. "Finish this, or I will tattle to our sisters."

"Beck sends them his love," Ethan said after several spoonfuls of soup. He made and then devoured a sandwich, while Nick sipped his drink and watched the fire.

"Is there something you're not telling me, Nicholas?" Ethan asked when the sandwich had also disappeared.

"I want you to think about something," Nick said, still staring at the fire. "But just think about it. I'm not sure I'm entirely comfortable with it myself."

"Think about what?" Growing up, the most harebrained schemes—also the most fun—were always Nick's, but Nick's tone was serious now.

"How would you feel about leaving your boys here, with me and Leah? We've offered to take her brother Trent's children for the nonce, and all four boys are of an age. They've had great fun these past few weeks, and we've enjoyed having them."

What the hell? "Leave Joshua and Jeremiah here? With you? You just met them, Nick, and why are you taking in Leah's brother's children? Belle Maison is large enough, I know, but it isn't as if the place is empty. What makes you think you can have my sons too?"

Ethan was on his feet by the time he finished, and pacing in a rising temper. A throbbing started up at the base of his skull; an old rage at Nicholas and his high-handed notions throbbed along with it.

"When Ford goes back to his father's house," Nick said, "Leah's brother John will have no company here his own age. I'm not asking that Josh and Jeremiah bide here permanently, but it might make sense in the near term."

Ethan scowled at him. "You aren't thinking. Of course they're having a romping good time here this summer, of course the little boys are becoming fast friends, but what then? What about when Trent Lindsey recalls he has an heir, and Ford is whisked away? What about when they have a falling out, and

Joshua and Jeremiah aren't such good companions for John anymore? What about when we have to separate them again, when they've already grown as close as brothers?"

Old, old wounds—wounds that should have long since healed—lurked beneath Ethan's volley of questions.

"I am only asking that you consider it," Nick said mildly as he rose, "and it is an offer, not a request. I would not have raised it now, but my impression was you intended to repair to Tydings fairly soon."

"Fairly." Ethan made an effort to rein in his temper. "We can discuss this later, but I am their only parent, Nick. I have to decide what is best for them."

Nick smiled at Ethan, all amiability, while Ethan wanted to wallop his brother, regardless of fatigue, headache, or backache. "Of course you do. Whether you want to or not. Good night, Ethan, and I'm glad you're here, safe and sound."

"Good night, Nicholas. You aren't too afraid of the storm to walk back to your rooms alone?"

"Go to hell, Ethan." Nick turned to leave but not before Ethan saw his smile. "And sweet dreams."

"Scream if you see the wolf," Ethan rejoined. Nick blew him a kiss and left, closing the door softly behind him.

Ethan sat by the fire, running a hand through his damp hair. He made himself another sandwich and lounged back, realizing part of his headache—not all—had been derived from hunger.

And some from fatigue. Ethan's mind, however, was still slogging through storms, including the hail of correspondence he'd picked up at Tydings after his visit with Beck. There were all manner of memoranda, letters, and reports from his factors and agents, but there was also a letter of resignation from the boys' latest tutor, who had been ostensibly holidaying with his sister in Bath.

Of course he was. Ethan gave a mental snort. More likely, Mr. Harold had been looking for a new position, somewhere far from Ethan Grey, bastard firstborn of the late Earl of Bellefonte, and his hellion offspring. It was a pity, too, because Harold had been making some progress with the boys academically.

Maybe Nick was right, Ethan thought as he negotiated the steps up to the bed. Maybe the boys should stay here. Ethan didn't like the idea, but he'd accommodated ideas he hated, and survived.

As his tired mind slowed then began to drift toward sleep, Ethan's last thought was neither of commerce, correspondence, his feelings for his younger brother, his station in life, nor the prospect of parting from his children. His last thought as he drifted off was worthy of Nick prior to that fellow's recent marriage.

It would have been deuced pleasant to snuggle up to a warm, sweet-scented governess and let her spin tales of ferocious wolves and brave little porkers, rather than battle storms in the mud, rain, and dark of night.

෴

When the sun rose on a glorious summer morning, Ethan rode out with Nick to survey the storm damage. While the horses splashed along muddy lanes, Nick commenced the interrogation Ethan had no doubt been spared the previous night:

What was Nick to do with their dear brother George, whose left-handed tendencies were ever a worry?

Ethan suggested foreign service, the Continent being more enlightened in at least a few regards.

Would Ethan attend Nick's investiture in the autumn?

Ethan replied in the affirmative, not feeling it necessary to add that the request touched him.

And why wasn't a man as good looking and wealthy as Ethan Grey remarried?

Argus had shied spectacularly at that query, almost as if the beast perceived his master's reaction to the question.

Ethan was equally leery of the afternoon's planned diversion—a picnic involving women, children, and all manner of noise, bother, and uninvited insects. Rather than subject himself to same, Ethan decided on the more familiar torment of dealing with his correspondence.

He opened the door to the library, thinking it would almost be a relief to bury himself in commerce, when he heard an odd, muffled sound from the couch over by the hearth. A dog, perhaps, having a dream, but Nick didn't have house dogs—he had house cats, instead, claiming they were prettier, quieter, better smelling, and capable of placating women and eradicating mice.

Ethan closed the door behind him and crossed the room, only to find the Belmonts' small daughter hugging a pillow, obviously in distress.

"I beg your pardon?" Ethan wasn't sure how one dealt with a balled-up little girl who had a death grip on a pillow. "It's Priscilla, isn't it?"

Big teary brown eyes peered up at him. The child whipped her braids over her shoulder and clung to her pillow. "Go away, please."

"I'd like to," Ethan said, lowering himself to the couch, "or better still, I'd like you to find somewhere else to wax lachrymose, but you are a lady, and I am a gentleman, so we'll have to muddle through. Here."

She glared at him past his monogrammed handkerchief, then sat up, scrubbed at her eyes, honked into the handkerchief, and proffered it to Ethan.

"You're to keep it, child."

"Is it a token?" Priscilla looked at the damp linen. "It smells ever so lovely, like fresh trees and Christmas. I'm too young to accept tokens, except from family."

So young and so artlessly charming. Thank God he had only sons. "It's a handkerchief. Now, why were you crying?"

"My heart is breaking." She sighed a larger sigh than one little girl ought to contain. "I will write much better stories after this."

"You will divulge the particulars of this tragedy, if you please. I have correspondence to tend to."

"Miss Portman is leaving me. She's says I have grown too smart for her, and it's time I had tutors, not just a governess."

Ethan settled in more comfortably on the couch, though the need to deal with his correspondence nagged at him. "You are suffering a consequence of growing up. These are ever more inconvenient than adults might represent."

"I hate it. Next I'll have to wear a corset, curl my hair, and learn to flirt."

Her tone suggested a worse fate had never befallen a young lady. "Don't panic. I think you have some time before those miseries beset you."

"Papa says the same thing, but he never wants me to grow up. He had only boys with his other wife, and I am his only girl."

"His only daughter for now." Ethan's eyes had told him Mrs. Matthew Belmont was in anticipation of a happy event. "You will correspond with Miss Portman when she moves to her next post, will you not?"

"I don't know." The girl smoothed out the linen on her lap. She had a grass stain on one bony little knee, and her pinny was hopelessly wrinkled. "I am not too smart for her, and she can be my tutor. She just wants to go, is all. I am mad at her for that."

Children were horrendously canny when it came to sniffing out adult prevarications. Little Priscilla's governess might well be simply tired of the child.

"Maybe she wants to leave while you still think she's smart and you still like her. She doesn't want you to be smarter than she is. Word of advice, though?"

Priscilla nodded, apparently willing to entertain a confidence from a man who looked like her friend Wee Nick.

"You can be angry any time you please," Ethan said, "but it could be that you are only picking a fight because you're hurt, and maybe a little scared—scared because you like Miss Portman and you might not like your tutors as much."

Priscilla kept her gaze on her lap. "I'll miss her."

And a child could miss loved ones passionately. A man, thank God, knew better.

"She'll miss you too," Ethan said, hoping it was true for the child's sake. "If you're really her friend, though, you want her to be happy. And I think you can trust your mama and papa to find you tutors you get along with."

Outside the door, a herd of small feet thundered past, young voices shrieking about pony carts, kites, and a race to the orchard.

"I have to go now." Priscilla scrambled off the couch, flung a curtsy toward Ethan, and raced to join in the happy affray.

Ethan closed the door as a rankling notion stole into his brain: Nick would see to it Joshua and Jeremiah had the best of tutors and nannies. He'd also *play* with them, as Ethan most assuredly did not. Ethan shoved that thought back into whatever mental dungeon it had sprung from and turned his attention to a pile of letters, some water stained around the edges. He was halfway through a reply to the steward of his sheep farms in Dorset when the library door again opened.

"Excuse me." The governess—Miss Porter? no, Miss Portman—admitted herself to the room and closed the door behind her. "I'm returning one book and fetching another. My pardon for disturbing you, Mr. Grey."

Ethan half rose from his seat and gestured toward the shelves. "Help yourself." He paused to rub his eyes. They'd been stinging more and more of late, and sometimes watered so badly he had to stop what he was doing altogether and rest them. He rose from the desk and came around to lean against the front of it, watching as the governess bent to put the large volume of fairy tales on the bottom shelf.

"It's Miss Portman, isn't it?"

She rose slowly, as if feeling Ethan's gaze on her, and turned. "Alice Portman." She bobbed a hint of a curtsy. "You are Nicholas's brother, Mr. Ethan Grey, father to Joshua and Jeremiah."

"You call the earl Nicholas?" Ethan concluded she was one of those plain women who'd grown fearless in her solitary journey through life. He respected that, even as he had to concede there was something about Alice Portman's snapping brown eyes he found… compelling. Her shape was indeterminate, owing to the loose cut of her gown, her dark brown hair was imprisoned in some kind of chignon, and her gaze had an insect-like quality as a result of the distortion of her spectacles. All in all, Ethan suspected she was a woman of substantial personal fortitude.

She held his gaze with a steadiness grown men would envy. "When I met your brother, he was mucking stalls in Sussex and content to be known as Wee Nick. I do not use his title now, because he has insisted it would make him uncomfortable were I to do so."

This recitation was a scold. Ethan mentally saluted her for the calm with which she delivered it. "No doubt it would."

She turned back to the books, but rather than bend down to the lower shelf, she sat on the floor cross-legged, as she'd sat on the rug the previous night. Then, she'd been swaddled in another plain, unremarkable dress, and banked with children on either side. For all her primness, she'd looked comfortable with the informality, if a little disgruntled to be interrupted.

Ethan's correspondence started whining at him, but his eyes still stung too.

"So what did you name him?" Ethan asked. "The wolf with the unfortunate predilection for onions, that is."

"That was a challenge," Miss Portman said as she surveyed the children's books on the bottom shelf. "Pris, being of a dramatic frame of mind, wanted to name him Sir Androcles of Lobo."

"Wasn't Androcles a lion?"

The governess turned her head and beamed a full-blown, pleased smile at Ethan. "Why, Mr. Grey, I am impressed, but Androcles was the young man who took the thorn from the lion's paw. The lion never earned his own sobriquet."

"Lobo is Spanish for wolf," Ethan said, his gaze straying around the room lest he betray a reaction to that smile. Ye gods, the plain, prim, buttoned-up Miss Portman had the smile of a benign goddess, so warm and charming it hurt to see.

"Pris is learning Spanish, French, and Italian from her uncle Thomas, who is a noted polyglot." Miss Portman chose a book, frowned at it, and put it right back.

"What's wrong with that one?" Ethan asked, amused at her expression.

"No pictures," she explained. "Who in their right mind prints a storybook for children without pictures?"

"Somebody trying to save money on production costs. Did the wolf acquire a name?" He was asking to be polite, to make small talk with somebody who was likely not much befriended below stairs.

"He acquired various names." Miss Portman chose another book and opened it for perusal. "Wolfgang Wolf was John's nomination. Ford, being our youngest, voted for Poopoo Paws Wolfbottom."

She said this with a straight face, which had probably made the children laugh all the harder.

"And the winner was?" Ethan hopped off the desk and crossed the room to help the lady to her feet. She frowned delicately—a puzzlement rather than a rebuke, Ethan surmised—then put her bare hand in his and let him draw her up from the floor.

"Lord Androcles Wolfgang Poopoo Paws Wolfbottom Wolf the Fourth," she recited. "Children like anything that makes the telling of a story longer and are ever willing to mention certain parts of the anatomy."

"I see." What he saw was a flawless complexion, velvety brown eyes staring up at him in wary consternation, and a wide, full mouth that hid a gorgeous smile. He stepped back and dropped her hand accordingly.

"I am off." Miss Portman edged around him in the confines of the shelves, and Ethan caught a whiff of lemons. Of course she'd wear lemon verbena. This was probably a dictate in some secret manual for governesses.

"You haven't joined the cavalcade of pony carts making for the scene of this bacchanal?" Ethan asked, standing his ground.

"I am not fond of equines," Miss Portman replied. "Nor of animals in general, though I can appreciate the occasional cat. I choose to walk instead. The exercise is good for me, and I am less likely to be ridiculed by the children for my fears."

"Shall I provide you escort?" Ethan heard himself ask.

Now where in the bloody, benighted *hell* had that come from? "It's a pretty day," Ethan went on, the same imp of inspiration not yet done with him. "I've missed my family, and I can work on correspondence any time."

She wanted to refuse him. From the fleeting look in her eyes, Ethan deduced that his company ranked below that of Mr. Wolfbottom Wolf after a large meal of mutton and onion sandwiches.

And wasn't that cheering, to find one's company distasteful to a mere governess?

"Don't let me impose, Miss Portman." Ethan offered her a polite retreat. A bastard, even a wealthy one with passable looks, learned the knack of polite retreats. "I can always saddle my gelding and join the party later." He saw his mistake when her eyes narrowed, saw she took the reference to his horse as a personal taunt.

"My apologies." He was not sorry, he was behind in his correspondence. "I meant no offense, but you do not seem at a loss for company."

"I am not," she replied, peering at him. "Your children need to spend time with you outside this house, and you can carry the blanket and the book. Shall we?"

Oh, she was good, reducing him to the status of her bearer and making him work for even that privilege. An idea blossomed in the back of Ethan's mind, borne of the realization she'd tamed the precocious Priscilla and could likely handle younger children even more easily. He let this idea unfurl in his awareness, where he could consider it from several angles at his leisure.

"Let me tidy up the desk," he said, "while you find us that blanket, and I'll join you in the kitchen momentarily."

"As you wish." She whisked off, her words implying Ethan had arranged matters to his own satisfaction, when in fact, he was at a loss to explain what he was doing trundling after a prim spinster to spend hours swatting flies and trying not to let the shrieks of children offend his beleaguered ears.

When he met Miss Portman in the kitchen, she sported a wide, floppy straw hat on her head, a blanket over her arm, and the book in her hand. She wore gloves as well, which should not have surprised Ethan, but disappointed him for some reason.

"There's a shortcut to the orchard through the home wood," Ethan said as they left the house. He'd rolled the book into the blanket and tucked the blanket under his right arm, leaving his left free for escort duty.

Except the lady was striding off across the terrace like she was intent on storming the Holy Land single-handedly.

Ethan waited by the back door. "Miss Portman?"

"Sir?" She perfectly matched his condescending tone. His own children could not have mimicked him more precisely.

"When one escorts a lady," he said, "one generally offers the lady his arm." He winged his elbow at her and waited. He was disproportionately gratified to see Alice Portman blush to the roots of her lovely·dark hair. Petty of him, but there it was.

"My apologies." Alice strode back to his side, put her hand on his arm as if he were clothed with venomous snakes, and fixed her bespectacled gaze straight ahead. Had she started singing some stalwart old hymn, he would not have been surprised.

"Is it really so distasteful, Miss Portman, to stroll with a gentleman on a pretty day?" Ethan asked, setting a deliberate pace.

"I am not used to the company of gentlemen." Gentlemen might have been "grave robbers" or "highwaymen" in the same inflection. "Most men don't know what to do with me if they know I'm a governess. I'm considered above the maids, but certainly not family. I'm not spoken for, but I'm not fair game, rather like taking holy orders. It can be awkward."

She was blunt, which he liked. At the rate they

were going, their progress would take some time. "I have the impression this might be awkward for the gentlemen, but not particularly so for you."

"I am content to be what I am," Miss Portman said, her posture unbending a little.

"So content"—Ethan's tone was as mild as the breeze—"that I found little Priscilla crying into her pillow in the library this morning, for her friend Miss Portman is abandoning her."

Miss Portman paused minutely in her forward progress, and Ethan regretted his comment. Her feet hadn't stumbled, but he sensed her resolve momentarily wavering.

"Priscilla is dramatic," she said at length. "She will learn one can survive the comings and goings of others in one's life."

"Not an easy lesson for a girl. Has she really outgrown you?"

Miss Portman turned her head to glare at him. "Yes, she has, Mr. Grey. Priscilla has her uncle's facility for languages, and while I can teach her some drawing-room French, I cannot by any means provide what she needs. She shows an equal propensity for mathematics, which I believe she sees as just another language, and she needs a teacher who cannot simply keep up with her but who can challenge and guide her. The intellect of a child must be nurtured carefully if learning is to be made a lifelong habit."

"Even the intellect of a girl child?" He said it to goad her, to keep the fire in her brown eyes and the animation in her expression. If his sisters could have heard him, though, he'd be minced meat. He should be minced meat, in fact.

She would have stomped off had Ethan not caught her hand.

"My apologies." He bowed slightly over her hand. "The question was unworthy of me, and you are right to take umbrage."

"Umbrage?" Miss Portman snatched back her hand. "Umbrage is taken by vicars and duchesses, Mr. Grey. I am *offended* you would question the appropriateness of developing a mind as talented as little Priscilla's. Given the unfortunate circumstances of her birth, her education might someday be all she has to fall back on."

"Mr. Belmont wouldn't allow that," Ethan said. Hell, Nick wouldn't allow that. "I wouldn't allow it."

"You barely know her," Miss Portman shot back, but her tone had taken on an edge of curiosity.

"I don't know her well, personally," Ethan said, "but I do know, personally, what it's like to be raised with only immediate family for company, Miss Portman. I know what it's like to have my mother's name as my own, what it's like to require letters and dispensations to be able to claim any tie to my titled father. Priscilla's parents can love her—mine loved me, after their fashion—but they cannot ease her path through life once she leaves their care."

She stomped along in silence beside him, and Ethan could only guess at the thoughts rocketing around behind her grim expression.

He was about to open his mouth to stumble through further apologies, when a rabbit bolted from the undergrowth, followed closely by a second of the same species. His companion startled, gave a muffled shriek, and then toppled sideways, her gloved hand slipping from his grasp as she fell.

Two

IN THE INSTANT BETWEEN LOSING HER BALANCE AND knowing she was going to fall, Alice had time for thoughts.

Please, God, not this, not now, with the arrogant and condescending Mr. Grey on hand to witness it, and only him to help me. Please…

"I've got you." The words were gruff, the grip on her arms ungentle, but the way Ethan Grey held her against his chest was secure and such a relief Alice hung there, catching her balance in something very like an embrace.

"I've got you," Mr. Grey said again, his grip relaxing, though he didn't step back.

And neither did Alice. The near fall had scared her; the near falls always scared her, had her heart hammering in her chest, her breath coming too quickly, and memories—the worst memories in her possession—obliterating rational processes.

Panic swirled close. Alice forced her breathing to slow rather than allow that panic any closer.

"Here." Mr. Grey tugged at her, his arm slipping around her waist as he guided her to a fallen tree large enough to sit on. He tossed the folded blanket over the tree and urged her down, sitting beside her with his arm still around her waist.

Ethan Grey was an awful man. He beat his children, and Alice hadn't once caught him smiling; but he was tall, strong, and solid, and he smelled of cedar and safety. When he urged her against him, she leaned just a little.

"You're pale as a ghost," he said, his tone displeased. "If I had smelling salts, I'd be waving them under your nose. Are you going to faint?"

She shook her head, though she had to swallow twice to find her voice.

"I have a bad hip," she said, eyes on her lap so he couldn't see her embarrassment. "When it gives out, it can lame me for a considerable time, and the house is not close."

"As if I'd leave you here for the gamekeeper to discover on his fall rounds some months hence. Does your hip pain you now?"

"You caught me in time." Though her hip did pain her. It pained her nigh constantly, and this little slip would mean a bad night at least. It could have been so very much worse. "My thanks."

"Hmm." He regarded her, no doubt seeing her lips pinched against pain, her complexion pale, and her composure—upon which she prided herself—eluding her. "Has your hip always been unreliable?"

He made it sound as if her hip was a shifty, shady sort of character, not a body part they shouldn't even be alluding to.

"I wasn't born this way." She glanced up at him, some of her irritation coming back, and wasn't that a relief, probably to them both. "It's worse if I'm tired, or I try to move too quickly."

"We're about halfway between the house and the orchard. What's your pleasure?" He stood with his hands on his hips, looking put out. That was some comfort.

"Press on," she said, trying to rise, only to find Mr. Grey's hand on her arm restraining her.

"Soon." His eyes—a startlingly handsome blue—lit with what had to be his version of humor. "Rest a minute longer, Miss Portman. You can do it if you put your considerable will to it."

She shot him a truculent glare, which caused his mouth—also curiously well formed—to quirk up in a smile. The expression was unexpectedly charming on him, taking years off his features and giving an astonishingly winsome aspect to her escort.

Manners compelled her to smile back.

"Is this hip of yours the reason you do not enjoy horses?" he asked, glancing around at the surrounding woods.

"In part," she replied, thinking again he talked as if her joint were naughty. "I can sit a horse if I have to, but it's very hard to get on and off, and I pay for the privilege."

"This is why God invented coaches, perhaps. Though for my part, they are mortally stuffy and cramped."

"One can see how this might be true for you."

"I cannot help my height, Miss Portman."

"I don't refer to your height, Mr. Grey." She shifted, testing her hip and wincing at the result. "I refer to what might be a familial tendency to take the reins rather than be a passenger."

"You still hurt." He treated her to a frown while some lunatic bird started chirping above them. "And yes, as a family we tend to charge forth rather than sit back. Shall I pass some time reading to you?"

"Fairy tales?" She resisted the temptation to smirk. "That might be entertaining."

"Not nearly so much as it might be were you to read to me."

"What?" She frowned right back at him, wondering if he was attempting to flirt with her in some backhanded way. "You could do better than Lord Androcles Wolfgang Poopoo Paws Wolfbottom Wolf the Fourth?"

"Not on my best day, but we might get the story actually read."

"And then it would be bedtime, Mr. Grey. Were you truly never a child? Nicholas would have me believe you were, but he likes to tease."

He eyed her up and down, his disapproval now encompassing her entire corpus. "I can see Wee Nick taking on the challenge of teasing you with some degree of relish, but yes, I was once upon a time a child, though it was long ago and far away, and a folly briefly concluded. I am debating fetching my horse to ferry you to our destination."

Alice waved a hand that had lost its glove—drat the luck. "No horses, please. If we take our time and avoid steep cliffs and earthquakes, I can manage."

"Very well." He rose, looking none too happy with her decision, which yielded a measure of satisfaction in itself. "If you please?" He extended his bare hand, and when Alice laced her fingers through his, he drew her to her feet, tucked his arm around her waist, and held her to his side.

"We are to promenade?"

"Let's see how you fare through the woods. If you're foot-sound, you can charge across the orchard at a dead run." She stiffened, contemplating a rousing good argument, then realized their verbal altercation would take place with his arm about her waist.

As that would hardly serve—and her hip hurt, and her escort was tall and strong—Alice set off at a sedate pace.

⤫

As he guided Miss Portman along through the sunlight and shadows of the old woods, Ethan had an odd sense of pleasurable discovery.

Alice Portman was in disguise. She looked all prim and tidy, not a hair out of place, but she smelled delectable—not just lemons, but something more too—spices both soothing and intriguing. And against a man's body, she felt quite... feminine. She was apparently wearing only country stays—a married man learned of these things, will he, nil he—and her breasts were pleasingly full. Then too, no corset on earth could disguise the feminine swell of a woman's hips.

"Are you in pain?" Ethan asked as they strolled along.

"A little," she admitted, but he wasn't fooled, so he moved slowly with her, mindful of her steps, and while his grip was snug, it was also careful.

"We're almost out of the woods," Ethan said, forcing himself to adopt a more conventional escort's stance. "You will take my arm, Alice Portman, and you will behave."

"Yes sir, Mr. Grey." She rolled her eyes, likely forgetting her straw hat had fallen down her back, revealing her face to Ethan's view. Nonetheless, she wrapped her hand into the crook of his elbow and honestly let him take some of her weight.

Priscilla spotted them first and came gamboling over to grab her governess's free hand. "We've made you a necklace of clover, and Papa showed me how to skip rocks, because Wee Nick was tossing the boys into the water, and boys don't skip as well as rocks, at least our boys."

"Ethan!" Nick's voice rang with pleasure as they crossed the green to the grassy bank of the stream. "You honor us. Now get out of those boots and help me repel the pirates trying to board my ship. Alice, release the prisoner into my custody. He'll be a good boy, or we'll make him walk the plank."

A chorus of juvenile voices took up the cry, "Walk the plank!" which Nick quelled by slapping water in the direction of the four sopping-wet boys trying to splash him back from the shallows.

For a total of five boys, if one included the earl.

There was no hope for it. Ethan aimed a scowl at the child capering around on Miss Portman's other side. "Miss Priscilla, you will not yank on Miss Portman's arm. We are setting a dignified example for my hopeless little brother."

"Younger brother," Priscilla corrected him. "I still have your handkerchief, Mr. Grey."

"Pleased to hear it," Ethan said, wondering if he could get out of joining Nick and his band of cutthroats in the stream.

"Go on." Miss Portman dropped his arm. "If you take Nick down, you will be a hero in the eyes of little boys throughout the realm."

And perhaps in the eyes of one governess. The notion had peculiar appeal.

"Until he takes me down," Ethan muttered. Nothing would do but that he spread the blanket, sit, and pull off his boots. "And his countess will fuss at him, but she'll be wroth with me."

"Whining, Mr. Grey?" Miss Portman offered him another one of the dazzling, heart-stopping smiles.

"Absolutely." Ethan stood up. "Can you manage?" He glanced down at the blanket meaningfully. When she only frowned, he offered his arm and got her settled on the blanket before pulling his shirt over his head and striding off for the water.

"Stand down, Wee Nick," Ethan bellowed. "I'll not have you terrorizing the peasants."

"We're not peasants," John said. "We're tars."

"Them either." Ethan winked at John, whom he hadn't said two words to in the previous three weeks. "Prepare to meet your doom, Wicked Nick."

Nick grinned an evil, piratical grin and dove for his brother. The water was only about two feet deep, perfect for making a huge ruckus without any risk of harm. The little boys squealed and hopped around, calling encouragement to their pirate of choice; the big boys bellowed and splashed and dunked each other repeatedly, until Nick and Ethan were both sitting on a log downed in the shallows, panting and licking knuckles scraped on the bottom of the stream.

"Now look what we've done," Nick said as the smaller boys began to roughhouse in earnest. "The seven seas will never be safe again."

"True, but at least our breeches stayed on."

The boys had been wading in their drawers, and when waterlogged and held around slippery little bodies by only a drawstring, Joshua's and John's clothing was being dragged into the briny deep.

"What on earth has Joshua done to his backside?"

Ethan slogged across the water toward his son, his brain taking a moment to comprehend what his eyes insisted was fact. He discreetly pulled up Joshua's sagging drawers and did the same for John before turning a thunderous expression on his brother.

"Nicholas Haddonfield, did you beat my son?" He kept his voice down, while both hands curled into tight fists.

"I did not," Nick said, keeping his voice as low as Ethan's. "He came to us like that, Ethan. Alice noticed it when she gave them a bath the first night, and brought it to my attention."

Nick's disclosure made Ethan want to hit someone— something—all the more. "*That* has been healing all this time? He never said a word."

Nick eyed Ethan's hand. "I asked him if he fell. He said he was bad and he deserved it."

"He's five," Ethan shot back. "How could he deserve a hiding like that?"

"So you didn't do it."

"You thought…" Ethan dropped Nick's gaze, his eyes going to his youngest son. "It had to hurt like hell, Nick."

"If you didn't do it, then who did?"

"I am ashamed to say I do not know." Ethan watched as Joshua's backside peeked into view again. "I suspect it was Mr. Harold, their tutor, but until I talk to Joshua, I can't say. I feel sick."

"I feel relieved," Nick said. "A man's children are his own business, but to think you might have done that to your son did not sit well with me or my countess. They're good boys, Ethan. If anything, they're too good."

Ethan wasn't listening. A muscle worked in his jaw, and he could feel the vein just beyond his hairline throbbing. His eyes were fixed on his sons, sturdy little men having a grand time on a summer day. To appearances, all was well with them, but Ethan still felt the urge to kill whoever had hurt one of his boys.

"Come on." Nick prodded him with an elbow. "I brought spare breeches, and you can borrow a pair. Into the bushes with us. Beware the savages, as we're fair game for attack."

When they'd changed their clothes, they returned to the blankets to find the boys still cavorting in the water—though their lips were blue and their teeth were chattering.

"Joshua and Jeremiah, out!" Ethan barked. "Now!"

They came right out of the water and presented their shivering little selves to their father, while John and Ford whined and dallied and made excuses to Nick.

Ethan bent down and wrapped each boy in a towel. "You will be dried off and dressed and eating yourselves sick while John and Ford are still dripping on their blankets." He grabbed for Joshua and rubbed the child briskly all over with the towel, until the shivering had subsided.

And if he stole a surreptitious hug in the process, he was the only one who knew.

❧

Alice glanced up from where she was reading the children a story, to see a groom leading an enormous golden gelding from the direction of the house.

"It's Argus," Jeremiah informed her in a whisper. "Papa's horse. Is Papa going somewhere?"

"I am not." Mr. Grey spoke from where he stood towering above the children. "Miss Portman requires escort back to the house, and Argus volunteered."

"Your horse?" Alice tried to scramble to her feet, but found she was lifted there instead by Mr. Grey's hands under her elbows. "What about the story?"

"Mrs. Belmont?" Mr. Grey's smile sported an alarming complement of perfect white teeth. "Can you or Priscilla finish the story?"

"Let me!" Priscilla yelled before her mother could respond. Mr. Grey passed the girl the book.

"We've no mounting block," Alice said. Also no sense, for the last thing, the very last thing she was going to do was climb onto that enormous golden beast. The idea of it made her chest pound and sent Hart Collins's taunts skittering through her memory.

"No problem." Nick appeared at her elbow, oozing friendly concern, the wretch. "We'll get you on board easily enough, provided you're willing?"

"I can't ride by myself." The admission hurt, even all these years later.

"Nor would I expect you to," Mr. Grey said as he swung up. "Nick?"

And just like that, Alice found herself gently deposited before Mr. Grey in the saddle, the horse ambling off in the direction of the house.

"Put your arm around my waist," Mr. Grey said as he guided the gelding away from the picnic spot.

"You're sitting gingerly, as if the saddle were too hot, and that will just make the horse nervous and you more prone to tipping off."

"You frequently ride about with damsels before you?" Alice tentatively slid an arm around Mr. Grey's lean waist, reasoning he'd done the same with her when they were on foot.

"I never ride about with damsels before me." He passed the reins to one hand and circled her waist with the other arm. He drew her back against his chest and left his arm where it was. "Relax, and I'll have you safely home."

Relax. She was on a horse large enough to rival an elephant, snugged up against an equally large, grouchy man who smelled too good, and he wanted her to relax.

"Is it the horse you're afraid of," the man asked when Alice was still barely letting her body touch his, "or is it me?"

"What have I to fear from you?" Alice didn't dare turn her head. It might upset her balance, the horse, anything.

"Nothing." He leaned back as Argus negotiated a slight slope, and Alice clutched his waist. "Easy." Mr. Grey straightened slowly. "It must have been a very bad fall."

Alice did risk peeking at him and wished she hadn't, because his mouth was exactly in line with her eyes. God above, it was a lovely sight. Those perfectly sculpted lips were the boon of a god both generous and perverse.

"It was a bad accident," Alice said. "I was dragged for quite some distance and lucky I didn't lose my leg."

Or her mind. She shoved the memory of Collins's cronies jeering at her back into its mental vault. The memory of Avis's eyes was a more difficult struggle.

"You're lucky you didn't lose your life. Being dragged is usually far worse than simply being pitched off. You'll tell me about it?"

What an odd request—until Alice realized he was trying to distract her from her perch before him. "Sometime. I don't even like to think of it."

"I know." His tone turned bleak. "You want to forget, but you never will, so neglecting the memory is the next best thing."

He spoke from experience, leaving Alice to wonder what a wealthy, handsome man like Ethan Grey had to forget. He was a bastard, true, but that hardly seemed to bother him. Perhaps the pain in his eyes stemmed from grief over the recent loss of his father. It might explain his distance from his sons, and even an occasional loss of temper with them.

"Nick said you were the one who noticed the marks on Joshua," he said, as if divining her thoughts.

"They were very angry marks," Alice replied, though this was hardly a more sanguine topic than her fall. "It must have hurt him to sit, but he wouldn't talk about it, so I had Nick give the boys their next bath. Joshua didn't want to talk to him either."

"I didn't do it. I didn't even know about it, and in a way, that's worse than if I had done it."

So she could remove from the list of Ethan Grey's numerous faults that of child beater. It was an odd relief, but she was willing to do it.

"One cannot keep one's children safe from all harm," Alice said gently. "Joshua thinks he deserved the punishment. You might consider talking to Jeremiah. He is very protective of Joshua and could not be happy to see his brother treated so poorly."

"Good suggestion. Is it the case you haven't yet secured another position, Miss Portman?"

Oh, no. *No, no, no.* Alice would have pokered right back up, except Mr. Grey's arm around her middle prevented it.

"I have not." She went on the offensive, despite her precarious perch and the fact that she was depending on Mr. Grey for her safety. "I am not well versed in the nuances of dealing with little boys, Mr. Grey. I do not know your sons well, and I am not cheap."

"Neither am I," he replied, amusement in his voice. "I will pay you exactly what I paid their previous tutors, if you'll take them on even a temporary basis."

She might have hopped off the horse and stomped away rather than conclude the discussion, but money was always a consideration, and with a bad hip, one didn't hop off eighteen-hand behemoths or stomp very far.

"How much?"

He named an astonishing figure, one that would allow Alice to add considerably to her savings. But no… These were boys, and two of them, and that was bad enough, but then there was Mr. Grey…

"I can't. They are active little fellows, Mr. Grey, and I cannot be responsible for getting them into the fresh air and sunshine each day as I should."

"I'll manage that part, if you'll handle the school-room and the rest of it."

"What is the rest of it?" She should hop off, bad hip or not.

"They'll have a nursemaid, of course, for tending

them at the start and end of each day. The grooms will supervise them in the stables, and I've enough footmen to toss cricket balls at them, and so forth."

Here was purchase in a negotiation she intended to win. "Not footmen. You."

"I beg your pardon?" He frowned again, but then made a little fuss over steering the horse, who no doubt could have found the barn blindfolded in a high wind.

Was he trying to scare her?

"You did not have your sons' trust, Mr. Grey," Alice said. "You can't simply command them to trust you. They have to see and experience you as trustworthy. You can't do that if you're shut away with your ledgers and they're off with a groom on their ponies."

This would nicely scotch his schemes, and without them having to argue about it. Alice congratulated herself on her brilliance as she relaxed against his chest. She was out from under his offer, and nobody need be offended. For the first time in years, she almost enjoyed being on a horse.

"Three days a week," he said, "I will spend at least an hour in recreation with both boys."

Drat. Her brothers had taught her some rudimentary gambling as she'd recovered from her injuries; being a governess had taught her strategy. She raised the stakes. "And you'll take a walk with each child once a week, weather permitting, or play cards, or somehow spend an hour with each child individually."

"I can do that."

"And you will join them for breakfast," Alice plunged on, concluding Mr. Grey must not be thinking sensibly. "And one evening meal a week."

Behind her, Alice felt Mr. Grey draw in a breath and go silent.

"Fridays would suit," he said at length, "and you must agree to join me at that meal too."

"Of.... of course." Alice felt her world slipping, and she inadvertently held more tightly to Mr. Grey, whose arm tucked around her closely in response.

"You'll have pin money and a clothing allowance besides," he went on, while Alice grappled with the import of their discussion. "And a half day every Saturday. Nobody is expected to work on Sunday at Tydings, including the kitchen. You will have two weeks paid in the summer to see friends, such as Miss Priscilla, and the use of a horse or pony trap, should you need it. We are agreed?"

Alice was quiet, stunned at how her world could change in the space of a half mile. She had not lined up another position because she preferred to deal with agencies to screen potential employers. Any place in London itself would not do, there being a surfeit of titles around the place, and Collins—may he rot slowly in a malodorous corner of hell—was liable to visit other titles from time to time.

Any household that had too many grown sons or uncles or male cousins was out of the question as well. Any place that expected her to ride with the children or march them about the estate every day of the week, any place that would not pay a decent wage or give her even a half day a week to catch her breath...

Mr. Grey was offering her more than she usually demanded, in every regard. He had no title; his children were dear and very much in need of someone who would care for them.

"This is temporary," Alice said as the horse shuffled into the stable yard. "You said this was temporary."

He nudged the beast to a halt. "I said I'd hire you even if you were only willing to take us on temporarily. I suggest we give the matter a three-month trial. If you are not content, we can agree to part at that point, but you must allow me at least that long again to search for a successor."

The condition was practical and would ensure the children did not suffer a lapse in studies. It also ensured that for six months Mr. Grey would not be left with the dilemma of finding another tutor.

"So it's a six-month position, at least."

"At least," he agreed, then swung off the horse, leaving Alice perched on the pommel, mind reeling. "Miss Portman?"

Alice glanced down to see Mr. Grey regarding her patiently from the ground. She put her hands on his shoulders and felt herself lifted easily from the saddle. Though Mr. Grey was careful to settle her onto her feet slowly, her left leg buckled when she tried to put weight on it.

"Steady." He held her still, letting her lean against him once more. "Give it a minute."

She bit her lip and blinked. "It's shot," she muttered miserably as the horse was led away. "The only thing that helps now is bed rest."

"Can you lean on me?" Mr. Grey asked, wrapping an arm around her waist. But he was too tall to be properly leaned on, and Alice hadn't the strength or the balance to hop up three flights of stairs on one foot.

She shook her head, feeling tears threaten, not exclusively as a result of the ache in her hip.

He muttered something that sounded suspiciously like "bugger this," and Alice felt herself being swept up against his chest.

"We'll have you surrounded by hot-water bottles in no time." He headed across the gardens to one of the house's back entrances.

"The servants' stairs are closer," Alice said, looping her arms around his neck. She hadn't been carried like this since she'd fallen off that horse, and though she was full grown and well fed, Mr. Grey carried her as if she weighed no more than little Priscilla. It was disconcerting, sweet, comforting, and awful, all at once.

He bent his knees a little at her door, so Alice could lift the latch, then he kicked the door shut behind them. Alice found herself gently deposited on the edge of the bed, facing a stern-faced Mr. Grey, who was glaring down at her, his hands on his hips. Without warning, he dropped to hunker before her and took one of her boots in his hands.

She stared down at him. "What are you doing?"

"Removing your shoes," he replied, unlacing her half boot as he spoke. "Bending at the waist is likely uncomfortable for you."

Protests dammed up behind the truth—bending at the waist hurt abysmally, though Alice nearly died of mortification and shock when she felt Mr. Grey's hands slip under her skirts and tug down her stockings.

"Mr. Grey!" She tried to scoot back on the bed, but that hurt like blue blazes, so she had to settle for glaring at him as he rolled her stockings like a practiced lady's maid.

"Oh, simmer down." His tone disgruntled, he

looked around and put the stockings on her vanity. "I was married for several years, you know, and it isn't as if I'll be ravishing you over the sight of your dainty feet."

Alice went still on the bed, all other indignities and imprecations forgotten. "What do you mean, you *were* married?"

"My sons are legitimate." He frowned at her, his hands back on his hips. "I would not wish bastardy on any child, much less my own."

"But you said you *were* married," Alice pressed. "You aren't married now?"

"I am not," he replied, cocking his head. "And were I not in polite company, and did it not sound insufferably callous, I would add, 'thank God.' My wife expired of typhoid fever a little more than three years into our union. I would not have wished her dead, but she is, and I quite honestly do not miss her."

"Mr. Grey! Surely you haven't voiced those sentiments before your children?"

"And if I have?"

"You would have much to apologize for," Alice shot back. "Much to be forgiven for. She might have been the worst mother in the world, but those little boys need to believe she was in some way lovable, much as they would need to believe the same about you, lest they see themselves as unlovable."

His gaze narrowed. "You presume to know a great deal about my sons."

"I knew well before you did that one of them had been birched too severely," Alice retorted. "And I know they need to regard their parents in some reasonably positive fashion."

"Well, then, fine." He ran a hand through his hair in a gesture Alice had seen his younger brother make often. "Your expertise confirms my choice of you as the boys' next governess."

Alice opened her mouth to say something, then shut it abruptly.

"I will take my leave of you." He stepped back from the bed. "A maid will be along posthaste. Will you want some laudanum?"

"No. Thank you, that is. No, thank you."

"Good day, then. I'll have our terms drawn up into a contract and provide a copy for your review."

She nodded, not even watching as he took his leave. Her hip hurt, and it was going to hurt worse in the next few hours, and she'd just made a devil's bargain with a man who smelled divine and handled her like she was a sack of feathers. Alice was tucked up in her night rail, a glass of cold lemonade by the bed, before she realized she was just as disgruntled with Mr. Grey for being widowed as she was for his handling her like she was a sack of feathers—and not even a female sack of feathers at that.

Three

ARGUS CHURNED ALONG AHEAD OF THE DUST AND racket of the coach, no doubt sensing the approach of home even though Tydings was still at least an hour distant. With luck, they'd beat the inevitable thunderstorm building up to the north.

Ethan had not slept well the previous night, his mind a welter of thoughts and feelings left over from his visit to Belle Maison. When he was a boy exiled from his home, he'd missed Nick so badly he'd cried at first, and a six-foot-plus fourteen-year-old male did not cry easily. Now that the old earl was dead, and he and Nick were free to be family to each other again, Ethan hadn't been able to get away fast enough.

And Nick had been hurt.

For all of Nick's glee over his new wife, all of his excitement at the prospect of having a family with his Leah, Nick had still known Ethan was dodging, and had let him go without a word. He'd merely hugged his brother tightly, then patted Argus and told the horse to take good care of his precious cargo.

Well, life wasn't a fairy tale, Ethan reasoned when

more of the same kind of musings finally brought him to the foot of the long driveway leading to Tydings.

"Papa!" Joshua was standing on the box, the groom's hands anchored around his waist. "We're home! I can see the house, and there goes Mrs. Buxton to fetch the footmen."

Ethan's housekeeper, Mrs. Buxton—Mrs. Buxom, among the footmen—was indeed bustling down the long terrace at the side of the house.

"Sit down, Joshua," Ethan called back. "Standing up there is dangerous, and Andrews will need to hold the horses. He can't be holding you as well."

Joshua dropped like a rock but bounced on the seat like any small boy would upon sighting his home. When the coach pulled into the circular drive in front of the house, footmen trotted up to lower the steps and began moving the luggage. The groom scrambled down to grab the leaders' bridles, and a stable boy come bouncing out of the carriage house to take Argus.

"Welcome home, Mr. Grey," the senior groom called cheerily, "and welcome, young masters. Did you have a grand time with your uncle in Kent?"

Joshua was jumping around on the box again. "Miller, we had the *best* time, and Uncle Nick is *even* taller than Papa, and he has a *huge* horse named Buttercup, and a *huge* house, and his cook makes *huge* muffins. Enorm…" Joshua paused and looked to his brother.

"Enormous," Jeremiah supplied. "And he let us ride his mare once, because we were very good, and we picked raspberries with Uncle Nick, and Aunt Leah is very nice, and there were other boys there, and they were all littler than us, but very nice, and we played Indians in the trees, and everything."

"Gentlemen." Alice Portman's pleasant tones glided into the ensuing silence. "I'm sure your papa will help you down now that we're safely home. Please don't run until you're away from the horses, and then I will expect you to give me a tour of your rooms once you're settled. What do you say to John?"

"Thank you, John Coachman!" both boys chorused. Ethan had swung off Argus, intending to get to his library with some cold, spiked lemonade and a small mountain of correspondence. Footmen were capable of getting the boys down from the high seat. Hearing both boys extol Uncle Nick's *huge, tall, enormous* virtues grated, though, so Ethan plastered a pleasant expression on his face and turned back to the coach.

"Here you go, Joshua." He held up his arms and hoisted the first child to the ground. "Up to the house, as Miss Portman said. Time to pester the grooms later. Jeremiah, down you go."

"Yes, Papa." Jeremiah stepped back as soon as his feet hit the ground. "Joshua, let's go. Miss Portman wants a tour."

"But I want to go see Lightning and Thunder," Joshua retorted, his chin jutting.

"Later, Joshua," Jeremiah said through clenched teeth. "We have to go to the house *now*."

Joshua's lips compressed into mutinous lines, but before Ethan could assert paternal rank, Miss Portman extended a hand in Joshua's direction.

"Come along, Joshua, or I shall get lost in a house as grand as this." She wrapped her hand around his. "And if I get lost, well then, I might not be found in time to read a couple of perfect gentlemen, and very fine singers, their bedtime story."

Joshua brightened. "We sang really loudly. I bet the horses' ears flippered around."

"I'm sure horses all over the shire were flippering their ears." Miss Portman slipped her other hand into Jeremiah's and led them off, chattering about horses in China and flippering ears.

"Prettier than old Harold," the groom remarked with the familiarity of long service. "Bet she reads a mean bedtime story."

"See to the horse," Ethan replied, watching as Miss Portman sauntered along with the boys toward the house. She should have waited for Ethan to escort her, but the view of her retreat was most pleasant, so Ethan kept his disgruntlement to himself. Joshua stopped, dropped her hand, and crouched to study the dirt—an insect, most likely, since Joshua was apparently going through a bug-studying phase—and Miss Portman crouched down to peer at the dirt right beside him, her skirts pooling on the dusty ground.

Argus, after balking for form's sake, let himself be led to the stables. The coach clattered away toward the carriage bays while the small parade of footmen hefted the luggage off to the house.

Still Ethan stood in the drive, wondering if he'd ever seen Mr. Harold once pause to study a bug? Seen him take either boy by the hand? Heard the man sing?

Had Ethan ever done those things with the boys himself? Even once?

The questions were vexing him several hours later as he made his way to the family parlor where Miss Portman would join him prior to the evening meal. Perhaps it was the effect of several hours at his desk, but Ethan realized he was looking forward to the next hour. Food was always a pleasure, but Miss Portman's presence was the added spice that had him glancing at the clock and wondering what she'd wear to the table.

She wore a frown and the same dusty traveling dress she'd had on all day.

While Ethan had bathed and changed into clean clothes.

"I see you did not change for dinner," Ethan remarked as the footman closed the door behind her.

Miss Portman eyed him up and down. "I was told you keep country hours and you do not change, when you bother with sitting at the table at all."

Ethan gave her the same up and down perusal she'd given him, though compared to a governess's virtuosic ability to communicate disapproval at a glance, he was a mere tyro. "I gather you would prefer to be spared this ordeal?"

She peered around the room. "Honestly, the chance to sit down and eat something appeals greatly."

"You've been standing the livelong day? I should offer you a drink, at least some wine."

She shook her head. "No wine. It does not agree with me, but thank you. And yes, I have been on my feet."

"If you're to forgo your gustatory glass," Ethan said, "why don't we go in to dinner, and you can regale me with the details of your day while we dine?"

"Because that would be unappetizing," Miss Portman informed him, her tone so wistful, Ethan felt his lips trying to quirk up. He offered his arm, keeping his eyes on the door instead of Miss Portman's face.

"As bad as all that?" he asked, leading her toward the folding doors to the informal dining room.

"As tiring. What have you done with yourself since abandoning your children in the driveway this afternoon?" A small silence followed, while Ethan observed the courtesy of seating a woman who delivered scolds as casually as others might offer pleasantries.

"Forgive me." Miss Portman closed her eyes and blew out a breath. "I am fatigued, and therefore cranky."

"And here I go, demanding you put up with me when all you want is to climb into bed. Are your rooms acceptable?" He poured her a glass of wine as he spoke, and passed it to her.

"They are lovely." She offered a tired smile, and Ethan noticed she had smudges of shadow under each eye and a slight droop to her shoulders. "The view of the back gardens is wonderful, and the balcony is a luxury this time of year."

"All the bedrooms at the back of the house have balconies." He gestured to the footman, who served the soup, then waved the man away. The remaining courses were put in the center of the table so the diners might serve themselves. When the footman had retreated and closed the door behind him, Ethan found a familiar frown on Miss Portman's face.

"You are going to be difficult because I dismissed the footman," he surmised. "You would rather have us discussing the weather all evening than allow us the privacy of a single meal?"

She answered him with a measuring look. "I would rather you had asked me if I were comfortable dining en famille."

Ethan sipped his wine and waited for her to take the first taste of her soup. "How did you spend your initial hours here at Tydings?"

"Chasing your offspring."

"You were touring the premises?"

"The grounds first." Miss Portman kept glancing around the table, as if looking for something or finding fault with the settings. "After two days of travel, the boys needed to stretch their legs, and then too, you've gone and gotten them ponies, whose acquaintance I had to make or civilization would crumble. When they'd burned off the worst of their mischief, we inspected the house from top to bottom, with particular attention paid to all the best hiding places for when Papa goes on a tear."

Ethan set his wineglass down. "I beg your pardon?"

"I gather it's a rare occurrence and mostly consists of a lot of yelling at solicitors and stewards, and cursing, and stomping about, followed by a slammed door or two and the sound of Argus's hoofbeats tearing off at a gallop."

"They told you this?"

"With great relish. You had best eat your soup, Mr. Grey. I do not intend to consume mine."

"Whyever not?" Ethan picked up his spoon, manners be damned.

"It has onions in it. They do not agree with me."

"And you are probably not partial to mutton sandwiches, either," Ethan remarked. He hadn't noticed the onions in the soup until she'd pointed it out. He liked onions in his soup, and if he were to eat mutton sandwiches, he'd probably like onions on them too.

"Nobody from the North is partial to mutton. But by all means, enjoy yourself."

Ethan put his spoon down, certain she was teasing—rudely, of course—but unable to detect a hint of it in her expression.

"It's gotten a bit too cool," he decided. "Shall we see what else the kitchen has prepared?"

Miss Portman's brows flew up. "Who sets the menus?"

"Haven't the foggiest." Ethan lifted the lid of a warming dish and found a tidy little quarter of a ham, with potatoes arranged around it. "The food shows up when I'm hungry, and the dishes disappear when I'm done. Ham, Miss Portman?"

"Please." She watched as he sliced her a generous portion, chasing little boys being a tiring proposition. "A bit less, if you please?"

"Less?" He cut off a corner of her intended portion.

"Even less. About half that, in fact."

He complied without comment and deftly moved it to her plate. "Potatoes?"

"One," she instructed, so he chose the largest one.

"Well, then." Ethan served himself portions that made his guest quite frankly goggle, a lapse in her manners he noted and politely ignored.

"Let's see what else awaits us." He uncovered a plate of roast beef. Another platter held a small roasting hen complete with bread stuffing, a basket of bread, and a tureen of dumplings swimming in more gravy.

"This will do for me," Miss Portman said, putting a bite of ham into her mouth.

"You're not having anything else? Nothing?" He had the oddest sense she wasn't being rude.

"This will do." She took a sip of her wine, grimaced, then set the glass down.

"Suit yourself." Ethan proceeded to put decent helpings of food on his plate, then to make his portions disappear with a kind of relentless dispatch that did not allow for conversation. And even as he demolished his dinner, he did so wondering how he would endure meals with Miss Portman for the next six months. When his plate was nearly clean, he looked up to find his guest regarding him curiously.

"Is this the kind of fare your sons consume?"

"I suppose." He sat back but did not put his utensils down. "Why?"

"Don't you see something missing from your table, Mr. Grey?"

"Dessert. Fear not, it will be here, as I do enjoy the occasional sweet."

"Not dessert," she replied, her tone annoyingly patient. "Something more conducive to the good health of a growing child."

"I'm not serving ale at my table, Miss Portman. We have it in the kitchen, and I'll occasionally have a pint, but it hardly adds to a genteel supper."

She eyed her wineglass balefully and forged ahead.

"Vegetables, Mr. Grey," she said on a long-suffering sigh. "You have no summer vegetables. You have nothing from the abundance of the good earth but potatoes. I know this will strike you as a radical notion, but children need vegetables, even if they should forgo the spicier preparations."

Ethan glanced around the table, nonplussed. At Belle Maison, there had been vegetables at every meal save breakfast. It was high summer, for pity's sake, when the garden was at its best.

He put his utensils down. "I am willing to concede the wisdom of your point. Henceforth, you will meet with Cook and approve the menus. I will have my desserts, though, Miss Portman. It's little enough to ask in life at the end of a man's busy day."

"Fear not," she quoted him. "I will agree with you—mark the moment—a little something sweet at the end of the day is a deserved reward."

Unbidden, the question of what Alice Portman might consider a treat at the end of her day popped into Ethan's mind. A fairy tale read to a rapt juvenile audience, or did she harbor girlish fancies to go along with her tidy bun and studious spectacles?

He took a fortifying sip of his wine and offered her a salute with his glass.

"A moment of accord," he noted gravely. "How unusual."

"I won't make a habit of it. The books in your schoolroom being a case in point."

"Oh?" Ethan resumed the demolition of his dinner.

"They are boring, for one thing," she said, sitting back and watching him eat. "And they are far too advanced, for another, and lack anything like the breadth of subject matter little boys require."

"You were a little boy once, perhaps, that you are expert on the matter?"

She leveled a reproving look at him, which he noted between bites of potato.

"There is more to a boy's education than drilling into him the dates of ancient battles, Mr. Grey. More to history than the Greeks, the Romans, and the British. More to languages than five declensions and four classes of verbs."

"You know Latin?" She was an intelligent woman—and he did not mean that insultingly, to his surprise—but Latin?

"Latin and Greek. Once you get the knack of the structure of the one, the other isn't so difficult to grasp."

"Good heavens." Ethan set his utensils down again. "What else has been stuffed between those ears of yours?"

"Astronomy is among my favorites," she confessed, casting a bashful glance at Ethan's half-eaten potato. "Mathematics, of course, including geometry and trigonometry, though only the rudiments of calculus. History, though I fear European history defines the limits of my command of the subject at this point. I am competent in French, but my command of modern languages is lacking. I read voraciously when I've the time."

"And what of needlepoint?" Ethan pressed, knowing he should have made these inquiries several days ago. "Tatting lace? Watercolors? A little piano or voice?"

She waved a dismissive hand. "I can mend what needs mending, and I'm a passable accompanist, but it hardly signifies."

"And why should the refinements of a lady hardly signify?" This bluestocking quality made perfect sense, given what he knew of the woman, but it impressed him as well. He liked a woman who didn't attempt to trade solely on her face and figure.

"They are not useful, Mr. Grey. The world does not need lace from me, though lace is charming. The world does not need a note-perfect rendition of the simpler Haydn sonatas at my hands, though music is a gift from God. The world does not need another vague rendition of some fruit and a towel, could I manage it, though painting is another gift from God."

"What does the world need?" He genuinely wanted to know.

"From me," she said, studying her plate this time, "it needs education. Were I proficient in those ladylike pursuits, I'd be a finishing governess. That is not my gift. I am far more interested in cultivating the minds of my charges than I am in assisting some schoolgirl in her quest to snatch up a spotty young swain of a few weeks' acquaintance."

Ethan propped his chin on his hand and surveyed her. "You are an anarchist, Miss Portman. And here I've placed the care of my sons in your rabble-rousing hands."

Her blush was all the more enchanting for being unexpected.

"You are teasing. Do you have all those books in your library for show, then, Mr. Grey? I hadn't taken you for a man driven by appearances."

"I'm not. I love to read." This was not a matter of pride; it was a simple truth. "One can't be managing business affairs every hour of the day, and reading is a solitary pleasure, suited to my nature."

"If you say so."

That was a governess's version of casting a lure. Even so, Ethan took the bait. "What?"

"You don't live alone here, Mr. Grey."

"Of course not. I dwell with my sons, and the servants and staff in my employ, and now—heaven be praised—with your very useful self."

"Have you seen your sons since the coach pulled up here today?" she asked in the same peculiarly quiet voice.

"I did, actually." He was pleased with himself to be able to say it. "Out the window, as they dragged you around the rose gardens. A charming tableau, made blessedly quiet by the distance involved. Better you than me, Miss Portman."

"They miss you," she said flatly. "Though God

knows why, Mr. Grey, as the concept leaves me quite at a loss. Now, if you will excuse me, I find I am intolerably fatigued, and though the meal has been appreciated, I must seek my bed."

She pushed back from the table and left the room before Ethan was halfway to his feet. He sat back down, his meal lying uneasily in his gut, and thought over the conversation.

He'd said something to push her past her limit, something... not funny. Cruel, perhaps, from her perspective. Well, there was no decoding the whims and fancies of females, bluestocking or otherwise. He eyed the table, intent on helping himself to more food, then changed his mind.

He'd been sitting too long, and this made for dyspepsia, so he took himself through the house, his wineglass in his hand, and headed for the back gardens. A man needed to stretch his legs from time to time if he was to have a prayer of remaining civilized.

Except his sons had been stuck in the coach for two days, and they had needed to stretch their legs. Alice Portman had reasoned that out; Ethan had not, and he wanted to smash the damned wineglass on the flagstones as a result. Because he was an adult, and civilized, he did not give in to the urge but wandered around in the moonlight until the shadows and breezes and pretty scents had soothed him past his anger.

Three floors above him, on her balcony, Alice watched the dark figure moving along the gravel paths. Moonlight suited him, though in daylight, he was deceptively golden. His hair was more burnished than Nick's wheat blond, and his features more austere. Still, he gave the impression of light, with his blue, blue eyes, light hair, and quiet movement.

He wasn't light, Alice concluded as she took down her hair. He was dark, inside, in his heart and soul. It still surprised her after she'd had days to observe him, but he looked so much like Nick, she still expected him to laugh like Nick, smile like Nick, flirt like Nick.

She missed Nick, and because it wasn't any kind of sexual longing, she could admit it. She desperately, pitifully missed Priscilla, and worried for how the child was going on.

In years of governessing, Alice had dealt with enough overly tired, cranky, distraught, fractious children to know if she didn't get herself to bed, posthaste, she was going to treat herself to an undignified, unproductive, useless crying spell. She was already hungry again, exhausted, in need of a bath, and facing a situation she should have examined more carefully before leaping into it.

"You're just discouraged," she told herself. "Braid your hair, get to bed. Things will look better in the morning."

But in the morning, things didn't look at all better.

In the morning, things looked much, much worse.

❦

"You will leave in the morning, Hart, and you will not come back in my lifetime." The Baroness Collins had never taken that tone with her son before. Not when he was a child, not when he'd been a young man, and not now, when inchoate middle age and a dissolute lifestyle were making him look like an old child, an aging boy becoming less and less attractive with the passing years.

Predictably, Hart bristled. "I'll damned well come and go from my own property as I please, madam. You would do well to recall upon whose charity you survive." He tossed back another glass of brandy, adding to the amount that had disappeared in the course of the conversation already.

"You are not safe here."

Somewhere in the depths of her maternal heart, the baroness could not allow her son to knowingly court danger, regardless that it was danger of his own making. "Your scheming and violence, your disregard for proper behavior, your disrespect of every woman you meet will be the end of you if you stay here in the North. I am not asking you to leave, Hart, I am insisting."

He paused before putting his empty glass down on the harpsichord. That harpsichord had belonged to the baroness's grandfather, and yet, she did not rise and remove the glass—not while Hart was in such a mood.

"You are insisting? How will you insist, dear Mama, when I cut off your allowance?"

Perhaps it was the French disease or the drink, but Hart's memory was growing faulty. "You cut off my allowance years ago, Hart. I manage on my portion." Which, thank her sainted papa's shrewdness, no venal, grasping son could touch.

He turned his back on her, making the bald spot on the back of his head apparent. He'd hate that, if he knew she could see it. Hart Collins was so vain, so unhealthy, that he'd see even the normal impact of time as victimization.

She did not wish her son were dead. In the manner he went on, he'd meet his end soon enough.

"I'll need money."

Of course he would. The old baron's solicitors were a pack of jackals well up to dealing with Hart's tantrums and bullying. Not one penny of estate money would get into Hart's hands until the very day it was due him.

"I have a few jewels." Those had belonged to her grandmother. "You will leave in the morning, Hart, and I'll write to some people I know in the South, who would welcome you to their house parties."

He was no longer welcome in Rome, and neither was he safe in Paris or Marseilles. His duns in London had already found him at the family seat in Cumbria and were becoming impatient.

The baroness unfastened the pearl necklace her grandmother had given her upon her come out and held it out to her son. In the flickering candlelight of the once-elegant parlor, the jewels looked like a noose.

Perhaps the English countryside would shelter him for a time. It was just a thought, not a wish, not even a prayer.

⟶⟶

Ethan slept badly, but got up early and heeded the impulse to get out of the house. Confinement never improved his mood, so he made for the stables after a quick breakfast. Miss Portman and her charges were not in evidence at breakfast, which suited him splendidly.

As he took his second-favorite mount out for a bracing hack in the cool of the earliest morning, Ethan forced himself to consider he might owe Miss Portman an apology. On general principles, it irked him to apologize to anyone, particularly when he wasn't quite sure where he'd transgressed.

One thing he'd realized as he surveyed the remains of supper: there had been nothing to drink except wine, and Miss Portman did not enjoy wine. He should have seen to it she was offered something else. Had she not been so provoking, he might have been a better host.

He let his gelding come down to the trot after they'd cleared every stile and fence between the house and the home farm. Maybe Miss Portman was peeved at him because he'd teased her for her degree of education.

But that explanation didn't feel quite right.

The horse halted without Ethan cuing him, as the realization sank in that Miss Alice Portman did not care one bean—a vegetable, mind you—how much Ethan teased her. She minded bitterly the way Ethan disregarded his children.

Bloody, bleeding hell.

He did not know what they ate.

He did not know what they learned.

He did not know how they passed their days.

He had not known his youngest had been harshly beaten, or why.

As the horse started walking forward, Ethan knew in his bones he was facing an opportunity—a challenge. He could continue as he'd gone on, largely trying to ignore that his wife had borne two sons, or he could transcend his pique and be the kind of parent his sons deserved.

The kind of father he himself had not had.

Which decided the matter, foot, horse, and cannon.

He did not want to be a father at all, but he was damned if he would do to his children what the old earl had done to him. The man had presided over his family as a benevolent dictator, but had been so badly informed regarding his own children he'd tossed Ethan away on the strength of ill-founded suspicion alone. Banished him.

That line of thought was worse than bleak, so Ethan patted his horse, turned for the stables, and mentally rearranged his day. He'd start with the nursery and find some way to talk to his children. It couldn't be that hard, after all. Miss Portman did it easily, didn't she?

But as he made his way through the house, he was accosted by a chambermaid hurrying down the stairs, eyes wild, cap askew.

"Oh, Mr. Grey, I don't mean to be getting above myself, but you best come quick. Mrs. B. is off to the village and Cook's abed and Mr. B. is down to the mill." She reached for Ethan's arm, then dropped her hand and dipped a little at the knees, as if she were resisting an urgent call from nature.

"I'm coming," Ethan said, keeping the irritation from his voice. "What exactly is the problem?"

"It's the new governess," the girl moaned as she turned back up the steps toward the nursery wing. "I think Miss Portman is dying!"

Four

ETHAN DIDN'T EVEN KNOCK. HE OPENED THE DOOR TO Miss Portman's bedroom and was hit immediately with a blast of warm, stale air. The curtains were opened, but the windows, which should have been cracked to let in some of the breeze, were closed tightly.

But he knew this scene—the bedclothes badly tangled; the air uncomfortably still; a hot, painful tension in the room.

"Close the drapes all but a little," he quietly directed the maid. "Open the windows, then bring me up some lavender water with ice, and a pitcher of cold mint tea. Sugar the tea. We'll need clean sheets as well, and some buttered toast, and the laudanum. Move quietly, or I'll know the reason why."

On the bed, Miss Portman tried to roll away from the sound of his voice.

"Miss Portman?" Ethan approached the bed sound lessly and kept his voice down. "Alice?"

The sound she made when she tried to draw in a breath was terrible, a wheezy bleat that struggled against itself.

He did not sit on the bed, as he knew all too well that giving Miss Portman any cause for anxiety would only exacerbate the situation. He did, however, note the location of the nearest pitcher and basin. And by the scant light coming through the drawn drapes, he saw Miss Portman had had a bad night.

Her braid was a disaster, her skin was pale, and beneath her closed eyes, there was still that grayish, drawn look of extreme fatigue.

"Alice?" He sat carefully on the bed, and her hand appeared from the covers to rest over her stomach.

Another horrible indrawn breath, and then, "No." It meant, he knew, no talking, no moving, no company. No hope, too, when the fear was at its worst. He reached out a hand, just to be sure, and laid the back of it to her forehead.

No fever, thank God, because this much discomfort might also signal some physical ailment.

"Alice?" He smoothed her hair back, noting she tolerated that well enough. "Alice, can you talk to me?"

"Go away." She tried to roll away, to draw her knees up, but then her eyes flew open. "Oh no…"

Ethan's wife had not fared easily early in her pregnancy with Jeremiah. He knew what that particular variety of "oh no" presaged, and in an instant had her sitting up beside him.

"Look at me," Ethan ordered. "You're at Tydings, you're safe, and your charges are likely stirring across the hall."

Another breath, just as tortured. "Want to die," Miss Portman murmured to her knees.

"I know." Ethan settled a hand on her nape and took a more soothing tone. "Look around you, Alice.

You're having a bad moment, but it will pass. Don't try to breathe, just let it happen. See your things there on the desk, your robe across the foot of the bed. Your spectacles are here on the night table. I expect you picked this rose when you were out strolling with Joshua and Jeremiah."

As he spoke, Ethan rubbed his thumb slowly across her nape. He matched his breathing to hers and felt her gradually calming. "Better?" Ethan asked.

She nodded, her gaze on the single red rose in a bud vase near her spectacles. He did not take his hand away. Soon, she might start to shake or weep, if her bad moments resembled his.

"Humiliated, but better."

"Was it the wine?"

"Spirits don't help." She tried to move, but he prevented it. "Nothing else on the table. Thirsty. Mostly, it's being in a strange place and being overly tired. I woke up…"

"You're safe, Alice. Tydings is boringly, unendingly safe."

Though he'd never thought of it that way before. As Ethan remained beside her, his fingers massaging her nape, he realized Alice hadn't been assessing his silver pattern or his table linen the night before. She'd been looking for a simple glass of water. She could have rung for it…

But she'd been running all afternoon, and she was new to the household, and she was Alice Portman.

"You need fluids," he said, again being careful to keep his voice down, and to fill a water glass only half-full. He propped an arm under her shoulders and held the glass to her lips, finding it worrisome—bothersome—that she didn't protest the proximity or the assistance.

"More."

"Soon. We have to accommodate your tentative digestion. Will laudanum help?"

"God, no. Laudanum makes everything strange, and that is worse than a spell of anxiety."

And her with that creaky hip. No wonder she had to be so careful with it, if she could not relieve her pain in the usual fashion.

"The breeze feels wonderful." She addressed her observation to the half-full water glass. "Thank you."

"It's still too hot in here." Ethan retrieved a tray from the chambermaid, then closed the door. He shouldn't be in Miss Portman's room, of course, but she shouldn't be having a damned spell of nerves because she'd over-done and awoken in strange surroundings.

"This is mint tea." He poured a glass half-full from a ceramic pitcher. "When my digestion is tentative, it seems to help." He put a basin on the night table. "This is lavender water, with ice. I don't know if it truly helps, but the scent is soothing, and I don't think it will hurt."

"You are prone to unprovoked sensations of dread?" She lay back on her pillows, sounding hopeful, as if wishing she were not isolated in her misery— except when it came to this ailment, each sufferer was profoundly isolated.

"Not as often as I used to." Ethan wrung out a cloth in the lavender water and folded it across her forehead. "I've learned to dodge much of what causes them."

"Which would be?" From the expression on her face, the cold cloth was a bit of divine relief.

Ethan frowned at her from his perch at her hip. "Any extreme can set me off. Too little sleep, too little activity, too little food, too little drink, too much exertion, too much change of company or conditions. I expect in your case, you needed fluids and rest, and you ignored those needs for two days. You're away from all that's familiar, and the change was not one you had much chance to contemplate."

Because he hadn't wanted her to have the opportunity for reflection.

"Perhaps." She took a sip of her mint tea. "I hate when this happens."

"I know." She would hate the indignity far more than the suffering. "But these moments pass, and then one is so pathetically grateful."

The maid appeared, having the sense to knock softly and close the door softly when Ethan permitted her to enter. She bore clean sheets and some buttered toast.

"No food." Miss Portman waved a hand weakly when the maid had left again. "I cannot, Mr. Grey."

"Yes, you can," he corrected her, taking the cloth from her forehead. "Just a bite or two, washed down with some tea. I'll help." She managed a very weak glare at him, which suggested the patient would live. He gently hefted her up, and while holding her forward against his shoulder, he arranged pillows at her back.

He straightened, looking her over as he did. "You did not threaten me with dire punishments for my presumptions, so you must allow you are not yet feeling quite the thing."

"I am making allowances for your unfamiliarity

with compassionate impulses." The words held only a
fraction of her usual starch.

"Two sips." Ethan held the glass to her lips, thinking
it odd that now that he had a moment to order her
around, he dearly wished she wasn't permitting it.

"I'll do it," she muttered against the rim of the glass,
wrapping her hand around his much-larger one.

"And now your toast." He set the glass down and
picked up the plate, tearing her off a bite right over the
plate so the crumbs wouldn't get on the bedclothes.
He held it to her lips, and she took it from him with
her hand.

"You are surprisingly solicitous," she said, munching
the toast, "if inclined to managing."

"Chew," he ordered, smiling slightly. "To be
accounted managing by one of your standards makes
my day complete. Two more sips."

She complied without argument. He suspected she
knew that goaded him too.

"The maid will be back shortly to do up your braid,
change these sheets, and remove the tray. Remain
silent, Alice Portman, and do not fuss."

He reached for her hand, which was cool in his grasp.

"Now," he went on, keeping his fingers wrapped
around hers, "you will not exert yourself for at
least the rest of this day. I will keep the boys out
of trouble, but I will also check on you, to make
sure you are sipping your tea, resting, and eating
enough to keep a bird alive. If that featherbrained
young lady serving you does not report to my
satisfaction, you will find yourself bearing more of
my company.

"You are a disgrace, Alice Portman," Ethan

informed her, "to get into such a state and not even ring for a damned maid. I am not happy with you."

He was pleased, though, for some unfathomable reason. He was pleased she was tolerating his fussing and scolding. Pleased to be of some *usefulness* to her. Pleased he knew what to do.

"You are excused from tonight's meal," he said very sternly. "And henceforth we will have water on the table at all times. You will rest, and you will acquaint yourself with your surroundings. Write the loved ones you miss, and otherwise take one day to adjust to your new surroundings. Do I make myself understood?"

She nodded when she probably wanted to dump her tea over his head. It was time to go, before he provoked her into a display of vinegar for his own reassurance. Still, he held her hand a moment longer.

It would be a good moment to tell her about his willingness to give parenting his children another try—a better try—but he kept his peace, even as he marveled at the delicacy of the bones of her hand. All women were small to him, given his height and muscle. Alice was taller than most, and yet to him, she was delicate and diminutive. And up close, she smelled good, of lemons and sunshine.

"I'll leave you in peace now." Ethan turned her hand loose and wrung out another cold cloth. "You sip tea, nibble toast, and let the maid brush your hair for hours on end. If you don't behave, I'll thrash you silly."

"I'll behave," she replied, smiling at him faintly. "My thanks for your assistance, Mr. Grey."

He rose from the bed and glared down at her. "Would you call me Ethan if I asked you to?" He should not ambush her in a weak moment, but there was no point trying to ambush her in any other kind of moment.

He'd asked. He'd actually put his wishes into the form of a question. This was a measure of his panic at seeing her ailing, though try as he might, he couldn't resent her for it.

"I would allow it, under certain circumstances, if you asked politely. Any governess worth her salt knows to reward proper manners, particularly when the result is such a marvelously nonplussed expression."

Her smile had nothing in it of buns, spectacles, or sensible shoes. Her smile was pure, lovely female benevolence, and it inspired Ethan to a reckless display of his best manners.

"I am asking, most politely, for the honor of my given name from you."

Because she'd back down. He knew she'd back down, plead her diminished capacity, and otherwise let him call her bluff.

Her smile grew yet more brilliant. "When circumstances don't require otherwise, I shall call you Ethan."

He smiled back—let her have a taste of her own good manners rewarded—then made a bid to knock her off her governess pins by leaning over and brushing a kiss to her cheek. "I'll stop by after lunch, and you had best be napping, or at least on the mend, or there will be unpleasant consequences."

He finished with an admonitory scowl, thinking this scolding business was almost fun. No wonder Miss Portman—who was looking gratifyingly, no, *marvelously* nonplussed—seemed to enjoy it so much.

⚬

"Papa?" Jeremiah scrambled to his feet, dragging Joshua upright with him, their astonishment at seeing their father in the nursery suite plain on their faces.

"Good morning." Ethan frowned down at them. "Gentlemen." He added it as an afterthought, and it earned him a wary exchange of looks from his sons. "Miss Portman is not faring well today, so we are cast upon one another's company. I am charged to get the both of you outside before it gets too hot, and then we will visit Miss Portman at midday. Now then…" Ethan's sons were gazing at him with disconcerting stillness. "What had you planned for the day?"

Joshua shrugged his little shoulders. "Nothing." He shot a puzzled look at his older brother. "Well, we didn't."

"Miss Portman said we'd have to see where we were," Jeremiah offered hesitantly. "She said there should be time for a ride and would discuss it with you."

"A ride might be just the thing." He'd ridden with them before, though the last time was months ago, and it was by happenstance. Still, it was a good place to start.

And it went surprisingly well, the ponies having been kept in work by the grooms during the boys' absence. Ethan rode Argus, who was too tired from his travels to provide his usual brand of entertainment, and the boys largely absorbed each other's attention as they walked and trotted their mounts through the woods. They were all headed back to the barn at the walk, the heat building, when Joshua turned to his brother with a questioning look, though no inquiry had been voiced.

Jeremiah shook his head emphatically, which inspired Joshua to stick out his tongue then whack his pony one stout blow with his crop. The little beast shot forward, Jeremiah's mount did the same, and Ethan and Argus were left to bring up the rear at a canter.

Shouting wasn't going to help. Ponies were wily little things, and these two were both sane, sittable, and sure-footed. His sons were standing in their stirrups, clearly accustomed to a hearty gallop from time to time. When Joshua aimed his pony at a stile, though, Ethan felt his heart rise up in his throat.

"Joshua, no!" Ethan bellowed, but the pony had seen the objective and wasn't to be pulled off his fence. At a dead run, the animal charged up to the fence and sailed over, Joshua grinning like a fiend on his back. Jeremiah cleared the same obstacle, but had the sense to shoot worried glances over his shoulder as Ethan popped the jump easily behind them.

Only when Joshua drew his pony up did he glance at his father. His grin evaporated as he recalled who their groom was that morning, though he patted his pony, who was rudely cropping grass after its exertions.

Ethan's lips pressed into a thin line. "Who taught you to jump like that?"

"Nobody taught us," Jeremiah piped up, ever protective. "The ponies just know, and it's shorter to get home if you hop the stiles. Shorter to get to the village too."

"So you *hop* them frequently at a dead run?" They had ridden the jump like little jockeys, their form flawless and relaxed.

"We canter them," Jeremiah said, his chin coming up. "Mostly."

So they'd cantered them the first time, and gone

screaming over forever after. Ethan did not know
whether to be proud or horrified.

"I suppose we'll have to get you proper hunting
attire, then. Cubbing starts in September."

He turned Argus without another word, feeling his
sons staring agape at his back.

"We're to ride to hounds?" Joshua's tone suggested
he could not believe such a thing.

"Cubbing." Jeremiah said, nudging his pony
forward. "It's not quite the same, but it counts."

"But, gentlemen," Ethan called over his shoulder
then stopped Argus and turned him to face the ponies.
"Tearing off that way in company is considered the
height of bad form, though I know between the two
of you, it's great fun to startle your brother's horse.
When we ride in company, though, there'll be none
of that, correct?"

"Yes, sir."

"Correct, sir."

"And now we will walk our horses out, for they've
exerted themselves mightily, but I see we're on the
wrong side of the fence, aren't we?"

Joshua and Jeremiah were exchanging one of those
puzzled, fraternal looks when Ethan surreptitiously
nudged at Argus's side with his spur, sending the gelding
back toward the stile at a brisk trot. The ponies fell in
behind without benefit of direction from their riders,
and they cleared the same obstacle, one, two, three, at a
more dignified pace but with the same excellent form.

When they gained the stable yard, the boys were
grinning, and whacking their ponies with appreciative
pats on the neck, and betting each other their ponies
could clear anything old Argus could.

"Let's not put it to the test," Ethan interrupted them. "And if I ever learn you were foolish enough to attempt an obstacle without me or a groom to supervise, I will forbid you to ride for a considerable while, not that I think either of my sons would be so foolish."

His sons surely would, but Miss Portman's favorite gentlemen might not.

❦

"Outside?" Joshua and Jeremiah grinned at each other. "Now?"

"I suggest you stop up in the playroom to mass your troops," Mr. Grey said, sounding very stern indeed. "Get a shovel from the garden shed and ask Tolliver where you might find some shade and a patch of earth to memorialize British military heroism. You will be expected back upstairs, with clean hands and faces, by teatime."

"That's five bongs of the clock," Joshua said. "Let's go, Jeremiah."

"And thus the Corsican monster meets his deserved fate," Alice said from her place on the bed. The boys bounced away from her sides, leaving her in blessed quiet—and quite at sea—with their father.

Mr. Grey—or *Ethan*, since they were in private— lowered himself to sit on the bed at her hip. He was inspecting her, not in any way trespassing against propriety.

"Thus my sons are given an excuse to be loud, get muddy, and plague the gardener."

"You would have made a tolerable governess, you know." Alice smiled at him, even knowing he was assessing her complexion, her eyes, and any other aspect of her person that might provide insight. "Disguising mud as British military heroism is ingenious."

"I suspect a fair amount of mud was involved at Waterloo, if the stories are true. You look better."

"Which is not saying much." Alice smoothed a hand over her quilt, not sure how to deal with an Ethan Grey who could outwit his sons and play nurse-maid to a governess. "I was in wretched shape this morning, and you have my thanks for your kindness."

He sat there at her hip, regarding her out of solemn blue eyes. He wore riding attire very well, and a faint odor of horse clung to the edges of his usual cedar scent. That she could enjoy any scent when blended with horse was a puzzlement.

"What will you do with your afternoon, Alice Portman?"

"I have many letters to write. I slept most of the morning. Perhaps I will tend to correspondence."

"A letter or two only." He frowned and tucked a strand of hair over her ear. The touch was not proper, but cowering in bed while bleating like a trapped sheep rather trumped all comers in the impropriety department.

"The headache and nervousness are slipping away, creeping back down into my vitals from whence they sprang."

"That's how it feels, isn't it?" He rose, making the mattress shift. "Where is Clara?"

"I sent her downstairs." Alice settled against the pillows, relieved to have the bed to herself though curious as to how Ethan Grey knew the exact contours of a bout of panic. "She is a dear, but twittery, and recovery from a spell like this morning's is facilitated by calm."

He said nothing, but stood at her window, where the curtains were drawn back halfway. While Alice cast around for something innocuous to say, he spoke over his shoulder.

"Why are the boys so concerned with death? As we rode in this morning, Joshua asked me if you were going to die. From a simple headache, such as I might suffer any day of the week—I told them you suffered only that—they leapt to making your final arrangements." Then he did turn, though he stayed across the room, leaning his hips back against the windowsill and crossing his ankles. "Or do I perhaps misperceive my children?"

Not a question she'd anticipated, but a sound one, and they could discuss it with a whole room between them. "I don't think you do. They know your father just died, and of course their mother died, which leaves them with only you."

"Only me." Even frowning, Mr. Grey was a handsome man. A handsome, largish man who looked perfectly comfortable to be visiting her in her boudoir. That came as a lowering realization since, despite his buss to her cheek earlier, it implied he could not conceive of improprieties transpiring here. "I haven't said anything to them about the old earl passing on, and they never met him."

"They know anyway. Leah explained to the little boys that you and Nick had the same father, and thus the boys' grandfather had died."

"Good of her." Ethan's—Mr. Grey's—Ethan's—frown intensified. "Barbara died in August. The night of the nineteenth."

This was not a confidence. Any governess learned

these bits of family history sooner or later. "How did she die?"

"Typhoid." He turned back around to stare out the window. "It is neither a tidy death nor quick."

"Were the boys here?"

"Of course. As was I. I wasn't going to let her die alone, regardless of the state of our marriage. She was ill for a good month, and sometimes the fever even seemed to abate, but then it spiked again. She was lucid from time to time and asked to see the boys when she was."

"And you allowed it?"

"I did. She was dying. I tried to keep them from touching her, but they did visit the sickroom on good days. Joshua was still in nappies. I can't think he remembers much."

While the boys' father probably forgot little.

"He might not have much recollection, but Jeremiah has no doubt talked with him at length about their mother, so Joshua thinks he recalls everything his brother does. It must have been very difficult."

"It was… hot."

Likely stifling in a sick room, stinking horrendously, humiliating for the patient and trying for the family. And this had gone on for weeks. Of course the children had a recollection of it.

With his back to her, Ethan went on speaking. "She… apologized. In one of her lucid intervals, she apologized for her…" Alice was sure he hadn't meant to say that, but to her surprise, he finished his thought softly. "For her betrayals."

Gracious heavens. Betrayals—plural. That could not be good.

"May I offer you the library?" he asked, facing her, his expression once again that of a solicitous host. "It will be cooler, and you'll have everything you need to tend to your letters. I've done most of my writing for the day, which leaves me the accounting, for which I do not need the desk."

The change in topic was a relief, probably for them both. "Cooler sounds lovely. I've been in this bed long enough, but I hardly think it will serve to have me in my nightgown below stairs in broad daylight."

He pushed away from the window. "This is my house, and if I permit it, then nobody will say anything to it. I am not an earl, in case you hadn't noticed."

Mr. Grey was more arrogant than any earl. Alice had met a few and was in fact related to one. "The gossips will say whatever they please," she retorted, "though not to your face, and maybe not to mine. If you'd give me a few minutes, I'll be right along."

"As you wish." He turned to go then rounded on her. "You are not to pin your hair up in some frightful concoction designed to aggravate a lingering headache."

She accepted this edict, because Clara had tidied her braid very nicely, and because Mr. Grey liked to have the last word. Alice regarded his retreat, noting that he walked like the lions she'd seen in the Royal Menagerie, slinky, silent, and graceful, but somehow menacing in their very elegance. She did not doubt Ethan Grey was capable of sending an enemy to his final reward, and as big as he was, it would be quickly done.

And what kind of thoughts were those? Alice eased from the bed and crossed to her wardrobe. Maybe the boys weren't the only ones preoccupied with death, but as to that, it was good to know the anniversary of their mother's death was approaching.

A capable governess kept her eye on such things, for they caused havoc when ignored. She slipped into the most comfortable of her old summer dresses, a short-sleeved, high-waisted muslin faded with age, and put her feet into a pair of comfortable house slippers.

Alice made her way to the library, composing a letter to her sister Avis in her head. She was halfway to the desk when she realized she wasn't alone. Ethan Grey sat on the couch, his papers and an abacus spread out on the low table.

Five

ALICE STOPPED ABRUPTLY AND FELT HER BALANCE WEAVE. "I did not know we would be sharing the room."

"It's a large room." His lips were moving soundlessly as he ran his finger down a column on a page. "A moment, if you please." He scratched something on the page then got to his feet.

"Ciphering appeals to me," he said with a slight smile. "There is one right answer, and when things balance out, one has a sense of satisfaction about one's work. The pen, ink, and paper are in here." He opened a drawer on the desk, coming near enough that Alice got a whiff of cedar. "The sand is in here, and wax and seal are here. I've rung for tea, but with lemon and honey, because you're probably ready for a change from the mint."

"Thank you. That was considerate of you."

"It was not." He set a penknife on the desk. "I was thirsty, but I am not intentionally rude."

Her smile widened to a grin.

"Well, not all the time," he amended, his lips quirking up. "I'll leave you to your correspondence."

He was back at his figuring, while Alice mused that he *was* intentionally rude, frequently, but acts of consideration and kindness, those he seemed to produce only with a struggle.

But produce them, he did. Alice settled at the desk and bent to her task, but she recalled the sensation of Mr. Grey's large hand on her nape, his body supporting hers while he rearranged the pillows, his voice low and soothing as he did what was needed to ease Alice's discomfort. He wasn't a flirt like Nick— thank God—but he knew his way around a female body, and for the first time, Alice wondered what sort of man he'd be in intimate circumstances.

She let her gaze wander over his broad shoulders where he hunched like a golden raptor with his ledgers. He was muttering again. From time to time he'd pounce with his pen on an inaccuracy, talking to the figures under his breath as if they were some sort of sparring partner.

"Got you, you…"

"You don't belong in expenditures, and you know it."

He was down to shirt and waistcoat, in deference to the heat, and he'd dispensed with his neckcloth. The tanned skin at his throat fascinated Alice. She'd had her face against that skin, felt the heat of it. She'd inhaled the clean scent of him and felt the urge to remain in his embrace, her face hidden against him, her body slack and safe in his arms.

"Don't know what to tell them?" he asked.

He was on his feet, leaning back against an arm of the sofa, regarding Alice with amusement.

"It's repetitive," Alice said. "My sister still lives

in the North, at the family seat." Though how Avis tolerated such proximity to the Collins estate was a mystery. "Both my brothers are from home, so one must write the same news twice, at least, if not three times. And then I need to write a simpler version of things for Priscilla, and a not-so-simple version for Leah Haddonfield and Reese Belmont."

"All those people are to know the illustrious doings of my boys' governess. I am impressed."

"You are not," she said mildly, stifling the urge to yawn. The library really was very pleasant, with a ceiling of at least twelve feet, clerestory windows over the French doors, and shade trees beyond the windows all contributing to a cool, airy feel.

"Have some lemonade," he said, pouring her a glass. "You've been scratching away for more than an hour, and I propose a recess on the terrace."

"A fine idea." Alice rose, held steady for a moment, then preceded him through the French doors to the shady terrace. "How do you suppose Waterloo is proceeding?"

"The Corsican has probably been routed halfway to Kent by now, several times."

"And covered with mud," Alice added, letting him seat her at a wrought-iron table among boxes of flowering lilies. "Your house is very pretty, Mr. Grey. Is that your late wife's influence?"

He studied his drink. "Barbara wasn't the domestic sort. Lady Warne—Nick's grandmother—pointed out to me after Barbara's death that I was always happier in the country. I began to take more of an interest in Tydings after that, but anybody can order the gardener to plant a few flowers."

"Not everybody does," Alice rejoined, declining to

point out that it was far more than a few. Roses ringed the terrace in thriving abundance, their fragrance blending with the breeze. A rainbow of beds of cutting flowers spread across the back lawns. "What had you muttering and threatening away the afternoon?"

The question was a bit beyond the bounds of what a governess might ask her employer, but then, this employer had kissed the governess. True, it had been a rhetorical kiss, a point made in the interest of some sort of debate, but it left Alice more conversational latitude than she might have assumed otherwise.

"I was working on the accounts." His smile was sheepish. "I get fierce when the numbers aren't as they should be. What of you? Have you completed your letters?"

"I haven't written to Nick and his countess." Alice hid another yawn behind her glass of lemonade. "He insisted I let him know we are safely arrived, because he didn't trust you to see to it."

"He wanted to know you hadn't left us in a fit of wrath."

"I will not hare off in a fit of pique." Alice sipped her drink, enjoying the cool of the glass against her fingers. "I would not do that to the boys. But why don't you write to your brother and spare me the effort?" One needed to make such a suggestion casually. Alice drew her finger around the cool, wet rim of her glass.

"Perhaps I shall. I should thank him for putting up with my darling sons, shouldn't I?"

"He was happy for Ford and John to have other playmates. One has the impression Nick will always enjoy having children around, and Leah doesn't seem to mind, when they make her dear Nicholas happy."

"Are you jealous of her?"

That was definitely not an employer's question to the governess, though Alice didn't resent his curiosity. Much.

"Oh, certainly." Alice considered her drink, which could have done with a touch more sugar. "Leah has the love of a good man, material comforts, a loving family, and the certain knowledge her dragons will all be vanquished before her morning tea. Few women are so blessed."

"Do you harbor a tendresse for my brother?" Ethan asked, swirling his drink slowly—casually.

An inquiry that qualified as *odd*. "Nick?" Alice snorted. "He is a shameless flirt and oblivious to the dictates of Polite Society. He was a prince with Priscilla and calls her his princess to this day."

Ethan wrinkled his nose, as if the noisy, busy child he'd met earlier in the summer was in nowise a candidate for a crown. "Were you somebody's princess?"

Alice considered remarking that they'd probably have a storm by nightfall, except Ethan's question was a version of what an employer might ask—*before* he allowed a woman to have the care of his sons.

"I was my papa's princess, and my brothers', as was my sister."

"And your brothers don't mind you traveling all over England to see to other people's children?"

That question, she did not want to answer. "Of course they mind. They are my brothers, and my older brothers at that. But they understand I need to make my own way. We correspond regularly, and when I'm in London, I try to see them."

"We'll be in Town for Nick's investiture, though if you need to see your family sooner, you've only to ask."

Alice smiled at him patiently. "You've spent one morning with your boys, Mr. Grey. You would not be so generous were it a long week of mornings, I assure you."

"If you need to see your family," he said again with peculiar gravity, "you have only to ask. We'll put you in the traveling coach, you can stay with Lady Warne, and the boys and I will manage. And you agreed to call me Ethan."

"Thank you." Alice cocked her head, seeing he was dead serious, and Ethan Grey's version of dead serious was serious indeed. "Ethan."

"Better." He sipped the last of his drink, and quiet settled around them. For Alice, it was pleasant and peaceful to be out on the shady terrace, sipping lemonade and enjoying a summer afternoon. Out in the sun, particularly if one were active, it would be hot.

"Shall we move a bit?" he asked, rising and extending a hand. "I promise to keep you in the shade."

"A little movement would be appreciated. I can become too accustomed to the indoors, and that is a waste of pretty grounds."

"I'm fortunate that Argus makes it worth my while to keep him in regular work. The consequences of neglecting a morning hack don't bear consideration." Mr. Grey—Ethan, now—tucked her hand onto his arm. Because his sleeves were turned back, and Alice with out her gloves, this put her hand on the bare expanse of his muscular forearm. "This path keeps to the shade and takes us by the stream. If my hearing serves, we are likely to come across a great battle on the way."

Alice strolled along beside him, thinking he was relaxing more the longer he was on his home turf. Lady Warne had been right to hint he should spend time in his own home, but then again, maybe it wasn't travel that put him out of sorts, but time with his brother, the earl.

"How was it you were separated from your siblings?" Alice asked when they'd gone some way in silence.

"A misunderstanding. The story of record, until recently, is I accidentally branded Nick's fundament with an *H*, and the old earl thought I was a danger to his heir."

"Nick's famous scar."

"You've seen it?" His eyebrows rose, but his voice dropped with some severe sentiment—censure, or possibly disappointment.

"I most assuredly have not, but not for lack of hearing him offer to show it to the dairymaids, the goose girl, the vicar's granny, and my own self. He says he was branded like a bullock because he was mistaken for one by a drunken herdsman."

"He would." Ethan's smile held relief. "Our father burned an *H* for Haddonfield into the harnesses and saddles and anything in the stables that might tend to disappear. Nick and I were fooling with the branding iron, I tripped, and Nick's nether parts got stuck with the hot iron. I'm told he did not ride for several weeks, but even then, he wasn't offended."

"No doubt he enjoyed having the maids tend his wound. But you were sent away for this?"

"Not exactly."

Alice heard the boys shrieking with glee over by the

river, heard the soft, summery sounds of the afternoon: birds singing, a breeze soughing through the oaks, a cow lowing for her calf. She forced herself to let out a breath and waited, because Ethan was not done answering her question.

"The earl came by our bedroom at night to check on his injured son," Ethan said, pausing on the path but keeping Alice's hand at his elbow. "He found Nick and me in the same bed, which happened frequently. We were great ones for whispering and plotting and rehashing our days so the younger boys couldn't hear us. I have no doubt we were sharing the same pillow. The next night his lordship found the same situation, and he concluded I had enticed my younger brother into an unnatural association. He feared for his sons, his legitimate sons, and so he sent me away."

"He thought you had enticed Nick…?" Alice said slowly, while a feeling like panic, but angrier than panic, took hold in her belly. "And, of course, you had not. Not in any way."

This explained much, all of it bitter and dreadful. Her instinct was to protect the boy he'd been, the boy who might somewhere still lurk inside him. She shifted, so her arms went silently around his waist and her head came to rest on his chest, hugging him as she would one of her charges. "I am so sorry, Ethan. For you, for Nick, and for your father. Did he ever apologize?"

"For his mistake, yes." His arms closed around her slowly, slowly. "He never knew all the consequences of his error, and I let him die in ignorance."

"That was kind of you," Alice murmured against his chest. "What an awful thing to do to one's children. You and Nick must have been devastated, and I'm sure your father lived to regret his decision."

She spoke in the plural, regretting the consequences for him, for his brother and father too, but she kept her arms around the man with her.

"It's in the past," Ethan said, and still he didn't let her go.

"Our entire lives are in the past," Alice snapped. "Your papa might have been a good man, Ethan. I hope he was, but he was terribly wrong."

"He was." Alice felt him take a deep breath. "He was about as wrong as a father can be. I loved Nick. I do love Nick, and I'd never…"

"You wouldn't," Alice agreed, stepping back and slipping her arm through his. "You absolutely would not, and neither would Nick. Your father was simply wrong, and we must allow that this happens with human beings, but we don't have to like it one bit or pretend it wasn't such an egregious error. I suppose you wanted to bellow at him in righteous anger, and he deserved at least that."

They paced along the path for a few yards while Alice seethed with upset for the man beside her. Fourteen was not so very old, especially not for a boy raised in the sheltered environs of an earl's country seat.

Ethan paused beside her and cocked his head. "I hear the boys. Shall we leave them in peace or find out how goes the war?"

"You are a man," Alice said, allowing the change in topic. "War will fascinate you. I am a female. It will appall me. Why don't you see to the boys and I will return to the house? I think I'm due for another nap."

"I should escort you," he said, hesitating. His scowl

was aimed briefly at her hip. "Come." He started to turn them around, to return to the house.

"Don't be silly. I am well enough to stroll through the shade back to the library. You'll tend to the letter to Nick for me?"

"Of course." He let her slip her hand from his arm. "And to the vanquishing of the Corsican and any chance-met dragons."

❧

Ethan found a dry, shady spot between the battlefield and the water, and sank to the grass to watch his children. They had such energy in their play, such unstinting commitment to the joy of having fun. And yet, they were mindful of each other. He and Nick had been like that. Ethan knew it; he just could not recall the experience of it. He let the boys frolic and splash and dunk each other for a good half hour in the name of washing off the mud of battle.

"Gentlemen!" Ethan rose to his feet when Joshua's teeth were chattering. "Time to report to headquarters!"

The splashing stopped, and the boys slogged up the bank, with Joshua walking right up to his father's leg and leaning on it, panting.

"Water is heavy," Joshua observed.

"But you are not." Ethan picked up the cool, slippery weight of his youngest, and swung him toward the pile of clothes. "We'll use your shirts to dry you off. Come along, Jeremiah. You're probably going to want to look in on Miss Portman."

"We are?" Jeremiah looked confused as he scrubbed at himself with his shirt.

"Of course you are. You must report your history

lessons to her, just as you did your earlier efforts regarding the fable of the heroic pismire."

"Pismire!" Joshua exploded into peals of laughter. "You're a pismire. Jeremiah Pis-a-miah Nicholas Grey!"

"Hush." Ethan tossed Joshua's shirt gently at the child's face.

"Or you'll thrash him silly," Jeremiah suggested, not just smiling but grinning.

Ethan nodded gravely. "I'll thrash him hysterical and change his name to Pismire Nicholas Grey."

"Oooh." Jeremiah pointed at his little brother. "Now who's a pismire?"

"You're both pismires." Ethan did not smile, though it was a near thing. "And you make too much noise. Gather up your shoes, and let's storm the fortress yonder. They're bound to have some victuals for a couple of weary soldiers like yourselves."

"I'm thirsty, too," Joshua said, gathering up two shoes and his shirt. "I forget where my smalls are."

"Here." Jeremiah tossed them to him. "But they might have ants in them—pismires for a pismire."

"Do they?" Joshua looked at his father worriedly, unwilling to touch the offending clothing at his feet.

"Hardly matters." Ethan snatched up the tiny underclothes. "You aren't in them. Now can we please move along?"

He shooed the boys into the house through the kitchen, pausing to make sure they got some lemonade and buttered bread, then had them stop off in the laundry for a quick, hot bath. Both boys occupied the same tub, to save time heating water and to encourage them to soak long enough to get some dirt off. By the time Ethan ushered them up the steps to their suite, they were both considerably more subdued than they'd been earlier.

"Shall we stop off to see Miss Portman?" Ethan suggested, knowing *he* at least was going to make a call.

"Let's," Jeremiah said. "She will want to know we went swimming, and saved the empire, and ate raspberries."

"Not in that order." Ethan did smile at the business of a boy's summer day. "But she will want to know."

They found her in her room, addressing a stack of correspondence. She was in her comfortable dress, her braid a little less tidy, her eyes tired but devoid of the choking worry Ethan had seen in them earlier.

"We've come to see how you fare," Ethan said, "and to regale you with tales of the day."

She smiled and sank onto her settee, patting the cushions on either side of her. "Come and tell me what has passed this day while I've languished for lack of the company of my dearest little gentlemen."

The boys gamboled over like the puppies they were, leaving Ethan to lower himself to the delicate chair behind Miss Portman's escritoire. Even on short acquaintance, his sons were comfortable with her. They tucked right up against her sides, cuddling in as if she were a favorite aunt—or uncle.

Absently, Ethan's eyes strayed to the letters stacked on the corner of the blotter. There were a half dozen or so, addressed in a tidy, flowing hand. His gaze fell on the top one, and he wasn't meaning to read, much less pry, but the name on the envelope was familiar to him.

So what, what in the bloody blue blazes, was Alice Portman doing writing to the private investigator kept on Nicholas Haddonfield's personal payroll?

Six

My dearest Benjamin,

You will be pleased to see I am no longer immured in the far, distant wilds of Sussex. I am now merely two hours' ride from you, at the estate of Tydings near Guilford in Surrey. My responsibilities here include two very charming young fellows, ages five and six. They are lively young men but a little more hesitant to go on than they should be, owing to past upheavals in the greater household.

The estate is pleasant in the extreme, my wages are generous, and my employer considerate, if sometimes a little gruff. His children love him, but he is a busy man, and I will endeavor to keep the lads too occupied to miss their father's attention much. The kitchen has become a bit lax, but this will soon be set to rights, I am sure.

You must be reassured, dear Brother, I fare well. I left the Belmonts on very good terms, but because I had been with Priscilla for almost five years, it was time to allow more scholarly hands to guide her development. I trust I will remain with the Grey *children for some time, though I am allowed these first months as a trial period. You are not to put your nose into my situation here, Benjamin, not directly or otherwise. Mr. Grey came with the very highest personal recommendations from the Earl and Countess of Bellefonte, among others. I will be safe here, and you are not to worry.*

I love you and miss you, and look forward to seeing you. We are to go into Town for Bellefonte's investiture. Until then, try not to be too serious or too busy.

> *Your loving sister,*
> *Allie*

◦◦◦

Alice was wearing a big, fat, cheery smile when she dragged the boys into the breakfast parlor. "Good morning, Mr. Grey! How fortunate to see you so early in the day."

"The good fortune is entirely mine." Ethan reserved the irony in his smile for Alice. "Joshua, Jeremiah, which of us will have the privilege of seating Miss Portman?"

Two little faces regarded Ethan blankly.

"Oh, very well." He stepped behind their governess, treating himself to a whiff of lemons. "I've had my first cup of tea, so I will demonstrate, but I won't be doing this every day. You fellows must occasionally pitch in. Miss Portman?"

She sank gracefully into her seat with a murmured, "Thank you, Mr. Grey," for the benefit of their rapt audience.

"Where do we sit?" Joshua asked, frowning.

"In the other two chairs," Ethan said. "Now, since

I am taller than either of you, I will prepare your plates, lest you pull the entire sideboard over while you search out your preferences. Joshua?"

"Can I see it?" Joshua gestured to the buffet laid out just higher than his line of sight.

"Of course." Ethan scooped him onto his hip. "Let's inspect, shall we?" He explained each selection to his son, answered more questions than one typical breakfast buffet ought to engender, and reached compromises that created a breakfast of more than just jam and chocolate.

"Jeremiah, you aren't going to let your little brother be the only one to eat well, are you?"

"I can see it," Jeremiah groused, though he was only an inch or so taller than his younger brother.

Ethan came down on his haunches and whispered to his son, "How am I to cadge a morning hug without Miss Portman gawking at me?" Jeremiah's dubious expression confirmed that Ethan was taking a gamble, but then the boy cracked his rare, dear smile and threw his arms around Ethan's neck.

"Good of you," Ethan whispered as he stood with Jeremiah on his hip then said in a louder voice, "If you want something that will last you until luncheon, you'd better tuck into some ham or bacon, or at the very least, get some butter on one of those scones." He soon had Jeremiah sitting before a fairly impressive plate of food, then resumed his own seat.

Ethan sat back to his meal, a queer little hitch in his chest. He'd not had breakfast with his sons before, though they were nearly old enough for such an informal meal, and he'd not known they were joining him today. But here they were, being gently guided toward proper manners by their enterprising governess, and Ethan felt a spurt of pleasure in their company.

They really were good boys.

And what had been wrong with their mother, that she hadn't seen that?

∽

Breakfast had gone well. Alice assured herself of this as Ethan proposed that their discussion of the boys' lessons be moved from the library to the shady walking path.

"That will serve. After a good meal, one wants activity."

And almost any time, it seemed *one* enjoyed having one's hand on Ethan Grey's arm, hearing his precise baritone, and catching his cedary scent.

As they stepped onto the path, Alice launched into a discussion of Latin primers.

"Boys don't find Latin useful at all," Ethan interjected. "Men like to toss around the occasional apt phrase, and sprinkle their conversation with wise sayings. It's the only Latin one uses after university, I assure you."

"You attended?"

"Cambridge."

"A rebel?"

"Nick went to Oxford."

She slipped her arm from his and stopped in the shade of an enormous maple. "The earl didn't even let you attend the same university? What was wrong with your father?"

"He was being protective, or so I tell myself."

"He was being an ass," Alice hissed, hand fisting.

"If ever there's a man who could protect himself from unwarranted advances, it's your dear *little* brother, particularly by the time he was sixteen or seventeen years old." She reined in her temper, since she had no business making such pronouncements. "With respect to French, I find the verbal nuances are better—"

Ethan stood quite near her, his expression amused. "You're very fierce, Alice Portman. I wish the earl were alive so you might blister his ears with your observations." He took her hand, and there in the lovely morning air, kissed her knuckles, as a knight might kiss the hand of a lady whose favor he wore into the lists.

This flummery provoked a blush and put all thoughts of primers to rout. "I am not fierce, Mr. Grey."

He smiled at her, likely for resorting to more formal address. And oh, that smile sent common sense gamboling after the errant primers. He was a handsome man in any mood, but distant, reserved, and *safe*. When he smiled, all the warmth in him was briefly visible, all the dearness that made him fret for his children and for his younger brother.

Maybe even a little for a governess. "I am not fierce," Alice said again, feeling an awkward confession looming far too closely.

"Will you elaborate on your supposed meekness, *Miss Portman*? I confess, my own conjectures cannot encompass such a flight."

He drew her by the hand toward a wooden bench in the dappled shade, and when he seated her, he did not drop her hand. Maybe he sensed the confession as well.

"Nick once told me your youngest sister, Della, is prone to breathing spells."

"She is." He seemed to have forgotten that their hands were joined. "They didn't start until after I left."

"If I were fierce, I would not be prone to spells when I can't breathe, I can't think, and every particle of my mind is filled with dread at my certain and imminent death. I don't even like talking about such moments, I get so anxious."

"And you suffered these spells at Belle Maison."

"Only two," Alice said, resisting the compulsion to take deeper breaths. She focused instead on the warmth—the improper and comforting warmth—of Ethan's fingers closed around hers. "Mrs. Belmont was with me, and she knows I'm prone to them, but Nick has seen me through one too, and it's unusual for me to have two in two weeks."

"I am making a list, Alice Portman, that starts with megrims, progresses to a bad hip, and includes these breathing spells. You have nightmares too, don't you?"

He spoke gently, but he *knew*. Somehow, this great, strapping, self-possessed man knew what it was to be reduced to an animal, cataleptic with fear and pain.

Alice managed a nod.

"I have gone for as long as three years without a spell." And even longer without discussing this nuisance with anybody. She focused her gaze on the patterns of sunlight and shadow dancing on the grass rather than stare at her hand enveloped in his. "I used to have nightmares."

Bringing up the topic had put a pinch in her breathing and a knot of unease in her belly. She leaned into him, just a little, hoping he wouldn't notice.

His arm settled around her shoulders, suggesting her hope had been in vain. "Before you came here, when was the last breathing spell, Alice? And don't think to dissemble."

She didn't dissemble, but she hesitated long enough to take a fortifying whiff of cedar, to concentrate on being this close to a man and wanting to be closer.

Surely that was a good thing? "In my room, after you'd offered me this post and I'd ridden the horse."

"Because," he said, his voice close to her ear, "any change brings with it anxiety and loss, even a change for the better. If you have more of these spells, Alice, what shall I do?"

She almost told him she wouldn't have a spell if he were in the vicinity, but here she was, dragging in slow breaths, even as she was tucked against him.

"It helps to be warm and to put my head down, and it helps if you can talk to me slowly and quietly, exactly as you did. You can't get anxious, and you shouldn't *be* anxious. The worst thing that will happen is I'll faint for a few minutes, and when I faint, I can breathe."

He was quiet for a moment, his fingers drawing a pattern on her shoulder.

"But until you faint, you will be certain the entire world is coming to a horrible, unstoppable end. You might do stupid things—run from friends when in unfamiliar surroundings, draw a weapon for no reason, cower in corners gulping for breath and awaiting certain death."

More awful knowledge. Thank God he didn't mention the worst of it. She might lose control of bodily functions. She had, for the first two years.

He shifted then and wrapped his arms around her, abandoning all pretense that his proximity was a casual misstep by an otherwise unassuming gentleman. The tension in her belly quieted; the hitch in her breathing eased. Her conscience fell silent as well, because the comfort—the sheer, glorious comfort—of his embrace was too precious.

"It might help too," he said, "if you put in your mind a picture of something good, something beloved and dear, and when you feel your breathing seize up and you sense your reason is deserting you, you bring that image to your mind and hold it hard."

She nodded against his shoulder while his hand traced the line of her hair where it smoothed past her ear.

"I will do my best to make sure you are not plagued with frightening thoughts or frightening people, Alice. I've found a lot of peace here at Tydings, and despite the racket and mayhem created by my sons, I think it's still a peaceful place."

He made no move to shift away, to end this unlooked-for familiarity. Instead, he repeated that caress in a slow, soothing rhythm, until the pleasure of it and the warmth of his body seeped into Alice's soul.

Her brothers were fiercely devoted, kindhearted men who would do anything for her, and yet she hadn't allowed them this. When Ethan Grey said he would do his best to shield her from upset, it was as if he took a vow, and the sense of sanctuary Alice felt was a steady flame in an oppressive darkness.

Because he *knew*. Somehow, without being aware of any of the details of her ordeal, Ethan Grey knew what she had suffered.

❧

Holding Alice Portman on a shady bench in the middle of a pleasant summer morning, Ethan felt as if he'd stepped off a cliff into some other morning in some other man's life. Women were no more than fixtures to him. As an adolescent, they'd fascinated him; in his marriage they'd horrified him; and he counted himself lucky to be largely indifferent to sexual desire in recent years. His sisters, Lady Warne, and Leah, they were women to be admired and protected.

As was Alice Portman, maybe more than any of the others, maybe more than all of them put together.

Alice had been wronged somewhere in her past, egregiously wronged, and while Ethan's mind knew that, his body was taking note of other things: Alice fit in his embrace wonderfully, like she wanted to be there, not like she had to tolerate this closeness. She had a pleasing shape, a pleasing scent, and soft, silky hair. He could feel the slow heave of her breathing against his chest.

The confluence of protectiveness and desire was disorienting. This was how one ought to feel about a wife perhaps, or so Ethan had once thought.

With an effort of will and the feel of Alice's soft curves burning into his memory, Ethan decided it was a good thing for a man in his prime to feel desire. It was in accordance with the plan of God and Nature, and no reason to be alarmed. Were he honest, he'd admit that not feeling desire for the past few years had been more alarming.

He could desire Alice Portman. This had to do not just with her steady brown eyes, well-disguised curves, and pleasant, tart scent, but also with her breathing spells and bad hip and nightmares.

He bent his head toward her, inhaled the fragrance of flowers and lemons, and idly—in a purely theoretical way—wondered if she could desire him.

❧

"Are you gentlemen *trying* to spook my horse?" Ethan inquired as both boys happened to pause for breath in the same moment.

"He dragged me off!" Jeremiah shouted, a note of hysteria in his voice. "He should have let go, and he bloody wouldn't, and he made me fall off, the sodding little bugger."

"You didn't hold on!" Joshua shot back, hands fisting. "You had the mane, and I didn't, you should have caught me, and you let me slide right off all the way down. You're a sodding little *pismire*."

Ethan lip's twitched, to hear the word fired off with such vehemence. He gestured to Miller, who nodded and came to stand beside Ethan, then trotted off in search of more tack when he'd gotten his instructions.

"Gentlemen." Ethan kept his voice quiet. "If you would kindly shut the hell up for one moment, I will tender my apologies."

Joshua cocked his head. "Huh?"

"Papa is going to apologize," Jeremiah said. "I think."

"He is," Ethan said, "for not warning you Argus sometimes kicks out when schooling piaffe in hand, and for putting you on double. Has no one taught you how to fall off?"

The boys exchanged glances when Miller appeared with a long lead line.

"No, sir," Jeremiah said. "I thought one didn't want to fall."

"Sometimes one does," Ethan countered. "For example, if Argus bolted with me and was heading for a low branch or a cliff, I might want to part company with him. Or if by chance I should become unseated and a fall is inevitable, then one wants to fall as safely as possible. I will demonstrate."

"You're going to fall off Argus?" Joshua goggled. "On purpose?"

"I am, but perhaps my waistcoat need not participate." He shrugged out of it, removed the surcingle from around the horse's belly, passed the saddle to Miller, grabbed a hank of mane, and swung up.

"How'd he do that?" Joshua asked Jeremiah. "Argus is tall, and Papa didn't use a mounting block or stirrups or *anything.*"

Miller stood in the center of the arena, the horse circling him on the long lead, while Ethan got his seat at the trot bareback.

"All right, you lot." Ethan kept his eyes front, settling into the rhythm of the trot. "Spook him."

Miller nodded at the boys. "You heard your papa. Spook that big golden devil, and unseat your papa."

"How?" Jeremiah asked as Joshua bolted past him.

"Pismire pony!" Joshua bellowed, waving his arms and charging right at the horse. Argus, true to his delicate sensibilities, shied mightily, giving Ethan the pretext he needed to slide gracefully over the horse's shoulder. Argus came to an immediate halt, allowing Ethan to swing back on.

"Again." Ethan nodded at Miller. "And put some effort into it, gentlemen. Argus will go to sleep otherwise, and so shall I."

It took a few more tries before Jeremiah got into the spirit of the game, but Argus got into it too, spooking horrifically, only to stand stock still as soon as Ethan had decamped. Ethan demonstrated both an emergency dismount, which ideally left the rider on his feet, and the less graceful variations thereon.

Ethan beat at the dust on his once-pristine shirt. "I think we can commend Argus on a job well done and turn our attention to your ponies." The boys turned to see grooms holding both ponies, and neither pony sporting a saddle.

"Up you go." Ethan hoisted Joshua onto his pony, then Jeremiah.

"I don't want to do this," Jeremiah said, staring sullenly at his pony's mane. Ethan considered his older son and those few brave words.

"C'mon, Jeremiah," Joshua said. "We'll get dirty, and we can scream like girls."

"He doesn't have to if he doesn't want to," Ethan said. "My intention was to have you practice only at the halt, and if you felt up to it, at the walk."

"It's stupid," Jeremiah declared, defiant eyes raised to his father's. "Why would you fall off on purpose if falling off is how you get hurt?"

"Am I hurt?" Ethan asked, holding his son's gaze.

"No," Jeremiah admitted. "But if Argus stepped on your head or your guts, you could be dead."

Death. Again.

Ethan wanted to shake the boy but kept his voice calm. "Do you think I would do anything to intentionally put you in harm's way?"

Jeremiah mumbled something then looked away.

"I beg your pardon?" Ethan's patience was strained, but Miller had led Joshua out of earshot and was letting the boy get used to a bareback ride.

"You hired Mr. Harold," Jeremiah said. "He was harmful. Langstrom wasn't much better."

"Mr. Harold caned Joshua. I know that, but it—"

"More than once," Jeremiah interrupted. "He caned him lots, and he made me watch, and he would make Joshua try to do things that were too hard just so he could cane him. He called us names and said we were the shame of the neighborhood."

"Ye gods…" Ethan's physical balance wavered, as if he'd sustained a roundhouse punch or had too much cheap liquor. "What else did he say?"

"A lot of things." Jeremiah sighed. "Mean things. I didn't understand all of them. He called Joshua a slutterswipe…"

"Guttersnipe," Ethan supplied, hauling back hard on his temper—for at whom ought he to be most angry but himself?

"Here's my difficulty," Ethan said. "I am sorry you ever had to deal with Mr. Harold. I wish I could thrash him silly. Bloody damned silly, in fact, and don't you tattle regarding my language, Jeremiah Grey. But Harold isn't here, and I want you to be safe when you're riding. Knowing how to fall is part of being safe. I didn't keep you safe from Mr. Harold, and I hate that, but I want desperately to keep you safe from a bad fall."

"I'll stop riding," Jeremiah decided, giving his pony's neck a wistful pat.

Ethan's heart began to beat in a slow, hard rhythm in his chest. "You love to ride, and you're very good at it. And then Joshua would have no one to ride with except me, and I'll wager I am not half the fun you are."

Jeremiah eyed his brother. "He gallops everywhere. You're better at swearing."

Ethan waited, heart thumping almost painfully,

because the mysterious juvenile cogs in his son's brain were clearly still turning.

"I fell before," Jeremiah said. "It hurt, but Lightning didn't do it on purpose. There was a rabbit."

"Pesky beasts, rabbits. Always darting out and looking so cute while they do." Ethan's heart beat so hard he could feel it working… like a rabbit's.

"Tell me," Jeremiah said, fiddling with his reins, "*if* I were going to practice falling, how would I practice it?"

"Carefully," Ethan said, his heart slowing a little, "and with people around who mean you only the best. You do it slowly, Jeremiah, in stages you can understand, and if you need to take a break, you insist on a break. *If* you were going to, that is."

"How would I start?"

"You relax," Ethan said, finding he needed to swallow a few times before going on. "You let your body relax, and you don't fight the fall. If you're traveling at speed, give up the reins, or you'll just jerk your horse's mouth before you lose them anyway. Try to slip down the horse's side, but tuck up to protect your head. Your horse will never try to step on you, so don't even consider it a risk." He went on, his voice gradually becoming more even and his breathing easing up.

"I'm ready," Jeremiah said, clutching the reins desperately and sending his pony in a plodding circle at the walk.

"All right." Ethan stepped away, making sure to keep his own body and tone of voice relaxed. "When I say 'pismire pony,' you relax, let go of the reins, and curl down along Lightning's side. He'll probably stop and give you a puzzled look."

Jeremiah nodded, his expression suggesting he contemplated the mental equivalent of a severe birching.

"Steady on." Ethan took another step back. "One, two, three... pismire pony."

He'd nearly whispered the last two words, and Jeremiah tipped, slipped, and tumbled off his pony's back. The pony halted, swished his tail, and sniffed at the little boy in the dirt. Ethan crouched down and met Jeremiah's eyes.

"You did it. I'm proud of you." He wanted to damn cry he was so proud.

"I did it." Jeremiah sat up and was promptly pulled into his father's arms. Wordlessly, Ethan hugged him—really, really hugged him. This wasn't a sneaky hint of a hug in the midst of a picnic hubbub. It wasn't a surreptitious, teasing hug while choosing from the breakfast buffet. This couldn't be construed as anything but a hug, plain, heartfelt, and sincere.

"I did it." Jeremiah said again, closing his eyes and laying his head on his father's shoulder. "I fell off."

"Splendidly," Ethan assured him. The pony spoiled the moment, pony fashion, by butting Ethan's shoulder, nearly pushing man and boy onto their arses in the dirt.

"Wretched beast," Ethan murmured, still holding his son. "Shall we see how your brother fares?"

"He'll be fine," Jeremiah said as Ethan set him on his feet. "He's little."

"I know what you mean. He seems to bounce through life."

"Is that bad?" Jeremiah watched as, at the halt, Joshua slid off his pony.

"No," Ethan said, thinking of another little brother

who seemed to bounce through life. "But he didn't bounce just then, did he?"

"No." Jeremiah grinned. "You don't bounce either."

"And neither do you, Jeremiah." Ethan smiled back. "But you fall beautifully."

❧

Ethan sent his sons up to the house, and off they went at a dead run. He turned toward the stables, intent on retrieving his waistcoat, knowing that hours of ledgers and correspondence awaited him in the library.

A cheering thought intruded: he and Alice had never quite gotten around to a discussion of the boys' curriculum.

And then the cheering thought was interrupted by the sight of a groom who had Joshua's pony, Thunder, trailing on a lead behind him. Thunder was rearing and propping, and for good cause. The groom was using the end of the leather lead shank to whack at the pony's neck and shoulders.

"Step on me, will ye?" the man shouted. "I'll show ye who ye can step on, ye hairy little shite. No damned manners, and getting fussed all day has ye spoilt rotten. The knacker would love to take a knife to yer tough little hide."

"Hold," Ethan said quite loudly as he approached the man, "and I do mean now."

The man nodded. "G'day to ye, guv. Little monster thought to stomp me good."

The little monster was still kiting around on the end of his lead line, eyes rolling at the potential new threat Ethan posed.

"Give him to me." Ethan held out a hand for the lead shank, keeping his voice quiet. "When did he attempt this violence?"

The man gestured to the stables, fifty yards distant. "In the barn. Just up and tromped on me boot."

Sturdy, if worn, heavy boots, Ethan noted. And the groom himself had the thick, muscular physique and dusty, worn attire of a typical plowboy.

Thunder, by contrast, was a Welsh pony, an elegant little equine standing about twelve hands. He was small enough to work the mines, about as small as a riding mount could be, even for a child.

"So you thought to discipline him here." Ethan stroked a hand down the pony's coarse mane. "To impress upon him the error of his ways, what, a quarter mile and ten minutes after the crime?"

"He's stubborn, that one." The groom eyed the pony balefully. "Takes a firm hand."

Miller came puffing out from the stables, just as Ethan would have bellowed for him.

"Problem, Mr. Grey?" Miller asked, using deferential address before an inferior.

"Did Thunder act up in the barn? Perhaps misbehave in hand or take advantage of Mr. Thatcher here?"

"Thunder?" Miller snorted and glanced at the now-quiet pony. "That beast doesn't know how to misbehave, unless it's to snitch a mouthful of grass. He dodged a little when a cat jumped up the ladder beside him, but it weren't mischief."

"A misunderstanding then," Ethan said. "Easily explained. Miller, you will see Thunder to his paddock, please?" Ethan gave the pony a final pat and passed the lead shank to Miller.

Thunder—a good boy of the equine persuasion—followed docilely.

"Mr. Thatcher." Ethan eyed the man coolly. "I trust Miller's judgment more than my own when it comes to horses. What have you to say for yourself?"

"Miller weren't leading the damned pony." Thatcher's chest heaved with indignation. "Them's dangerous, ponies are. Them's quick and mean and belongs in the mines with both eyes put out."

"How did you come to work in the stables?"

"Came to help with the last harvest in the fall," Thatcher said. "Miller took sick in the winter. I stayed on."

And Ethan had trusted Miller to sort out the bad apples that had come in with the harvest.

"Stay away from the ponies, Thatcher. Another such misunderstanding, and I will turn you off. Ponies can easily be made mean, but that pony belongs to my son and is none of yours to make mistakes with. Do we understand each other?"

Clearly, Ethan was making an enemy. The man's eyes narrowed, his expression closed, and his gaze went to where Miller was turning the pony out with Lightning, who bucked and cantered up to his mate in welcome.

"I understand ye clear enough." In a cavalier display of rudeness, Thatcher spat his words, turned his back on his employer, and stomped off. Which confirmed to Ethan he should have fired the man, plain and simple. He'd have Miller find a pretext for doing same, but leave it in his stable master's hands. Some of the joy of the morning was tarnished, but not all.

He could find Alice and interrogate her regarding

Latin primers and whatever else she'd been prosing on about before more important matters had come under discussion.

He smiled as he turned back toward the house, but paused before the peach tree, not intending to grab a snack but merely to assess the ripening crop. As he stood in the tree's shade, he spied Alice walking hand in hand with a tall, dark-haired man in riding attire. It wasn't anybody Ethan recognized, and Alice was a fair distance from the house. As he debated intruding—a gentleman did not spy—Alice stopped and wrapped her arms around the man, holding him in a fiercely close embrace.

Seven

ETHAN LEFT HIS CHAMBERS FOR THE LOWER FLOORS OF the house, his toilet repaired sufficiently for the noonday meal.

His mood, however, was not in good repair at all. He caught the eye of the footman at the end of the corridor. Tall, blond, handsome—like Nick, of course. "It's Davey, isn't it?"

The fellow smiled, revealing surprisingly good teeth. "That would be me, Mr. Grey."

"Be warned. The boys like you." Ethan hurried off, stomach growling, mood deteriorating apace. If Alice Portman had a gentleman caller, she would in nowise be hanging about Tydings for even her probationary period. No woman in her right mind chose govern-essing over matrimony.

Where was Ethan supposed to find another governess, and how was he supposed to explain it to the boys?

"Mr. Grey?" Mrs. Buxton stopped him at the foot of the steps. "We've set lunch in the dining room. Miss Portman said there's to be a gentleman for company.

She's in the family parlor with the gentleman, and she asked the boys to join the adults at table."

Ethan's eyebrows rose, as this was presumption upon presumption. "She did?"

"She certainly did," Mrs. Buxton nodded, sails filling with righteousness.

"Then she must have had good reasons," Ethan said before the housekeeper could launch her first volley. "You will tell the kitchen I'm sure lunch will be exemplary, particularly the vegetable dishes."

"Aye, sir." Mrs. Buxton looked confused, but bobbed her curtsy and disappeared, no doubt to inform the kitchen they were in Ethan's crosshairs.

His mood sank further when he heard genuine, hearty laughter as he approached the family parlor. Alice's suitor was apparently a charming bastard, making Ethan realize he hadn't heard her laugh yet—not like that. Alice Portman was overstepping, and—to take a maliciously appropriate leaf from her own book—she could have done Ethan the courtesy of asking.

He swept into the family parlor without knocking, as it was his goddamned house, and Alice was practically sitting in the man's lap.

"Miss Portman." Ethan barely nodded. "I see you have an unanticipated guest."

"Grey." The man rose, and Ethan saw his face for the first time. "A pleasure to see you again. My sister has said only nice things about you, so I know you're hiding something."

God above. Ethan stuck out his hand on reflex, as he did indeed know the man.

"Alice is your *sister*?" Ethan managed, mental gears

whizzing. If Benjamin Hazlit was Alice Portman's brother, then why weren't their last names the same? By God, if Alice were married. His mood halted mid-plunge and reversed itself: she might be *widowed*…

"My younger sister." Hazlit's smile was faintly mocking. "I am reporting for inspection, because we haven't seen each other for some weeks. My apologies for not sending word in advance, but I was in the neighborhood. You have a lovely estate, at least what I've seen of it, and Alice says the house is just as pretty."

"My thanks," Ethan said, recovering a few of his wits. "Has Al—Miss Portman offered you something to drink?"

Alice smiled at him, and this Alice—who laughed, who welcomed a brother much respected in Polite Society—bore little resemblance to the woman who'd clung to Ethan beneath the maple tree.

"We were waiting for you, Mr. Grey," she said. "I apologize for not warning you, but Benjamin tends to show up for an unannounced call whenever I change positions. It's always a pleasant surprise to see him."

There was a plea in her smile, for forbearance, maybe. She hadn't invited her brother here and probably wasn't entirely glad to see the man. And for Alice—Ethan knew this about her—there would always be something unpleasant about any surprise.

"Family should always be welcome," Ethan said. "Let me ring for drinks. Something chilled might do. Lemonade?"

He could be a creditable host, and he slipped into the role by dint of will. Lunch passed pleasantly, with Hazlit quizzing the boys as if Alice were the charge and they the supervisors.

Joshua grinned at his governess. "If you forget our story, Miss Portman, we'll make you go to bed without supper."

"If you send her to bed without supper," Hazlit said, "she might be cranky the next day. Out of sorts, grouchy—you know what I mean?"

"Miss Portman is never out of sorts," Jeremiah said, all seriousness. "She says moods and vapors do not become a lady whose task is as important as hers."

"And that important task would be?" Ethan gestured to the footman to top off everyone's glass of lemonade.

"Keeping us out of trouble," Joshua said. "It's a lot of work, Papa."

"I can imagine. Shall we take our drinks to the terrace so the kitchen can get to the work of tidying up?"

"It's my turn!" Joshua bumped his brother aside with a stout application of a pointy little elbow to a fraternal rib, and stood behind Alice's chair. She rose and waited while Joshua wrestled the chair back.

When the boys had departed for the next installment of Waterloo, the adults enjoyed the shaded end of the terrace.

"I think I'll go fetch a hat," Alice said. "I might want to see this famous battle site, but the sun is quite fierce." The men stood, and Ethan turned to see Hazlit regarding him with the same speculation Ethan was aiming at his guest.

Ethan arched an eyebrow. "The point of your sortie wasn't to fawn over your sister, though you get marks for being a good brother. What do you want to know?"

Hazlit saluted with his drink. "You share your brother's gift for plain speaking, which suits me far better than pettifogging inanities. Alice seems happy here."

"Provided she looks after my children, there is no reason why she can't be happy here. But we are not addressing your primary concern, are we?"

"We are not," Hazlit conceded. "Alice may rejoin us at any time, so let me be blunt." When Ethan said nothing, Hazlit's near-smile made another fleeting appearance. "It's like this, Grey. None of us, save my sister Avis, who rusticates in Cumbria, uses our actual family name. Hazlit and Portman hang somewhere nearby on the family tree, but several branches back."

"And you resort to this subterfuge, why?" Ethan took a slow sip of his drink, not sure he wanted an honest answer but damned certain he'd extract one.

"My sisters were involved in a scandal some twelve years ago," Hazlit said. "They were not to blame, and they've lived exemplary lives ever since. Avis adjusted by burying herself at the family seat and becoming what Wilhelm and I call an instant spinster, though she was quite young at the time. Alice, who was even younger, adjusted by becoming utterly independent. She will not take one penny of her family money, and believe me, there is ample."

"Why are you telling me this?" Old scandals were the worst kind. They tended to rise up and sink their teeth into one's present life, and not let go until a high price had been paid. And yet, it made sense. Alice's bodily symptoms were evidence of a kind of haunting, and nothing haunted like a brutal scandal.

Hazlit swirled his drink. "I'd like your word, if the details of Alice's past come out, you won't cut her loose over it without giving me time to step in."

A bad scandal indeed. "You assume I would cut her

loose. I myself have been on the receiving end of more than one scandal."

"One doesn't want to presume," Hazlit said. "And your most notable scandal involved the woman whom you chose to be the mother of your children."

Hardly. "Your tact is appreciated. My wife was a tramp, which is exactly what I should have expected when I married my mistress, isn't it?"

Hazlit shrugged. "Not if she loved you. Women are complicated. They can be more loyal than Wellington's foot soldiers, when they choose."

Society's most discreet investigator would need tact like that. "She did not choose, and then too, your sister has condescended to find employment in my household, when my antecedents are worse than suspect."

"Alice is the last person to hold bastardy against anyone." Hazlit snorted. "Her last charge, Priscilla, was not legitimate. There were rumors that my half brother was not legitimate."

"And will he be calling upon my governess unannounced as well?"

"Unannounced gives a man clues he wouldn't have otherwise been able to gather."

"Such as?"

Hazlit gave his host a measuring glance. "Such as you are too much of gentleman to eavesdrop, and you are enough of a papa to spend a summer morning in the stables with your sons. Beneath your tailored attire, you have the muscles of a yeoman, which suggests you are not prone to gentlemanly idleness. Your children are welcome at your table and even welcome to speak at table. Your staff is competent, your grounds well maintained, and you call my sister Alice, which means she's given you that honor."

"It is a rare honor?" Ethan heard himself ask.

"Outside of family? Your brother Nicholas; Matthew Belmont; Thomas, Baron Sutcliffe, by virtue of his relationship as Priscilla's uncle; and now... you."

The other three were married. Happily married.

"I will not abuse the privilege," Ethan said. "Have you more questions for me?"

"What happened to her predecessor?"

An insightful, uncomfortable question. "As to that..." Ethan ran a hand through his hair and turned to survey his back gardens. "I chose poorly, and my sons paid the price. His name was Harold, tall, blond, the epitome of the earnest English scholar, devoted to his calling. I'm not sure what the boys learned from him, except to fear the birch rod, and me."

"How long was he here?"

"Since the first of the year," Ethan said. "Your sister is a lovely change of approach for them, and though I do trust her, I have no intention of allowing anybody such unbridled control of my children again."

"That's all you can do," Hazlit said, sympathy in his eyes. "You vow to be vigilant and never let it happen again, and you pray until God must go deaf from your ceaseless begging."

Ethan regarded him at some length. Such an invitation was not to be declined.

"It must have been a very bad scandal," Ethan said. "Is this how Alice was injured?"

"It is. Her injury doesn't seem to be bothering her though."

"Her hip gives out on her if she takes a bad step,"

Ethan said, pouring them both more lemonade. "Then it pains her for a while. And the breathing spells? You know she had two while at Belle Maison?"

"She didn't say," Hazlit said slowly, new respect in his eyes at this confidence. "Change can bring them on, situations that feel out of control, sudden frights."

"So she controls children, and thus orders her universe," Ethan said. It was a sound strategy. Ethan himself controlled businesses, which were probably more predictable than children.

Hazlit looked... disgruntled. "You notice things."

Alice told him things, too, which he wasn't about to admit to her brother. "From a man of your calling, this is a fine compliment."

"It is. This is a kind of compliment too, Mr. Grey: if you cause my sister any substantial distress, by being difficult to work for, by being a sorry excuse for a parent, by so much as looking at her with that well-honed imitation of patrician condescension, I will meet you. Your choice of weapons."

Despite an affable tone, there was a thread of steel in Hazlit's dark eyes. Ethan gave him credit for rattling a loud sword.

"She has my children in her care, Hazlit. I will be as demanding, sorry, or condescending as I must be to ensure they are safe with her. I appreciate your protectiveness, but Alice is your grown sister, whereas Jeremiah and Joshua are my little children."

Hazlit's half smile bloomed into the complete version, illuminating his face with a startling charm. When he smiled, he looked more like Alice and less like some avenging Saracen warrior masquerading in civilized attire.

"We understand each other, Mr. Grey. Now let's rehearse our chitchat, because no hat could take this long to tie. How is Wee Nick?"

"Managing," Ethan said. "He will do a good job by the title, and he's chosen the right countess, but he dreads all the Parliamentary nonsense."

"He'll take to it well enough when he sees his first bill pass," Hazlit said. "But you'd better get your brother George on a shorter leash. He's cutting a bit of a left-handed swath."

"We were hoping he'd take ship, but Nick ignores the problem," Ethan replied. "Perhaps I should take it on."

"Somebody should try," Hazlit said. "George is a good soul, not out to harm anybody, but the parsons get to screaming, and the newspapers want a sensation, and next thing you know, somebody's harmless brother is swinging for what goes on every day in many a great house, dormitory, or back alley."

"You needn't preach to me. I'll talk to him."

Hazlit turned, his expression softening. "Here comes my dearest Alice. Sister, I am taking my leave of you. Mr. Grey clearly appreciates your talents and will be a biddable employer. Kiss me now, and write often."

They didn't just kiss the air beside each other's cheeks. Hazlit kissed his sister's cheeks, and then her forehead, but he held her close even a moment after that, the expression on his face oddly pained.

"Thank you for coming, Ben," Alice said, and Ethan would have sworn her eyes were getting misty. He wasn't about to thank Hazlit for leaving him with a teary female, for pity's sake.

"Be well, Allie. I'm here if you need me."

She nodded her thanks and let him step back. He bowed slightly to Ethan then retreated, his pace, to Ethan's eye, a little hasty. Alice stood beside Ethan, silent, until her brother disappeared into the stables. A funny little gulp of breath gave her away.

"Oh, for God's sake." Ethan spun her gently by the shoulders and wrapped her in an embrace. "He's only going to London, and you can have him out any time."

"I m-miss him," Alice said miserably. "He's such a good brother, and I pushed him away, and this is all we have, and it's my fault."

"Hush. Brothers understand these things, and you have more with your Benjamin than I do with my younger brothers or sisters."

"I miss Avie too," Alice watered on. "I miss her so much. I haven't seen her for five years, and that's my fault too."

"You are a terrible person," Ethan assured her gently. "An awful sister and a disgrace of a governess. You should be banned by royal decree. Children should see you held up as a bad example, except my children, of course, and your name should replace Beelzebub's as the imp of Satan. New sins should be named after you…"

He felt her shoulders twitch, and then she was aiming a soft, damp smile at him.

"Thank you." When she should have stepped back, she bundled back in against his shoulder. "I'm all right until I see them, Ben or Vim, and then I go completely to pieces, but I miss them too."

"I cried when I saw Nick for the first time in years." He could say this to comfort her, and because she couldn't see his face. "He cried too."

"Of course." Alice nodded against his chest. "When I saw Avie, I cried."

There had been nothing *of course* about it, not until Alice pronounced it so. Ethan would consider that later. "What is wrong with this sister of yours, that she makes you cry only every five years?"

"She doesn't leave Blessings and its surrounds," Alice said, and she did step back—alas. Ethan proffered his handkerchief for her use. "She clings to the place. I can't stand the thought of it."

"I love Belle Maison," Ethan said, missing the feel of her plastered against him. He linked his arm through hers by way of consolation and began a progress toward the battlefield. "Going back there made me recall the painful years of not being allowed to go home. It tainted the good memories."

She sniffed at his handkerchief before using it to blot her eyes. "You need more good memories. You'll bring the boys back for another visit, maybe at the holidays. You'll pop out to check on Nick and Leah, and your sisters. I think they worry about you, by the way."

"My sisters? We used to call them the Furies when they were little, so passionate were they in their loves and hates. I cannot wait to see what manner of gentleman takes each of them on."

"Do you suppose they were curious as to which lady you wed?"

"A bastard approaches marriage differently," Ethan said as they heard the first childish shrieks of glee. "Did honor not compel me, I would not have offered for Barbara, and I do not intend to find myself offering for anybody else."

Alice peered up at him. "Why not? A woman loses everything by marrying. She becomes property, her children are chattel, and she has no money of her own, no authority over her own life. What could marriage cost a man that's any worse than that?"

"Interesting perspective." Ethan resisted the urge to pat her hand on his arm. She'd perceive the gesture as avuncular, and deserved his cooperation in her attempts to restore her dignity. "From my end of the trade, I give up the right to choose any other woman as the mother of my children, I provide for her every need, and all I can do is hope she's faithful, or at least discreet, and kind to my children."

Alice smoothed her fingers over his knuckles. "You did make an unfortunate choice."

"We fought bitterly," Ethan said, pausing out of sight of the warring armies. "And loudly, and often, but it pleased her somehow. I wasn't raised with antipathy between the earl and his wives. I'm sure they had spats, but not before the children, and not so… viciously."

He could reveal this much and have it be a relief, not a humiliation, or not much of one.

"My brother claims a mean woman will outstrip a mean man any day," Alice said. "I'm sorry, Ethan, that all you knew of marriage was unhappy. You deserved better."

He was, to his astonishment, coming to think he had too. "We patched things up somewhat when Barbara fell ill. Even before, I realized it didn't matter to Barbara what we fought about, as long as she could get me to lose my composure. The last thing I wanted was to ally myself with a cruel intimate."

"Well said," Alice murmured. "Cruelty finds us often enough we needn't seek it out."

He wanted to hold her again, to press her soft, feminine body along the length of him and give and receive the comfort of simple touch.

And he wanted to toss her over his shoulder, cease this useless talking, and plunder her charms until her legs were locked around his naked flanks and she was whispering his name—a thought not nearly as astonishing as it should be.

He settled for a kiss.

⊱⊰

The Baroness Collins put aside her letter, though correspondence was usually a welcome respite from the solitary monotony of penurious rustication. As a widow, she had peace, though, and peace was no small treasure.

Hart did not have peace, and never had. He'd gone from spoiled boy to rotten young man, making trouble with the help, and then with the neighbors. His mischief had gotten him all but banished to the Continent, where English coin went further toward procuring the lifestyle Hart believed was his due.

His current hostess was pleased to have a baron among her guests, but also tacitly complained about Hart's treatment of the maids. Maids bore an unfortunate lot in life, but the smarter ones knew how to work that to their advantage. The baroness could not spare much concern for the maids.

Her concern was not even for her son, but rather, for the younger Portmaine girl, said to be governessing in Surrey. The letter cheerily informed the baroness

that Hart's next destination lay in Surrey, and that was
not a good thing.

Not a good thing at all.

❧

Ethan Grey's company was seductive, and not just
in the erotic sense. Alice was coming to think she
could tell him anything—tell him *everything*—and
he'd absorb all her terrible sorrows and secrets without
thinking any less of her.

And yet, there was a carnal attraction, too, all
the more appealing for the way he could receive or
bestow a difficult confidence without flinching. The
notion of genuine intimacy with him, intimacy of the
body, mind, and heart, beckoned irresistibly.

His kiss was a surprise, though Alice recovered
quickly. A soft, careful touch of his lips to hers was
enough to inspire Alice to twine her arms around
Ethan's neck. She sighed against his mouth, in relief
and satisfaction. She had not imagined their mutual
appeal, not conjured it from loneliness and fancy.

He pressed his mouth more firmly to hers and let
his hands slide down to her hips, an embrace that
anchored her even as it transgressed beyond a stolen
kiss. Alice wiggled a little with the pleasure of it, and
brushed her thumbs over his cheeks, a slow, learning
caress that both satisfied and stirred the peculiar ache
in her middle.

And then she should have eased back, because
a pleasant kiss was ricocheting around in her body,
becoming a demanding, intensifying, stubbornly focused
prelude to all manner of mischief. Instead, Alice sank
more snugly into him, letting her breasts press against

his chest. Lest he abandon her for her forwardness, she took his bottom lip between her teeth.

He muttered something, *God in heaven* maybe, and against her belly, Alice felt unmistakable evidence of male arousal.

Ethan slipped his tongue along her lips, and she went up on her toes, hungry for him. She met him, shyly at first, but he went slowly, always asking, never demanding, and she was soon exploring him as carefully as he was her. Her tongue rubbed along his; her hands traveled over his shoulders to his back, through his hair, and along his arms; and her body leaned into his embrace.

"Alice..." The dratted, enchanting man tried again to ease away. "The boys are just through the trees."

"Boys?" She was kissing his *neck*, tasting the salt and cedar of his skin, wanting to rip off his shirt and kiss him everywhere.

"Joshua and Jeremiah," he reminded her, his arms still wrapped around her. "My sons."

"We should stop?" Whyever...? She kept one hand resting on his shoulder for balance. With the other she petted his chest through the fine tailoring of his shirt and waistcoat.

"Yes, love." Ethan's breathing was ragged. The chest she'd like to learn intimately was heaving. "We should stop." He tucked her closer, so Alice could feel his heart thudding along beneath her cheek. "Just let me hold you."

She wanted to kiss him some more, endlessly, wickedly. She could not lift her face from his shoulder though, because his hand cradled the back of her head.

He was, however gently, defending himself from her advances. "Oh, dear."

"None of that, love. I kissed you first."

She stood in his embrace, her hands linked around his waist, and cast around for something to say. An apology came to mind, even a tender of resignation, but then she felt Ethan's arousal, a rigid presence against her belly. She eased her body away from his, though she didn't take a step back.

"I am afraid to look at you," she said, nose still buried at his throat. "I am mortified." Men could not help their responses, not even a man as self-possessed as Ethan Grey.

"You are lovely," Ethan corrected her. "We merely got a little carried away on the basis of confidences exchanged. I gather it's been a while for you?"

He sounded hopeful, not embarrassed. She did pull back enough then to see his face. "A very long while. You?"

"Years." He tucked her back against him, out of kissing range. "Long, long years."

"You don't seem to be out of practice," Alice remarked on a sigh.

"Oh, shame on you." Ethan nuzzled her crown with his chin. "I am inspired by present company and trust the same is true for you."

This was not mere gallantry. He sounded as flustered as she felt—which was no end of reassuring, though it did not change their circumstances. She mustered a smile and slipped her arms from his waist. "I did not expect this to happen."

His eyes shuttered, suggesting her observation was not what he wanted to hear. "You did not expect it to happen, or you wish it had not happened? I can manufacture an apology if you absolutely insist."

"I did not expect it." Alice managed a few steps of distance and turned her body so she would not see him and his blue eyes and his broad shoulders, much less any evidence of their kiss. "If we are honest, we will admit neither one of us wants a complication."

"A single kiss does not a complication make." Bless the man, he was going to see reason, though he didn't sound happy about it.

"It doesn't." Alice's smile felt bleak. "But you are my employer, and neither of us wants marriage, so we must deal with the question of intentions."

"Must we deal with it *now*?"

His voice told her he'd come closer. If he touched her again…

"I was crying, and then I plastered myself all over you, and I know men are prone to… well, no, we need not parse this quite yet."

"Good. I really would not want to cause you hurt, Alice. If you're offended, you must tell me, and I will take myself off to Town or go sea bathing or something until we can pretend this kiss did not happen."

That he could pretend any such thing was lowering in the extreme. Alice reached for pride but found only rueful humor. "I don't think a single unexpected kiss merits anything so drastic as sea bathing."

She risked a glance at him to find he was smiling crookedly.

"No sea bathing then. Will you come inspect the battle with me?"

"I think not." Alice tugged her floppy straw hat up from her back to her head. "Today is Friday, so we will have the children to join us at dinner. I will spend the afternoon writing out next week's lesson plans, though, and hope we can proceed with a bit more structure starting Monday."

"A little more," Ethan said. "I don't think the boys have had a real break here at home for at least a year, when I hired Harold's predecessor."

"They had a nanny before that?"

He looked pained, which was fine. Alice was pained, to be kissing him one minute and then find he was happy to discuss his children the next. While she wanted to… to *climb* him, to knock him flat on his back and kiss him for the rest of the summer.

"They had nannies." He lifted a hand and traced his finger along her hairline. "You'll be all right?"

Maybe he wasn't so happy to discuss his children.

"I will be fine," Alice said, going up on her toes to brush her lips against his. "Just fine."

He nodded but didn't say anything more. Alice turned and made her way up to the house and left Waterloo for Ethan to deal with.

⚜

Where did a governess learn to kiss like that?

Was this raging, pounding need what had driven Nick from one bed to the next with any willing female?

What if the boys had seen them?

What had he been thinking?

And *when* could he get his hands on her again?

Ethan did not turn directly for the stream, but took a circuitous path that kept to the shade of the home wood and took him farther from his children's shouts and battle cries. He came to a clearing, one graced with a little gazebo, and sat himself down on the steps to consider the developments of the past hour.

What he wanted—besides the freedom to plunder his governess's charms without any consequences—was to talk to his brother. Nick wouldn't laugh, and he would understand, and if there were answers to be had from greater experience of women and intimacies with them, Nick would share the answers.

But Nick was far away, and Ethan had imposed on him enough for one summer.

God in heaven, what a lovely, lovely kiss.

Ethan's steps took him to the Tydings stable, where he busied himself saddling one of his spare mounts. Waltzer was a big, muscular dark bay, with the personality of a puppy dog.

"He'll be fresh," Miller said. "Mind you walk him out in this heat, guv."

"I'll be careful," Ethan replied, securing the girth. "I'm not out for any great feats of athleticism, but it's been a trying day."

"You didn't let Thatcher go," Miller said as he handed Ethan the bridle.

"I should have." Ethan took off the headstall, and had to smile as the horse obligingly dipped his big Roman nose, trying to find the bit. "I shall, if you see him so much as forgetting to scrub a bucket."

"Ponies are tough."

Ethan straightened and glared at his stable master. "That pony carries my son around. Thunder doesn't need to be tough. He needs to be the safest mount I can provide for Joshua, and that means no gratuitous beatings."

"I take your point."

Ethan didn't say another word, just led the big horse out to the mounting block and swung up. With his usual willingness to please, Waltzer cantered off, only kicking out behind once when he passed a paddock full of yearlings.

Having permitted the horse to express his good spirits, Ethan brought him back to the trot and turned him into the woods along a track that met up with the stream. A bridle path ran parallel to the far side of the water, so Ethan let the horse splash across then turn away from the house and grounds toward the cool of the deeper woods. The path would take him past several of his neighbors' properties, and by agreement, was available for the enjoyment of all whose land bordered it.

"Well met, Grey," a voice sang out on an approaching chestnut.

"Heathgate." Ethan drew up as his neighbor approached him. The chestnut was as handsome as all of Heathgate's mounts, but this one was also particularly elegant.

"Is that a *mare?*"

"You think your brother is the only one who can appreciate the fairer sex in another species?" Heathgate asked. He still had the same gimlet-hard blue eyes he'd had as a younger man, the same dark hair, and an even leaner, more unreadable face. Oh, and for the last fifteen years or so, he'd sported his grandfather's lofty title too. Ethan might not have chosen to settle at Tydings had he known Gareth Alexander would be one of his neighbors.

He owed the man, owed him for intervening long ago in a situation most would have quietly run from, and owed him even more for never once bringing it up.

"Nicholas hasn't the luxury of considering gender before size, sanity, and soundness in his personal mounts," Ethan said. "She's very pretty."

"She is." Heathgate's smile was fleeting as he patted the horse's neck. "And a lady of particulars. How fare your boys?"

Parenting was a useful source of small talk, though Ethan had never appreciated this before. "They are busy. We've just come back from several weeks with Nicholas and his countess at Belle Maison, and picked up a new governess in the process. I have only two children, and yet it seems they cause enough mayhem and activity to bring the entire house down on occasion."

"It gets easier," Heathgate said. "My last one was easier than the first one, and thank the gods she's a girl, because my marchioness was determined Lady Joyce have a sister."

"Two will be my limit. Your family thrives?"

"Loudly. Hence the appeal of a quiet hack. Constantina here could use a chance to catch her breath on the way home."

The words held a careful invitation. "I'll join you," Ethan said, because to do otherwise would be rude. He liked Heathgate, had liked him before his acquisition of his grandfather's title. The marquess cared not one whit for Society's opinion, and he'd married where his heart led, despite his wife being merely a viscount's spinster daughter. There was really nothing not to like.

Except Heathgate had seen Ethan in the worst, most vile, degrading moments of Ethan's life. The knowledge lay between them, assiduously ignored every time they met.

So... onward to more small talk.

"My sons have recently demonstrated to me their

affinity for jumping their ponies," Ethan said. "At a dead run."

"Of course. They're boys."

"And thank God," Ethan went on, "they're on a pair of game ponies. But Joshua and Jeremiah will soon acquire more of my height, and I was thinking something from your brother's stable might serve as a next step."

"Ladies' mounts? I suppose the principles are the same. Greymoor found my son James's first pony, as well as Pen's. You might corner Greymoor at a gathering of the clan at his place on Wednesday. I'm sure his countess would be happy to send along an invitation."

And just like that, another turning point loomed before Ethan. He'd owned Tydings for seven years, and yet he didn't socialize, didn't trade calls, didn't expect to be invited to share a drink or a meal with his neighbors. First, he was of questionable *ton*, being illegitimate, but then he'd committed a far worse transgression by marrying his mistress. Even had the neighbors been amenable, the idea of turning Barbara loose on the unsuspecting gentry of Surrey had been unthinkable.

And then the boys had come along, his marriage had gone utterly to hell, and a couple of years later, Barbara was gone.

"It's just some food and drink with the neighbors, Grey," Heathgate said. "A picnic, with children rocketing about, pall-mall balls whacking into the dessert table, babies needing attention at inopportune moments, and papas being told to wipe cake off that one's mouth or put it on this one's plate. We do it mostly for the ladies, but also for the cousins."

"How old is your oldest?" Ethan asked.

"He looks to be the same age as yours," Heathgate replied, his expression patient.

"Joshua and Jeremiah haven't been in company much," Ethan said. "They did fairly well at Belle Maison."

"So bring as many footmen and nannies and dogs as you need to keep them in line, or try to. Each of my children has a separate nanny. They spell each other, the nannies, that is, but the happiness of my entire kingdom turns on the morale of my nannies." The marquess sounded absolutely sincere.

"One understands, sometimes, why women can be hysterical."

"One does. So you'll bring the boys? We gather around four, when the heat starts to fade and the babies have had their naps, and we don't stay late, because the older ones get cranky if they're out too long."

That a marquess should know these things was reassuring.

"I'll have to bring their governess, Miss Portman." For any number of reasons. "She will enjoy getting acquainted with the neighbors, I think."

"Your governess has some odd connections," Heathgate observed as his horse stepped carefully over a fallen log.

This oh-so-casual comment crossed over from small talk to something more significant.

"Her last position was with some squire's daughter down in Sussex for five years. How could her path have crossed yours?"

"Not mine. I don't know if she told you, but her brother is Benjamin Hazlit."

And how did Heathgate know such a thing? "Your snoop of choice. Nick's too."

Heathgate did not dignify that with confirmation. "Hazlit spent the night with us last night, as he sometimes does when he and I have much to discuss. Felicity likes him, and he told her he was calling on his sister, Miss Portman, this morning. Her ladyship dug in, as she will, and extracted from him his sister's location."

"Impressive, your marchioness." Was this why there was a neighborly invitation now, after seven years? The titled neighbors wanted to look over Hazlit's sister? Had Hazlit put them up to it? "I think Alice likes her privacy, and I know I like mine."

"We all appreciate privacy. Hazlit more than any of us."

"He said there was scandal." Ethan paused, not sure how much to say. "He didn't ask for me to keep it in confidence, so I don't suppose there's harm in telling you."

Heathgate waved a gloved hand in impatient circles. "Out with it, Grey. I've known you half your life, and you know my discretion is reliable."

An oblique reference, but valid.

"I don't know what the scandal involved, except that both sisters were affected, and the siblings not at the family seat all use different names to avoid the repercussions of the scandal. There is wealth of some sort, and an estate in the North, but Hazlit told me only that much."

"He's a closemouthed devil, but there are more scandals hanging on my family tree than Hanover has princes, Ethan. Let sleeping dogs lie, and all that."

That Heathgate would use Ethan's name was a slip. They hadn't ever assumed such familiarity and probably never would, out of consideration, not for Heathgate's great title and consequence, but for Ethan's dignity.

Heathgate smiled. "Have I offended? You can be honest, you know. My wife always is, and it has toughened me considerably."

"You have not offended. You do surprise me, though."

"Probably for the first and only time. I will tell Greymoor and his countess to expect you with your entourage on Wednesday, rain or shine."

"My thanks." Ethan nodded by way of a mounted bow, and let his companion take the branch of the path that would lead back to Willowdale, while Ethan turned around, overdue to investigate Wellington's progress against Bonaparte.

Eight

"YOU ARE COMFORTABLE WITH WEDNESDAY'S OUTING?" Ethan asked Alice at breakfast the next morning. The boys had taken off with Davey to try to dig a pond suitable for the reenactment of Trafalgar, though Davey was under strict orders to keep the ocean blue smaller than the size of two horse troughs.

"What I want doesn't matter," Alice said. "My charges will go off to socialize with the neighbors, and I will attend them." Her lips were compressed into a prim line, and she was taking only the smallest sips of her tea.

This testiness on Alice's part wasn't about an invitation to picnic with the neighbors, though she was probably not looking forward to that. Ethan regarded his boys' governess and concluded she was unhappy with her employer, and maybe, were she honest, a little bit with herself. Ethan was unhappy with himself, too.

Alice was under his protection, plain and simple. In the dark hours after midnight, he'd decided he wasn't to be kissing her, importuning her, or—if he could even figure out how to manage such a thing—flirting with her. She seemed to be sending him the same message, not in so many words.

"I've known Heathgate since well before he succeeded to the title," Ethan said. "We've been neighbors for years, but this is the first invitation I've been issued. Refusing would have been unpardonably rude."

Alice sipped her tea, not meeting his eyes. "I understand, Mr. Grey."

Mr. Grey. To hear her address him thus in that tone of voice rankled exceedingly. "There will be other boys to play with. I'd think you'd see that as a good thing, Alice."

She closed her eyes at his use of her name, and Ethan felt his temper spike.

"Good God." Ethan covered her teacup with his hand when she would have raised it to her mouth again. "It was one harmless, albeit passionate, kiss, Alice. Will you punish my children as well as me for that single lapse?"

"I'm not punishing anybody," Alice said, drawing her hand away from the teacup. "I'm simply not looking forward to being amidst a bunch of twittering ladies and their titled menfolk."

Ethan considered that and turned loose of her tea.

"They were thoroughgoing rascals as younger men, but both of the Alexander brothers have settled down in recent years. They tend to their business and their land. They raise their children and dote on their wives. They're domesticated, Alice. They won't, unlike your employer, be stealing kisses from you in bushes. And for the record, I married my mistress. Some would say that makes me the biggest rascal in the shire." More fool he.

"You didn't steal that kiss."

"I am heartened to hear it. Even such a one as I frowns upon larceny."

"Stop it." Alice tossed her napkin on the table and got up, pacing over to the window.

"Stop what?" Ethan rose and stood just behind her. Kissing and taking advantage were deplorable and inexcusable, and he would never do such things again. Probably. There was nothing in the code of gentlemanly behavior to prohibit inhaling a woman's fragrance though, or admiring the slope of her breast from a discreet angle.

"You refer to yourself as if you're some reprobate off the hulks." Alice crossed her arms over her chest, still facing away from him. "In the company you describe, you will be among the better behaved, I'm sure."

Ethan took a step away as a disturbing notion got hold of him. "You're not sure at all. Are you ashamed to be seen with me, Alice? Or with my children?"

"Of course not," she shot back, expression gratifyingly horrified. "How could you think that?"

"Because others have been. If you aren't concerned about being seen in our company, then what on earth is the problem?" She turned her back again, and Ethan had to strain to hear her.

"How will we get there?"

What queer start was this? "It's within walking distance, if we take the bridle path. The boys would likely take their ponies, and were I left to my own devices, I'd ride Waltzer."

Ah, but walking was hard for her, and so was riding. Ethan almost smiled with relief. "I'll help you. You can take Waltzer, and I'll be up on Argus, how's that?

Waltzer is a capital fellow, very willing to please, and as solid as a plow horse."

"A plow horse?" Alice's cheeks lost color.

"Yes. Very docile, biddable, sensible, that sort of plow horse."

Was *this* what had her in such a taking? She was afraid to ride?

"We could send you in the coach," Ethan said, "along with whatever contribution we're making to the picnic, and extra clothes for the boys, in case they should spill their lemonade, for example."

"Would anybody notice?" Alice asked, her voice small.

"Nobody will think twice about it," Ethan lied glibly. "If we bring along some blankets, the boys' hoops, a pillow or two, it will not be remarked. But, Alice?"

"Ethan?"

He was back to Ethan, and that was good.

"I would like to teach you to ride."

She drew in one shaky breath and shook her head.

"No." She shook her head again. "No and no. It is good of you, and I appreciate your generosity, and you have my thanks, but no. Absolutely not."

"What if I rode with you," Ethan posited carefully, "and we took the stirrups off the saddle?"

"Removed the stirrups? How would that help?"

"I assume you were dragged because your foot caught in the stirrup. No stirrup, no getting caught."

"How can you teach me to ride sidesaddle? Do you even own ladies' saddles?"

"I own several," Ethan said. "I'd hoped, at one point, to at least be able to hack out with my wife. She ordered a number of habits, for riding both to the left and to the right, but never wore a one of them."

"That is a waste. But no, I cannot imagine I would survive five minutes in the saddle without having a breathing spell."

"You didn't have a spell the last time you rode with me," Ethan said. "We covered nearly a mile on Argus. It isn't much farther than that to Willowdale."

She turned to face him, her expression troubled. "I know you want to do this for me, and I appreciate it more than I can say. But once I get on that horse, I will feel like you are inflicting torture on me. It feels so high up, and all I can recall is bouncing against the ground, the horrible pain, and knowing I was going to die."

That was not all she recalled. Ethan knew she recalled all manner of odd details, and each one could trigger an entire panorama of awful memories.

"In the intervening years, Alice, you haven't died. You didn't die then."

"I wanted to."

And in her mind, Ethan knew, the bad fall was part and parcel of the scandal Hazlit had alluded to. God above, he knew what that was like. Ever since his first week at boarding school, Ethan had been unable to stomach the smell of a barrel of pickles. If the scent hit him without warning, he'd still become ill. When he met people named Hart or Collins, he flinched mentally and tried not to shake their hands.

Pathetic, but after all this time, he no longer castigated himself for these weaknesses. They were the instincts of a man who wanted to live to see his children grown, and that was a good thing.

Ethan turned Alice by the shoulders then dropped his hands. "You will be safe on any horse I put you on. I promise you that."

"You can't promise me that. Nobody can promise that. The most competent rider in the world can be tossed when his horse steps in a rabbit hole or takes a bad spot in the hunt field."

"Your brother said there was a scandal." Ethan kept his gaze on hers and let the words stand alone, an invitation for Alice to say more.

She paced away from him. "Estrangement from one's brothers might not be entirely bad. Why on earth would Benjamin burden you with such a confidence?"

"Two reasons." Ethan watched as Alice drew in on herself, arms wrapped around her middle. "First, he wanted to explain the different last names, though he might have simply allowed me to conclude you are half siblings, as it's common enough. Second, and I think it the more compelling concern for him, he demanded that should this scandal erupt anew, I give him a chance to ride to your rescue before I toss you over the transom to whatever wolves and vultures are waiting to devour you."

She wrinkled her nose. "And you didn't call him out?"

"I have siblings, Alice. For several years I could barely learn how they went on, or let them know the same regarding me. Your brother cares about you."

Alice dropped her arms and marched back to the window. Outside across the gardens, Davey, sans livery and flanked by a boy on each side, a shovel over his shoulder, ambled toward the stream. "I suppose now you want to know the whole of it?"

"Not unless you want to tell me. I've endured scandals of my own, Alice, and telling you about them would neither abate the pain of those memories nor raise me in your esteem."

"It might." Alice smiled the faintest, sad smile. "Just to know you didn't die either, it might."

"I haven't yet." Ethan's smile matched hers for sadness.

"Was Barbara the reason you didn't reconcile with Nick?"

"In a manner of speaking, yes." He thought for a moment, trying to choose words and sort out how much to tell her. "When I met Barbara, it was nearly eight years ago. I'd been down from university for several years, but I spent my time on my commercial endeavors, crass as that might seem. I wanted to be able to support a family in appropriate style, and quite honestly, I enjoy commerce." He flicked a glance at Alice's face but saw no judgment there. Yet.

"Barbara approached me at some function where I was escorting Lady Warne. I'd never go about in society unless Grandmother inveigled me into it. Lady Warne suggested Barbara was exactly the kind of diversion I needed, and I've never regretted an impulsive decision more."

"You didn't care for her?"

"It's hard to explain," Ethan said, and what was he doing, imposing his past on her, when she was the one who was supposed to be confiding in him? "I had kept very much to myself, at school, at university. There were reasons, and they seemed like good ones at the time, though it left me appallingly unsophisticated with respect to the ladies and Society in general. But she was persistent, available, and physically appealing."

And this characterization of his past was not mendacious, but it was different from any previous descriptions he might have given of it.

"You were besotted."

He'd been horny, plain and simple, and wretchedly, painfully inexperienced with women. "Parts of me were besotted, perhaps, and Barbara was adept at reading people and being what they wanted, for a time anyway."

"Do you suppose she intended to conceive your child?" It was a bold, personal question, but the whole discussion was outside the bounds of propriety, and Ethan rather liked it there.

"She admitted as much on many occasions," Ethan said, wincing in memory of the way Barbara had laughed at his incredulity over her conniving. "I was the most gullible fool ever to stumble up a church aisle."

"That is…" Alice sank back down onto a seat at the table—Ethan's seat, in fact. "That is the most heinous, despicable… that is like rape, but worse, because in addition to a betrayal of one's vows, it's willfully inflicting on a child enmity between the parents. It's an abysmal… I am so sorry."

In a few words, she'd gotten to the heart of years of misery and conflict, summing up even more heartache than she knew. He wanted to kiss her again.

"I was sorry too, for a while, but now I have the boys, and I consider I got the better of the bargain."

There was no sadness in her smile now. She beamed radiant approval at him, and that made him want to kiss her too. "Oh, you did. You very certainly did, Ethan. They are wonderful boys, and you will always be glad they are yours."

Ethan saw such a light of longing in Alice's eyes, he had to look away. God above, the woman wanted children. She wanted children of her own, and she'd be a wonderful mother. And yet Barbara, to whom children had been merely pawns, was given two, while Alice was denied any of her own.

"You'll ride with me." Ethan patted her hand briskly. "Say you will, just once, to give it a try and shut me up."

"You won't let this alone, will you?"

Never. Maybe he couldn't give her children, but he could give her this. "I've told you more about my wicked past than I've told my own brother. I'm not asking you to trust me with the details of your own unhappy history, Alice, I'm asking you to trust me to keep you safe for a few minutes on a very reliable horse."

The two were related. He'd bet Argus on it.

"Very well, but I have no proper attire."

Victory without bloodshed, the best kind. "That's my girl. You won't need it, because we'll start off astride."

"You won't take me up like you did before?"

"That has to be the worst way to ride a horse," Ethan scoffed. "Yes, I get to put my arms around a pretty lady, but you are trying to balance contrary to the movement, which makes no sense."

"You did not think I was pretty." Alice snorted, then put a hand over her mouth as if to recall the words.

"You are pretty." Ethan had never been more sincere. "And your scent is delightful, as is your form. And while you went above stairs and couldn't catch your breath, I went above stairs and thanked the Almighty for a governess with a bad hip."

So to speak.

Ethan saw he'd silenced her, and shut his maw before he said even more. When had he become so damned loquacious?

He tapped her nose with a single finger. "Go

put on some half boots. Meet me in the stables in thirty minutes."

She could change her shoes in five minutes, and what Ethan had planned behind the privacy of his locked bedroom door would also take about five minutes—all three times.

❧

Alice's mind went in two directions at once. Part of her was preparing for a nasty breathing spell; another part was suggesting if she'd just glance down at the horse's neck, she could find the reins to pick them up.

But that she could *not* do, lest she see the ground yards and yards away, so she fished with her fingers in the thick mane until she encountered leather. "I've got them."

"Now we just sit here." Ethan's voice was right at her ear, his cedar scent was a soothing fragrance on an otherwise horsy breeze, and his chest was a solid presence at her back. "We're well trained, and we know we don't take a step until my lady tells us to. I don't think it's quite as warm today as it was yesterday."

Hang the bloody weather. "Neither as hot nor as humid."

"I asked you what you'd consider a treat by way of reward when we saddled up. You never answered," Ethan reminded her pleasantly. His hands were resting lightly on her waist, and but for that, Alice knew, she knew in her bones, and muscles, and organs, she'd fall and be dragged again.

"Getting off would be my best treat." Though in the barn, when Ethan had mentioned a treat, she'd been helpless not to gaze at his mouth. "How long do we sit here?"

"Until you tell him to do something else, but I want to know your next-best treat."

Alice gave the smallest, most useless tap of her heels. "And I want this to be over."

Waltzer moved one front hoof then swung his left ear forward and back.

"Again," Ethan coaxed. "He wasn't sure you meant it, and he's asking for clearer orders."

Alice felt her shoulders move with the depth of her breathing, but she gave her mount a firmer tap, and he moved two steps then flicked his ear again. She wanted to pat him for being such a careful horse, but that would mean moving her hands, which were gripping the reins for dear life.

"Try again," Ethan said. "This time, let your seat go a little too, or he'll think you mean go with your heels but stop with your seat."

"My *seat*?"

"Your hips. Here." He pressed against her waist and angled his hands down, as if to rock her hips in the saddle. "You recall the motion of it from your childhood rides. Just think about it when you tap him again."

Alice tried it, and the horse started walking at a very sedate pace.

"Oh, God. Now I have to steer."

"Not necessarily. He'll go forward in this direction until he lumbers up to the fence, and then he'll stop and ask you what you want next. Watch."

Because she couldn't do anything else and breathe, Alice did as Ethan suggested. The horse stopped, sighed, then turned his head around to peer at Alice's knee.

"What next?" Ethan interpreted. "Just tap again,

and because he's already looking around to the right, he'll probably saunter in that direction."

It took two tries, but the horse was rapidly figuring out the game.

Ethan kept his hands on her waist. "I think you might steer, if you wanted to."

Hang him and his helpful thoughts. "Oh, no, I couldn't. We'll just find our way to the rail again."

"Let's be very daring." Ethan dropped his voice. "Try another turn to the right."

"Ethan, *please* don't make me do this."

"We'll stop when you say, Alice, though I think you could steer us back to the mounting block."

She bit her lip, because she didn't want to get off all the way down to the ground. Just as she tentatively tugged on the right rein, the gelding began to shuffle along in that direction.

"Can he read my mind? Or did you make him do that?"

"You did it. You looked at the mounting block, you probably leaned toward it, and you picked up the right rein. Now why is it," he went on in the most conversational tones, "you won't tell me what your second-best treat is?"

"Hush," Alice hissed. "He's coming to the mounting block."

Except he'd approached at an angle, and because the previous three times the horse had asked, the lady had told him to bear right, Waltzer, being an obliging soul, sauntered past the mounting block and strolled off to the right.

"Oh, blast and damn," Alice wailed. "Now what?"

"Such language. Now you simply steer him back

toward where you want him, and this time, we'll ask him to stop."

"I can't. They don't go when you ask. They don't stop when you ask. They turn by themselves, and they're just too big…"

"You're doing splendidly, but think of wee Waltzer as a little boy, Alice. You have to tell him how to go on, and when you're crossing a busy thoroughfare with a small child, you take his hand firmly. To Waltzer, there are many distractions, such as every blade of grass, every dropping, every breeze and sunbeam. You must make your directions clear, so it's easy for your charge to know his task."

In the midst of that little homily, Alice's hips had finally started moving in rhythm with the horse's walk. The image of the horse as a child in need of guidance tapped some vein of confidence unknown even to her, because she wordlessly directed him back to the mounting block, but this time, steered him left as they went around it. Ethan kept silent behind her but kept his hands on her waist as well.

"And now," Ethan suggested a few minutes later, "you must tell him he's doing well."

"You're doing well, Waltzer. You'd best keep doing well." And Ethan Grey had best shut his helpful, interfering, gorgeous, handsome mouth.

"Oh, that was encouraging to a lad who's trying his heart out for you. He doesn't understand your words, Alice."

"So you tell him." She was beginning to think her best treat would not be forbidden pleasures with Ethan Grey, but rather, to fashion a gag for him.

"Pet the boy. Put both reins in one hand and pet him on his neck. He'll be your devoted and humble slave."

"Devoted *and* humble." Alice carefully arranged the reins and leaned forward slightly to pet the animal's neck.

"Tell him."

"Good boy, Waltzer," Alice said softly. "Very dear, good boy."

"Well done. Now take me home, Alice, and don't spare the horse."

She actually nudged a little with her seat and steered the gelding on a direct course for the larger mounting block, then halted him right alongside of it.

"Oh, well done, indeed. And off we go."

"Exactly, how?" Alice kept her eyes forward, because she'd done well so far by not looking at the ground. "I know how to do it with a stirrup, but this…"

"It's simple. Waltzer will hold absolutely still while I get off, and then you will let me assist you."

"How do you know he'll hold still?" In the time it had taken Alice to state her question, Ethan had slid over the horse's tail, landed on the ground, and hopped to the top of the ladies' mounting block.

"Rest the reins on his neck, Alice. He won't budge, since he understands his exertions are done."

Alice put the reins down and tried to breathe. Bad things could happen during a dismount. Awful things. "Ethan, please get me off this animal."

"Arms around my neck," he coached. "Hold tight, and I'll lift you out of the saddle on three." Except the scurrilous varlet lifted on "one," and Alice was on her feet, standing in his embrace, before she could even close her eyes in dread.

"See?" Ethan smiled down at her. "You're safe and sound, Waltzer is dutifully catching a nap, and all is well."

"Oh, Ethan." She slumped against him, needing the physical support—surely she was entitled to that? "That was awful. That was the worst... I can't..." She huffed out an enormous sigh, feeling lighter and looser than she had in years—despite the trembling in her knees. "It wasn't awful. It wasn't awful at all. You'll give Waltzer a treat?"

"Waltzer is given a regular ration of oats for his efforts. I'm interested instead in the treats that would appeal to you."

His smile was approving and genuine, almost tender. Alice was about to go up on her toes and seize for herself a sample of the treat she most desired when a patrician voice called out from the back of a large black horse over by the arena gate.

"Greetings, all. Have I come at a bad time?"

Nine

WHY HAD SHE WAITED SO LONG TO *TRY* SIMPLY controlling a horse? Alice had been on a strange horse when she'd had her accident, a beast she'd never seen before, much less ridden, and she'd been in a panic even before she leapt onto its back and found the stirrup leathers much too long for her legs.

And having ridden again… this was heady stuff, this feeling of lightness and joy, something she would never have predicted. Had the Earl of Greymoor not come calling, Alice would have hugged Waltzer and kissed him on his big, horsy nose.

"Miss Portman?" A single knock on her door told her Ethan Grey was not going to allow her more solitude.

"Come in," she called, hopping off the bed. She wanted to throw her arms around him too, and squeal like little Priscilla in a happy moment.

"One notes you are smiling, madam. This is encouraging."

"I can breathe." She beamed at him shamelessly where he lingered near the door. "And I met an earl."

"A half-smitten earl." He did not sound pleased

about this. "Once he'd dispensed with the issuance of a social invitation, Greymoor complimented your eyes specifically and called you pretty when you'd abandoned us. He barely bothered to inspect me or my property."

"I did not abandon you." An *earl* had called her pretty, though the earl was clearly smitten with the small blond girl he'd had up before him.

"You most certainly abandoned me," Ethan groused right back, taking a couple of steps into the room. "Little Lucy rifled the entire library before tossing a book directly at her papa's lemonade, managing to provide him, his shirt, waistcoat, and cravat quite the cold bath. I was obliged to loan the man clothing and entertain his offspring while he made himself presentable."

He sounded quite pleased with himself, lending clothing to an earl attacked by a toddler.

"You poor thing. Having to manage a single, adorable child for an entire five minutes. The boys will be so proud of you."

"*You* are supposed to be proud of me." He ambled closer then stopped by her escritoire. "Lady Lucy is accounted a woman of particulars, and I convinced her not to shatter my hapless eardrums with her caterwauling."

Had they teased each other like this before? "Children are sometimes fascinated with strangers. You should be pleased, nonetheless. Generally, the young have good instincts about people."

"How you flatter me, Miss Portman." He offered an ironic bow. "May I take it you are none the worse for having ridden with me? Be honest, Alice."

Alice. The way he used her name was sweet, special,

and a little stern. "No trouble breathing. I cannot credit it. For the past twelve years, any time I have been at the mercy of a horse, I could not manage it."

"You managed it today. I am pleased for you, Alice Portman."

Alice recalled the feel of him at her back on the horse, steady, solid, and calm. She grabbed her courage with both hands and locked her gaze with his. "Pleased enough to help me try again?"

"Of course."

How easily he assented. "It might not go as well. In fact it probably won't."

His lips quirked up. "Or it might go better."

"I would settle for being able to start, stop, and steer at a placid walk," Alice said. "I would be thrilled with that, to be honest."

And when was the last time she'd been thrilled with anything? Anything save her employer's kisses?

‌⁓

"You look so serious." Ethan frowned at Alice, wondering what went on inside her busy head. Her second venture in the riding arena, between tea and supper, had gone without incident, much to his relief. "Are you doing as the jockeys do at Newmarket and reliving each moment of your ride?"

She walked along beside him in silence for a moment, the evening sun finding red highlights in her hair. "Hardly that. I am contemplating the contrasts in my life."

"This sounds weighty. Shall we pursue the topic while we stroll?" He offered his arm, and she took it, something that might have been a minor struggle between them only days ago. "Tell me about these contrasts in your life, Alice Portman."

"When I lived at Sutcliffe," Alice said as they reached a gravel walk that turned toward the stream, "we had such quiet. Days and days of quiet, nothing louder than Reese's voice in conversation with my own."

"It sounds Gothic." Also like a waste of at least two women. "Were you happy there?"

"I enjoyed Reese and Pris," Alice said, "but it was a bleak place. Most of the servants did not respect the lady of the house, which meant a great deal of work went undone. We managed our own mending, much of our own cooking and cleaning. If we wanted a bath, we carried the water, or it would not come up hot."

"You lived as if you had no servants." As if she *deserved* to have no servants. "Shall we sit? The evening grows pretty, and we are not at the end of this discussion."

"We aren't?" Alice settled on a bench at the base of a venerable oak. The tree was so large two people on the bench could both lean back against the trunk comfortably.

"We are not." Ethan lowered himself beside her and wondered idly how many kisses the tree had witnessed. "The topic is contrast in the life of Miss Alice Portman."

"So it is," Alice said. "In any case, my life now is different from what it was for five years."

"Different, how?" Ethan let his back rest against the oak and crossed his ankles. He did not take her hand, not when she was working up to confidences of some sort.

"Sutcliffe was peaceful. Predictable, stable, and safe."

"You aren't safe now? Should I be concerned?"

"Safe…" Alice huffed out a breath. "It's hard to define what I mean by that. Relative to my time at Sutcliffe, my time since then has been a constant uproar."

Uproar was not a good thing. Something cold trickled down Ethan's spine, so he went on the offensive.

"You wanted a quiet rural post, and instead you find yourself dealing with an oversized, widowed social misfit, riding a comparably oversized horse, and a neighborhood full of titles suddenly expecting you to provide your charges—among whose number I might include myself—for socializing."

If she left them… that cold sensation congealed into that familiar and unhappy acquaintance: dread.

"I feel as if," Alice said slowly, "the mild breeze I'd used to sail along in my little boat has turned into a fickle gale, tossing me in all directions at once."

"You're knocked off your pins. It isn't a pleasant sensation."

"I thought you were going to say, 'I'm knocked off my horse,'" Alice said softly. "And maybe that's it. I feel a little of the same disorientation as I did then, when I was minding my girlish business one day and then literally knocked off my horse the next."

Rage at her malefactors warred with the compulsion to take her in his arms.

"Your disorientation is understandable. The sensation will likely fade in time, as you gather more confidence in your changed circumstances." But always, upset like this took too bloody much time to fade. Years and lifetimes.

"It isn't…" Alice bit her lip and colored up furiously. "It isn't just my circumstances."

Ethan had to lean closer to catch her words, which had the effect of filling his awareness with lemon verbena. "I beg your pardon?"

"It isn't just my circumstances," Alice said a little more loudly. "I am knocked off my pins by… you."

Silence, as Ethan studied Alice's profile, from the compressed line of her lips, to the brilliant blush on her cheeks, to the quiet misery in her eyes.

"Alice?" His voice was carefully neutral. "Can you explain yourself?"

He gave her credit for turning to face him, despite the blush trying to swamp her dignity. "You are part of this gale-force wind, Ethan Grey. You…" When she might have risen and paced off to a safe distance, he laced his fingers around her wrist.

"Tell me," he commanded softly. "Please."

And because of that one entreating word, he knew she would.

"You touch me," she said, dropping her gaze to her lap. "When I had such a bad breathing spell, you weren't too fussy to offer comfort to a mere governess. At Belle Maison, on Argus, you put your arms around me, and I did not fall. Here, on the horse, you don't let me fall, and then too…"

"Then?"

"You kissed me," Alice said, her voice dropping again. And Ethan realized that she'd gone long years without a friend, but far longer years without a kiss.

"I kissed you," Ethan said, "but you kissed me as well." He was fiercely glad to recall this.

"And there is the problem."

"Are you making too much of a single incident, Alice? You aren't going to leave your post over some backward female notion of protecting my honor, are you?"

"It isn't that one kiss. It's that I want another."

Thank God for all His mercies. "Does this have to be a problem?"

She was female, and she was Alice, so his question was rhetorical.

"Of course it's a problem. You are my employer, and by all rights, if you're kissing a decent woman, you ought to be doing so in the interest of finding a mother for your boys. You need not humor a lonely governess."

"Good God." Ethan shot to his feet and jammed his hands in his pockets. "Is that why you think I kissed you?"

"You're kind, though you're shy about it." Alice rose as well, her chin coming up as her blush faded. "I know this about you, and I know as well that in the years I've been in service, I haven't exactly had to fend off the advances of drooling hordes of fevered men."

"I should hope not!" Ethan looked at her in consternation. "You wear those great ugly glasses that distort your lovely eyes, you scrape the most glorious hair on God's earth back into an old woman's snood, you dress as if in half mourning for your former life and in gowns that hide the most luscious…" He glared at her then reached for her with both hands, anchoring her by the upper arms and bringing her flush against him.

"I did not kiss you out of some condescending motive like pity, Alice. I kissed you because I had to, and I have to."

He framed her jaw gently in his hands, angling her

face toward his, and then brushed his lips across hers in a whisper-light warning caress. When she made a yearning sound, he joined their mouths and gathered her to him.

"Ah, God, Alice…" His sigh held longing, humor, and resignation to go with her name, and then got down to kissing her in earnest. One hand slid down her back, to press her tightly against his groin; the other drifted to her nape and buried itself under that scraped bun, and held her captive for his mouth.

He did not plunder, not exactly. He tasted and hinted and suggested, until Alice's tongue was tangling with his, and her breathing was accelerating. Her hand found its way into his hair and, if anything, she was pressing her body eagerly to his.

Eagerly!

Which would lead them… Ethan withdrew his mouth and rested his chin on her crown. He wasn't about to let her go, not when she rested against him nigh panting with the effects of a brief, fully clothed kiss.

"Dear Almighty God," she whispered. "Dear Almighty, Everlasting God."

"Amen."

Alice raised her face from Ethan's chest and regarded him curiously. "Are you laughing at me?"

"Good heavens, no." Ethan stepped back, ignoring the shriek of disappointment echoing through his body. "I need to sit, Alice, and so do you."

Though she at least wasn't hiding her arousal.

And arousal itself was a relief for Ethan. He'd begun to conclude his capacity for unbridled passion had prematurely aged. In almost two decades of sexual experience, he couldn't once recall being so physically enthusiastic about a woman so quickly. He'd learned caution at a high price, but with Alice…

"I'll go," Alice said quietly, and Ethan realized she was sitting a few inches from him on the bench, primly not touching. To blazing hell with that. He threaded his fingers through hers and drew her wrist to his lips, because nobody was going anywhere just yet.

"Back to the house? Or you'll sail your little skiff right out of my life, out of the boys' lives, and find another bucolic retreat where you can once again impersonate a forty-nine-year-old spinster?"

"You can't allow an immoral influence around your children," Alice said with soft insistence. "I can't allow it."

"Well, that's all right, then." Ethan reached out his free hand and drew it down Alice's hairline. Her bun should have been in shambles, but it was like her today, well anchored in the proprieties. "If we're to remove all pernicious influences from their lives, then I'll merely accompany you, and they'll be free of both our wicked selves."

"You're not wicked."

"But you, who were the kissed, not the kisser, are somehow Satan's imp?" He looped his arm across her shoulders and scooted to tuck himself against her. She wasn't going to bolt off to her lesson plans until they'd come to some understandings, and—given her endless determination—that meant it could be a long evening.

"You are a man," Alice said, a hint of exasperation in her voice.

"You noticed. How fortunate. I was at risk of forgetting it myself."

Alice scowled at him. "You were not. You're among the most masculine people I've met."

"Because you're a governess, sweetheart. You don't exactly consort with the dragoons and the grenadiers."

"I have brothers, Ethan Grey." She was getting her dander up, which relieved Ethan no end. That meek, defeated version of Alice Portman made him want to howl and break things for her. "And my brothers have acquaintances, and I've been in your brother's household, and Mr. Belmont's, and Baron Sutcliffe's. No governess goes into service without a keen wariness regarding a man's animal urges."

"And you are prepared to tell me about these urges? Say on, Alice. I'm all ears. My own urges haven't been in evidence since shortly after Joshua was conceived, so you likely know more about my urges than I do."

Her brows went up as the meaning of his words sank in.

"Hushed your scolding with that one, didn't I?" Ethan muttered, surprised that Alice remained sitting snug against him, making no move to withdraw her hand from his. "Well, it's the truth, my dear. I married unwisely, and life hadn't exactly handed me the instincts of a libertine before that. The realization that my wife was a bad choice rather killed my appetite, and in the general sense, not just for her."

"But Joshua…"

"Is five years old. It has been a long, long six years." During which, he silently added, he'd heard a constant string of tales regarding his brother Nick's prowess in the bedrooms of London's demimonde, each more impressive than the last.

Alice's gaze became concerned. "Are you sure he's your son?"

Now who was prying confidences from whom? And yet, Ethan wanted the truth between them.

"He is my son in every way that counts." Ethan dipped his face against Alice's hair as he spoke, needing the comfort of lemon verbena and Alice. "My wife might have known a different truth, but I have never regarded it as relevant."

"Why are you telling me?"

Ethan raised his face and spoke slowly. "Could it be I trust you would never do anything to hurt a child?" And perhaps, his conscience added, he was damned sick of carrying this alone? Wondering if the boy might somehow find out and turn on the only parent he'd known?

Taking his brother with him...

"You love him," Alice said staunchly. "Joshua would be devastated to think you aren't his papa. What was wrong with your wife?"

"Marriage was wrong with her," Ethan said tiredly, even as Alice's immediate defense of him warmed his heart. "Marriage to me was wrong for her, anyway. And when I would not oblige her intimately, she had an affair. She was angered by my neglect of her and fought back with the only weapon she felt she had. My lack of expertise with the fairer sex was such that I could not see the corner I drove her into."

"Oh, Ethan." Alice did lean into him then, bringing her hand up to the back of his head and holding him as much as he was holding her. "You deserved so much better."

"I am beginning to think perhaps I do." He wanted

better, and that was a start. "But I suspect you do not mean what you say."

"You think I'd lie to you?" Alice drew back and resumed her frowning. He was coming to adore that starchy, prim expression on her face, because it was such a pleasure to relieve her of it.

"I think you do not divine the direction of my thoughts, Alice Portman," Ethan replied, and in his chest, he felt his heart begin to beat with a slow, palpable throbbing. He was going to lay himself open to intimate rejection, and he knew it. He chose to do it, though, because wanting and not having was better—far, far better—than never wanting anything at all.

"So elucidate your thoughts for me," Alice said while her fingers tightened around his.

He could prevaricate and hint and complicate what was simple and precious. His regard for Alice would allow none of that.

"I want you," Ethan said. "I want your body under mine, overcome with desire. I want to share intimate pleasure with you, to drive you to incoherence with longing and satisfaction." He wanted that desperately. "I want the taste and scent of you filling my senses, the texture of every inch of your skin burned into my memory. I want to hear you cry my name in the dark, Alice Portman."

Before she could formulate a scathing set down, Ethan charged forth, determined she should hear him out.

"I know, Alice, you will not countenance marriage, and I suspect this relates to having been mistreated in your past. I do not account myself any sort of bargain as a husband, in any case, and would not offend you by presenting myself as a candidate for your hand. But I can offer you pleasure and joy and... friendship, or some version of it."

"You are propositioning me." She sounded astounded rather than offended.

"I am offering you a liaison," Ethan clarified. "Though I can exercise enough restraint to assure you I would not get you with child."

"And if I wanted a child?"

Ethan battled back joy that she'd even ask such a thing. "No bastards, sweetheart. I can't do that to a child of mine, nor would you want it for our child either."

He fell silent but remained beside her, giving her time to recover from what was clearly an unanticipated overture, while he tried not to contemplate their options if she did—despite his best intentions—conceive a child.

Such thoughts blundered perilously close to *hoping*, and Ethan knew better than to countenance that folly.

"I'm not without experience," she said softly, turning to rest her head on his shoulder.

If she'd expected him to stiffen, pull away, or physically display disappointment, he was determined to confound her. He pulled her closer and kissed her temple.

"God, Alice, neither am I. For you, I wish I could be." It was an odd, heartfelt sentiment he would never be able to explain to her. "Were you mistreated?"

"No." Ethan heard a silent "but" following her denial. "I was engaged, when I was sixteen, and could once again walk without much of a limp. My brothers had seen to it I was well dowered, and a young man

I'd known most of my life offered for me. He was of decent family, and I saw him as my means of leaving Cumbria and its memories far behind. I accepted him, on the condition we'd leave the area and settle elsewhere. America would have done for me, or the Antipodes. I just needed to get away."

"And this young man," Ethan conjectured, "the one you refer to as decent, he took liberties, thinking you would not cry off after that no matter what, and then announced he had no intention of taking you anywhere."

Alice's smile was rueful. "More or less."

"But you," Ethan went on, "having a spine of Toledo steel, did cry off and left the poor idiot without a wife, her dowry, or a semblance of his honor, which was exactly what he deserved. I am proud of you."

"Proud of me?"

He had surprised her, and he was damned glad of it. "There is no explaining the courage it takes to face down the judgments and expectations of Polite Society. Did your brothers try to dissuade you?" Ethan tried to recall where his dueling pistols were stored in the event he did not approve of her answer.

"Benjamin knows the whole of it, and he understands my decision."

Bastard. "He never told you he was proud of you, that he admired your fortitude and integrity? He never told you the scoundrel wasn't good enough for you in any regard?"

Alice looked away. She scuffed her half boot against the dirt. "He brought me South. He keeps an eye on me."

He had kept that eye from a distance, when the man by reputation was well able to provide a roof over her head. Ethan made a note to locate those dueling pistols.

"Mr. Durbeyfield thought he was doing me a favor." Alice turned her head, and Ethan thought she might have sniffed at his shoulder. "I was, in the local parlance, touched with an unfortunate past, which he was willing to overlook."

"So that he could get his lying, smug, unworthy paws on your dowry. Your brothers should be ashamed."

Alice sat up then and cocked her head at him. "Perhaps they are. I always thought they were ashamed of me… Men are odd creatures. But dear."

Dear was encouraging. Ethan would shoot her brothers some other day, because *he* would like to be dear to her. Dear and desired; it was a frightening, exhilarating, and ambitious combination. He hadn't his brother's charm or his title or his tremendous amatory experience, but Alice was on this bench, tucked obligingly against Ethan, not Nick.

It was enough to keep Ethan on the bench all night, if she'd allow it.

"We should be going," Alice said. "They'll be ringing the bell soon for supper, and the boys will be looking for me."

"You're going to make me work for it," Ethan decided. "Good girl."

"Work for it?" Alice let him assist her to her feet.

"You do not respond to my offer, Alice, and it's an offer that requires a yes or no answer. If you refuse me, I will understand I do not appeal to you as a woman finds a man appealing. I will not enjoy the rejection, but neither will it destroy me." He hoped. "If you reject me, you will continue to be the person to whom I entrust the education of my sons, a respected member of my household, and safe at Tydings from any unwanted advances, including my own." *Damn it.*

"We simply ignore this extraordinary discussion and both kisses?"

Ethan smiled over at her. "We pretend to, as best we can."

"And if I accept your offer?" Alice kept her eyes focused ahead, depriving Ethan of the insights they might yield.

"You decide." Ethan dropped his voice. "You decide if I come to you or you come to me. If we join in a bed or in the hay mow or on a blanket in the woods. You decide if you remain in the position of governess—I think you like it, for one thing, but it protects your reputation and mine, for another—or we find another governess. You decide."

He liked—he adored—the idea of them deciding *together* something as significant as who the boys' next governess should be.

She turned her face up to the dying sun as she walked along. "I cannot abandon the appearance of propriety, and I am wicked for admitting I'd even consider such a thing. You do kiss exceedingly well, though, and you…"

She trailed off, while Ethan waited.

And waited. He what? Got her on a horse? Would die to keep her safe? Made the loneliness and doubt recede when he took her in his arms?

For she surely did that for him.

"I have much to think about," Alice muttered. "We would have to be very discreet."

She was considering it—considering allowing him to

become her lover. "I can be discreet." Ethan ushered her up the terrace steps at a sedate pace, when he wanted to vault them three at time. "And so can you."

"Give me a week, Ethan. At least a week."

A week was seven entire days and nights, an infinite procession of moments. How could a yes-or-no decision take that long?

"You may have as long as you please, Alice. It is a lady's prerogative. I will see you at dinner?"

"I think not. Some solitude will allow me to clear my head."

"As you wish." He saw her guard relax a trifle before he swooped in and pressed a soft, lingering kiss to her cheek. "I will see you at breakfast and in my dreams." He left her there in the golden evening sunlight, her fingers pressed to her cheek.

Ten

"IT'S BUTTERCUP!" JOSHUA SPOTTED THE BIG MARE first, and only his father's bellowed command stopped the boy from galloping the remaining distance to the stable yard.

"Uncle Nick!" Joshua yelled from the back of his pony. "Uncle Nick, we're home!"

"You may trot," Ethan allowed, because they were nearing the arena. "You too, Jeremiah." Ethan drew his horse to a halt and waited beside Alice's mount when the boys' ponies started forward at the faster gait.

And here their outing had been going so well. "It appears my brother is paying a visit. Shall we greet him?"

"I suppose I have no choice?" Alice looked around as if seeking a hiding place.

"You can dismount here. Go on up to the house if you wish, but Nick will see the sidesaddle and ask questions."

"I'm being silly." Alice nudged Waltzer forward at the walk. "Nick will tease me, though, and I'd as soon avoid that."

Her reaction, far from enthusiastic, held a petty

kind of reassurance for a man whose overtures took a week to consider. "Nick will behave, or he won't be welcome under my roof."

"Don't be dramatic," Alice murmured as they neared the barns. "He never means anything but fun."

Ethan was torn between a guilty pleasure that on the face of the entire earth, there was at least one woman whose heart didn't leap for joy at the prospect of spending time with Nick, and an odd disappointment. Having been assured Alice was not attracted to Nick, Ethan wanted her to like his brother.

Nick came out of the barn looking golden and splendiferous in riding attire. "Can these be my little nephews? You've grown just since leaving Kent." He knelt, so the boys could try to strangle him with hugs around his neck, then rose with a nephew on each hip.

"Ethan." Nick smiled up at him. "I've found some urchins to take back to Kent with me. I think this one will be a boot boy and this one a potboy. Or maybe I'll keep them until they grow into a matched set of footmen for my lady. She'll be the envy of Mayfair when she goes shopping."

"Not shopping!" Joshua screeched dramatically. "Please, Uncle Nick. I want to be a stable boy."

"Then go put up your pony," Nick said, setting both boys on their feet. "If you're quick about it, you can help put up Buttercup, too, while your papa introduces me to the lovely la—*Alice?*"

Nick's expression went from that buccaneer's charming grin, to consternation, to a beaming, genuine smile in a succession of instants.

"I see you've met." Ethan swung down and came around to assist Alice from her horse lest Nick usurp that pleasure for himself. "Alice Portman, may I make known to you your friend Wee Nick. Nicholas, you'd best shut your mouth if you're to extricate yourself from this without catching a fly."

"Alice Portman." Nick shook his head as Ethan lifted her from the horse and set her on her feet. "You prevaricating, deceitful, naughty girl. The air in Surrey is most certainly agreeing with you."

Alice smiled at him. "Nice to see you again, Nicholas, but you knew I'd been taught how to ride."

Nick's smile tilted back toward flirtatious. "I'm not complaining about hiding your ability to ride, sweetheart, though it's a pleasure to see you in the saddle. I'm taken aback by your ability to hide a siren in governess's clothing."

"From you," Ethan muttered, loud enough for his brother to hear.

"Point taken," Nick said, still regarding Alice thoughtfully.

"Alice was willing to make the effort to get on a horse for the boys, because she's to accompany us to Greymoor's picnic on Wednesday." Ethan handed his horse off to Miller. "We can toast her with some cold cider or something stronger, now that the morning's ride is accomplished. May I assume you'll stay at least the night?"

"Am I welcome?" Nick asked. "I debated sending you a note, but can make other arrangements easily."

Nick was studying the arena, the trees, the barns... perhaps thinking Ethan would turn aside his own brother. "You will always be welcome, Nicholas. Now come up to the house and let me feed you as best as I can. The staff has Sunday off, and we make do."

"Alice? Will you be joining us, or will you tarry here with your charges?"

"I do not supervise them in the stables," Alice replied, but her eyes shifted to Ethan, clearly seeking guidance.

"Come." Ethan tucked her hand over his arm and did not look at Nick. "You must celebrate your success with Waltzer and supervise Nick and me as we raid the larder." Alice slipped her arm from Ethan's as they reached the back entrance.

"If you gentlemen will excuse me, I'll change out of this habit."

"If I must." Nick said. "But not until I tell you again how fetching you look, Alice. Turn yourself out like that on the Ladies' Mile, and you'll leave a trail of love-struck, callow swains."

"Callow swains of any description are of little appeal."

Ethan let her go, noting that Nick, for all he was happily married, watched the twitch of her skirts with unabashed admiration.

"It's the glasses," Ethan said because he'd been guilty of the same oversight, and without Alice's presence, some of his possess—*protectiveness* ebbed. "And that bun, and all those sack dresses, and her..." He waved a hand around. "Governess airs."

"Yes. Governess airs are excellent camouflage. Are we really to fend for ourselves in the kitchen?"

"We are. Fear not, though. I've figured out where the bread and butter hide, and which key opens the larder."

"You have a very pretty property, Ethan." Nick followed his brother to the kitchen. "I've ridden by from time to time, but the walls and hedges make it hard to see much from the lanes."

"Why didn't you stop by?" Ethan washed his hands, then extracted a loaf of fresh, white bread from the bread box rather than watch Nick's reaction to the question. "Did you really think I'd not be home to you?" Because until Barbara's death, he might not have been.

"I didn't know."

Ethan started cutting the loaf into exactly even slices. "You've always had my direction."

"And you've had mine. I see now your property is in excellent repair, your stables full of handsome horseflesh, and your house larger than any of ours, except for Belle Maison itself. I've worried about you when I didn't need to."

Was that resentment in Nick's tone, or hurt? "Because I'm well off?" Ethan fetched a half wheel of cheese from the larder and again put the knife to use. "You can slice some of the ham hanging in the hallway, if you don't mind."

"You're well off enough to remarry," Nick observed, using a basin in the sink to wash his hands before he went to work on the ham.

Ethan wrapped the cheese and took it back to the pantry, then fetched a bowl of ripe peaches, which reminded him of Alice.

Rather than comment on Nick's observation, Ethan fished in the drawers and cupboards until he found everyday cutlery, linen napkins, and plates. Nick's arrival on a Sunday was something of a mercy, allowing them privacy while they tried to find a rhythm with each other.

"So how did you get Alice on a horse?" Nick asked, carrying bread, meat, and cheese to the table.

"She knows how to ride." Ethan put salt, pepper, mustard, and butter down next to Nick's tray. "She just needed an incentive to deal with her understandable fears."

"Reese Belmont said she'd been hurt trying to report a crime of some sort." Nick carried the pitcher of lemonade to the table, while Ethan opened a bottle of sweet white wine and found glasses.

"I don't know the details." Ethan set the wine on the table to breathe. "And I don't want to know them unless Alice wants me to. It must be bad, though. Hazlit was out here, strutting and pawing like a papa bear."

"Hazlit?" Nick's eyebrows rose. "My Benjamin Hazlit?"

"He's Alice's brother. I assumed you knew they were related." And wasn't it gratifying to know something Nick did not?

"I had no idea," Nick muttered. "How odd."

Ethan poured them each half a glass of lemonade, added a portion of wine, and took a seat across from Nick. "For what we are about to receive, we are damned grateful, amen."

"Amen." Nick reached for the bread. "I cannot fathom Benjamin Hazlit confiding in you, Ethan. Meaning no offense, but the man's lips are closed as tightly as a king's coffin."

"His younger sister works for me," Ethan said, waiting for Nick to finish with the butter. "He told me he'd call me out if I offended Alice, and I had to like him for it."

Nick set the butter knife down, his expression distracted. "You like him for threatening you?"

"He's protective. I would want our sisters to be able to count on us for the same. Mustard?"

"Please." Nick accepted the mustard and set it down beside his plate. "I feel as if… First, you find a lovely woman where Pris's starchy little governess was standing when last I looked. Then you turn up living not in some gothic horror but on a gracious, perfectly pleasant and prosperous estate. And now you tell me Benjamin Hazlit is revealing family secrets to you, and you like him for threatening your life. Maybe the ale was bad at the last posting inn I stopped at."

"What did you expect, Nick?"

"I don't know. For Alice to be holed up in her room, reading over the boys' school work, you to be scratching away at your infernal correspondence, Tydings to be somehow grimmer. I don't know."

"Are you disappointed?"

Nick smiled self-deprecatingly. "Maybe. You don't need rescuing, do you? Mustard?"

"Please." Ethan accepted the mustard and tried not to flinch at the question. "Reserve judgment on whether I am in need of rescuing until after the picnic. Greymoor himself came by to issue his summons for this bacchanal. I found him likable enough, and might have to return his call."

"You don't visit?" Nick scowled at his plate. "Not even Greymoor or Heathgate or Amery?"

"I know Heathgate slightly." Ethan sipped his drink, wishing it was something more fortifying than this bland concoction Nick favored. "I'm hardly his social equal, and why would I visit the others?"

"Because that is what one does in the country, Ethan Grey." Nick directed a pained stare at his drink. "You visit, and you talk about the hunting and the shooting and the crops, or the lack of hunting, shooting, and crops. You bump into each other riding out. You cadge a Sunday meal after church. You stay for a pint at the local inn. You stand up with the wallflowers at the assemblies."

Ethan remained silent, regarding his brother levelly because he honestly did not know what to say.

"I'll shut up," Nick said. "Pass me that tray. Growing boys need sustenance."

Ethan passed him the tray and the butter and mustard.

"I don't go to church," Ethan said. "I don't ride to hounds, I don't go to the assemblies, and I don't frequent the local watering hole."

"Ethan?" Nick's voice held consternation and concern.

"I do ride out," Ethan allowed, "and thus I bumped into Heathgate. I've met Greymoor and that other fellow."

"Amery," Nick supplied. "Have you met Westhaven?"

"Not that I recall."

Nick put down his glass with a soft thump. "You can't live here in legendarily pleasant surrounds, cut off from all around you. It isn't... It isn't right."

"Not right for you," Ethan said, his tone mild. "But I accomplish a great deal, Nicholas, when I'm not dancing, visiting, gossiping, and watching a pack of dogs tear an arthritic fox to pieces."

"Miller told me you've promised to take the boys cubbing this fall," Nick said, apparently willing to reserve further sermons for later.

"They need to know the protocol if they're to be gentlemen, and they ride well enough."

Nick set his second sandwich down only half-eaten. "I feel like you've gone away, like you grew up and became somebody my brother could not have turned into. You were not like this as a boy."

"Like what?" Ethan was truly curious, but concerned too, because he could see Nick was getting genuinely upset with him.

No, not with him, *for* him.

"You enjoyed people," Nick said. "You joked with the stable boys, flirted with the dairymaids. The little girls wanted you to read them their stories and braid their hair and check under their beds at night. You beat Papa at cribbage and led me into one silly prank after another. And now…"

"Now?"

"You *accomplish a great deal*," Nick said in exasperation. "You may not write to your brother but once in seven years, but you accomplish a lot. You'll take your boys cubbing so they learn their manners, but you don't call on your neighbors, nor they on you. You're a good-looking, wealthy widower, but you won't stand up at the assemblies. You probably make more money year by year, but you couldn't be bothered to tell me you were married, much less widowed, much less a father twice over. What happened, Ethan? What on earth happened to you?"

Nick's tone was so bewildered, Ethan couldn't have been offended if he'd wanted to be, and he did not want to be.

Nor would he tell Nick what had happened. Not ever. For his own sake, but equally for Nicholas's sake.

"I grew up, Nick. It wasn't my choice, entirely, but I'm doing the best I can with it."

"Is this how you felt about me, when all the wild talk circulated about my womanizing?"

Ethan pursed his lips. "Felt how?"

"Like some strange man was using your brother's name," Nick said. "Doing things your brother wouldn't, and saying things he'd never dream of uttering?"

"No." Was that how Nick felt? "I worried, Nick. That much carrying on isn't about having the occasional recreational tumble."

"It wasn't." Nick scrubbed a hand over his face. "How did we ever get onto such gloomy topics?"

"You are disappointed in me," Ethan suggested gently. "I am socially backward, reclusive, and much preoccupied with my commerce."

"And all of that"—Nick waved his big hand again—"would be of no moment, Ethan, but are you *happy*?"

Ethan had stopped asking himself this question at the age of fourteen. It had no bearing on anything.

"Happiness is a luxury," Ethan said, staring at his empty glass. "If it comes to pass, it should be appreciated, but life doesn't owe us happiness. I am content, Nick, and much less unhappy than I was when Barbara was alive. If that makes me evil, then so be it. Before she died, we learned what it meant to hate each other, though fortunately that was not the last page of our dealings. I did not marry well, and you did. Can we leave it at that?"

"For now." Nick looked mightily disgruntled at the idea. "It isn't that simple."

"No," Ethan agreed, rising, "it isn't, but you are my first houseguest in the seven years I've been here, and I am not inclined to spend your afternoon rehashing ancient history. How long can you stay?"

"Miller mentioned that George might be out this way," Nick said, getting to his feet.

"I've invited him and Adolphus both. We'll see if he accepts."

"Let's say I'll head back to Kent on Thursday morning. My business in London is done, and if I can spend time with George, I'll consider my travels a success."

"You may already consider your travels a success," Ethan said, pausing with the pitcher in one hand and the wine bottle in the other. "I am glad you're here, Nick."

"I'm glad to be here." His tone and his expression suggested this was not an entirely genuine sentiment.

Ethan set his burdens on the counter. As younger men, they might have settled this—whatever *this* was—with a round of fisticuffs. "I know you mean well, Nicholas, but please bear in mind, I am not you, and I am not the affable, innocent boy with whom you shared your childhood."

This was an understatement the proportions of which defied description. Ethan wasn't going to tell Nick that, either.

Nick sidled along the counter and hooked a beefy arm around his brother's shoulders. "You are my brother, and if you are not happy, it's hard for me to be happy."

"We aren't boys anymore." Ethan wanted to pull away, but that would hurt Nick's feelings. "You can't create happiness out of a long summer afternoon, two boys, bare feet, and a cold stream."

Nick didn't say anything. He just put his other arm around Ethan and hugged him until Ethan stepped back and resumed tidying up their lunch.

❧

"It's Sunday," Ethan said as he crossed the threshold to Alice's room. "You cannot be working, Alice."

"Says who?" Alice put down her pen and capped her inkwell. Why was it that Ethan Grey in riding breeches, boots, and waistcoat looked handsomer than any man she'd laid eyes on? His sleeves were rolled back to the elbow, exposing tan muscle dusted with golden hair. She wanted to lay her cheek against that forearm, taste the strength in his wrists.

"Almighty God gave us the example of resting on the Sabbath." Ethan ambled over to her escritoire and peered over her shoulder. "Because I am the almighty lord of this property, I condone the notion. What are you about?"

"Making a list of Latin aphorisms," Alice said as Ethan leaned over and scanned her work. Her imagination suggested he inhaled through his nose, but then, so had she.

"Why do you laugh?" Ethan quoted. "Change the name and the same can be said of you."

"That one's too long, though your boys do a great deal of laughing."

"More lately." He remained half-bent over her while Alice tried to lecture herself into ignoring him. "This is an interesting collection, Alice Portman. Is Hazlit's Latin as facile?"

Ethan straightened and crossed to sit on her bed. The door was open, and nobody was about, but still, sitting on her bed was intimate, and Alice liked the look of him there—heaven help her.

"It is not, and neither is Vim's."

"What of your sister, the one you haven't seen for five years?"

"Avis." Alice's smile dimmed. "She was neither a bluestocking nor given to competing with our brothers." She did, however, run the entire estate of Blessings so their brothers could lark about all over the realm.

Ethan ran a hand over her pillow, and Alice's insides became muddled. Just like that, drat him. "Have you made up your mind about going to visit her?"

"You were serious when you said I might?"

He did it again—ran his palm over the linen and wreaked havoc with Alice's composure. "We can agree, I think, I am generally serious."

Not as serious as he wanted people to think. "I've written to Avis, suggesting she might come south, and I could come north, and we'd meet in the Midlands, but there hasn't been time for a reply."

Another stroke over her pillow, over the very spot where she laid her head. "Can't your brother send one of his famous pigeons? He must have some flying between Blessings and his southern residence."

"I hadn't considered Benjamin's pigeons. Even if he has such, they can carry only very brief messages."

He rose and turned to smooth over the covers where he'd sat, and the back of him was no less unsettling to look upon than the front. "You should send such an invitation. I am here, in fact, to issue a summons to you."

"To me?" Alice tidied her papers and set her pen in its stand. "It's Sunday. One may not be summoned."

"Nicholas has taken it into his head to make muffins and has asked you to attend him and the boys in the kitchen."

Alice rose, relieved—truly and honestly relieved—to

be getting Ethan out of her bedroom. "If I have to go, then you have to as well."

"Nick didn't include me on the writ," Ethan said as they made their way down the back stairs. "You are female, so he assumes you will know where things go in the kitchen."

"I avoid the kitchen. Your cook is a cantankerous and territorial old dame. Mrs. Buxton made it clear Cook is not to be trifled with."

"Valid point, but Cook also consumes a fair amount of the cooking sherry and takes her Sundays off to heart." Ethan lowered his voice and bent near as they walked along. "I think she has a follower."

"Or a drinking companion."

"Who has a drinking companion?" Nick asked. He stood at the kitchen counter, a towel around his waist as an improvised apron. "If there's any drinking going on, I'd like to be informed. Joshua, stop kicking the drawer and find us three clean spoons. Jeremiah, we'll need some mugs of cold milk to sustain us."

Ethan quirked an eyebrow at his brother. "Perhaps we, who have been mucking around the stables, ought to wash our hands, hmm?"

Nick's expression was arrested. "Good idea. Boys, wash up, and then step lively. Uncle Nick is hungry for muffins."

Ethan scanned the counter, where ingredients were lined up in recipe order. "You're not going to drown the apples in cinnamon, are you?"

To the ears of any governess, the question was laden with challenge from one boy to another.

Nick propped his fists on his hips. "You blaspheme on the Lord's day, Ethan Grey. I do not drown my apples in spices, but I am not stingy with cinnamon or cloves."

"So you completely overpower the equally worthy, less pungent flavors," Ethan scoffed. "As usual."

"You could do better?" Nick glowered at him, the boys watching the exchange with round eyes.

"I always have." Ethan's smile appeared exactly designed to goad a younger brother.

"You're on." Nick slapped his towel against the counter. "Alice and the boys will judge, and may the best muffin win."

"Muffin him silly, Papa," Joshua said.

"Make yours double enormous, Uncle Nick," Jeremiah joined in.

"Joshua Grey!" Nick turned to his smallest nephew in mock offense. "How can I name you one of my seconds if you're rooting for the other team?"

"I can root for Papa and be your second. Miss Alice can be Papa's second."

"Alice?" Ethan crossed his arms over his chest. "This is a matter of honor, and my sons are turncoats. That leaves me you or the pantry mouser."

Alice plucked the towel from Nick's hands. "I'm your man, Mr. Grey." She gently whapped the towel across Nick's chest, while the boys hooted and shrieked with glee.

When she was left alone in the kitchen an hour later, and the boys had dragged the men out to the garden, Alice did not immediately start to clean up. Instead, she sat down with a cup of hot tea and enjoyed the silence. If anyone had told her two weeks ago she'd be participating in a duel-by-muffin between two grown men, she would have laughed.

And this afternoon, with Ethan, his brother, and his sons, she *had* laughed. That set her to thinking about the recipe that was her life—too much caution and observation, not enough participation or spice.

She was thinking so hard she didn't hear the door open or the footsteps behind her. A pair of lips settled on her cheek, and her first instinct was to melt into the kiss, except...

"Nicholas, behave yourself for once."

"I was thanking you." Nick smiled at her and slid onto the bench across the table from her. "You looked so serious and pretty sitting there, staring at your teacup as if it held the answer to all life's mysteries."

"I'm English. A good cup of tea does hold the answer to many of life's mysteries. That doesn't excuse your kissing me, Nicholas, and I'll thank you to keep your lips to yourself in future."

"Or what? You'll paddle my backside?"

"As if you'd mind."

"Did I truly offend?" Nick asked, his smile fading. "If I did, I do apologize."

"You nearly did, except I know you are harmless. You left Ethan outside with the boys?"

"I did." Nick rose. "I am off to fetch some paper and pencils from the library. Ethan suggested we sketch designs for a tree house. When will the muffins be ready?"

Alice rose, because dishes had never once in the history of kitchens washed themselves. "The muffins won't be ready until Wednesday next. Shoo, or I'll issue another edict."

Nick scampered out of the kitchen, his hands playfully covering his behind, so Alice had to snap a towel at him for good measure. She turned around, intent on piling dishes in the sink, only to find Ethan lounging against the hallway door, observing her with a slight smile.

"Forgive my brother his airs. The title weighs on him heavily."

Alice took down an apron from a peg. "I think it does, too. Bring me some hot water, please, and I'll get these soaking." He brought her the kettle from the hob, and leaned in to kiss her jaw as he did.

Alice smiled, closed her eyes, and forgot entirely about the dishes. "You're as bad as your brother."

"That scamp did not offer to help with the dishes."

"He did not. If you and Nick are in the house, who is with the boys?"

"They popped down to the paddocks to stuff carrots into the shoats named Lightning and Thunder." Ethan refilled the kettle, and the reservoir in the stove for good measure. He tidied up as Alice rinsed things off and added them to the collection soaking in the big kitchen sink.

"Ethan Grey, did you just finish my tea?"

"There was only one cold swallow left." Ethan brought her the empty mug. "Shall I make you another?"

"So you can pilfer from that too? I think not. What are you... Oh, Ethan."

He'd come up behind her and linked his hands around her waist to pull her back against his chest. She kept her hands in the water, closed her eyes, and enjoyed the simple, warm proximity of him.

Ethan's voice rumbled at her ear, as she felt his lips graze her jaw. "I told myself I would not pester you, but you look so desperately pesterable, with the apron around your waist and your mouth all pinched up like that."

"And my hands sopping wet and not a towel within reach. I used to think you weren't anything like Nick, you know?"

"How could you think such a thing?" Ethan murmured, and dear Jesus, was that his *tongue* tracing her ear? "We are both tall, blond, blue-eyed, and of an age. We have features alike, and we both make excellent muffins, though mine are better."

"Turn loose of me." Alice wiggled a little against him, but not to get away. "Somebody could come along, and this isn't how you preserve anybody's reputation, Ethan Grey." He stepped back, slowly.

"You are a woman of considerable resolve, Alice Portman. Right now, I do admire you for it, but I cannot like it."

"I'm crushed." Alice fluttered her lashes dramatically. "Go find your sons and collect your brother before I'm interrupted again by some errant pair of lips. And do not think of peeking into that oven, Mr. Grey, or you'll forfeit the contest."

"That wasn't one of the rules."

"And neither was it good sportsmanship to try to cozen a judge." Alice gave him her best The-Governess-Is-Not-Happy glare. "The other team is guilty of the same, so I will not assess a penalty."

"I will take my leave." Ethan executed an elaborate bow. "If you see my opponent, tell him I'm at the stables, corrupting his seconds."

"Out!"

Eleven

Horses needed the occasional drink, especially in warmer weather. At least the coachy looked apologetic when he insisted Hart Collins pause on his journey between house parties.

Boring, staid, excruciatingly proper house parties held by those whose social aspirations meant a title—any title at all—would find welcome in their midst.

"Very well." Hart Collins stood beside the coach and surveyed the unprepossessing village green. "But if I sicken from drinking the dog piss that passes for ale in such surrounds, be it on your head, John Coachman."

"Aye, milord."

The coachy would have a nip too, of course. The man drove better drunk than sober, something Collins did not hold against him—a drunk being less inclined to carp about timely payment of his wages.

The inn was, like its setting, tidy, clean, and completely unremarkable. A bucolic Tudor exponent of English respectability such as Collins occasionally pretended he missed when dealing with the infernal heat and insubordinate servants in Italy.

And sometimes, the barmaids in such establishments were not averse to earning a few extra coins. Then too, the horses would move along more smartly if they were given a chance to blow, after all. One shouldn't neglect one's cattle.

"A proper squire would come in occasionally for a pint."

The speaker was hunched over the dark, polished wood of the bar, and his tone suggested this was not the first drink with which he fueled his discontent.

"Hush, ye, Thatcher. We don't all of us need to cast our business to the wind. Mr. Grey pays his tithes and minds his own." The rebuke came from a plump matron sitting in the snug with the unsmiling specimen who must have been her yeoman spouse.

"He can well afford to pay his tithes," Thatcher retorted, straightening. "Man's a bloody nabob, and watches every coin."

Yokels would ever complain about the gentry, the gentry would complain about the nobs, and the titles would complain about the Crown. Merry Old England was predictable, at least.

Collins stepped up to the bar. "A pint of your best, and some decent fare."

"There's ham and cheese, and bread just out of the oven," the bartender said while pulling a pale pint. He wasn't an old man, but he had the self-contained quality of most in his station.

"Ethan Grey's cheese," Thatcher spat. "You purchase your goods from a man who's too high and mighty to patronize the only inn in the neighborhood."

Ethan Grey?

"That's enough from you, Thatcher," the conscience

in the corner piped up. "Most would be spending their free time with family, not biting the hand that feeds them." She sent a significant glance at Collins, a clear reminder that foreigners—those from outside the parish—were not to be parties to local grievances.

"This Ethan Grey," Collins said, sliding his drink down the bar and taking a position next to Thatcher. "He's one of the landholders hereabouts?"

"Owns one of the prettiest properties in the shire," Thatcher replied. "Imports his sheep and cattle, keeps a prime stable, but spoils his wee brats rotten and thinks he's too good for the rest of us—and him nothing but some lord's bastard, or so they say."

Sometimes, just when it seemed those fickle bitches known as the Fates turned their backs on a man, they were in fact leaving in his hands the means to solve all his problems.

Ethan Grey had children—small children. "Is this Ethan Grey tall, blond, and blue-eyed? Serious as a parson?"

"*More* serious than Vicar Fleming," Thatcher groused. "A hard man and hardheaded. Hard on the help what gives him an honest day's work."

From the scent of Thatcher and the dirt on his boots and clothes, the man was a hostler of some sort. In pursuit of self-interest, Collins was willing to have truck with even such a one as this.

"And you say he's wealthy and dotes on his children? Come, Mr. Thatcher. Perhaps you'd like to share in the plebeian offerings that pass for sustenance at this establishment."

Thatcher looked momentarily wary, until the bartender put a plate of sliced ham, cheese, and brown bread on the bar.

"I'm a mite peckish," Thatcher allowed.

Collins picked up the plate with one hand and his drink with the other—a surprisingly mellow summer ale. "Come along. I have a few questions for you."

As they made their way to a corner table as far as possible from the bar and the snug, Collins's mind began to spin possibilities. Across the room, the bartender scrubbed out a mug with a dingy white rag and said nothing.

ex∞

When Nick returned to the kitchen, he brought paper, pencils, and a gum eraser, and sat at the work-table. Alice peered over his shoulder as he sketched, startled at the whimsy of the structure on the page.

"You could really build that?"

"Of course." Nick didn't look up. "It would take some doing. On a raised structure like this, we might have to paint the boards before we build, which means being able to see how the whole fits together from the raw lumber."

"These are like your bird houses, but bigger."

"And one must plan safe entry and exits, because little boys don't generally fly. Bring your tea over here, Alice. I'm about to interrogate you."

"So interrogate," Alice challenged him as she took the bench opposite him at the table. "Be warned I'm not the tattling kind."

"It's only tattling if somebody has misbehaved. Are you happy here?"

Not the question she'd anticipated. "Happier than I thought I'd be. Overwhelmed too."

"Overwhelmed?" Nick frowned at his sketch. "I'm

not sure I can credit that such a thing is possible. They are good boys, Alice. How can you be overwhelmed to be teaching them their sums and declensions? Priscilla was overwhelming, with her wild imagination and careless heart."

"Wild imagination?" Alice took a sip of her tea, aiming a pointed look at the sketch on the page. Nick had designed a two-story affair patterned to blend right into the surrounding foliage, complete with birds and a birdhouse secreted among the leaves and branches.

"Wild." He used the eraser the better to shade the foliage, while the scents of cinnamon and clove filled the kitchen. "The stories that child concocts should be published." He frowned at his sketch then paused to help himself to a sip of Alice's tea. "You put cinnamon in this, and you're dodging my question."

"The boys are busy," Alice said, "and you're right. Academically, they are well within my abilities."

"But?" Nick set his sketch aside and regarded Alice closely, all hint of teasing gone from his features.

"But I realize I am tromping around Tydings like a mountaineer, Nick. I used to go for days at Sutcliffe without leaving the walls of the manor. My hip hurt, true, but here, it seems the more I walk, the less it hurts."

"This overwhelms you? And why didn't you just tell us you stayed indoors because you hurt?"

Yes, why hadn't she? "It doesn't bother me much now. That's a change, a big change. Miss Portman," she said with some consternation, "does not enjoy the outdoors."

Nick cocked his head. "But you do. You were positively beaming on that horse, Alice. You were enjoying the outdoors and being on horseback."

"That overwhelms me too. Before this week, I'd gone twelve years without managing a horse, Nick. I'd avoided titled company, but ended up on the arm of an earl here in Ethan's gardens, and we're off to do the pretty with more of same on Wednesday. It makes my head swim, to tell the truth."

"I'm a title." Nick swiped more of her tea.

"You're just you, for which I am grateful."

"So are you overwhelmed with joy, or worries?"

"Both." Alice peered at her almost-empty mug. "Then there is your brother."

"Ah."

What a man could do with one syllable. "He overwhelms me too."

"It's the family charm. We're endowed with it in proportion to our size."

"Abominable man." Alice stalled by sipping the last of her tea. "Ethan is charming, and you should not mock him."

Nick sobered. "I don't mock him, and I don't understand him either. He used to have charm to burn, Alice. I was convinced, growing up, he would have made a much better earl than I, and I used to pray he'd end up with the title, though it was a legal impossibility."

"Why would he have made the better earl? You're the heir."

"Ethan is so much more of a man than I am. He's not just smarter, he's wiser. He's not quite too big, whereas I have the dimensions of an ox. He never descended to chasing skirts out of immature resentment of life's responsibilities. He managed to dust himself off after Papa's wrongheaded foolishness, and he comprehends finances with an intuition I lack. He's just… better. I am glad Leah did not meet him first."

"Have you told him this?" Alice asked, wondering why women were considered less rational than men.

"He would just give me that cool, kind smile of his." Nick scrubbed a hand over his face. "He'd tell me he hadn't any idea what I was going on about, then change the subject. It unnerves me."

"Why would that unnerve you?"

"Because the old Ethan, my brother Ethan, would have argued me right out of my positions, because they are not entirely logical—I comprehend that—and he would have done so without causing me to resent his superior reasoning. He took a first in mathematics, you know."

"And his Latin is excellent. Where did he go to school before Cambridge?"

"Stoneham," Nick replied. "Some dreary place up north. Lady Warne about tore a strip off Papa when she got wind of it. I gather it is not a congenial environment, as boarding schools go."

Alice felt the tea in her belly abruptly curdle. "God above. Stoneham is not far from Blessings, Nick. It's a horror."

Nick's hand went still, the eraser poised above the whimsical sketch. "A horror? What constitutes a horror, Alice? And don't spare me the details."

"Adequate academically, and probably not too harsh for the typical meek younger son, but for an earl's disgraced bastard… Stoneham is one of the places boys go when they're sent down from the better schools. There's an assumption at such institutions that 'boys being boys' means many boys will be hurt, deprived of their meals, beaten, and worse."

Nick looked heartsick, a disquieting thing on a man so large and generally sunny. "What you describe is bad enough. Ethan did nothing to deserve such a fate."

"Some would call such a fate an opportunity. He got into Cambridge, and did well there."

"What aren't you telling me, Alice?" Nick met her gaze squarely, but Alice could see him steeling himself for her reply.

"My half brother Vim attended Stoneham at one point," Alice said. "He came home with a broken arm after only a few weeks of the Michaelmas term. He got crosswise of some baron's lordling and was attacked by a gang one night on the way to the privy. He lost the hearing in one ear for most of a year as well, and we weren't sure he'd be able to see out of one eye."

Nick stood, almost knocking the bench over. "At Stoneham?"

"At Stoneham. And from what Vim said, the proctors and deans regarded this as tolerable behavior between young men of unequal standing."

"Because your brother was a bastard?"

"He wasn't. He was my mother's son from a prior marriage, wealthy, much loved, and very bright. His family was right at hand and outraged on his behalf."

"Ethan was there for two years. He didn't leave the premises even once." Nick scrubbed a hand over his face again, and his gaze slewed around toward the door. His expression was tortured as he backed away from Alice. "I have to... You'll excuse me."

And then he was gone, leaving a sketch of such whimsy and grace on the table, Alice thought it worthy of framing and hanging on the schoolroom wall.

❧

"You look a little tired," Ethan remarked, pushing off the doorjamb to Alice's room and settling himself at her escritoire. The desk wasn't far from the bed, but Alice was relieved he'd stopped there.

And… disappointed.

"I am tired. I sleep better here at Tydings than I did at Sutcliffe or Belmont Hall. I think it's because the boys keep me moving, and not just about the house, but all over the grounds."

"Does it bother your hip?"

"At first, yes. It ached, but now it seems stronger." A good deal stronger. How had this happened in just a few weeks?

"Maybe the riding helps. Are you ready for tomorrow?"

"I will be relieved to have it over with, though the boys are looking forward to it and promising to be on their best behavior."

"I'll bring Davey," Ethan said. "If there are three adults to manage two little boys, we might stand a chance."

"You aren't to manage them. You're Mr. Grey, the invited guest, and Davey and I will see to the children." To remind him of the hierarchy reassured Alice, or it ought to.

Ethan rose and ambled the short distance to the bed, coming down beside her. "I wish you did not see yourself as subordinate."

With his weight on the mattress, Alice was pitched against his side. "I don't see myself as subordinate. I see myself as *employed*."

"You don't have to be," Ethan went on. "Your brother said there's a great deal of family wealth."

"There is, and when I'm too old to keep up with a

child, I'll have need of it. Benjamin invests my share, and it does quite nicely."

Ethan had turned his head, as if he'd study Alice's ear. The thought was unnerving. "I'd be happy to speak with him regarding some worthy projects. I don't bruit it about, but I am occasionally called to Carlton House to whisper in the Regent's ear regarding his finances."

Whisper in the... "You're *what*?"

"That's my reaction as well." Ethan looked a little puzzled. "I peer at the records for that monstrosity he's building in Brighton, assess which roads ought to be improved in which order, that sort of thing. Suggest a few investments that might turn him a profit. He's an intelligent man, is Prinny, and in a difficult position, but he does listen and seldom forgets what he's heard—unless he's passed out or far gone with some other sin."

"Sin. Always a worthy topic in lofty circles." And in the bedrooms of lowly governesses.

"Are you contemplating the sin of fornication with me, Alice? Do I dare hope you are considering such a thing?"

"Ethan." Alice made herself pull away. "The door."

"It's closed." He nuzzled at her neck.

Alice shut her eyes and angled her jaw. "It's not locked."

"Alice?" Ethan's gaze was curious, but in his eyes, Alice saw banked heat.

She shook her head. "I am not suggesting we... sin right here and now. Your sons are across the hallway, probably still whispering and plotting about tomorrow, and they could interrupt at any moment."

"A gap in my strategy," Ethan chided himself as he rose and went to the door. "And now the door is locked."

His walk as he crossed the room this time was the relaxed, feline glide Alice usually observed. The grace was there, and the power, but the purpose had changed. He was stalking her, closing in on his objective with single-minded determination.

"This isn't the right time, Ethan."

"Agreed. You are nervous of me, and I would reassure you."

Was the gazelle nervous of the lion? "You won't hurt me," Alice said, believing it. He wouldn't hurt her physically, for all his size and muscle.

He peered down at her. "Of course I wouldn't. I promise you that."

To her consternation, he dropped to the floor before her, stuffed a pillow under his knees, and wrapped his arms around her waist.

"Ethan?" Alice's hand settled on his golden hair, unable to resist touching him in such a docile pose—such a deceptively docile pose.

"Nick and George went at it just before dinner." Ethan laid his head in her lap, resting his cheek against her thigh. "They all but resorted to fisticuffs in the grand fraternal tradition."

"That would be a rousing match. Nick is nigh half a foot taller than your brother George."

"And carrying considerably more muscle. They were spoiling to get a piece of each other, but I couldn't allow it."

"What were they arguing over?" Alice asked, stroking Ethan's hair then feathering her fingers over his cheek, forehead, and jaw. To touch him this way was lovely; to hear his troubles and worries was lovelier still.

"Each accused the other of behaving badly without regard to the family's sensibilities or his own safety," Ethan summarized, "and they were both right."

"Nick was a tramp," Alice said flatly. "I hope his wife understands this about him. His ability to remain faithful to her should not be taken for granted."

"I know." Ethan nuzzled at Alice's hip. "That feels good, what you're doing."

"You are tired." He was tired and cuddled in her lap, and who would have thought him capable of such a thing?

"I am." He sat back, and took off his neckcloth and unfastened the collar of his shirt. "So I won't trouble you for long." He tucked himself against her again, and then went still, until Alice's hands found him once more, and he let out a quiet sigh.

"George was at university until this summer, wasn't he?" Alice asked as she kneaded the muscles of Ethan's neck.

"Good Lord." Ethan's sigh was louder. "That feels heavenly, and yes, George has just completed his formal education. He's agreed travel would complement his studies nicely."

"Travel?" Alice switched her grip with one hand and cradled Ethan's jaw with the other. "As in, on the Continent?"

"For now." Ethan shifted his shoulders, wedging himself more snugly against her. "George prefers the intimate attentions of men, and this is unsafe behavior."

"Unsafe?" Alice knew her tone held more than a

touch of dismay. "It's considered immoral, unsanitary, and felonious."

"You judge him? How is it any more immoral than carousing the way Nick did, or taking to wife a woman only tolerated on the fringes of Society as I did?"

"I understand you and your brothers haven't been saints, Ethan, but George's preference could get him hanged. I suppose this is why Nick wanted to use his fists."

"It is," Ethan muttered, sounding drowsy. "And George was just as frustrated, because he envisioned Nick with diseases that could have taken his reason or his ability to ensure the succession, or blotting the family escutcheon with his peccadilloes."

"George has a valid point. I suppose both men were insisting they'd been careful, but obviously not careful enough if each knew of the other's risks."

"They were able to see that." Ethan shifted to rest his face against Alice's other thigh. "Nick apologized, as some truly dreadful gossip devolved to George as a consequence of Nick's behaviors, and George agreed essentially to go on reconnaissance and see if there might be some places he'd enjoy living abroad."

These were familial confidences. A governess did often learn of them, but *not* from the master of the house as he cuddled against her lap.

"Seems a shame." Alice let go of Ethan's neck and brushed her hand over his hair in a slow, soothing caress. "You just meet your brother George as an adult, and he's sent away to avoid scandal."

"He's choosing to travel to avoid a grim and unnecessary death. I'd rather lose George to the charms of Paris than to death."

"But what a sad choice, hmm?" Alice leaned down and wrapped her arms around Ethan's shoulders. It wasn't a sexual embrace. Nothing they'd done since locking the door had been sexual. She breathed in the cedary scent of him and felt a desire to protect him from having to part from his brother, from any of his brothers.

"Let me brush out your hair." Ethan ended the embrace, remaining on his knees before her, hands on her hips. "I'll leave you in peace then, and you can dream of me."

She wanted to keep touching him, to keep comforting them both by touching him. "I don't think dreams of you will be peaceful."

"They'll be pleasurable." Ethan was up on his feet in one lithe move. "My dreams of you certainly are."

"Such talk." Alice's lips compressed rather than let a smile show.

"Come." Ethan tossed the pillow back on the bed and drew her to her feet. "I said I wouldn't stay long, and I am a man of my word. I've been longing to see what you look like with your hair down, so stop stalling."

"You've seen it down," Alice replied, but she let him guide her to her vanity. How dangerous could it be to let him simply brush her hair?

"I've seen it coming down, and I've seen it in a braid. That isn't *down*."

"It's just hair."

Ethan said nothing, taking the glasses from her nose and then letting his hands rest for a moment on her shoulders. The gesture quieted her, brought her calm inside, where she still wasn't quite settled enough from her busy day to contemplate sleep.

"Relax, Alice." Ethan held her shoulders. "I will merely brush out your hair and bid you good night."

She waited, but instead of getting down to work, Ethan's hands massaged her shoulders, then her neck, until Alice was leaning forward, her forehead resting on the arms she'd folded on her vanity.

If this be seduction, then let it never end.

"Better," Ethan murmured, and only then did Alice feel his deft fingers sliding pins from her hair. He worked with a kind of methodical rhythm, until her braid swung free, then he easily unplaited her hair, leaving it flowing down her back.

"So pretty." In the mirror, she watched while he brought a handful of her hair to his nose. "And this is why you smell of lemon verbena."

"I keep sachets with my clothing too," Alice said as Ethan trailed her hair down her back. "It's a perky scent, suitable for a governess."

"Perky." Ethan's lips quirked. "Tart, bracing, unexpected, with an underlying allure." She thought, from the husky note in his voice, he might start in kissing her neck. She loved it when he kissed her neck—he'd already taught her that about herself—but he took the brush to her hair, sweeping it in long strokes that tickled her back through her nightclothes.

"You like this," Ethan mused as he divided her hair into three thick skeins. "Left or right?"

Alice stifled a yawn. "I switch off. I'm right-handed, so over the right shoulder is easier."

"Then I'll do you a left-handed braid." He got it just so, not too tight, not too loose, and positioned to lie over her left shoulder. When he finished, he rested his hands again on her shoulders.

"Thank you." Alice could not hold back this yawn. "You have a nice touch with a brush, Ethan."

He smiled at her reflection in the mirror. "So nice, I've put you to sleep."

Hadn't that been his aim? "I do feel more ready for rest now. Thank you."

He held her chair, and as she got to her feet, Alice felt a little frustration that he wouldn't use their proximity to kiss her further.

"Good night." She met his gaze, finding his expression half-amused, half-veiled.

"I wasn't going to do this," he muttered. He drew her closer and dipped his head. When he settled his lips over hers, Alice snuggled in against him, relieved to be in his embrace. It was an easy, undemanding, friendly kiss, with Ethan's mouth moving slowly over hers, his tongue lazy.

"Good night, Alice," Ethan said, drawing back only the half inch necessary to permit speech.

She rose on her toes and fused her mouth to his, causing Ethan's lips to quirk up when she went foraging with her tongue.

He tolerated her quest for a moment, then drew back and tucked her face against his chest. "You need your sleep, and if you toy with me, I won't answer for the consequences."

His words did not initially sink in, because Alice was making an investigation of the taste of his neck and throat, but the stillness in his body—and rising hardness pressing against her belly—did.

"You are serious."

"I desire you mightily, Alice Portman."

"Alex," she corrected him. "My real name is Alexandra, but that isn't a governess name."

"Alexandra." His hand smoothed over the back of her head. "You honor me with such a confidence. It's important."

"It's just a name." She rested her forehead against his chest.

"It's just *your* name," Ethan corrected gently. "Just *your* hair, just *your* trust. *Yours*, Alexandra." His arms around her were gentle yet secure, and she felt the sting of tears. To hear her name, her real name, was such a gift, particularly spoken with the near reverence he gave it.

"I'll leave you now," Ethan said, but he held her a moment longer. "Nick and I will ride out with George in the morning. You sleep in. The day will be trying."

She nodded, not wanting him to go, but slipping her arms from his waist when he kissed her forehead, then her nose, then her lips.

"Good night, Ethan." She smiled as he turned at the door to blow her a kiss.

"Good night, Alex." He smiled back, and then he was gone.

But not before Alice caught a glimpse of Nick leaning against the wall outside the boys' room, arms crossed over his chest, expression thunderous.

Twelve

"WHATEVER WENT ON IN ALICE'S ROOM," NICK rumbled ominously, "it had better have been with the lady's consent."

"And a pleasant good evening to you too. Are you spying on me, Nicholas?"

"Maybe." Nick pushed away from the wall with his back. "I came up to say good night to the boys, as their papa was supposedly doing."

"I said good night to them and to their governess."

Nick looked disgruntled, like a man who was spoiling for a fight, only to realize there was nothing to fight over. "She deserves more than a quick tumble, and you'd best not be trifling with her."

"I agree." Ethan took Nick by the arm and turned him down the hallway. "This is not the place to air your concerns. Did you leave me any of Heathgate's whiskey?"

"We did. George is a lightweight, for all he's newly down from school."

"A mere child. So explain to me, worldly earl that you are, how it is Alice deserves more than a quick tumble and not trifling with."

"The rules are simple, and because I played by them, and played hard for years, I will recite them for you: You may dally wherever an experienced woman consents, provided her husband has his heir and spare. If you get a single woman pregnant, you must insist on marriage. Never bother virgins, for they require inordinate care and get romantic notions. Widows are a law unto themselves."

Nick could have stitched his blighted rules into samplers, so sanctimonious was his tone.

"Alice wouldn't marry me if I were given a damned title by the Regent," Ethan said. "And for the record, Nicholas, I merely kissed her." And brushed her hair, and cuddled in her lap like a lonely cat, and kissed her some more, and held her, and could not wait to do more of the same.

"So you're taking your time. That's good. It gives Alice time to come to her senses."

"And send me packing?" Ethan asked as they reached the library.

"No." Nick smiled a little. "She'll have you proposing and be accepting your suit."

"I can't expect that. There are certain things that can befall a man in this life which permanently reduce his expectations, particularly with respect to matrimony. Alice seems to have a similarly jaundiced view of marriage," Ethan replied, crossing to the decanter. "More for you?"

"Yes. I abused that whiskey earlier today. This evening, I offer it only my most sincere respect."

Ethan poured two drinks, handed one to Nick, then eyed the French doors.

"It's lovely out," Nick said. "You can see the stars,

unlike in Town, and the crickets are singing. Why don't you think Alice would marry you?"

"She's been badly spooked," Ethan replied as they found some chairs on the terrace. "Very badly spooked, though I don't know the details. Something to do with her sister and the scandal and so on. She has her own money and works only because it affords her a badly needed excuse to remain away from the family seat."

"She told you all this? I've met some self-contained women in my time, Ethan. Alice takes first honors in that category. Reese Belmont lived with her for years and never knew she had siblings."

"I am not Reese Belmont. In any case, I think Alice is a governess because she adores children but believes she won't have any of her own." And why it had become necessary to share that insight was a mystery as imponderable as the stars.

"Sad. The people who have children are not necessarily the people who deserve them."

"So I've thought." Ethan sipped his drink, trying to ignore the way Nick peered at him in the dim lighting.

"You're thinking of your late wife and possibly your dear self."

"Oh, possibly." Ethan took another sip. "This really is a fine whiskey."

"I'm not letting you change the subject this time, Ethan. If Alice were willing, would you marry her?"

"She isn't willing," Ethan reminded Nick, *and himself*. "But if she were—the boys love her already, I can barely keep my hands to myself... I wouldn't deserve a lady like her." And there was the irrefutable, bedrock truth. He would *never* deserve a woman like her.

"She's a governess," Nick scoffed. "Maybe by choice, but she's a governess, Ethan. What's not to deserve?"

"She's a lady, Nicholas. In every sense of the word, she's a lady, and in every sense of the word, I am a bastard. Is there any more of that whiskey?"

He handed Ethan the rest of his drink. "I miss my Leah."

"A good woman is always worth missing." Ethan took a sip and passed the drink back to Nick. "A good woman misses you too."

"I miss her more," Nick grumbled, taking his sip and returning the drink.

"Of course you do." Ethan accepted the glass. "But if you take your lonely little self up to bed, you might see her in your dreams, and when you wake up tomorrow, you'll be that much closer to holding her in your loving arms."

"You are sending me to bed before I embarrass myself with maudlin behavior." Nick rose, accepting the last swallow of the whiskey.

"Or I do." Ethan remained seated. "Sweet dreams, your lordship, you've had a trying day. But, Nick?"

"Lordship me again, and I will have to thrash you, and then Alice will thrash me, aided by your offspring."

"You're doing well," Ethan said, staring off across the dark gardens. "With our siblings, with me, ditching Papa's weasely jackals—with the earldom— you're off to a fine start."

"Blather." Nick bent to kiss his brother's cheek. "Utter, senile, meaningless blather."

Ethan waited until Nick's footsteps had retreated

into the house before murmuring to the night air, "Love you too. Always have."

❧

Alice arrived to Lord Greymoor's property as part of a veritable entourage. Ethan, Nick, and the boys were mounted, *as was she*, followed by Davey and a groom on horseback as well. The coach had been sent ahead, with changes of clothing for Alice and both boys, several baskets of ripe peaches, a hamper of the requisite enormous muffins, a wheel of Danish cheese, a pall-mall set, and a bottle of peach cordial for the lady of the house.

"It's a good thing you're riding," Ethan said as they emerged from the bridle path. "There's hardly room in the coach for a grown person."

"I didn't know you imported cheese," Nicholas said from Alice's other side.

"Import and export. English cheddar is among the best cheese there is," Ethan said. "You are not to gallop up the drive, Joshua Nicholas Grey. Nor you either, Jeremiah."

Nick looked pleased. "You gave him my name?"

"I gave them both your name. Alice, we're off Tydings property. Is Waltzer behaving?"

"He's a perfect gentleman. Just like my smallest escorts."

Nick frowned at his mare's mane. "I'm behaving. She must be unhappy with you, Ethan."

"Hush, Brother. We're about to make our grand entrance. Will I do?"

"Will you do?" Nick snorted. "I have a bet with Miller that Lady Greymoor has invited at least a half-dozen eligible young ladies to inspect the widowed and wealthy Mr. Grey. You could have eight little boys, a hunchback, and a squint, and they'd be delighted to make your acquaintance."

"You're jaded, Nicholas." Alice offered this reproof because Ethan was sitting noticeably straighter on his horse. "You narrowly escaped a Society marriage, so you can't see simple neighborliness for what it is, and any young lady would be delighted to make Ethan's acquaintance." Every young lady with any sense, in fact, a thought which dimmed an otherwise beautiful summer day.

"Hah." Ethan smirked at Nick, but Nick got even by assisting Alice from her horse and leaving his hands just an instant too long on her waist.

"Behave, Nicholas," Alice said, "or I will tell the boys you want to spend the entire afternoon with them." Nick's hands dropped as if burned, but he was saved from a reply by the arrival in the stable yard of Lord Greymoor and a pretty, petite blonde.

"My heart." Nick wrapped the woman in a careful, if enthusiastic hug. "The day just grew more fair as I gaze upon the visage of my dearest little countess."

The countess extricated herself from his embrace with an exasperated smile. "Save that balderdash for your horse, Nicholas, who probably takes it even less seriously than I. Introduce us, please."

Nick made a proper job of it, introducing first Alice then Ethan, then presenting the boys. If introducing the governess to such august company was unusual, no one remarked it.

Greymoor, dark-haired, blue-eyed, and of a height with Ethan, bowed over Alice's hand. "I do not ride a mare upon whom I might practice my flummery. You'll have to do with a simple 'Lovely to see you again.'"

Lady Greymoor met Alice's gaze. "Humor my husband, please. Nick started it, but don't encourage him. Mr. Grey, we expect you to be a good influence. They are in short supply at this gathering. Now, Miss Portman, you must accompany me inside, where we will get you into something more comfortable than that habit, while the men start snitching from the desserts. Greymoor, our guests need libation, and somebody ought to find James, William, Pen, Joyce, and Rose so the children might get acquainted."

She swept Alice toward the house by the simple expedient of linking their arms. Alice knew with a certainty the men were admiring the view of their retreat.

"You are no governess," Lady Greymoor remarked as she led Alice into the house.

"I beg your pardon, your ladyship?" Alice almost stopped walking, but such was Lady Greymoor's forward momentum that Alice was tugged along anyway.

"At least you're not a tart, like Mr. Grey's late wife," she went on. "Not that a tart is necessarily a bad choice. Greymoor was something of a tart when we wed. His brother was a very bad example, and there were extenuating circumstances. Your clothing was sent up to a guest room."

"You need not accompany me," Alice protested. The woman was a countess, for all her youth, and the hostess of the gathering.

Lady Greymoor turned a charming and alarmingly determined smile on her. "I very much do, and I am to let you know Lady Warne will join Mr. Grey for dinner at Heathgate's on Saturday. You're to let Mr.

Grey know, as fair is fair, and the men won't see it done. What lovely hair you have—I've often wished I weren't so infernally blond, but Greymoor claims we make a stunning couple."

Lady Greymoor took down a green silk summer dress Alice had sent over with the coach. "We can't tarry up here, since the menfolk are unsupervised and Mr. Grey a stranger among them."

It took several minutes for Alice to change, and Lady Greymoor insisted on redressing Alice's hair. All the while, Alice was subjected to a gentle inquisition.

"So how fares our Mr. Grey?"

"Are the boys going to public school? The oldest must be almost seven."

"They never seem to ride out as a family, do they?"

Alice was soon in her green silk, her hair repinned, and her meager store of knowledge regarding Mr. Grey plundered. She did not tell her hostess his kisses were sumptuous and his smile worth waiting days to behold.

"Do not let my brother-by-marriage put you off with his consequence," Lady Greymoor suggested, taking Alice's arm to escort her through the house. "Heathgate is a man with eloquent eyebrows, but he can be intimidating, unless you're family. Any questions?"

"I think not." In truth, she had too many to choose one.

"Good." Lady Greymoor grinned as they emerged onto a side patio. She took a look at the expression on Alice's face and frowned. "You haven't moved about much in Society, have you?"

"I'm just a governess, my lady."

"Hah." Her tone was firm and very uncountess-like.

"Steady on, and I'll find you safe passage, but the menfolk need to be dealt with. My lord?"

Lord Greymoor turned an amused smile on his little countess. "My love? I see Miss Portman is sporting that dazed, uncomprehending look so common to your new acquaintances. Let me take her around, and you can turn your wiles on Mr. Grey."

"You're a dear." She rose on her toes and kissed her husband's cheek. "I thought I was going to have to prevaricate."

"Perish the thought." Greymoor winged his elbow. "Miss Portman, you've yet to meet my cousins." Alice was drawn away as she saw the countess marching off in the direction of Ethan and his sons.

"I really think I should see to the boys, my lord."

"I see a braw young footman hovering with their kite, Miss Portman. Resistance will get you nowhere. My lady claims you are not a governess, and she will have her curiosity satisfied."

"What are you implying, my lord?" Alice allowed a little starch in her tone, because coming from a man, the accusation might have a prurient connotation.

Lord Greymoor shrugged muscular shoulders. "We will have to ask the countess what she implied. You are certainly prettier than any governess I ever had."

❧

"They won't wake up until tomorrow," Ethan said as he regarded his sons, sprawled on blankets on the floor of the coach. "Davey will see them to their beds, and Clara will get them undressed."

"They played and played and played." Alice brushed

a lock of hair from Joshua's closed eyes. "You'd think they never knew people their own age existed."

Ethan turned to his brother, who was hovering near the wheelers. "Will you ride back with us or join John on the box?"

"I'll keep John company. I had rather a deal of that whiskey, and the night air will clear my head."

"Then I am your escort, Alice," Ethan said. "Our mounts should be ready by now. Nick, don't wait up. I know you've an early start."

"Until morning." Nick saluted his brother then bent to kiss Alice's cheek. "Sweet dreams, lamby-pie. Remind me never to oppose you at pall-mall again."

"Grey?" The Marquess of Heathgate emerged from shadows near the stables. "A word before you go?"

"Excuse me." Ethan nodded to Nick and Alice, and joined his host's brother.

She waited by the horses in the gathering darkness until Ethan rejoined her, content to let the men talk business or breeding stock or whatever was too unrefined for her delicate, tired ears. The marquess—who did indeed have eloquent, dark eyebrows—took a polite leave of her, and Ethan boosted her onto Waltzer's back.

Though whatever passed between the two men, it hadn't been about imports or commerce. The rising moon revealed Ethan's features to be cast in granite, as remote and cool as a statue's. The horses were back on Tydings land before Ethan bestirred himself to speak, and while Alice was concerned for him, she also had to marvel that she was happy—happy, content, and relaxed—to be on a horse's back.

"Tell me you at least had a pleasant time, Alice."

"Pleasant enough. The ladies are nice, if a bit fierce."

"I'm to join them again on Saturday," Ethan said, "for dinner. I wish I could take you along. I found them a rather intimidating lot myself."

He was being honest. Perhaps it was the spirits consumed in some quantity earlier in the day, but Alice found that honesty touching. "And yet they're friendly, and their regard for Nick sincere."

"I cannot decide if Nick and the countess were lovers. Greymoor is extraordinarily tolerant, if that's the case."

"Not tolerant," Alice said. "The earl and the countess are close and devoted, and she's quite young. I doubt Nick would have dallied with her, but I doubt even more strongly she would have permitted it."

"I cannot picture it," Ethan said. "She's barely five feet tall, while he's six and a half feet plus. I can't think it would be a comfortable union."

"Do all men think in such blunt terms?"

"Yes, we absolutely do, about four hundred times a day. And I am not a particularly lusty fellow."

This too was honesty, which Alice found... appalling. "I disagree, sir. I've kissed you, and I pronounce you very, very lusty, but also very discriminating."

By the light of the rising moon, he turned in the saddle to regard her. "That is one of the nicest things anybody has said to me."

"So it must ring true." And she must not belabor the point and spoil the moment. "This isn't the way we came."

"It's another path." He drew rein as they gained a little clearing with a gazebo in it. "Let's enjoy the night for a moment, shall we?"

Men. Their stratagems never ceased, and they called women calculating. "You'll behave?"

"Get off your horse, Alice." Ethan put his hands around her waist and lifted her easily to the ground. He didn't let her go, but held her against him until her arms stole around his waist. "Let's get something clear between us: I will not ever press my advances on you without your willingness. I could not, in fact."

In contrast to his stern tones, his hands on her back were gentle.

"What does that mean?"

"Kiss me," Ethan whispered, sealing his lips over hers. He took his time, but it wasn't a cheerful little good-night indulgence. He brought her body close against his and angled her head with one large hand so she could not have avoided his kiss. His tongue was in her mouth, coaxing and teasing and implying a carnal rhythm that set up a low hum of need beneath the pit of Alice's belly.

"Touch me, Alice," Ethan whispered. "Put your hands on me."

God above, it was a timely invitation. Alice wanted to burrow into him but settled for running her hands over his shoulders and arms. She swept her fingers through his hair, cradled his jaw in her palm, and rubbed her body along the length of his.

"Feel this." Ethan took her hand and brought it to the evidence of his arousal. "This is proof I want you, and badly. But, Alice?"

She looked up at him in the moonlight, knowing if he took his hand away, she'd indulge the dangerous desire to shape and stroke him through his clothes.

"If you show me you don't want me," Ethan said,

letting his hands fall to his sides, "I can't sustain this. My flesh softens. I cannot consummate the deed. I am incapable of joining with you without your consent."

"You're capable now," Alice said, trying to make sense of his words as she explored his length. "And other men don't require consent."

"I'm not other men. I have to know you're not just willing, Alice, but enthusiastic about becoming intimate with me."

Alice gave up the fascinating feel of him and stepped back. This topic was awkward and one he apparently needed to belabor. "I think we need to talk."

"Come." Ethan held out a hand and led her up the steps to the bench inside the gazebo. "We'll talk."

Something about him was off, not quite distracted, but not at ease. "Are you angry?"

"I'm... upset. Heathgate imparted some disturbing news, and I'm aroused, as proximity to you does that for me. But my ears function, and Nick understood my admonition to seek his bed."

Men did not lightly admit to being upset. "Will I get another lecture from Nick in the morning about the need to tread lightly with his dear brother?"

That earned her a smile, bashful and a little exasperated. Alice catalogued it with the other smiles she'd hoarded up. "He lectured you? I would have liked to have seen that."

"I'll summon you next time. Greymoor preached at me too."

The smile turned a trifle irritated. "I hardly know the man. What sermon could he possibly deliver when he's hardly been a saint himself?"

"Your late wife was a trial," Alice explained gently.

"I am not to put you through that again. He was very oblique, all 'one would be disappointed' and 'one observes,' but I was given to understand that dealing with you dishonorably would be frowned upon. Your neighbors are protective of you."

And the man's eyebrows were every bit as fierce as his brother's, despite his tendency to smile often when in company with his countess.

"You couldn't deal dishonorably, not if you sprouted horns and a tail, you couldn't. Still, I'm surprised Greymoor said anything."

"He assumed the rights of a protective brother." Alice reached a hand toward Ethan's thigh then dropped it. "Your wife must have been quite something."

She wanted to touch him, not simply sit beside him in the moonlight, and yet, she wanted to hear what he had to say, too.

"I chose very, very poorly, as did she. I like where your hands were, Alice Portman, so why don't you touch me while you talk to me?"

He took her hand again, but only set it over his groin, then let his own hands fall away. Alice traced the considerable length of him, the breadth, trying to visualize what her hand stroked.

"I want to see you," Alice said. "Really see you."

He said nothing. Just unbuttoned his falls and then let his hands return to his sides. How long had he been waiting for her to ask?

"Look your fill. Some women find the sight alarming."

"I'm not some women," Alice said, regarding his lap dubiously. "That's what I wanted to talk to you about." Though why she'd bring up the topic now was a puzzle.

"You told me you're not without experience, Alice." Ethan stroked his knuckles over her cheek. "I couldn't consider joining with you, otherwise."

"I have more experience than I wanted," Alice said on a sigh. "Or the wrong experience." Her hand shaped him again, but still only through the loosened fabric of his breeches. "That scandal we haven't talked about? I need to let you know the particulars."

"If you need to. *Only* if you need to."

The words caused her heart to lurch painfully but sweetly too. She could love a man who placed entire authority over such a topic in her hands, one who cared not one whit how wicked and sorry her past had been.

"You really don't want to know, do you?" Alice drew her hand away, only to find Ethan's fingers closing around her own and bringing it back.

"I have suffered some scandal," he replied, closing his eyes as if to savor her touch. "And once somebody knows those things about you, it can become a burden between you. Heathgate…" He paused while Alice slowly drew down the flap of his falls then eased him free of his breeches. "Heathgate has that kind of knowledge of me. I'd relieve him of it if I could."

"You'll tell me." Alice stroked a finger over the velvet head of his member. God in heaven, he was magnificent. "Someday?"

"If you want to hear." He kept his eyes closed as Alice's finger—just her finger—circled the soft, soft skin of his crown. Gently, Alice's hand closed over his shaft.

"Tell me how to please you, Ethan," Alice whispered. "I want to know how to please you."

Thirteen

THIS WAS NOT WHAT ETHAN HAD PLANNED WHEN he'd brought Alice here, though it was what his body had planned the moment he'd laid eyes on her. Ethan closed his hand over Alice's and taught her the easy, loose stroke that pleased and aroused in equal measures.

"But not faster or tighter, or I'll spend." He was going to spend, but he'd rather not lose control until he had the privacy of his rooms. Alice was a lady, not some doxy, and while not a virgin, she apparently lacked experience.

"This feels good to you?" she asked, shifting her grip slightly.

"Divine, but slow down, Alexandra. It can be too good."

A considering silence, while Ethan's arousal strained at the leash of his self-discipline.

"There is no such thing as too good. Let me pleasure you, Ethan. I want to."

"Shouldn't," he muttered, letting his head fall back and his hips move in counterpoint to Alice's strokes.

"Kiss… Please, kiss—" He opened his eyes, searching for her. Thank all the gods of the night, she knelt up beside him and gave him her mouth. More roughly than he intended, he palmed the back of her neck and opened his mouth beneath hers, devouring her as his free hand cupped her breast.

She returned his kiss fiercely, growling at him as she knelt above.

That growl sang like an angel chorus through Ethan's body.

A man gave up hope sometimes, because it was the only way to preserve his sanity. Ethan Grey had long since given up hope that desire might ever again be driven by not just his body, but also his heart.

When he kissed Alice, when he gloried to feel her hands upon him, he kissed hope itself. She was not simply a woman to him; she was Alice. She was all manner of pleasures and possibilities long since forsworn, and her touch said he could be that for her too.

"Holy…" His hand fell away, fumbling in his pocket for a handkerchief. "Perishing… Almighty… Alexandra…" His hips shoved hard against Alice's grip, and his fingers closed over hers, forcing her to hold him snugly. His last coherent thought was that he should have tried harder to make this moment last.

"Oh, God… love." His hips went still, but he kept his hand wrapped around hers, while his forehead fell to Alice's shoulder. "Forgive me."

"Hush." He felt her lips against his hair. "Just hush." She used her free hand to locate his handkerchief. Male passion was not a tidy business, and it took her handkerchief as well as his to deal with the aftermath.

"Was that comfortable, to be held so tightly at the end?"

Ethan gave her a weak smile. "Pray God you hold me that tightly often and soon." He brought her hand to his lips and kissed her knuckles. "Do you forgive me?"

Her expression shuttered as she folded up the handkerchiefs. She wasn't overly fastidious—one more thing to treasure about her. "Forgive you? I do not comprehend the transgression."

"I was selfish and vulgar and grossly... ungentlemanly," Ethan began. "I did not plan this, Alice." His hand traced her jaw. "I want it to be perfect for you. I want to be perfect for you." That was a troubling realization, for he was doomed in every attempt at the goal.

"Perfect would be boring. This wasn't boring." She slipped her hand over his cock where it lay meek and receding against his groin. "I coupled with Mr. Durbeyfield once," she said, her voice detached. "It did not *stir* me. He hiked my skirts and pushed around a bit while breathing leeks on my person. It wasn't uncomfortable, but it was awkward, and hardly worth marrying for."

He should be incapable of responding, given how she'd sated him, and given this peculiar turn of conversation. He was a brute, a boor... a man sharing the summer moonlight with his lady. "If you keep that up, you'll be stirring me."

"I would like to stir you." Alice gripped him more firmly. "For it stirs me to see you so... overwrought."

Spare me from determined women, Lord, but not quite yet. "I should have more control next time," Ethan said, "and you should have less."

"Less?" Alice cocked her head. "Control over what?"

"Slow down, sweetheart," Ethan said, bringing her closer for a kiss. "At least let me pet you a little."

"Pet me?" She drew back. "I'm not a cat."

"No, but I want you to purr like one. Put away your toy for now, and let me have some time with mine." Even in the shadowed moonlight, Alice's features were fraught with misgiving.

Ethan spelled it out for her. "You wanted to give me pleasure. Will you allow me the same?" Fairness apparently won him what coaxing might not have, because Alice nodded once then drew in a breath, as if he'd called upon her to recite.

"What must I do?"

Trust me. "You must be honest with me. I want to learn what touches you like more, which you like less. I want to learn how to please you, and how to not offend you."

How to *pleasure her.* He wanted to learn that more than he'd wanted to learn anything, ever.

"Offend me?" Alice regarded him curiously.

"Leeks," Ethan said. "Leeks can offend."

"I see." She shifted and rested her back along the wall of the gazebo. Ethan sat beside her, his genitals half-exposed in his rumpled clothing. He started to tuck himself up, when Alice's hand on his stayed him.

"I didn't really look at you before. Mr. Durbeyfield wasn't so obliging."

"I can be very obliging." If it killed him, he could be as obliging as she needed him to be. Slowly, Alice drew him from his clothing again. "If you tell me Mr. Durbeyfield taught you how to bring a man off, I'll kill him. I won't call him out, I'll flat murder him."

And this was not hyperbole.

"You taught me to do that, to *bring a man off*." Alice stroked over him with curious, delicate touches. He was rapidly growing hard again, despite his every attempt to think of… the smell of wet chickens, tomato aspic, the feasibility of growing peaches commercially.

"Where are you in your cycle, Alice?"

He should not have asked that. Should not. Next he'd be asking her if she knew what a sheath was.

"I would need to consult a calendar. Did you like it when I brought you off?" She used the vulgar term as if trying to decide how it translated into Latin.

"Did I like it?" Ethan looped an arm around her shoulders and stilled her hand by virtue of closing his fingers around hers. "No. I did not *like* it. If I live to be a hundred… Stop squirming, woman. I did not like it. I have no words for the degree to which I will humble myself for the honor of repeating that intimacy with you. No one has seen fit to bestow it on me, and really, Alice…"

"Are you lecturing me?"

Ethan gave up on a sigh. "I am goddamned babbling. You have reduced me to babbling. You've pleasured my brains out. Kiss me."

She did. By God, she did, and not with the sleepy contented passion of a woman whose desire had been sated.

"You astound me, Alexandra." Ethan pushed her head to his shoulder and withdrew a small silver flask from his waistcoat pocket. "My pocket pistol is loaded with peach brandy, so sip carefully, and spare a nip for a poor undone fellow, if you please."

She took a cautious sip. "I like it."

"The brandy, of course." Ethan took a heftier swallow and passed it back to her. "One more, for you anyway."

Her gaze went to the part of him most pleased with life at the moment. "I like touching you, but you seem upset."

Precious, perceptive woman.

Ethan took the flask from her, capped it, and returned it to his pocket. "I am simply stunned you would be so generous, so bold, so unbelievably… ah, love." He gathered her to him, burying his face against her hair as inspiration struck. "Thank you. It isn't enough, but I mean it. Thank you." And to himself he added a vow that she'd know equal pleasure from him, and soon. He would have said as much, but his throat had developed a tickle, and his eyes were stinging from the brandy.

When those annoyances had receded, he managed to ask, "More brandy?"

"Not just this moment." She settled more comfortably against his side. "For this moment, I have all I want and all I need."

Ethan could not have agreed more, so he closed his eyes and sent up a prayer of thanks. Tomorrow he'd start worrying over how selfish he'd been; tomorrow he'd consider the news Heathgate had given him; tomorrow he'd deal with sending his brother back to Belle Maison; tomorrow he'd brace himself for Alice's inevitable second thoughts and regrettable bouts of common sense.

Tonight, Alice had bestowed such a gift of pleasure, trust, and intimacy on him, he could only be grateful and at peace.

Dealing with illiterates was inconvenient, requiring that a man frequent awkward locations after dark. A baron should not have to trouble himself thus, but it seemed Ethan Grey—yes, the same Ethan Grey who had authored much of what discommoded Hart Collins to this very day—had grown wealthy and respectable in recent years.

Collins was inclined to renew his acquaintance with dear Ethan, or at least with a substantial portion of Ethan's money, and so he waited for Thatcher in the trees behind the village green.

When that worthy came lumbering out of the shadows, bringing the scent of horse and ignorance with him, his question was predictable. "You've the money, then, Baron?"

Always the money.

"You'll get your money when I see results. Now, tell me about these little boys and how I might best avail myself of one of them."

When that worthy came lumbering out of the

"By God, they got up." Nick's tone was pleased as he spied his nephews coming down the path to the stables.

Ethan was not pleased. "I was hoping they'd sleep in. They were up quite late last night. Miller"—Ethan turned to find his stable master at hand—"if you'd saddle up the ponies and Argus?"

"The ponies are saddled up, and Argus is already groomed, but he's fresh," Miller cautioned.

"He's always fresh. I'll take the boys for a hack this

morning when we've seen Nick off. It will take their minds off the departure of their dear uncle."

Nick turned a glower on his brother. "And who will comfort me? I'll be traveling clear to Kent all by my little lonesome."

"Leah," Ethan retorted. "It's part of those vows, best as I recall. Gentlemen, good morning. Can we assume you want to ride as far as the village with me and Uncle Nick?"

"Can we?"

"May we?"

"Of course, and we'll keep an eye out for the foxes coming home from their night of hunting. Of course, Argus might want to stretch his legs a little." Miller's cursing could be heard peppering the morning air.

"Or stretch his legs a lot," Nick surmised. "Does he bite, Ethan?"

"Of course not," Ethan scoffed. "But he and Miller have a certain good-natured antagonism that involves threatening to bite, and nearly stomping on feet, and narrowly pulled punches with cursing and dirty looks all around. If I die, Miller gets the horse."

"I understand," Nick said. "And if Miller died, the horse would be inconsolable."

"Who's dying?" Jeremiah asked, leading his pony out.

"I'm dying to get home," Nick said, "but I will miss my favorite nephews. When next I visit, I expect to see a tree house or two gracing the property."

"When will you come again?" Joshua asked, leading his pony.

"Soon. My friend Lord Val has asked me to attend the opening night of the symphony, and that's little more than a month away. Up you go." He swung each boy onto a pony, checked his mare's girth one more time, then climbed aboard Buttercup. "Ethan, you're holding us up."

"Apologies for the inconvenience," Ethan replied as Argus curvetted around on the end of his reins. "My boy is feeling frisky today."

"A coincidence," Nick muttered. "This boy misses his countess, and he's feeling frisky too."

Ethan took the reins, slipped them over the gelding's head, and swung up in the single instant during which Argus held still. Immediately, the horse began to prop and spin and misbehave.

"Nicholas"—Ethan's tone was bored—"lead us down the driveway. If he thinks his audience is leaving, he'll settle right down."

Nick obliged; his expression was disgruntled.

"I like a horse with spirit, Ethan," Nick said as Argus settled down to merely passaging, "but that one looks like a lot of work."

"He is," Ethan said, sitting the prancing horse easily, "but he'll jump anything, he's never taken a lame step, and when it comes down to dicey moments, he makes sensible choices."

"Still, I've no doubt your grooms won't ride him, so he likely gets rank as hell when you're gone for any length of time."

"Uncle Nick said *hell*," Joshua crowed from behind them.

"I sure as hell did."

"Damn, my ears are good," Joshua recited his part of the litany.

"My grooms won't ride him." Ethan ignored an uncle's willingness to corrupt his nephews' manners, because revenge was a certainty when Nick's children were old enough. "Greymoor has taken note of him and offered to keep him for me if I need to travel. If I can stick on this horse, Greymoor can do it while taking tea."

"Generous of him, and the horse would benefit."

"Your friends are being kind," Ethan said quietly, because the village was only a few minutes' ride, and some things needed to be said. "To me and to mine."

"My friends, your neighbors. They'll be your friends if you let them, Ethan."

"We'll see," Ethan replied as Argus finally settled into an honest trot. "Friendships take time."

"And you've such a busy calendar?" Nick pinned his brother with a look. Right there in front of the children, he pinned Ethan with a visual dire warning.

"No, but I had a thought for you to ponder."

Nick turned his attention back to his mare. "I'm listening."

"The Bellefonte earldom owns a vineyard in France, as I recall, and properties in both Spain and Portugal. I suspect George would look in on them for you, if you asked. I own either land or businesses in Switzerland, Germany, and Denmark, as well as France, and I'm thinking of asking him to add them to his itinerary."

"You own land in all those places?"

"They all make very good cheese, the German states have access to terrific stores of lumber, the Danes sail to every known port, and I've a little vineyard of my own in France, though I'm thinking of converting it to peaches."

"Peaches?" Nick looked impressed. "Just how wealthy are you, Ethan?"

Ethan looked around uncomfortably but saw his sons were engaged in a rousing argument, and named a figure.

"More or less." He shrugged. "Values are always fluctuating."

Nick gave a low whistle. "My brother is a bloody cheese nabob."

If they were boys—and they would never be boys again—that epithet would have become Ethan's moniker for at least a span of weeks.

"When one hasn't much else to do, and one is willing to travel in times of war, profit seems to happen. I didn't mention my holdings to impress, Nicholas, but to point out that between us, we could keep a foreign agent busy more than full time. And George is acquainted with several languages."

"It's a good idea. A very good idea, in fact. I'm guessing Lady Warne might put him to use too. She has holdings of her own."

"I'm to see your grandmother this weekend," Ethan said as they approached the village green. "She's to be my dinner partner at Heathgate's on Saturday."

Nicholas's blond brows drew down in an expression much like Joshua's fleeting bouts of thoughtfulness. "Give her my love if you have to admit you've seen me. Let's get Buttercup a drink, shall we?" Nick swung down and led his mare to the communal trough on the village green. It was an excuse to prolong their parting, but Ethan was grateful for it. He'd said good-byes to Nick before, and even a few in the recent past, but this one felt more… personal.

Nick turned to his nephews, who sat on their ponies looking uncertain. "You gentlemen will behave for your papa and Miss Alice. You will build a tree house or two and send me sketches of them. You will take your baths and eat your vegetables and go to bed when you're told, so you grow up as big and strong as I am."

"I only want to be as big as Papa," Joshua said, "but I don't want you to go."

"Joshua Pismire Grey," Nick intoned sternly, "if you make me cry in front of my older brother, I will tickle you silly." He feinted with his fingers, causing Joshua to giggle and curl away. "That's better." Nick carefully hugged his smallest nephew then turned to Jeremiah.

"You have a special mission," Nick said, leaning down and whispering something into Jeremiah's ear. "You can tell Joshua when I've left. You'll need his devious–little–brother assistance."

"Don't worry, Joshua," Jeremiah assured him. "It's something good."

"And you." Nick turned to his brother, who'd dismounted to watch the partings. "Come here, Ethan Grey." He held out his arms, and Ethan stepped into his embrace. "Don't be a stranger."

For the first instant, Ethan endured the embrace. This was a skill learned of necessity, an ability to temporarily vacate whatever aspect of the mind catalogued and experienced bodily perceptions: the sandalwood scent of Nick's soap, the soft thump of a leather-clad hand between Ethan's shoulders, the exact contour of his brother's muscular body.

And then something… let go. Something emotional sighed along with Ethan's body, and the endured embrace became a quick, shared hug.

"My love to the ladies," Ethan said, stepping back, "and safe journey home, Nick."

"Thanks for the hospitality, and look after my nephews." He was on his horse and cantering away before Ethan could say anything more, and really, that was for the best. The morning air had put the damned tickle back in Ethan's throat.

"Will you miss him, Papa?" Joshua asked.

"I'll miss him silly," Ethan said. "I can still see him"—could still feel the echoes of that hug—"and I miss him silly already."

"Me too."

"Me too."

Argus did not miss Uncle Nick, silly or otherwise, and reminded his owner of that by tossing his head so Ethan almost lost his grip on the reins.

Ethan scowled at the horse. "Bad pony. Spoiled rotten, you are." He was in the saddle before Argus could comment further. "Gentlemen, shall we let them stretch their legs?"

"You mean trot?" Jeremiah asked.

"Canter?" Joshua's tone was hopeful. "Gallop?"

"We'll play master and field," Ethan said. "Joshua, you're the master, and we'll follow you. You can't go anywhere Argus can't follow, so no low-hanging branches, and mind you don't lead us into danger. We're silly, drunken gentlemen out from Town for a little hunting, and we can hardly sit our horses, because we've had too much of Mr. Grey's famous peach brandy."

Both boys looked fascinated at this spate of paternal nonsense. In the distance, Ethan heard Buttercup's hoofbeats fade away.

"I can decide how we get home?" Joshua clarified.

"Anywhere on the lanes and paths," Ethan said,

"or on Tydings land. Take us across a planted field, though, and the steward will want me to thrash you."

"I know that," Joshua scoffed. "Hey, Jeremiah— remember when we were chased by pirates?"

The next thing Ethan knew, he and Argus were watching eight little pony hooves disappear at a furious gallop. Ethan let Argus bring up the rear, glad the horse seemed to understand his job was to trail the ponies. Joshua led them over stiles and banks, across ditches and logs, over the stream, back over the stream, and into the bridle paths criss-crossing the woods.

"Hold up!" Ethan yelled to his sons, but they'd seen Heathgate's mare as soon as he had, and pulled up so hard their ponies were practically sitting. Heathgate had angled the mare right across the path, but turned her when he saw the ponies come to a stop.

"And here I thought I was saving a couple of run-aways," the marquess drawled. "Fancy riding, gentlemen. My boys would be envious. Morning, Grey."

"Good morning, your lordship," the boys replied politely enough.

"We were out riding with Papa," Joshua added helpfully. "I was the master, and he and Jeremiah were the field."

"I see. My compliments, Grey, for I've neglected to introduce my children to that particular means of scaring the hair off a parent. Shall we let your horses blow a little?"

"Papa?" Jeremiah looked uncertain.

"His lordship means to walk them," Ethan said, "and since your ponies are heaving like bellows, it's a good idea." Even Argus had settled down over the course Joshua had chosen. Ethan let the boys pass him, then fell in beside his neighbor.

"I almost didn't get my ride in this morning," the marquess began. "Too much peach brandy. You'll want to provide a few flasks to the Regent and get his imprimatur on it. Have you considered what I told you last night?" Heathgate asked, quietly enough not to draw the children's notice.

"Not much. Hart Collins is a subject of the Crown. He was bound to return to England someday."

"You could bring charges," Heathgate suggested.

"Right. And have the whole world know I was incapable of defending myself? Only to have one of his cronies testify I enticed the man, or Collins was nowhere in the vicinity, and as I was facedown over the top of a barrel, how could I know for certain who was violating my person?"

Discussing the matter in the pretty summer morning seemed blasphemous, but the topic had lingered in Ethan's imagination—a reptile lurking in the muddy marshes of his memory—since the moment Heathgate had called him aside the previous night.

"You bring the charges," Heathgate said. "You don't expect to prosecute them."

"He's a member of the bloody Lords, Heathgate." Ethan spoke tiredly. "I'm a bastard who married my mistress. Bringing charges would be a joke, and as far as my family is concerned, a joke in poor taste."

"It's your choice, but you will likely run across him sooner or later, or Nick will, because he's a member of the bloody Lords too—as am I, come to that."

Ethan shot Heathgate a look, but the man was impossible to read. "No offense intended."

"Likewise. I thought you should know he's back."

"My thanks for the warning."

"You never told your family, did you?" Heathgate pressed. "Not even Nick."

"Especially not Nick." Heathgate had kept his peace on this most unfortunate subject for nearly twenty years. It was a relief, in a way, to have it in the open, but the old humiliation was there as well.

"Why not? He's your brother, the head of your family, and he loves you cross-eyed."

"He loves me. I love him." Hence Ethan would never bring up at least two very personal subjects with his brother.

"If I had a bottle of whiskey for every time I've heard him brag on you or reminisce about his perfect childhood with you, I could get the Royal Navy drunk." Heathgate paused and eyed the children.

"Your point?" Ethan inquired, *very* politely.

"You are trying to protect your brother," Heathgate said gently, "because it will hurt him to know what you've suffered. It will hurt him more you didn't think him worthy of your confidence. I have a younger brother, you will note, and speak from experience."

Ethan sighed, not sure if being a marquess gave one the right to divine minds or hearts. "The incident in question left me more deeply ashamed than I care to discuss."

Heathgate watched the ponies before them. The boys were concocting another scheme involving pirates on horseback. "Do you have any idea how much shame a man can build up when he has the wealth and the temper to pitch a nine-year-long tantrum? There were times I got some toothsome, titled young idiot drunk and indulged in all manner of foolery on a bored whim. Or I'd take women to bed, knowing they would not guard their hearts, and liking it better for being able to strike at them that way. I won fortunes from men too drunk to hold their cards and was only too happy to collect on their vowels, regardless that it would beggar them and put their women on the charity of relatives."

"This recitation doesn't flatter you, Heathgate." Ethan could not take his eyes from his horse's neck. "Why burden me with it?" Though Ethan suspected he knew—there were many situations in life that yielded a harvest of regret and shame.

Heathgate let out an exasperated sigh. "I have lifetimes of regrets I should be ashamed of, and I am. But you are ashamed of being a victim. If somebody did to your Joshua what was done to you, would you be disgusted with Joshua? Would you want him to be ashamed of himself?"

"For God's sake, don't be ridiculous. He's just a boy, and of course I would not want him ashamed of being the victim of a crime."

"You were fourteen," Heathgate said, "and set upon by six boys older, bigger, and stronger than you. They laid in wait, they plotted this violence, and they carried it out against you, knowing you had none to aid you. And yet you don't feel compassion for the boy you were. You feel ashamed of him. One can only wonder, Ethan Grey, what your own father might have done had he learned of your fate."

Heathgate urged his horse forward, having mercifully had his say. He engaged the boys in a pleasant discussion of foxhunting, climbing trees, and what it must be like for poor young Lord Penwarren to have a twin sister. Ethan was so lost in thought he didn't hear his children laughing at something Heathgate said, or realize his horse was for once being docile, until he was almost hit in the face with a low-hanging branch.

Fourteen

"IT'S AN INTERESTING MIX OF NEWS," BENJAMIN Hazlit reported as he lounged in a comfortable chair in the Marquess of Heathgate's library. His arrangement with Heathgate, as with most clients, was that nothing was written down. For the sake of security, his reports were made in person, except under rare circumstances. This meant his clients had to meet with him face-to-face, and usually in their homes, since most of them would have been loath to be seen calling on him.

And meeting them face-to-face gave Benjamin all manner of opportunity to learn about them and placate his own well-hidden curiosity.

"Well, don't beat about the bush, Benjamin." Heathgate paused while a footman brought in a tray. "Lemonade, cider, or something stronger?"

"Cider." Heathgate's version of something stronger was usually a whiskey too smooth and rich to be profaned by business conversation.

Heathgate passed him a tall glass. "I'll send a little something else along for your private delectation when we're through."

"I won't refuse." Not that sane men refused Gareth Alexander, Marquess of Heathgate, much of anything. "And now that you've impressed me with your manners, here's what we know: Hart Collins has been traipsing about the Continent since Waterloo. Before that he was holed up on some Greek island. But to pick up the story closer to the beginning, you need to know, after leaving Stoneham—one of several institutions to send him down—he finally made a try at Oxford, where he lasted not one term. Cambridge flat wouldn't have him, so he took himself back north to Papa's barony and seemed to make an effort to grow up."

"A successful effort?"

"Hardly." Benjamin paused to rein in his disgust. Heathgate needed information, but not every fact in Benjamin's head was pertinent to the marquess's inquiry. "He was engaged to the local equivalent of the darling of the shire, an earl's daughter, but the engagement ended amid some hushed scandal, and then he was off. Scotland first, Scandinavia, even the Americas, before returning to Europe. He pops back to England from time to time, but never for long. One can live cheaply on foreign shores, but Collins hasn't acquired the knack."

"He comes back when he's out of funds?" Heathgate's expression gave away nothing, but Benjamin knew the man well enough to sense heightened interest. "Too bad I've not set foot in a hell for years. I could probably ruin him in a single night of hazard."

Heathgate's tone said he'd enjoy that evening's work a bit more than a night at the opera.

"Doubtless, you could, and you need to get out more, old man."

"You should have a wife and children, *old man*. Except then you would not be available for my little queries and investigations. What else do we know about Collins?"

Benjamin met glacial-blue eyes, knowing his lordship might well be planning that outing to the gaming tables. The notion appealed to a protective older brother's instincts mightily.

"He came into the title about five years ago, and his papa did what he could to tie up the unentailed wealth. Collins is back now, wrangling with the solicitors and getting nowhere. I have personal reasons to keep tabs on the man, particularly if he should malinger in the vicinity of the family seat."

Heathgate refreshed their drinks. "For once the solicitors are of use. And what of Collins's accomplices?"

"Two are dead. Both soldiers who didn't come home. One has emigrated to America, another has the living at some obscure little crossroads in Derbyshire, and the fifth is in the hulks."

"Can we buy the clergyman or the debtor?"

"The debtor, of course." Benjamin named a sum Heathgate's marchioness might have spent on a single entertainment during the Season. "And the arrangements have been made."

"Benjamin, you are frighteningly thorough. What of the clergyman?"

"Has his eye on a more lucrative living," Benjamin replied. "I've not approached him. The element of surprise would be in your favor."

"Best send someone to deal with him. Have either the debtor or the clergyman been in touch with Collins?"

"The clergyman. Collins had him invited to some

house party, and the man dropped the Lord's pressing business and came by post."

"So Collins has something on him. What we have is worse, I'm sure."

"Conspiracy to commit a felony is serious. I must point out you're doing this all on your own initiative, and I can't help but wonder if Mr. Grey would appreciate it. He seems to have moved on with his life."

Or with something. Benjamin wasn't sure exactly what, though Alice appeared to be in better spirits for it.

"Hmm."

The tone of that syllable piqued Benjamin's instincts. "Heathgate, you can't play God. An incident like this would have been the undoing of a lesser man, particularly when Bellefonte was no help to his son whatsoever. It's only with the old earl's death Mr. Grey has managed some sort of rapprochement with his siblings. Besides, my sister is half in love with your Mr. Grey, and that makes me a little protective of the man."

Heathgate looked unimpressed. "She's governess to his boys."

"She's his social superior," Benjamin countered, an edge lacing his voice. Heathgate might have resented the title years ago, but he understood the order of precedence well enough. "She's lovely, well damned dowered if she'd but allow it, and deserving of only the best. If she's chosen him, then I will respect her choice, and I will not let you bring the man grief."

Heathgate's eyebrow swooped aloft. "You come close to threatening a peer of the realm, Benjamin. I'm impressed."

"Stow it." Benjamin snorted. "If I thought your

intent was contrary to Mr. Grey's interests—or my sister's—I would never have undertaken this task."

"And here you work so hard to create the impression you have no loyalty, save to coin of the realm."

Benjamin sipped his drink placidly. "Don't be tiresome, *your lordship.*"

"My intentions are not contrary to Mr. Grey's interests, but this moving on with his life you refer to does not comport with either his brother's or my impression of the man. He does not socialize, he does not belong to a club, he does not ride to hounds with the locals except for the informal meets, and he does not attend services. Until recently, I'm not sure he knew which son was which. He sits, like a spider, in the middle of a financial web and spins money at a rate that impresses the Regent."

"And this is a crime, to do what one does well?"

"To let life go by in every sphere save one is a tragedy. My marchioness says we have neglected our neighbor, and my conscience has agreed with her, as it is wont to do. He has not moved on with his life, Benjamin. I know when somebody is mired in their past, because I've been in the same slippery ditch myself."

"It still isn't like you to interfere, conscience or not." Personal disclosures were not like Heathgate either, much less unflattering personal disclosures.

"I won't interfere. I will simply ensure Mr. Grey has the information necessary to make prudent decisions in a timely manner. He does that well in the commercial realm, and if your sister's affections are returned, he should be motivated now to do so regarding personal matters as well."

"I would not want you for an enemy, Heathgate."
Benjamin rose and set his empty glass aside.

"My sentiments as well." Heathgate set his glass aside
too, his face creasing into a startlingly charming smile.
"Now that we've covered my neighbor's situation,
come to the nursery with me. James, Will, and Pen will
want to see you, and Joyce will want to see me."

"Your marchioness will want to see you." And to
his credit, Benjamin managed to sound not the least
envious as he made that observation.

⁓

The anniversary of Barbara's death came and went,
and when Ethan realized he noticed the significance of
the date only in hindsight, he had to consider he was
putting Barbara's death behind him. For the previous
two years, his mourning period completed, he'd gone
off to hunt grouse in Scotland or Cumbria—or to
pretend he was hunting grouse.

He'd consider it sport when the birds were given
guns to defend themselves, though he'd never dare
express such an opinion to another.

He continued to meet up occasionally with
Heathgate on the bridle paths, and sometimes with
Lords Greymoor and Amery as well, all of whom
were fascinated with their offspring's every peccadillo
and sniffle.

This would have been a trial, except Ethan was fascinated himself. His children entranced him, with their
funny little opinions, their odd fears, and their willingness to be silly over nothing. He liked the way they'd
argue fiercely with each other one minute, and then be
off to whisper in the corner the next. He liked the way

each boy understood the other, and even in the midst of pitched battle, would tread lightly in certain areas.

He liked that they were affectionate, particularly since Uncle Nick's parting admonition to Jeremiah had been a whispered order to tickle Ethan at least every other day. That wouldn't last—boys grew up and acquired dignity—but it had given Ethan a pretext for hugging his children and wrestling with them in the grass from time to time.

And if the children weren't thawing years of reserve, Alice certainly was. She was shy of her own body, but eager regarding Ethan's. She'd touch him in little ways throughout the day if they were alone—smooth his cravat, take off his spectacles, squeeze his hand—and she was something else entirely at night.

Scholars were a curious lot, and Alice was inherently a scholar. She took off his clothes and studied him. She touched and tasted and even listened to his body, pressing her ear over his heart or lungs and then, satisfied he was quite alive, over his belly.

"It's how you diagnose a colicky horse," she'd said, frowning up at him.

And then she'd listened to him laugh.

They hadn't made love—yet. Not in the traditional sense of the phrase, anyway. Ethan told himself he was giving her time to change her mind, but in truth, he wasn't ready. He blamed his unreadiness on Gareth Alexander, Marquess of Heathgate, neighbor and Inconvenience at Large.

Since Nick's visit, Ethan had felt the presence of neighbors in his life, and not just on his bridle paths. Twice, the boys had been invited to Willowdale to play with Heathgate's children. Twice, Ethan had been to dinner, once at Heathgate's, once at Greymoor's. They were an informal, affectionate lot, even when the children were not in evidence. The only one of the group with whom Ethan felt truly comfortable was Amery, the quietest one of the bunch.

The hardest shock to bear was that these people touched him, physically. The ladies kissed his cheek and took his arm as if he were a long-lost cousin. The men were forever cramming themselves together on sofas and settles, sipping their drinks at the end of the day. They teased and fell silent, alluded to the occasional problem, and laughed gently at one another. It puzzled Ethan to be included in such goings-on, and he was growing to tolerate it better than he would have predicted.

Growing almost comfortable with it, except every time he began to lose track of his separateness, he'd look up to find Heathgate watching him. The marquess's eyes held the same questions he'd battered Ethan with the day Nick left: Why don't you feel compassion for the boy you were? Why do you feel ashamed of him?

And Ethan wished, as the air began to take on a hint of autumn, he could talk to Nick. Now, when Nick was busy with his earldom and his new wife and six other siblings, Ethan let himself miss his brother. He didn't want to burden Nick with superfluous confidences, but he missed his brother.

He just… missed him.

❧

"Miss Alice?" Joshua was preparing for a midafternoon nap, which was unusual. That he was accepting the need without protest was more unusual still.

"Joshua?" Alice sat on his bed. He looked a little

pale, but then, he was an Englishman's son, and Alice had never seen his color high.

"If you said you wouldn't tell a secret," Joshua began, "but then something else happened, so you had not just one secret, but two, does the first promise not to tell mean you can't tell the second time either?" Alice frowned and tried to puzzle through the riddle that was part logic and part little-boy inquiry into the heady topic of manly honor.

"Give me an example."

Joshua's brow puckered in thought. "If I saw Papa up reading past his bedtime, but I promised not to tell, then I saw him doing it again, should I tell?"

"Before you tell, you should confront him directly and give your papa a chance to explain, unless you think it isn't safe to do so."

Joshua fingered the hem of his coverlet. "Papa doesn't hit. Why wouldn't it be safe?"

"I don't know. I once didn't tell my brothers something, because I was afraid they'd go try to beat up someone for me, and I didn't want them taking that risk."

"Are your brothers as big as Papa?"

"Not quite, and they were quite a bit younger at the time. Now close your eyes. Do you want me to read to you?"

"Yes, Miss Alice." His yawn was genuine, and before Alice could select a soothingly familiar story, he was asleep.

"Is he all right?" Jeremiah's voice was laced with anxiety.

Alice smiled at the boy hovering in the doorway. "I think he's just worn out from trying to keep up with his brilliant older brother. He'll be fine."

Jeremiah came to stand beside her, looking down at his younger brother. "I heard him ask about secrets."

"It was a good question."

"Did you ever tell your brothers?" Jeremiah asked, still frowning at Joshua's sleeping form.

"I did not," Alice said, wondering what mysteries were churning in Jeremiah's too-busy little brain.

"Maybe you should. I think I'll take a nap too."

"You don't have to," Alice said. "If you're not tired, it can just make it harder to sleep at night." And God knew, the last thing she wanted was for the little boys to be up wandering around when she was misbehaving with their father at night.

⤳

Ethan slipped behind Alice in the library and wrapped his arms around her waist, feeling her curl back against him on a sigh. "Can I ask you something?"

Lemon verbena had become his favorite scent. It brought to mind not just Alice, but the sheets on her bed, where Ethan had spent many pleasant hours.

"You've asked me a great deal lately, Ethan Grey: my favorite flower, my favorite author, my political opinions, my name day, and my birthday."

He hadn't asked her to make love with him, and they both knew it. She wrapped her hands over his at her midriff. "Ask me, Ethan."

"We have on occasion mentioned the scandal in your past," Ethan said. "If there were scandal in my past, personal in nature, would you want to know?" The answer to this question mattered, and had something to do with Ethan's reluctance to consummate their dealings, much as he wished that were not so.

Also with his inability to go for long without touching her.

"I know about your wife." Alice slipped from his hold and turned to face him, defeating his hug-her-from-behind-so-she-won't-see-your-face strategy. "And you've told me Joshua may not be your son. What could be more personal than that?"

"Joshua is every bit my son. But about the scandal, you'd want to know?"

"If you wanted to tell me, I'd be happy to listen, but what befell you in the past matters a great deal less than who you are now, at least to me."

Bless this woman. "Even if it's a very bad business, Alice?" Ethan looked past her, out across the back gardens in the direction of the Marquess of Heathgate's holdings. Part of him wanted to tell her, not to weather her reaction, but to repose his whole self, past, present, and future, in her keeping. "Even if it's something that might make you ashamed to consort with me?"

"I could never be ashamed of you, and as to that, we don't quite consort, Ethan. This is beginning to puzzle me, because I am willing, and you seem interested, and yet we don't... Have you lost interest?"

She sounded bewildered and a trifle hurt. He could not abide either.

"No, never." Ethan jammed his hands into his pockets to keep from reaching for her. "But conception is an issue, and the timing hasn't been right." That was true, as far as it went.

"I don't understand."

"Your courses came just after..." Ethan paused, searching for delicacy. "After the picnic at Heathgate's."

"And?"

"And I would not importune you at such a time." Ethan felt color rising across his cheeks. He took her by the wrist and pulled her to a printed calendar hanging behind his desk. There were marks on it in pencil— ships arriving, contracts due, payments to be made—but he tapped his finger on the date of the picnic.

"I think you started your courses here." He shifted his finger two days. "Am I right?"

"You are." And it was Alice's turn to blush. "How did you know?"

"Your breasts were more sensitive then." Ethan kept his gaze on the calendar. "And you were… affectionate and quiet, but would not encourage certain types of advances, and then you asked me to let you catch up on your sleep for a few nights."

"And you took that to mean I was indisposed?"

"I hoped it meant that." Ethan glanced at her fleetingly, not sure whose modesty he was sparing. "Not that you were having second thoughts."

"Why would you think that?"

Ethan's gaze went back to the calendar. "Perhaps we might finish with our earlier topic?" He was dodging. He knew it, and she knew it, but they tacitly agreed not to confront the knowledge—yet.

"Please. I can't help but feel embarrassed you should know of these things and I would not."

"I kept a mistress," Ethan reminded her, "a woman with whom procreation was my last intention. The knowledge became relevant too late to do me any good."

"This is very… intimate."

There, on that date a few days after the picnic, Ethan had made one small mark—a little cross, and the significance of it was known only to him and her. He liked that; she was probably mortified by it.

"Personal, and having a child with someone more personal yet, whether the act is intended or not."

A look passed across Alice's face, one of stark, undisguised longing. Ethan dared not comment on it, for having a child with Alice—many children with Alice—would be a gift of miraculous proportions. She might be dallying with him out of curiosity and loneliness, but she would love her children.

He could trap her with that love, just as Barbara had trapped him with duty.

Ethan wrenched his thoughts back from that moral precipice and completed his explanation of contraceptive timing.

"And you think Barbara lied to you regarding her cycle?" Alice worried her lower lip, her expression disgruntled.

"I know she did. I interviewed her lady's maid when Barbara announced her pregnancy. I wasn't visiting her very often at that point and had bought her a parting gift, so I wasn't as attentive to her calendar as I might have been. After we married, Barbara boasted of her scheme to me."

Alice's eyes filled with ire. "She tricked you. Is Jeremiah even yours?"

"Painful question." Though Alice's mind, confident with facts and knowledge, would have leapt to it. "The same lady's maid kept careful track of her mistress and went everywhere with her. She assured me my wife was too set on having my wealth to give me any cause to repudiate her before the license was procured."

"Some comfort there, I suppose."

"Some little comfort. Once we were wed, the magnitude of our unsuitability only grew."

"She was not remorseful."

That succinct observation gave Ethan a pang, for it pointed to a larger reality: Barbara *had* expressed remorse—not loudly, not often—though Ethan had not offered her forgiveness, not until it was too damned late.

"Her brazen infidelity was the excuse I needed to stop trying, to stop deceiving myself." To give up hope. "We struck terms, with me agreeing to support her in the style she preferred, and Barbara agreeing to do nothing to harm our child, and at least exercise some discretion. When I was certain I'd found reliable staff for the nursery, I kissed my son good-bye and went traveling as often as I could."

"I am so sorry." Alice wrapped her arms around his waist and hung on. Ethan said nothing, but held her to him in the quiet of the library, wondering why'd he'd burdened her with his unhappy history.

And yet these disclosures, while by no means the worst of his past, did not bring the awkwardness they might have with another.

These confidences.

"It's in the past," he said softly. "I have two wonderful sons, I tell myself Barbara is at peace, and I have much to be grateful for."

"You do. We both do." She looked right at him when she said it. "I want you to come to me tonight. I'm not going to change my mind, Ethan, and if you are, you'd best tell me now."

"Tomorrow night," Ethan said, thinking of that small mark on the calendar. "It will be safer. And I won't change my mind, either, Alice. If we're to develop a conscience at this stage, it will be your doing."

She slipped from his embrace and went to stand at the French doors, looking out over the gardens that were in the riotous, slightly untidy glory of late summer. "I would feel a greater burden on my conscience if I did not consummate our dealings, Ethan Grey, than I would if we suddenly succumbed to a false piety now."

He said nothing, realizing he shared her sentiment. Again, he slipped his arms around her from behind and pulled her back against his body. He wanted to give her words, to tell her he cared for her, but it wouldn't be a gift to speak of his feelings.

Alice had offered him a sort of friendship, an intimate friendship that would include pleasure and companionship for a time. If he cared for her—hell and the devil, if he *loved* her—he'd give her that, and not impose his own dreams and wishes on her.

"You are very dear, Ethan Grey. Promise you'll come to me."

"I promise." Ethan kissed her cheek and gathered her more closely. He'd never stood quietly with Barbara like this, never been content just to hold her and treasure her closeness. She hadn't wanted it, had made it clear she hadn't.

"It's Friday." Ethan reminded her. "Will you and the boys join me for dinner?"

Alice turned to smile at him over her shoulder, and in that instant, Ethan lost a piece of his heart. Her eyes were clear, steady, and pleased—maybe pleased to have secured his intimate attentions as a lover, but also pleased simply to take a meal with him and his sons.

Fifteen

WHEN HE JOINED ALICE AND THE BOYS AT DINNER, Ethan looked a little tired, but pleased to see his children. The boys must have sensed their father's fatigue, because they were subdued—for them—as well. Alice herded them up to bed then occupied herself with duty letters to her siblings Reese, Priscilla, and Leah.

A soft tap on her door had her glancing up, expecting to see Clara with some laundry or fresh wash water.

"You're sending off the monthly epistles?" Ethan kept his hands in his pockets as he peered over her shoulder. "Have you heard much from your brother Benjamin lately?"

"I have not, which isn't so unusual. I think your brother is keeping him busy, among others."

"He is. I've been meaning to tell you Nick has reason to suspect I'm legitimate, in the legal sense." He studied her mundane correspondence as if it were a complicated column of figures.

"Does this matter to you?"

"It does." Ethan sat on the bed, facing her.

"Though not in the sense you think. It matters because Nick is afraid we're not related, or he was. Seems my mother was married to some soldier, about whom she neglected to tell the earl when she went larking about with her betters."

"Maybe she thought her soldier was dead." Alice watched as he pulled off a boot. "It doesn't change who you are."

"So I told my fretful little brother." Ethan smiled at her, his expression tinged with an odd tenderness. "And it really doesn't matter to you, does it?"

He was determined of late on ascertaining her opinion on every irrelevant detail.

"Of course not, except it impacts upon you. What are you doing, Ethan Grey?"

"Getting comfortable." He pulled his second boot off and set them beside the bed. "And don't look at me as if you've never seen me comfortable before."

"I thought you said tomorrow night…" She trailed off as he shucked out of his breeches and smalls, then pulled his shirt right over his head.

"I did say I'd come to you tomorrow night." Ethan pulled back the covers then ambled around to stand behind Alice. "And I will, but there's somewhere I'd like to take you tonight, if you'll allow it."

"Dressed like *that*?" Alice closed her eyes when she felt his fingers at the hooks of her dress.

"One gets there most easily in just this attire." Ethan bent to kiss her nape. "Besides, I love the way you look at me when I'm naked."

And she loved to look upon him, but this, this complete nudity in a well-lit room was more than just a pushing aside of clothes by moonlight. "I suppose you want me that way too?" Alice bent forward so he could reach the rest of her hooks.

"Say it." He leaned down near her ear. "Ethan wants me naked."

"Ethan wants me to blush myself silly."

"We'll blow out the candles," he said as he started on her laces, "if you really don't want to see me as God made me."

"You as God made you is one thing." Alice struggled for reason when Ethan drew her to her feet. "Me as God made me is another." And where on earth was she to affix her gaze?

"Another." Ethan drew her dress over her head. "Another entirely glorious thing."

"Ethan…" She stood barefoot, in shift and loosened stays, knowing he was looking at her.

He waited until she found the courage to glance at him. "This is part of it, this simple, mundane sort of trust. I want to see you, just as you wanted to see me. I like the sight of you. I want to have pictures of you in my head, to appreciate and treasure. We can do this in the dark, if you like, but I'd really rather you let me see you, even if it's just this once."

"I do like looking at you," Alice said, letting her gaze travel the muscular expanse of his chest, down past his flat stomach, his groin, his legs, and over every lean, sculpted inch of him. She nodded at his erection. "Does that inconvenience you?"

"Mightily," Ethan said with a slight smile. "Stop trying to change the subject."

"You'll have to do this. I haven't the nerve."

"You're just shy." Ethan's smile broadened, blinding her with its warmth. "Hold still." He

untied her tapes and bows and had her naked as Eve
in less than a minute, her braid swinging freely down
her back.

"God in heaven, you are lovely, Alexandra. How
could you be shy about sharing this?" He walked
around her, as if she were some treasure from antiq-
uity, a marble goddess come to life at Tydings. "I feel
sorry for Mr. Durbeyfield, I'll say that much."

"Can we please, *please*, get under the covers?"

"There is no place on earth I would rather be than
naked under the covers with you," Ethan replied
with an odd gravity. Alice didn't wait to decipher his
mood. She hopped under the sheet, ignoring the view
she gave Ethan of her backside. The mattress dipped
as Ethan's greater weight joined her, and then he was
over her, balanced on his forearms.

"Ethan?"

"That would be me." He kissed her cheek. "And
you are the lovely Miss Portman. Attend me, Miss
Portman, for I've a lesson to impart, and you're the
kind who appreciates learning."

She brushed his hair back. "You are ridiculous,
Mr. Grey."

"Disrespect will be punished," Ethan informed her
sternly. "Seriously, I want you to heed me."

"I'm listening, Ethan." How could she not listen
when he was naked, lying on top of her, all warm and
lean and touchable?

"I've asked you before to be honest with me.
It's more important than ever with what we
undertake now."

"I know. I will not play you false, Ethan. I hope
you know that."

"I do know it, and you have the same promise from me, but this is a different kind of honesty. You have to tell me if I'm asking too much, if I'm going too fast, if I'm hurting you."

She gently pushed his head to her shoulder. "Hush. Enough talk. Tell me what I must do to please you in this bed."

He angled back up, her meager strength nothing compared to his determination. "Promise, first. You'll tell me if you don't like something, if you're the least bit uncomfortable with it."

"I promise. Now stop fretting. I took off my clothes for you, sir, and not so you could lecture me to sleep."

"Wench." Ethan nuzzled her ear, which tickled, mostly. "Now you're going to talk to me."

"Oh, more talk." Alice huffed, then squeaked with alarm when Ethan shifted off of her. "Where are you going?"

"To a better listening post," Ethan said, tucking her against his side. "Think back, Alexandra, to all the times we've been affectionate, and tell me what touches you enjoyed the most."

"That is a ridiculous question," Alice scoffed, hiking her leg across his thighs—how bold he'd made her. How wonderfully bold. "I like it all, every bit of it, which makes me wanton, I suppose." What a lovely notion. She was proud of herself to consider it.

He hiked her leg a bit higher and drew patterns on her knee with one finger. "It makes you passionate and open-minded. But what do you like the best?"

"It isn't so simple to choose. Your kisses are exciting and wicked and wonderful, but the way you use your hands on me…"

"Yes?" That one finger on her knee was a case in point, bespelling her with a tactile pleasure she would never have guessed a knee might feel.

"You know where to touch, Ethan." She sighed mightily, for this recitation wasn't in any governess manual. "And no matter where you touch, it brings me pleasure."

∽∾

Alice's words lodged in his soul, because Ethan knew—he knew without asking, without questioning, she didn't mean simply his erotic touch. She liked it when he tapped her nose with his finger in the middle of some argument, when their hands brushed over the teapot at breakfast, when he pulled rank on his sons and assisted her to a seat.

To her, he was not dirty, shameful, second-rate, or anything less than deserving of her caring and respect. He could not have joined her in this bed had she thought him in any way unworthy.

And yet, direct questions were getting him nowhere on his stated agenda of the evening.

"Do you like it when I rub your back?"

"I *adore* it. If you want to make me purr like a cat, you put those big hands of yours on my back, Ethan Grey."

"Easy enough," Ethan said, rolling her to her side. He glanced at his hands, pleased for once at their size. He spent the next few minutes honestly rubbing her back, and she spent those minutes sighing and wiggling and sighing some more. When she'd had her fun, he let his hand trail down lower, over her buttocks.

Which earned him more sighing.

So he shifted around, to explore her breasts, and while she went still at first, she was soon arching into his hand, covering his knuckles with her palms.

"You like this?" He gently tugged at a nipple while ruthlessly ignoring his own arousal.

"Oh, that is *naughty*. Don't stop."

"Naughty" and "don't stop" were a compelling combination. Ethan eased her over to her back then replaced his fingers with his mouth.

"Ethan." It was a groan, a plea for mercy and a plea for more. Alice's hands winnowed through his hair to hold him to her, and her back arched in offering. Ethan felt her body slipping free of its restraints, even as his own was clamoring to join with her.

Slowly, so slowly it nigh killed him, he let one hand drift down her sternum, over her ribs and belly, to the curls shielding her sex.

"Spread your legs for me, Alexandra." Ethan spoke in a near whisper, savoring every syllable of her true name and every inch of her silky skin. "Let me touch you." She complied, restlessly lifting one knee to turn her hips toward him.

"Patience," Ethan chided, fastening his mouth over her other nipple.

"Ethan." Her voice was a little raspy and more than a little urgent. "This isn't comfortable."

He raised his head to consider her expression. "Do you want me to stop?"

"No!" She sounded sure of that. "But you can't expect me to enjoy being so... overwrought."

"I can." Overwrought was a mere beginning. He left his hand where it was, his fingers drifting over her mons. "Give me a little more time."

"Kiss me." She glared at him, clarifying that this was an order, not a request.

"Of course."

He treated her to a voracious kiss, not like anything he'd given her before. He consumed her, challenged her, teased and demanded and had her mouth clinging to his, even as her hands tried to map every inch of him. She found his nipples, sending a bolt of arousal straight south through his body. She found his buttocks and made him groan with the pleasure of being pulled close where she wanted him close. She kissed him back, to make demands of her own, only to fall utterly still when Ethan caressed her sex with two reverent fingers.

"Oh, holy saints, Ethan…"

He whispered his fingers across damp, intimate flesh.

"What are you doing?" Alice asked, circling his wrist with her fingers.

"Pleasing you, I hope." He leaned in to kiss her, a soft, voluptuous distraction from the lust raging through him, then shifted to take a nipple in his mouth.

"Ethan, I can't…" Her chest was rising and falling, but she said nothing more, just panted her desperation.

"Move, love. Move against my hand the way I've moved to your touch. Move the way your body wants to. Move toward the pleasure."

She undulated against his hand, taking long moments to find synchrony with his rhythm, and then she still didn't seem to know how to go on. Ethan realized she'd never trod this path before and was ignorant of the destination—another reason to shoot the leek-loving Mr. Droopyfield on sight.

Ethan slowed his hand, letting her catch her breath, then abruptly shifted to a fast, light stroke.

"Let it happen." Ethan's voice was urgent as he felt the sensations welling in her body. "Let yourself go. Come for me."

She arched into his hand, hard, repeatedly. She called his name, she dug her fingernails into his wrist, and she didn't stop until her breath was a harsh rasp and her body was a warm, replete bundle of naked womanhood against his side.

"That's my lady." Ethan's arms came around her, and she clung with surprising strength. His hands stroked slowly over her back, her arms, her shoulders, until Alice's breathing slowed.

"What was that?" She sounded bewildered, and a touch disgruntled, no doubt out of sorts to think some parcel of knowledge had been kept from her ken.

"I hope it was pleasure." For him, it had been nothing but pleasure, far eclipsing the lust still throbbing in his body.

"Is that what you feel?" Alice tucked her nose against his throat. "When you..."

"When you bring me off?" Ethan finished for her. He could feel her blushing against his neck. "Probably, or something very like it." Except he could do it only once, while she could repeat the pleasure endlessly. He wouldn't inflict that knowledge on her just yet, not when she seemed almost upset by her experience.

"I feel empty," Alice said on a shuddery sigh. "It was pleasurable, Ethan, profoundly, but now..."

His hold tightened around her protectively. "Now?"

"I feel lonely and worried," she said. "Like I could have trouble breathing if I let myself. That can't be normal." He wrapped his arms around her and cuddled her snugly to his body, offering her comfort, reassurance, and a different kind of pleasure in the secure warmth of his embrace.

"Better?" he asked a few minutes later.

"Better." She nodded, burrowing against his chest. "So is this what Nick shared with half the demimonde?"

He let her change the subject but felt a spike of exasperation that Nick—dear, bedamned Nick—should join them in the bed.

"Not quite. Physically, perhaps something similar, but emotionally, Nick would not have joined with someone capable of admitting the loneliness."

So there, Nicholas.

"He'd want a woman to lie?"

"I think the point of the kind of dalliances Nick sought was for everybody to lie, to pretend such matters could be undertaken only superficially."

"God above." Alice paused in an exploration of his collarbone with her tongue. "What a lot of poppy-cock. I've never done anything so intimate and lovely and overwhelming in my life. I could not abide the thought of sharing such a thing with a near stranger."

And that is a large part of why I love you.

"I thought I could. I was wrong." That he could say so to her was another part.

He held her to him, treasuring the feel of her naked body in his arms, until Alice levered up and speared him with a look.

"I want you in my mouth."

"I beg your pardon?" She was already shifting up and across him, intent on her goal. She curled up at his side, her cheek resting low on his belly.

"No sass from you, Ethan Grey. We have talked about this, and I have kissed you here." She took his erect cock in her hand. "Fair is fair. There's such a lot of room in this bed, too, we shouldn't let it go to waste."

Ethan didn't even have time to be thankful he'd bathed earlier, before Alice's lips were closing over him.

His hand tangled in her hair. "You don't have to do this. It isn't a ledger account, to keep balance or score."

"Hush," she admonished, gently cupping his testicles.

They *had* discussed this on one of Alice's scholarly tours of his body; they'd discussed it as something beyond naughty, and moved on to less fraught topics.

"Naughty" and "don't stop" collided again in Ethan's mind as Alice gained confidence in her welcome. She explored him carefully and thoroughly, and tried different touches and approaches, until she found the combination that had Ethan's hips slowly undulating.

"Sweetheart"—Ethan's voice was urgent—"I'm close... Too close."

She sealed her mouth around him and sent him past too close to that realm where reason and restraint were dim memories. His body bowed up, and she plied him with ruthless devotion until he was panting and spent, his only movement the caress of his hand in her hair.

"Everlasting... powers." Ethan wanted to gather her up, to tug her back over him, like a blanket, like a comforting lemony blessing, but he was simply incapable. Alice remained where she was, nuzzling his parts as she cradled him in her hand.

"Easy," Ethan cautioned. "I'm... sensitive. No sudden moves, please."

Alice shifted, sitting up and reaching for the glass of water on the night table. "I was sensitive too. I wanted to cry."

He smiled at her admission, misdirected though it was. She offered him the glass when she'd had her fill, and he took it, pleased at the small sharing. When she set the glass aside, she tucked herself against him without him having to ask, and his gratitude for that assumption—that they would want to hold each other—nearly did make him cry.

"So this was my warning shot?" Alice asked, her hand once again finding his flaccid penis. She held him gently, though not in a casual way either.

"In what sense?" Ethan liked that she touched him this way, loved it, in fact. There was reassurance in the gesture of insecurities he hadn't known he still had.

"Tomorrow night, you'll come to me again, and it will happen all over, but we'll be... joined."

"I pray to God that's so. Having second thoughts?"

Alice gave his cock an admonitory little tug. "Hush with that question, or I'll make you stand in the corner."

"But you'll spank me first, won't you? I've been very naughty."

"You are the furthest thing from naughty, but I think you'd like this spanking, wouldn't you?"

"Any touch from you would be to my liking."

She climbed over him, and while he missed the feel of her fingers around his cock, Ethan enjoyed the press of her breasts against his chest.

"Don't be shy." He caressed her bottom, shaped the smooth, warm female wonder of her. "Cuddle up."

"I'm not..." Alice frowned against his chest. "I'm untidy."

"You want a handkerchief? Or would you instead let me feel this luscious untidiness that follows when a woman is well pleased in bed?" He patted her bottom

again, a more businesslike affection that urged her
down against him.

"Naughty, naughty, naughty." Alice sighed, easing
her hips down. Ethan bumped up, letting her feel
the softening mass of his penis against her damp sex.
A body kiss, a cozy, intimate kiss of parts that made
Ethan ridiculously happy.

"With you, I'm the friendly sort," he said,
sweeping her braid down her back. "And I like to
feel you near me."

"Feeling's mutual," Alice said, stifling a yawn. "I
don't mean to be rude, but my eyes are heavy."

"Go to sleep, love." Ethan kissed her temple. "I'll
be gone by morning, but back tomorrow night."

"I shouldn't," Alice protested as Ethan felt her
lashes sweep a butterfly kiss to his chest.

"You should. Sleep in my arms, Alexandra, and
dream of me, for I will certainly dream of you."

While she drifted into the arms of Morpheus, he
was a long time holding her and considering what
it meant to love a woman for the first time in more
than thirty years on earth. He'd wanted to love his
wife, tried to talk himself into believing lust and initial
infatuation could mature to something more. He'd
wanted to fall in love, to find someone to whom he
could entrust his heart, his future, his children.

Well, he had the children, and now he had a
woman to treasure and cherish and intimately appreciate. It was enough; it was more than he'd hoped
to have when he'd consigned himself to marrying
Barbara—so much more—and it was enough.

❧

Alice awoke the next morning to see her curtains whipping in a damp breeze. The overcast that had rolled in during the night had let her sleep later than usual, so she hurried through her morning toilette, until a slight sensitivity in her private parts had her blushing and recalling the events of the previous evening.

Ye gods, ye gods... so that was sexual pleasure? That was the great prize given to the married and the naughty unmarried?

She couldn't imagine sharing so intimately with any other man, and with that insight, she gained some understanding of Ethan's claim that he could not make love with her unless desire was mutual. She did not want just the glorious sensations, she wanted *Ethan*. She wanted his arms around her, his voice in her ear, his scent on her skin, his hands stroking her flesh.

She wanted his confidences, his dreams, his hopes, and his rare playful gambits. She wanted his headaches, his extended family in Kent, and his stubborn determination to get her back up on a horse. She wanted not just his lovely body, but his entire heart.

Oh, dear.

Alice collapsed onto the bed and considered what it meant, when she longed for a man to trust her with his heart. This could not be a good thing, not when the man was a confirmed widower who'd endured one miserable marriage for the sake of his children. Not when he was so wealthy the Regent turned to him for financial advice.

Not when he'd been so carefully honest with her, assuring her he was beyond ever remarrying.

Oh, dear. *Oh, God.* She'd fallen in love with Ethan

Grey, and where did that leave her—besides looking forward to the coming night?

Alice had always thought love could only come to her slowly, a gradual shift in emotions from respect to affection to the kind of abiding regard her parents had had. She had never expected this tumult, this drama of the emotions, would befall her.

There was no fighting it. Her feelings were subject to neither reason nor logic, and all she could hope for was to keep her sentiments behind her teeth, where she would not embarrass Ethan with them.

Or herself.

So they would make love tonight, and in the privacy of her heart, Alice would love Ethan too. When he tired of her, her heart would break, but she'd be prepared for that. Her idea of heartbreak had shifted, though.

Heartbreak was no longer a vague, bothersome sense that she'd be unhappy for a while. Heartbreak was worse and better, she decided as she pinned up her hair. When Ethan set her aside, she'd be devastated at the loss of him, but she'd also be richer for having shared with him what lovers shared, even temporarily. It would be enough. It was more than she'd thought life would offer her, and it would be enough.

Sixteen

"HOW OLD IS UNCLE DOLPH?" JEREMIAH POSED THE question to his father as their horses walked back to the barn at the end of the one weekly ride that did not include Joshua.

"Nineteen, maybe." Ethan realized he wasn't quite sure. "Or maybe eighteen. I don't know. Why?"

"He's still at school. He's been at school a long time."

"Not so long. Dolph spent only a couple of years at public school, and he's been up at university for two years, I think. Before that, he was tutored at home, as you and Joshua have been."

"You went to public school," Jeremiah said, his tone diffident.

"I did, for a few years, as did your uncles Nick, Beck, George, and Dolph. Do you want to go to public school?"

Ethan's tone was equally casual, though a cold knife of anxiety sliced at his guts. Children did go away to school as young as six, and Ethan wondered at their parents for allowing it. Was Jeremiah somehow so unhappy he wanted to leave home?

"A young man goes away to school," Jeremiah said, his gaze even more intent on his pony's mane, "and you said I'm on the threshold of young manhood."

"I did say that. Give me your reins, Jeremiah."

Jeremiah looked puzzled but complied, and watched as his father tied the reins to a ring on the front of Waltzer's saddle.

"Up you go." Ethan grasped Jeremiah under the arms and lifted him from the pony's back to the front of Ethan's saddle. Waltzer paused, adjusted to the new load, and sauntered on while the pony obediently trailed beside the horse.

"You might have asked." Jeremiah looked down at his pony and reminded Ethan for all the world of Alice Portman when she was displeased with her high-handed employer.

"I might. I'm sorry. Next time I will. What is this interest in public school? Are you ready to leave your papa and strike out on your own?"

"Soon. Joshua should come with me, and he's still too young."

"I'm glad he's too young." Ethan had one arm around Jeremiah's waist, which meant he could feel the tension in his son's body.

"Why would you be glad about that? Miss Alice says we're growing like magic beanstalks," Jeremiah said, fiddling with the horse's mane.

"Why?" Ethan paused and tried to find words to explain the hole in his heart, in his life, in his soul, that would result if his children left his household now. He was just coming to know them, to be a father to them in any meaningful sense, and here his six-year-old—*his six-year-old*—was calmly suggesting

Ethan abandon them to the likes of Stoneham and Hart Collins.

"Because, Jeremiah Nicholas Grey, there is nobody I love the way I love my sons, and I would miss you very, very much."

Before him, Jeremiah stopped fiddling with Waltzer's mane. "You would? You'd miss us?"

"Because I love you." Ethan emphasized the words Jeremiah had tried to ignore. "Because you are my family, and too soon you will grow up and become a young man who wants to make his own way in the world. Then I will have to let you go, but I won't like it then, either."

"Even when we're old, like Uncle Dolph or Uncle George?"

"Even when you're old like me. I didn't go to school until I was fourteen, Jeremiah, and then only because my father thought Nick and I should be meeting other boys our age." This was a lie, but Ethan forgave himself for it before the words had left his lips.

"Fourteen? That's twice as old as me, and more."

As I, Ethan thought with a parent's inherent need to edit grammar. He kept his parental editor quiet and hugged his son instead. "It's forever from now, and there are plenty of young men who go to university without ever having gone away to school."

"I don't want to go," Jeremiah said on a huge sigh. "Mr. Harold said we ought, because we were an embarrassment and gutterswipes."

"Guttersnipes. It means orphans or little criminals in the making. Children who have no supervision or manners or home."

"I have supervision and manners and a home,"

Jeremiah said with a touch of defiance. "Mr. Harold was wrong."

"Very."

And when Jeremiah might have burdened his father with yet more memories of the execrable Mr. Harold, Ethan chose that moment to tickle his son gently. "Are you ready to return to your own saddle?"

"Not yet. I like it way up here. When can Joshua and I have bigger ponies?"

"Horses, you mean?" Ethan tousled his son's hair with a gloved hand. "Not for a while. Joshua is a demon on that pony, and I'm frankly scared of what he'd do with a larger mount."

"Thunder and Lightning are good boys," Jeremiah declared staunchly. "I wouldn't want to sell them."

"So we won't. This estate can support a couple of ponies who've done their share of work." Ethan did not examine too closely the notion that other children might come along to interrupt Thunder and Lightning's retirement.

"We don't have to sell them?" Jeremiah turned to regard his father. "Mr. Harold said the only things more useless than me and Josh were those fat, lame ponies of ours. He said they should go to the knackers, because they were a complete waste of money."

An accurate description for Mr. Harold. Ethan batted aside the paternal guilt following that sentiment.

"Mr. Harold was likely jealous. Your ponies are first-rate, and you ride them like a pair of Cossacks. And Jeremiah? It's ill-bred to mention it, so I beg your discretion, but what we do with our wealth is none of Mr. Harold's damned business."

"You said damned. I won't tattle. Do you think Miss Alice will ever canter?"

If Ethan had his way, her heart at least would be galloping that very night. "I don't know. For her to get on Waltzer, much less to hack out at the trot, took a lot of courage. We should be proud of her."

"She's proud of us. She tells us all the time. I like her, even if she makes us do lessons."

Ethan tolerated another filial inspection and realized Jeremiah had cast one of his subtle lures. "I like her too, Jeremiah. I like her a great deal."

"More than you liked Mama?" Jeremiah sprung the trap with casual innocence.

"That's complicated." Ethan searched for useful truths amid the painful and surprising realities. "I will always treasure your mother because she gave me you and Joshua, but she's in heaven now, and we are left here to live out our lives without her. I do like Miss Alice a lot, and I respect her. Those are probably the same feelings you have about your mother's memory."

"Sorta." Jeremiah started to braid a hank of mane. "Mama wasn't always nice."

"Nobody is nice all the time."

"She yelled." Jeremiah shrank back against his father's chest as he spoke. "She yelled *a lot*, at you, and at us too."

"Some people yell." Ethan tried to keep his tone level, but God above, Jeremiah had barely been out of nappies when his mother had died. Was his only memory of his mother her temper? "It doesn't mean they don't love you. I yell. Uncle Nick yells."

"He yells, but mostly when he loses his ball in the weeds. Uncle Nick went to public school too."

Back to this?

"He did. A different one than I did."

"Mama wanted to send us away." Jeremiah gave another one of those sighs, as if his entire soul was heaving away a burden, and Ethan felt his heart breaking. He wanted to argue Jeremiah out of these memories, to tell the boy Barbara had only been teasing or exasperated or trying to raise Ethan's temper in response, but he couldn't. Barbara had been fiendishly expert at ferreting out Ethan's sensitive issues, and though they'd argued about everything at some point, she'd honed in on public school as one of the most sensitive issues of all.

Ethan pressed a kiss to his son's crown. "Isn't it interesting that your mother is the one who did go away, thankfully to a better place, while you and Joshua are here, with me, right where I want you?"

"I don't miss her," Jeremiah said, undoing the braid. "Sometimes I go look at her picture so I'll remember what she looked like. Mostly I try to remember for Joshua."

"It's all right not to miss her. And you were very, very little when she died, Jeremiah. I'm surprised you recall her at all. My mother died when I was little, and I can't put my finger on any particular memories, though the scent of lilies makes me think of her. I used to look at her portrait too."

"Was she pretty?"

"She was." Ethan realized it was true. "She was tall and blond and had happy eyes."

"Joshua has those. Miss Alice is tallish, but not blond, but her eyes are happy too, mostly."

"And she's pretty," Ethan reminded his oldest son. "Maybe even prettier than either of our mothers."

That seemed to address the topic to Jeremiah's satisfaction, because he remained quiet—and up before his father—for the entire remainder of their ride. When Ethan and Jeremiah turned up the lane toward the Tydings stables, the Marquess of Heathgate emerged from the bridle path on his chestnut mare.

"Greetings, your lordship." Ethan wasn't exactly glad to see his neighbor, though he was glad to have Jeremiah up before him. "Finding some peace and quiet on a summer morning?"

"Nearly autumn." Heathgate smiled at the boy, a surprisingly friendly expression Ethan could not recall seeing before. "Master Jeremiah, good morning. Did you finally wear that pony out?"

"He did." Ethan answered for his son, unwilling to hear Jeremiah explain to his lordship that Papa had plucked him off his mount's back for sentimental reasons no grown man would want to confess to another.

"Enjoy your place of honor while you can, young man," Heathgate said. "Another year, and you won't be fitting so handily in your papa's saddle."

"Another year, and Papa will buy us horses from Lord Greymoor."

"Down you go for now." Ethan settled his son on the pony's back. "Look after your beast, and tell Miller to get his lazy arse out here to tend to his lordship's mare."

Yes, Ethan's gaze said as he met Jeremiah's, *Papa said arse.*

"Yes, Papa." Jeremiah winked at his father, and Ethan had all he could do to keep a straight face as he dismounted.

"Sometimes"—Heathgate's voice was thoughtful—

"the hardest part about being a parent is not laughing. That young man is going to break hearts when he's older. He has the family good looks, and he pays attention."

"Sometimes he pays too close attention."

"And then they ignore you completely," Heathgate commiserated, climbing off his mare. "If children sat in the Lords, it would be a very different place. Probably better."

Ethan regarded his companion as Miller led their horses away. "Do you spread sedition like this among your peers?"

"Of course. It isn't treason to speculate on methods of improving governance, though that's hardly why I trotted up your lane."

Ethan walked in silence beside the marquess, realizing the call wasn't entirely social. With a sense of foreboding, Ethan escorted his lordship to the house, signaled a footman, and led his guest into the library. "One hopes you came to enjoy a cold drink and a little neighborly company."

"One can hope that," Heathgate countered when the door was closed, "but one would be attributing to me a delicacy of manners I lack."

And the true Marquess of Heathgate subtly stepped forward.

"You don't come bearing another picnic summons, do you? Pardon me. They are invitations, not summonses."

"More like writs of habeas corpus, issued by the womenfolk."

"Right." Ethan did not smile, since having Heathgate in his home was not quite comfortable. He liked the man, respected him, and enjoyed his family.

And yet, he made Ethan... uneasy.

"Tydings is pretty," Heathgate said, glancing around the room. "Greymoor claimed this was so, and was intrigued that you've achieved a graceful home without a lady in residence. Did your late wife take the place in hand?"

He was clearly stalling until the refreshment had been delivered, and Ethan was willing to delay whatever Heathgate came to tell him.

"Barbara was not much inclined to domestication," Ethan said. "I've done what I thought necessary to the place, and thank you for the compliment."

"I knew the lady." Heathgate turned his attention to the view beyond the French doors. "You are kind to her memory."

Ethan was not going to ask his neighbor in what sense he'd known Barbara. She'd taken lovers before and after they'd married, and she'd been a devastatingly attractive woman—physically.

Heathgate surveyed his host. "You are silent. I wasn't one of her amours, if that's what you're wondering, but you probably knew exactly with whom she disported, where and when."

"I kept close enough track of her," Ethan responded, and then—thank God—the footman's tap on the door provided a distraction. When Heathgate was ensconced in a cushioned chair, a cold glass of lemonade in his hand, Ethan settled in the opposite chair and consciously relaxed his shoulders.

Heathgate withdrew a thin sheaf of papers from his waistcoat. "You won't want to leave this where it can be easily stumbled across by prying eyes."

"What is it?" Ethan set the papers aside, sensing instinctively he did not want to know their contents.

"My notes, taken when interviewing Benjamin Hazlit regarding certain individuals I'd asked him to investigate."

The idea of Heathgate and Hazlit coupled like hounds on a scent made Ethan's blood run cold.

"This would be of interest to me?" Ethan wanted to toss the papers out the French doors, but kept his expression bland.

"I've already warned you Collins is back in the country," Heathgate said. "I thought it prudent to know what he and his former associates were up to, so I set Hazlit to the task."

"In God's name, why?" Ethan rose, unable to maintain a cool facade. "It's damned near twenty years in the past. Why do you insist on bringing this up?"

"I don't know." Heathgate sipped his drink, a man in no hurry to cease prying into Ethan's old wounds. "Greymoor's countess claims I have a cruel streak."

"You surely didn't discuss this with your sister-by-marriage?" Ethan's voice was tight, and he let his temper show in the glare he leveled at his guest.

"I haven't discussed your personal business with anyone. Not even Lady Heathgate knows the details, and I do not keep secrets from my wife."

"I wish to hell you wouldn't discuss this with me."

"I don't believe that's so." Heathgate rose and went to stand beside Ethan where he stared out his mullioned windows. "You don't like what I know of the crimes against you, Ethan Grey, but you'd like it even less were you completely alone with the knowledge yourself. You'd begin to doubt your memories, tell yourself you exaggerated and embellished when you did not and you do not. Read those notes, my friend. Those jackals ambushed you once. You must not let them ambush you again. Think of your sons and your family."

"I am thinking of my sons. What would you have me do? Turn myself in to the constable as a sodomite to implicate Collins in something easily dismissed as distasteful schoolboy nonsense?"

"You don't have to do anything." Heathgate put a hand on Ethan's shoulder and just let it rest there. To be touched by another man while discussing Hart Collins was at once unbearable and oddly comforting.

Heathgate removed his hand, but apparently wasn't done passing out advice. "There's a middle ground between calling Collins out in some misguided attempt at revenge and ignoring him completely. The middle ground is to be informed and prepared, and thus to give yourself the upper hand if and when he acts. He has lingered longer in England this time than at any point previous, and no longer has the funds to debauch his way across the Continent."

Ethan let out a held breath, his mind comprehending Heathgate was offering him wisdom, even if his body was more prepared for a fight. On some level, he'd been prepared for a fight ever since the day Collins had assaulted him as a boy in the Stoneham stables.

"We're not boys anymore," Ethan said. "What makes you think Collins is any threat to my peace of mind at all?"

Heathgate's glacier-blue eyes gave away nothing. "I saw the condition they put you in, and that wasn't schoolboy nonsense, and believe me, having attended Stoneham for four years, I saw plenty of nonsense. Something is wrong with Collins. He was tossed out of at least three other schools for either extreme violence or incidents similar to the one you were involved in. There's probably a word for the kind of man he is, but if he were a horse, I'd put him down."

"He did the same thing to others?" The heart in Ethan's chest took up a heavy drumbeat, not dread exactly, but a sense of the moment bearing portents with far-reaching effects. "How many?"

"At least two others whom Hazlit spoke to personally," Heathgate said. "Hazlit says Collins was engaged briefly, but the lady wouldn't have him. And as quickly as Benjamin has assembled a very thorough report, the man has to be nigh notorious. Then too, Hazlit has some personal animosity toward Collins which I do not doubt goes back as far as your own. They're both from Cumbria, though Hazlit keeps his antecedents quiet. You'll read the notes?"

"I will." The idea of Collins originating from the same shire as Alice made Ethan want to retch.

Heathgate continued to study Ethan. "You wonder if it's ever going to completely go away, don't you? You bury yourself in your commerce and immure yourself here in the woods of Surrey, and all the while, in the back of your mind, it lurks, waiting to pounce."

"Do you expect me to admit that to you?" There were depths to Heathgate, and not necessarily happy ones.

"Oh, of course not." Heathgate's smile was humorless. "Whatever you're dragging around, whatever memories you're trying to ignore, they don't learn their proper place until you turn around and stare them down."

"Have you taken up hearing confessions too, your

reverence?" Ethan's tone was dry, just short of desperately disrespectful.

His guest's expression was utterly serious. "My name is Gareth. I will thank you to use it henceforth, should we be informally private."

Ethan's eyebrows rose, for such an invitation was beyond peculiar—also blatantly flattering. As neighbors, someday Ethan might have been expected to address the marquess simply as "Heathgate," but never by his given name. Only a brother might have presumed to call him by his name.

"I will read your notes, Gareth." Ethan said the name carefully, feeling the strangeness of it, but thinking the name suited the very masculine specimen before him. "And you have my thanks for taking an interest in my situation."

"I'm off, then. I've invited James and Will to ride out with me tomorrow morning, weather permitting. Amery might bring Rose if he can't weasel out of it, but the boys learned you mean to take your two cubbing this fall, and so you see before you a doomed papa."

When Heathgate dropped a subject, at least he dropped it entirely.

"Cubbing is harmless enough," Ethan said as he walked his guest to the front door. "I have no appetite for true blood sport."

"Neither do I, but Nick enjoys it, doesn't he?"

"I think he enjoys a good gallop and a romp with the hounds. A man his size is not permitted to cringe at a grisly death, or to sympathize with poor Renard."

"A man his size?" Heathgate's gaze traveled Ethan's length, which exceeded his own by a couple of inches.

"I am a veritable sylph compared to my brother. Just as you are ancient compared to yours."

"Just so." Heathgate pulled on his gloves. "My marchioness found a gray hair on me yesterday. Don't have daughters, my friend. They age a man as sons cannot."

"You're a font of wisdom, at least today."

"'A prophet is not without honor, save in his own country,'" Heathgate quoted. "I have to dispense my wisdom where it will be appreciated—so see that you heed me."

Ethan let him have the last word because, after all, the man had made sense—except for that blather about daughters. But rather than head back into the library and read the damned notes, Ethan turned the other way and sought his younger son. He had plans for his day, and his night, and reading sordid history did not comport with those plans at all.

❧

The gentry were proving accommodating, suggesting to Baron Collins that he'd been remiss not to frequent English house parties in years past. While enjoying fine food, decent drink, and the occasional housemaid—or footman—Collins could keep an eye on Ethan Grey and meet easily with that handy tool known by the locals as Thatcher.

"I can't be sneakin' about like this," Thatcher grumbled. "Miller watches me, and the work won't do itself when I'm waiting for ye to come strollin' along."

"Stable work is completed before dark," Collins retorted. "And I wasn't about to risk hanging felonies without corroborating your characterization of Grey's situation."

"Ye done what?"

A handy tool often sported a dull blade. "Without making sure Grey is as rich as you say he is. Many a fine lord is living on credit."

"He ain't a lord. He's a right bastard."

"He's a wealthy man." An affront to the natural order, that was, when the scion of an old and noble house had to scrounge for accommodations while a lowly bastard prospered. "He will soon be much less wealthy."

Except as Thatcher reported the routine in the stables, Collins realized the timing of his plans would be delicate. Ethan Grey's stables were busy, with grooms on hand at all hours and the tyrant Miller overseeing every detail. Worse, the children were closely supervised, and Mr. Grey himself often in company with them—and having Grey about would not do at all.

"I shall be patient," Collins decided. "I've waited nigh twenty years to put this particular upstart in his place. I can wait a bit longer."

Thatcher shuffled away in the shadows, leaving Collins to study the edifice up the hill from the paddocks.

Ethan Grey had indeed prospered, and that… that simply wasn't to be borne.

Seventeen

"I LIKED SLEEPING WITH YOU," ALICE ANNOUNCED when Ethan let himself into her room. The hour was late, approaching midnight, and she'd already donned her summer nightgown and wrapper, though the evening was decidedly more autumnal.

"I liked sleeping with you too." Ethan smiled to see her already out of her clothes. She no doubt thought she'd foiled his desire to see her naked as she undressed, silly woman. "And I'm sure I'll like it even more tonight."

He drew her to her feet from where she sat at her writing desk and wrapped his arms around her. She was all warmth, soft curves, and fresh lemony fragrance, and Ethan felt arousal stirring just to be holding her. There was more to his reaction, too—a kind of mental sigh, to have achieved the sanctuary of her embrace.

"It isn't too late to change your mind, Alice," he whispered near her ear. "I won't think less of you if you send me packing."

"At least you can think," Alice said, kissing his jaw.

"I've been useless all day, watching the hands of the clock crawl forward, wondering when the sun decided it would choose today to refuse to set."

"The days grow shorter. You are impatient." And may she always regard their joinings as eagerly.

She subsided more snugly against him. "Impatient, also a bit anxious."

As was he, truth be told. Heathgate had picked a miserable day to come to call.

"I do not like to see you anxious," Ethan said, kissing her forehead. "Shall we get under the covers?" Before she noticed that despite his anxieties, Ethan's body was anticipating lovemaking.

"I won't have a breathing spell," she said. "Not with you."

"I'm glad." *Neither would he, not with her.* Ethan stepped back enough to undo the sash of her night robe. She surprised him by whipping her nightgown off over her head and scrambling under the covers.

"You'd like to watch me." And how pleased he was that she did. Alice perched up against the headboard, fingers laced around her knees. Ethan did not consider himself a vain man, but the heat in Alice's gaze would make any fellow willing to strut before her.

He made no attempt to turn his disrobing into flirtation—he was too interested in joining her in the bed. When he was naked and his clothing folded on the clothespress, he climbed into bed and stretched out beside her. "What shall we talk about?"

"Talk? We're naked in bed and again, you want to talk?"

"I do." Ethan drew his finger down her nose. "As a younger man, I failed to appreciate the pleasures of visiting with a lover in bed. I was all business, so to speak. I don't want to be all business with you, Alexandra."

"Not business then." Alice made as if to nip his finger. "I'll tell you Joshua has made some real strides in his reading."

"I was slow to read." Ethan leaned in and kissed her eyes, one then the other. "Nick was much faster and had to help me."

As soon as he said his brother's name, Ethan expected a bolt of regret... that never came.

"You read all the time. Do you ever read to the boys?"

"I read to Joshua, once. He was quite small and ill, and his mother had just died. He was barely speaking himself, but the sound of my voice soothed him."

"Children know when someone cares." Alice laced her arm under his neck. "And they know when someone doesn't."

"Jeremiah had some interesting questions along that line on our ride today." Ethan shifted to his back, so Alice lay tucked along his side. He was astonished to realize that talking this way, about the boys, about anything, was not just a ploy to relax Alice's anxieties.

This talking, cuddled up on her big bed, was a comfort to him as well.

"Jeremiah wanted to know if I missed his mother and claimed he himself did not, because she yelled a great deal and threatened to send him off to boarding school as soon as may be. I add it to the list of things I must try to forgive her for."

"Was boarding school on Jeremiah's mind today as well?" Alice scooted, bringing her near leg up over Ethan's hips.

"It was." Ethan drew his finger down her nose again, and right on down her midline under the covers to her mons. "He was concerned I would send him and Joshua away when Joshua turned six."

"You didn't mock him, did you?"

"I hugged him," Ethan said, curling down to bury his face against Alice's neck. "I told him I would be miserable if he wanted to tear off into the world so soon, and Alexandra, I meant every word."

"Oh, well done, Ethan." Alice hugged him to her. "Well done, indeed."

They were quiet for a long moment, Ethan letting himself bask in her approval and affection and in the rare knowledge she loved his children the same way he did.

"I think your sons are happier now than they were at the beginning of the summer." She stroked the back of his head as she spoke, and Ethan wanted to hold so still that she never stopped, so much did he like the way she touched him.

"They are," Ethan said, picking up the reins of the conversation. "As am I."

"Oh, let's make it unanimous." She sounded so pleased with herself. "Though I wasn't exactly unhappy previously."

"I'm pleased." Ethan brushed his mouth across hers. "Pleased you're happy with us. Joshua asked me if I thought you'd ever canter."

"Ah, do that again. Please."

He willingly obliged, in part because his efforts to ease her closer to lovemaking with words and simple bodily proximity were having their effect on him. He kissed her with the slow, relaxed savoring of a man who knows he has all night, hours and hours, just to move to the next step.

When he began to explore her mouth with his tongue, Ethan felt Alice shift on the mattress, her limbs relaxing, her spine lengthening.

"Kiss me back, love," Ethan coaxed, his tongue teasing past her lips. "Come out and play with me."

He paused, his mouth a hairsbreadth away from hers, waiting for Alice to arch up and brush her lips against his. She repeated the caress twice more, until Ethan pressed her mouth open beneath his. She twined her arms around his neck with a slow, languorous sigh, and Ethan felt his heartbeat kick up a notch.

The barest hint of a misgiving skittered through his vitals, but not for the usual reasons. He wasn't experiencing the old uncertainties or ambiguities; he had no doubt he and Alice belonged in that bed together. He was neither unsure of himself sexually nor fearful of inexplicably losing his desire for her. He experienced an instant's hesitation only because he wanted this night to be better than right for her. He wanted it to be perfect.

And then Alice pulled her body closer to his and found his lips with her own. She welcomed him into the kiss and then welcomed him further, her legs spreading as Ethan shifted his body over hers.

The doubts Ethan battled—not just that night, but many nights in the past twenty years—vanished. He knew what to do, knew how to express his caring for this woman with his mouth and his hands, and body. This was Alice, whom he cared for greatly, and with her, for this one night at least, all would be well.

He closed his eyes, let himself feel the wonder of

her naked body beneath his, and gave himself up to the loving.

❧

When Ethan began to kiss her in earnest, a bolt of anxiety went through Alice's body and her mind. She lost track of the kiss and began to fret, even as Ethan's tongue glided sinuously over hers: What if she couldn't breathe? What if this night left Ethan with a disgust of her? What if she couldn't enjoy what he was trying to share with her? She hadn't cared with Mr. Durbeyfield, being only a little bit curious and a lot bored. With Ethan, God help her, she cared a great deal. Cared too much, and hence, the worrying gathered momentum.

But then he shifted, bringing his body carefully over hers in an embrace that caged Alice between Ethan and the bed. For all of her adult life, she'd hated being confined, hated any sort of entrapment. To be anchored under him this way should have made her frantic to escape.

A different panic gripped her, though. She wasn't frantic to escape. *She was frantic to get closer to him.* She did not like being confined—maybe nobody did. But she saw it was also true, true in a blindingly new and stark way, that for all her adult life, she'd been profoundly *lonely*. And what Ethan offered her was not confinement, but rather, intimacy. He offered her the closeness that had nothing to do with confinement and binding, but instead sought to free her.

With Ethan's body sheltering hers, his naked strength surrounding her, she felt that paradoxical sense of being utterly in accord with another and yet utterly unfettered, and she wanted intensely—desperately—to bring that feeling closer. She spread her legs, letting him settle against her, and wrapped her arms around him.

"Easy," Ethan murmured, grazing her jaw with his nose. "There's no rush, love. None at all."

Alice felt the impressive length of his erection against her belly. "I want you closer."

"Soon," he assured her, pained humor in that one word. "Wrap your legs around me."

He whispered his request again before she opened her eyes, brushed the hair back from his forehead, and shifted the angle of her hips to accommodate him.

"Like this?" She kissed his shoulder then scraped him with her teeth. He tasted clean and warm and faintly of the lavender sachets Mrs. Buxton hung in all the wardrobes.

"Like that." Ethan dipped his head to kiss her mouth. "Now guide me to you."

Alice left off using her tongue to taste his flesh. "Guide you?"

"Take me in your hand," he said, holding her gaze steadily, "and guide me home."

Ethan remained poised above her, his gaze locked with hers. There was both challenge and reassurance in his gaze. He would not subject her to the kind of fumbling she'd known before with another man. He was not going to allow her to passively tolerate intimacy either, but most of all, he was not going to allow her to be disappointed. Not in him, not in herself, not in what they shared.

Alice saw all that before she closed her eyes.

He nuzzled her throat. "Take my cock in your hand

and show me where you want me. I'll wait all night, if you want me to, but that means you wait too."

Logic, and at such a time. Alice tucked her face against his shoulder and brushed her fingers over the soft skin crowning his member.

He could wait all night, she was sure of that—and equally sure she could not.

❧

Ethan felt a tentative brush of Alice's fingers over the head of his cock. He thought of accounts payable and boiled cabbage and the recipe for Miller's horse liniment, and even tried the Lord's Prayer in Latin, but Alice closed her grip around him and brought him snug against her damp sex.

He had to kiss her.

"God above." He exhaled unsteadily, resting his forehead against hers but unable to resist her mouth for long. He sealed his lips over hers in a hot, open-mouthed, needy plea for some kind of immediate joining. Her tongue met his, and it was all he could do not to roar into her body, tongue, cock, fingers, *anything*.

"Ethan, *please*…" Alice tried to move against him, to take him into her body on her own initiative, but Ethan feinted with his hips.

"Behave," he said. "We savor this." He emphasized his words with the barest hint of forward movement of his hips, and Alice abruptly ceased her attempts to rush their joining.

"Better," he murmured, then, "relax, my love. We're not going to hurry this."

She could not relax. Beneath him, Ethan felt the tension in Alice's body, felt the tight, shallow breaths she expelled against his neck. He wanted to believe she was simply aroused past bearing, but she was so tight around the tip of his cock, he had to suspect she was simply anxious.

"Breathe, love, and recall your promise."

She opened eyes that had been tightly shut, and peered at him in the dim light as he brushed his fingertips over her forehead. "My promise?"

"You'll tell me if you don't like something or if it's uncomfortable. If you ask it, I will stop."

"I don't want you to stop," Alice replied, sounding more resolute than aroused.

"And I don't want to be stopped, but you promised."

He held himself against her, applying a firm, steady pressure but making no move to advance more deeply into her body. She wanted him, of that he was confident, but she lacked the experience to know her body needed time.

"It isn't supposed to be this difficult," Alice muttered.

Ethan pressed more firmly into her.

"Tell me how it's supposed to be," he said, laying his cheek against hers.

"Easy," Alice replied, sounding a little bewildered, "and sweet and pleasant."

Merciful God. He was about to explode, and she expected a tea party. "This is pleasant," Ethan said, kissing her lingeringly.

"I feel… discontent."

"Discontent is good," Ethan murmured before slipping a hand down and closing it over her breast.

"*That* is good."

"Not just good. Lovely, beautiful, dear…" He caressed and stroked and gently kneaded, all the while holding his cock against her, but just shy of real penetration. When Ethan closed his fingers around her nipple, Alice groaned, and using her ankles for leverage, heaved her hips against him.

He allowed it and slipped that first hot, glorious, wet inch inside her body.

"Shame on you, Alexandra. I'll kiss you silly for that."

She turned her head to hasten her fate, and Ethan obliged by covering her mouth with his again. She came out not to play, but to tease, entice, coax, and madden with her mouth and tongue and sexy little sighs. "Ethan, I need you."

He applied a hint of pressure to her nipple and let her have more of his cock when she arched tightly against his hand. This required such concentration of him, he decided it qualified as a form of prayer.

"More," Alice whispered. "More, *now*."

From somewhere, he found the self-restraint to deny her, distracting her with his tongue in her ear, his teeth on her earlobe, then his lips closed around her nipple as she growled low against his temple.

Alice's fingers tunneled through his hair to hold him to her, then tightened in desperate pleasure as he suckled.

"Damn you," Alice rasped. "Ethan, I am *begging*… Ah, God, yes…"

He pushed steadily forward, until he was *inside*.

Then he paused, knowing they had a distance yet to travel.

Alice raised her head, regarding him with a world of bewilderment. "Why did you stop?"

"I'm not stopping." Ethan laid his cheek against her temple. "I'm marshaling my reserves."

"Your reserves?" Alice flopped back against the pillows. "Reserves of what?"

"Passion," he said softly, easing his cock forward one blessed, beautiful, profoundly pleasurable inch, then easing back the same distance.

"Don't stop." Alice closed her eyes at this, the beginning of their real joining. "Don't you dare stop, Ethan Grey. Not *ever*." She let out a mighty not-as-discontented sigh, and some of the tension went out of her as Ethan slowly worked himself more deeply into her body.

"I like this. Ethan, I do like this."

"With you, I love it," he replied, his voice equally soft and just a little strained as he struggled to keep his rhythm easy and relaxed, and struggled not to speak words he wasn't entitled to burden her with.

He would not tell her he loved her, not with words, but he tried to communicate it with his body. He joined them by slow, tantalizing increments, until he was gliding easily into her depths and she was arching up to meet him. Her breathing deepened, and her body became more fluid in its undulations. Beside her head, her fingers opened and closed convulsively on the pillow until Ethan stroked his thumbs over her palms.

"Ethan, I can't…" She lost the words as he added the first hint of power to his thrusts.

"You can." He stroked her palms again. *"We can."* He laced his fingers with hers, and that gesture provoked a soft moan as Alice buried her face against his throat. Her fingers tightened on his, and she tried to hurry him with her hips and arch up against him.

He untangled one hand and wrapped an arm under her shoulders to hold her tightly to him. With Alice anchored snugly in his embrace, he let her have the deep, solid thrusts she'd been begging for, and in moments, she was shaking and clinging and coming apart in his arms.

He resisted the urge to drive her higher, to glory in her satisfaction as he might when they had more experience with each other. When he felt her body easing, he let himself go just enough to outdistance his own control.

He'd intended to permit himself a gentlemanly measure of satisfaction, but Alice's passion came roaring back to life, another orgasm heaving her up against him in hard panting demands for more. His arousal crested higher and higher, beyond his control, then beyond his comprehension, until they were a mindless union of striving bodies and entwined souls inundated with unbearably intense pleasure.

"Holy Everlasting God." Ethan wasn't aware he'd spoken aloud until Alice responded with a panted "Amen."

His hand cradled the back of her head while they breathed in rapid counterpoint with each other.

"Don't move," Alice said. "I feel like it could happen all over again."

"You tempt me." Ethan's voice was raspy and desperate, for he'd love to see her undone yet again.

"Don't… you… dare," Alice warned, closing her inner muscles around his softening length.

Oh, *Lord*, and she was this clever, this passionate while damned near a virgin. "Point taken. For now."

Gradually their breathing slowed, and Ethan was able not just to hold her to him, but to stroke his hand over her face, her hair, and shoulders.

"I have to hold you, Alexandra, but you are not to move just yet."

"As if I could."

Her smugness was a lovely, lovely thing, well worth the loss of a man's wits, his dignity, and every shred of his self-control. When Ethan shifted and the remains of his erection slipped from her body, she whimpered, and her fingers curled into fists on the pillow.

"I'll be back." Ethan kissed her nose and extricated himself from her embrace, tossing the sheets back off them both as he left the bed.

Alice watched him, fastened her gaze on his glistening cock, and watched while he washed off. He wrung out a clean flannel for her in the wash water, reminding himself next time—please, merciful heavens, let there be a next time—to keep some heating closer to the hearth.

"Spread your legs, love." He sat at Alice's hip and gazed down on the flushed, rosy front of her. "You are so lovely. I could just look at you and bring myself off."

"Is that what you did inside me?" She was watching him, her gaze soft and luminous in the candlelight. "Bring yourself off?"

"No." Ethan took her hand, put the cool cloth in it, and then pressed her hand to her sex. "*You* brought me off, spectacularly, I might add." Alice looked bashfully pleased with that, as he'd meant her to be—too pleased to be self-conscious about her ablutions.

As he watched her with the same shameless fascination she'd shown him, Ethan realized he loved her *and* he adored her.

"I enjoy this, Ethan. With you…" Her voice trailed away as if even words were too much effort. She slapped the cloth back into his hand.

"I will look forward to inflicting this pleasure on us both in future." Ethan eyed her sex, wishing he could light a hundred candles, the better to admire her by. "You are not sore, then?" He rose and rinsed the cloth again, hanging it over the edge of the washbasin before returning to the bed.

"You didn't answer me," Ethan said as he rejoined Alice beneath the sheets. "Talk to me, Alexandra. I'll fret that I was too demanding, too rough, too precipitous, too…"

She stopped him with a finger over his lips.

"Hush." She pushed him to his back and straddled him. "You are too desirable, too skilled, too generous, too careful, too worried, entirely too handsome, too dear, and inside me…" She cuddled down onto his chest.

"Inside you?" Ethan's hands came up to stroke her back, to learn yet more of the wonder of her.

"Too perfect," Alice finished, her tone smug and wistful at once. "I had no idea, Ethan Grey. No earthly idea, and I account myself a woman with an excellent education and a good imagination."

"You have a wonderful imagination, though I've only ever heard you turn it to wolves, witches, and sea monsters."

"Interesting point, and you are none of those, but, Ethan?"

"I'm listening," he said, though it was difficult to hear her over all that singing in his soul.

"I was worried," Alice said, her voice getting softer. She nuzzled at his shoulder for a moment before raising her face to meet his gaze.

"Tell me these worries, that I might disabuse you of them."

And he meant that. He wanted her passion; he
wanted her worries, her everything.

"I was worried." Alice ducked her face against his
sternum. "Worried I would have a breathing spell, that
I would not be skilled enough to please you, that it
would all be awkward and embarrassing and regrettable."

"And?" Ethan's caresses were purposely slow and
soothing, but he'd known some of the same worries,
and too often—with others—they'd been justified.

"And…" She hunched down more tightly to his
chest. "I never want to leave this bed, I never want
to put my clothes on, and I never want to let you out
of my sight."

His hands slowed further, for her honesty and
forthright speech reached into his shadowed soul like
beams of summer sunlight, but God Almighty, how
to respond?

Alice cocked her head to peer at him. "I suppose
I should not have said that. You will forgive me my
emotional excesses. I am all at sea."

"Your sentiments are reciprocated." He wanted
to say more but dared not. Not yet, and maybe not
ever. That she felt the least bit possessive of him
was… precious.

She lifted her face to his again, though this time she
was smiling at him.

"You aren't just being gallant, are you? I am not
accounted a sentimental woman, you know. I understand the intended nature of our dealings, Ethan."

"Hush." He gently pushed her back down into
his embrace lest she lecture him on the intended
nature of *her* dealings with him, and break his heart
all unknowing. "You need not retreat from honest

feelings, Alexandra. In fact, you must continue to set the better example for me in this regard."

"Me? Set an example for you?"

"You are brave to be so honest. I admire your courage."

"I am not brave. I am weak, wicked, and likely very foolish for disclosing my feelings to you."

"No." Ethan drew his fingers over her features. "You honor me, and you show me a kind of trust of which I hope to be worthy. I have not..." He gathered his courage and leapt headlong into an abyss of trust, because on this point he needed to be very clear.

"I have not *belonged* to anyone, Alexandra. When I was a boy, I thought I belonged to Bellefonte or to Nick or at least to Belle Maison. I was wrong. I thought I'd belong to my wife, but again, I was wrong. I haven't even truly belonged to my own children, at least until recently. If you do not want to let me out of your sight, it suggests I might belong a little to you, and I would be honored to think it so."

"You are mine," Alice said in fierce, certain tones. "In this bed, Ethan Grey, for the hours you share it with me, you are mine."

Ethan closed his arms around her. "And you are mine." And not, he silently added, just when we are together here. "Go to sleep, my love, and worry not. If you never allowed me another moment in your arms, I would still be forever in your debt."

"And I in yours."

In the darkest hour, before even the kitchen or the milkmaids rose, Ethan wakened and silently lectured himself to leave Alice in peace. The warmth of the bed was perfect though, and the feel of her in his arms...

His sigh of bliss—or perhaps his growing erection—wakened the lady around whom he'd wrapped himself.

"Go back to sleep, my dear." He brushed a kiss to her cheek. "You need your rest, and as to that, I will not come to you tonight, either, that you might have your sleep."

And that her inexperienced body might adjust to intimate relations.

Alice trapped his hand against her breast. "I do not think I will rest nearly as well without you as I do with you. Why is that?"

Ethan flexed his hips a little, enough to snug himself into the curve of her buttocks. "Because we fit."

"We do," Alice said, wiggling back a little against him. "You are a comfortable bedfellow, Mr. Grey, despite your penchant for hogging pillows."

Mr. Grey. He thanked a generous deity that he had lived long enough to hear her call him Mr. Grey naked in bed.

"You kick," Ethan said, pleased to no end she liked to cuddle with him.

"Never on purpose. If you don't come to me, I will miss you."

"If I don't come to you, you can be sure I am missing you as well. Now, leave off showing me your favorite toys, and try to get a little more sleep."

Alice reached around and closed her fingers around his cock. "My favorite toy is lacking some starch."

"Temporarily." Ethan held still while she caressed him, and he felt—God help him—lust roaring forth at her touch. He sat up and still didn't move beyond her grasp.

"Alexandra?"

She met his gaze, still holding his cock in a gentle grip.

The courage came more easily this time. "I leave you now, but part of me stays here with you, too. I would not go were it simply a matter of our pleasure—I hope you believe that."

"Of course you wouldn't." In the shadows of a setting moon, Ethan saw a grin spread across her face. "I would not allow it." She tugged his cock once for good measure then dropped her hand. "How will I face you at breakfast?"

He folded down over her and covered her chest with his own. "With a smile, at least. You must not feel ashamed. This has been a night of more beauty than…" He kissed her rather than attempt poetry.

"I'm not ashamed. I am overwhelmed and moved and pleased and grateful."

"Grateful?" Ethan levered up and considered the notion. "I should tell you that the gratitude is all mine, but who am I to tell you what to feel? I am grateful too, and nobody is going to talk me out of it. Now, sleep and dream of me."

He kissed her forehead, not daring to do more, drew the sheets up around her, and silently dressed in the dark. By the time he padded barefoot to her door, she was asleep, breathing easily, and he hoped, dreaming of him.

He moved silently down the hallway, turning the corner to move through the darkened house toward his own rooms, one floor down. He paused, though, and listened to a door opening in the nursery wing just behind him. The creak of the door was followed by a soft tap.

"Miss Alice?"

Jeremiah's voice, tentative and worried.

"Miss Alice?" Another tap, more definite, but Ethan was not about to let a child's nightmare or wet sheets disturb Alice's slumbers.

"Jeremiah?" Ethan hoped his impression of a papa coming to check on his children was credible. "Is something amiss?"

"Papa!" A wealth of relief flooded the boy's face. He was down the hall and wrapped around Ethan's legs in an instant. "Joshua doesn't feel well. He's hot, and he says he hurts all over."

Eighteen

Fever. BARBARA'S FINAL ILLNESS HAD STARTED WITH fever. Memories of helplessness and panic clawed their way into Ethan's mind.

"Let's see to your brother," Ethan said, picking Jeremiah up and returning him to his room. "It's probably just a passing cold or sore throat. He's been sick before, and I daresay he'll be sick again." He kept his tone brisk to hide his anxiety, but any minor illness or injury could claim a child's life. Colds turned into lung fever; cuts became infected; a bump on the head became a coma.

"Shall we fetch Miss Alice?" Jeremiah asked, glancing longingly at his governess's door.

Ethan hugged his son for reassurance. "Let her sleep for now. If Joshua is ill, we'll need to take turns sitting with him, and Miss Alice will need her rest. Joshua?"

"Papa?" The child's voice was groggy.

Ethan set Jeremiah down and sat on the narrow edge of Joshua's bed.

"Your brother says you are unwell." Ethan laid the back of his hand on Joshua's forehead. "I am inclined to agree. You have a fever, sir."

"I'm hot," Joshua muttered, shifting restlessly in his bed. "And I hurt, and my throat hurts, and I have to pee."

"The last is easily taken care of." Ethan flipped back the covers and hoisted Joshua from the bed.

"C'mon, Joshua." Jeremiah took his brother's hand, and while Ethan tried to calm the rising flood of panic in his gut, both brothers made use of the chamber pot.

Joshua blinked at his father and knuckled sleepily at one eye. "Is it time to get up yet?"

"Not quite." Ethan looked his son over. No red spots were emerging on the child's body, so the illness wasn't chicken pox. What else could it be? Barbara's typhoid had started just this way. "Joshua? Is your stomach at all sore?"

"A little." Joshua yawned as he stood before his father. "Here." He pushed on himself. "Not a lot, but achy."

Ethan ran a hand through his hair. "Back into bed with you, and back to sleep if you can manage it. We'll have you feeling better, though it may take some time and cooperation on your part. Jeremiah, I'll set Davey outside the door, and you'll call for him if there's need before I'm back."

"Yes, Papa." Jeremiah sounded worried but not as badly spooked as he'd been when Ethan had found him.

"I'll be back soon to make sure you're sleeping." He mustered a mock glower for Jeremiah's benefit. Joshua's eyes were already closed.

God above, Ethan was going to be sick, so miserably did anxiety choke him. He was standing beside Alice's bed without knowing how he got there, hating that he had to wake her but unable to manage otherwise.

"Sweetheart?" He crouched beside the bed, bringing his face level with hers. "Alice? Love? Wake up."

Her eyes drifted open, and she smiled at first then caught the worry in his eyes.

"The boys?" she guessed, flinging back the covers so fast Ethan had to rise and step away.

"Joshua is ill," Ethan said, hearing the tremor in his voice. "A fever, aches, and his stomach is sore."

"The bellyache might just be hunger," Alice said, grabbing her nightgown then tightly belting her wrapper. "He's been sleeping more lately, and I should have guessed he was coming down with something. It isn't the season for flu. Did you look at his stomach to check for chicken pox?"

"I looked at his arms," Ethan said, feeling a measure of relief. Alice wasn't ringing for a maid; she was preparing to deal with this herself. "No spots on his arms."

"They usually emerge on the belly first, but often not until the second day of illness." Alice tied her hair back with a ribbon then turned to regard Ethan steadily. "Children get sick, Ethan. If I had a week off for every time Pris came down with something, I'd be on holiday until May Day. You can't overreact."

Ethan ran a hand through his hair. "Joshua has all the initial symptoms of typhoid."

"If it is typhoid," Alice said, wrapping her arms around his waist, "we have a long, hard battle ahead, but he's a very healthy young fellow, Ethan, and we'll give him the best of care."

"Barbara had the best of care." His arms went around Alice automatically, and he held her just as desperately as he had at any point in the previous night. "Barbara died. It took weeks, and she suffered terribly, and Joshua is just a small child."

He buried his face against Alice's neck, lest any more such sentiment unman him.

"Ethan," she said, gently stroking his nape, "your son is small but vigorous, and he loves life. He loves you, his brother, and his pony. I daresay he even loves me a bit. He has much to live for, and we're going to help him."

He stepped back, though it was an effort.

"So sensible." And he didn't resent her for it; he treasured her all the more.

"Governesses pride themselves on being sensible. Now, off to the kitchen with you, Mr. Grey. Tell Mrs. Buxton what's afoot, and let her know we'll need willow-bark tea and feverfew for the fever and aches, a tisane of slippery elm for Joshua's throat, some cold water to bring the fever down. Then take yourself to the library to find us some decent reading books. And, Ethan?"

He paused with his hand on the doorknob, relieved to have something constructive to do.

"He will be fine," Alice said. "You must believe that, and you must reassure his brother of that."

Just as Alice was reassuring him.

❧

"Medicine for the boy, ma'am." Davey offered Alice a cautious smile when he met her at the door to the boys' room not ten minutes later. "Mr. Grey said you was to eat as well. There's tea and toast." Davey motioned to the tray as he set it on the table in the boys' room. "Mr. Grey said I'm to remain in the hall in case the boys need anything, so mind you ring if there's more you want. When Master Jeremiah wakes, I can set one of the other fellows to bide by the door, and take the boy to the stables to groom the ponies."

"That will help. Watching one's brother fall ill is no way for a boy to spend his day."

Davey gave a little bow and withdrew, but Alice had been glad for his presence. A governess could be the loneliest of creatures, neither family nor quite one of the upper servants.

She realized, as she pulled a rocking chair up to Joshua's bed, she felt a sort of belonging as a member of the household staff. She didn't belong to the other servants, or they to her, but all of them belonged to Tydings. And she belonged to the master of Tydings, for as long as he would have her.

And a little bit—more than a little bit—she belonged to the boys who slept so soundly in their beds. They'd stolen and stormed into her heart, into the empty place left by Priscilla's absence, and by the absence of any children of her own. She loved them for themselves, but loved them as well for being Ethan's sons, the little boys who were towing a big quiet man from shadows to sunlight, one pony ride, one tickling session, and one impertinent question at a time.

Joshua Nicholas Grey was not going to die. Alice would not allow it. She'd let down her sister and knew the bitterness of long regrets. She was not going to let down Joshua or Jeremiah or Ethan.

⤟⤞

Joshua continued to sleep, then awaken only to complain of his aches, sore throat, and fever. As uncomfortable as he was, Ethan knew the illness was likely to worsen at night. If it was typhoid, it could go on for weeks...

"Barbara's illness started off the same," Ethan said when Alice drew him across the hall into her room. He'd hovered near his son more and more closely as the day went along, first bringing his correspondence upstairs then abandoning any attempt at productivity. Jeremiah, at least, had gone out to the stables with Davey and groomed both ponies, then repaired to the hallway to beat Davey at Patience.

"Joshua does not have cramping of the bowels," Alice reminded him. She'd probably made the same point a half dozen times earlier in the day. "Intestinal distress is a hallmark of typhoid."

"I was tempted to send for Nick." Ethan looped his arms around Alice's waist and held her loosely, when what he wanted was to clutch her to him. "I thought about sending for him—Nick is the head of our family and travels easily and often—but I simply informed him Joshua was ill with fever and aches, a sore throat, and a tender stomach."

"You want Nick here because this is the first real illness in your household since your wife died. That's understandable, Ethan."

He didn't argue with her, but she didn't have the whole truth, either. No one did now, save Ethan, and he should probably leave it that way. Probably, but what if Joshua didn't recover?

He turned his thoughts from that hopeless outcome and extracted a promise from Alice to meet him in the garden for a walk before the light faded. She'd been in the sick room all day, and Ethan knew inactivity wasn't in her nature.

He left the nursery, able to do so only because Alice was with him in a way he could not have anticipated. He'd desired her, despite her severe buns, thick glasses, and governessy primness, because some part of him must have sensed this other beauty hidden as effectively as Alice's physical attractiveness.

Where she committed, Alice Portman stuck to her guns. She would no more leave Joshua's care in the hands of the maids than she would cast Ethan aside because he was gruff, lacked polish with the fairer sex, and hogged pillows.

She belongs to us, Ethan assured himself as he searched out Mrs. Buxton and ordered two baths and a hot meal. Alice did not yet know it, but she belonged not just to Ethan but to his boys as well.

And if there were a merciful God, they would find a way to keep her.

He was prowling in the library for books—Joshua and Jeremiah loved their stories—when his eyes strayed across the notes Heathgate left him regarding Hart Collins. They were sitting in plain sight, which was no doubt foolish, so Ethan folded them up and stuffed them into his waistcoat pocket. Choosing a storybook proved challenging, for Ethan had no idea which the boys had read, so he stacked a half dozen under his arm and headed back to the third floor.

When he gained the nursery, Jeremiah was sitting on his tidily made bed, watching Joshua sleep.

"He's going to die, isn't he?" Jeremiah's voice was steady, but when he drew in a breath, Ethan heard the worry filling him up. Ethan pulled up a rocking chair and lifted his firstborn onto his lap.

"From this?" Ethan glanced at Joshua too, and the

hectic pink spots on his cheeks. "Anything is possible, but I don't think so."

"Mama had fevers. She died."

"Right from the start of her illness, your mother had terrible trouble with her bowels, and Joshua hasn't had any. He has, however, been sleeping like an old dog, which makes me think his illness is different."

"I wanted the ponies to know what was going on. They would worry."

"Ponies are like that." Ethan hugged his son gently. "Governesses too, I think."

Jeremiah snuggled closer to his father. "Miss Alice doesn't act worried. You can tell if you look at her eyes, though. She doesn't like Joshua being sick."

"None of us do. If I don't want her to get sick, I'd best see Miss Alice gets some fresh air."

"I'll stay with Joshua." Jeremiah scrambled out of his father's lap. "I'll call Davey if Joshua wakes up. Don't worry, Papa. I'll look after him."

Ethan left on Jeremiah's childish assurance—there would be no moving the boy, in any case—and reasoning the sooner a papa left, the sooner he could return. He found Alice in her room, a shawl around her shoulders.

"It gets dark so much earlier," she said, "and I can smell autumn in the air."

"September has always felt melancholy to me," Ethan said, tucking her hand over his arm. "Summer is over, the land is preparing to go dormant for winter, and darkness presses in."

Then too, September was when the public schools began their academic year.

"My father used to hate it, because the boys went

back to school in the fall," Alice said as they made their way to the terrace. "I hated to see them go. The house always felt so much more alive with them around, but I liked the quiet, too."

"So you could read your books," Ethan guessed as they emerged onto the back terrace. "It is cool out, isn't it?"

"Cool and beautiful. Look at the moonrise."

A big fat yellow moon was drifting up through the trees, spreading its silvery light over the asters and chrysanthemums. "I'm glad we're out here to see this."

"You're warm enough?"

"I'm fine." Alice smiled, but even by moonlight, Ethan could see she was tired. He settled an arm around her shoulders as they walked and felt her arm steal around his waist. They eventually found the bench under the oak and watched as the moon rose over the gardens. Conversation wasn't necessary, just the peaceful moonrise and Alice's company.

As close as they'd been in her bed the previous night, Ethan felt just as close to her now.

"Shall we return to the house?" Ethan asked. "I've ordered you a bath too, but trays in the library for us first."

"Food sounds good. Worrying is hungry work, and soon enough all the vegetables will be in the cold cellar." They made the distance in companionable silence. Ethan held the door for Alice then touched her arm.

"Let me have your shawl." He drew it from her shoulders and folded it before handing it back to her, and the expression on Alice's face gave him pause.

A small thing, to fold a lady's shawl for her. Some

might say presumptuous; others might say husbandly. All that mattered was what Alice would say. "What?"

"Nothing." Alice tucked the shawl over her arm. "To the library?"

"For sustenance, though I want to go bounding up those stairs and stare Joshua back to health."

"Come eat, Mr. Grey, or the food won't be hot."

He was storing up a treasure house of her various *Mr. Greys*: stern, affectionate, reassuring, passionate...

Ethan let her draw him into the library, where a tea cart was crowded with dishes. The ambrosial scents of roasted beef and fresh bread wafted up from steaming trays. He stared at his plate when they took places side by side on the couch. "I can't eat all of this."

"You can." Alice flipped her serviette onto her lap. "You skipped lunch and tea, and you are a substantial fellow who needs his sustenance. If you fall over in a swoon, I won't be able to catch you. Salt?"

"Please." Ethan unfolded his napkin and began cutting his roast of beef. "Good Lord, this smells delicious. Will you marry me?"

"Of course not." Alice smiled at her plate. "You're out of your head with hunger, fatigue, and worry. I could use that salt when you're done with it."

Ethan stuffed a bite of meat into his mouth, utterly flummoxed at the question that had come from his lips. Where on earth—where in heaven or on earth—had those words come from? He'd meant them, of course, but thank God Alice had taken them as teasing.

They consumed good beef, green beans, fresh bread, pears, and cheese, limiting their discussion to the meal.

"More salt?"

"Excellent roast."

"This cheese goes well with the fruit."

One remark after another, each reassuring Ethan that his proposal had indeed been taken in jest. No harm done. To Alice, at least. He chewed mechanically, wondering if it was better to be rejected as only proposing in jest, or to be rejected because he'd meant each word with his whole heart.

When they finished their meal, Ethan chased Alice off to soak in a hot bath. She went without protest, perhaps sensing Ethan wanted some time with his sons. When she rejoined Ethan in the nursery, Jeremiah slept, and Joshua dozed in Ethan's arms.

"I wanted to hate him when he was born," Ethan said. Alice settled near him on the end of Joshua's bed as he spoke. "He was the ultimate symbol of my failure as a husband, as a man. And yet…" Ethan gazed down at his son. "One day, he smiled at me and grabbed for my nose. Jeremiah wanted to hold him, and the nursery maids wouldn't countenance such a thing. I held Jeremiah with one arm and the baby with the other, and I was… lost."

"You're not lost now. Not you, not Joshua, not Jeremiah. You've found each other."

"We have. I don't intend to lose either one of my sons."

Alice gave a fierce little nod. "That's the spirit."

"But I nearly did, Alice." Ethan started rocking slowly. "I convinced myself my children were red-faced, squalling, malodorous, ceaselessly needy little beasts. How could I have been so wrong?"

"You weren't wrong. You've described the average

baby, though you left out the part about how irresist-ibly lovable they are."

"Irresistibly," Ethan agreed, kissing Joshua's fore-head. "He's still hot."

Alice reached out and laid the back of her hand on Joshua's forehead.

"No hotter than he was this morning. I think he'll be fine, Ethan, though I've never seen this illness in another child."

"Nor have I, and my siblings were forever coming down with this or that ailment. We lost two babies, further down the line from Nick and me."

"A large family seldom sees all the children survive to adulthood. My mother was fortunate all four of us did."

Ethan cuddled his son a little closer. "One marvels such a slight person should create so much noise for the sheer hell of it."

"He does it in part to keep Jeremiah from growing up too fast."

"That one." Ethan's gaze traveled to where his older son slept on his side. "He reminds me of myself now, while Joshua reminds me of myself as a child."

"Quite a contrast. It's hard to imagine you as devil-may-care as Joshua, but time changes us."

"Some of us. You're exhausted, Alice. Why don't you lie down across the hall, and I'll rouse you if Joshua should worsen?"

Alice rose tiredly. "I'm going to set a good example for you. I'm going to get some rest because I most assuredly do need it." She leaned down to brush a finger down Joshua's cheek then bent to kiss the top of Ethan's head. "Wake me when you need a break, Ethan, and no heroics. Jeremiah will explode with worry if you fall ill."

Ethan let her go, though just the one little whiff of her lemony scent brought peace to his soul. Alice turned to leave, pausing to pull the covers up over Jeremiah and tuck them in around him more snugly.

I love her. For those little maternal gestures and how naturally they come to her with these children, I love her.

Alice opened the door then stepped back abruptly. "Nicholas?"

෴

One didn't mistake Nick Haddonfield's presence, and there he was in the corridor, looking large, wind-blown, and worried. Alice stepped back to let him into the nursery.

"Ethan sent a pigeon, and the roads were dry, and I don't suppose…" Nick peered past Alice to where Ethan cradled Joshua in the rocking chair. "Is Joshua all right?"

"Nicholas." Ethan rose, Joshua sleeping in his arms, and surveyed his brother. "You traveled all this way because my son is ill?"

"He's going to recover, isn't he?" Nick's gaze traveled from his brother to his nephew. "He looks fevered."

Alice tried to fathom the currents swirling between the two brothers, because Nick wasn't just worried about the boy.

"Joshua started a fever last night. I can't believe you came."

"I'll leave in the morning," Nick said. "I know I'm not invited, but I was worried, and I also know what a sick child can mean to a parent's peace of mind…"

Ethan shifted his son and extended a hand to his brother. "I am glad you're here. I am really, honestly glad you're here." The words sounded heartfelt. As Alice watched, Nick's features smoothed.

He'd been uncertain of his reception. The Earl of Bellefonte had been prepared to be politely rebuffed by his own brother—or perhaps, not so politely.

"He's sleeping very soundly," Nick observed. "Has he been bled?"

"I'll not have it," Ethan replied, laying Joshua in his bed and drawing up the covers. "He's weak as it is, and bleeding never did anybody I know of any good."

"I see." Nick looked uncomfortable again.

"You don't agree?" And now Ethan sounded wary too. Jeremiah stirred in his sleep, while Alice didn't want to leave Ethan and Nick alone.

"I brought a physician with me, Ethan, and please hear me out."

Ethan straightened the covers around Joshua and brushed a hand over the child's forehead. "I'm listening."

"Fairly doesn't like bleeding either," Nick said, "and he's a member of the Royal College, but he also apprenticed to a ship's doctor. He's not just an old windbag spouting Latin and carrying around a jar of leeches."

"I should hope not. Is this the fellow I met at Papa's funeral?" Still, Ethan regarded his ailing child.

"You did, but my manners are remiss. Alice, a pleasure to see you, though you look exhausted."

"She is," Ethan rejoined, holding out a hand to Alice. She crossed the room at this gesture of invitation then nearly stumbled when Ethan captured her hand and drew her against his side. "I've kept her up to this ungodly hour because she is in charge of Joshua's care, and my gratitude to our Alice is without limit."

Our Alice. She hoped it meant his, Joshua's, and Jeremiah's, and maybe even a little bit Nicholas's too.

Nick grinned at her. "Didn't take you long to have him eating out of your hand. Let me fetch Viscount Fairly. He'll want to talk to Alice before ordering her off to bed."

Nick was back in a moment, bringing with him a tall blond man whose looks Alice would describe as beautiful but unsettling. In the dim light, it took her several minutes to discern that his eyes were two different colors, one blue and one green. Those eyes bore a light of kindness, though, and she was profoundly grateful to Nick for bringing some real medical expertise to the situation.

"Your patient," Alice began, "is five going on six and answers to Joshua Nicholas Grey. He is as rambunctious as the day is long, and generally quite, quite sturdy. About a week ago, we noticed his energy flagging, and he began taking afternoon naps and coming down late for breakfast. Last night, an hour or so before dawn, his brother, Jeremiah, found him fevered."

"Other symptoms?" the physician asked.

"Body aches, particularly in his neck, tummy, and upper arms, and this great fatigue. His throat is sore, but it doesn't seem severely painful. His appetite is off, though his bowels do not pain him. He drinks all the vile potions we force on him then goes back to sleep. He's just… ill."

"I don't want to talk out of turn," Fairly said, "but given the symptoms you've listed, I can bet it isn't typhoid, malaria, or cholera, neither does it smack of lung fever. We might have some version of influenza here, but I'd like to examine the child, if you don't mind waking him."

"I'm up." Joshua struggled to sit up in his bed. "Is that Uncle Nick?"

"I'm up, too," Jeremiah chorused. "Joshua, do you have to pee?"

"In private," Joshua intoned truculently, glancing at the four adults in his bedroom.

"You can use my room," Alice said. "I'll have some food and drink put together for our guests." She slipped from the room, hoping that between the physician and the little boys, neither Ethan nor Nick would do or say anything untoward.

❧

Despite Joshua's illness, despite the lateness of the hour and the relative crowd in the children's room, Ethan watched Alice go.

Nick's smile as Ethan's gaze collided with his was sweet and knowing.

Well, what of it?

When the boys returned, Nick excused himself as well, muttering something about seeing how Alice fared in the kitchen.

Joshua peered at his father before climbing back into bed. "Are you leaving, Papa?"

"Good heavens," the physician said, "he can't leave, because then we'd have no one to make the introductions, and wouldn't that be awkward?"

Joshua smiled tentatively at that sally, while Jeremiah's expression was unconvinced.

"Viscount Fairly," Ethan began, "may I make known to you my sons, Master Jeremiah Nicholas

Grey, and your patient, Master Joshua Nicholas Grey. Boys, his lordship is a physician who was good enough to come here with Uncle Nick."

Jeremiah took his father's hand and aimed a worried look upward. "You won't let him bleed Joshua?"

"I will not," Ethan said. "No matter how Joshua begs and pleads and longs for a truly impressive scar. Now back into bed, both of you."

"Yes, Papa." Joshua's voice conveyed fatigue, even in two little words.

The physician sat on the child's bed. "Joshua, I must have your assistance if we're to find an answer to what's plaguing you. Will you give me your hand?"

Joshua complied and was taught how to feel a pulse by holding two middle fingers against Lord Fairly's wrist. They compared pulses and tongues and heartbeats and breathing sounds, aches, and pains until Joshua was yawning again. All the while, Fairly had plied the child with questions, probed gently for soreness and swelling, and conducted a far more thorough examination than the interrogation-and-prescribing Ethan had usually seen pass for medical science.

"You're tired now?" Fairly asked Joshua.

"Beat. I can't stay up at all."

"Then go back to sleep. You've been very patient with me, but I think you're wise to be sleeping so much, Joshua."

Joshua flopped down onto his bed. "I'm just tired."

"You're smart," Fairly countered, pulling the covers up over the boy. "The more you sleep, the sooner you'll heal, so sleep to your heart's content."

"G'night, Papa." Joshua cracked his jaw and closed his eyes. "G'night, Doctor."

"Good night, Son." Ethan pressed a kiss to Joshua's brow. "Sweet dreams. And you"—Ethan turned to spear Jeremiah with a look—"your brother is going to be fine, but he needs rest, so no keeping him up with your usual ruckus."

"I don't make a ruckus," Jeremiah protested, but he was smiling bashfully. "Unless Joshua makes one with me."

"Like the time you climbed down the tree in the middle of the night," Ethan reminded him, "and tried to take your ponies for a romp when there was no moon at all. Dream of that, why don't you?"

"Good night, Papa." Jeremiah turned to his side, probably the better to keep an eye on his brother. "And good night, Lord Fairly."

Ethan led the physician from the room, closed the door quietly, and rounded on him. "You're sure of that? Sure Joshua just needs to rest?"

"As sure as a physician can be," Fairly said, "which is short of certain but well past maybe."

Relief coursed through Ethan, leaving a light, exhausted feeling and a need to see Alice and share the news with her. "Let's go downstairs. Alice will have put together something to eat, and I don't trust Nick not to be bothering her."

"Bothering her? I understood your brother to be devoted to his countess."

"He is, but he's Nick, and he and Alice are friends of some sort, and those whom he cares for, Nick must bother, particularly the females."

"I see." Clearly, Fairly didn't see, but he was too polite to comment further. Polite or exhausted.

"You must have ridden like demons," Ethan said as they neared the kitchen.

"Nick lit out as soon as your pigeon landed. I live west of him, so I was on his way. Letty said I must come, because she would not fare well were illness to befall Danny or Elizabeth, and Nick would never ask if it weren't important to him."

"I gather Danny and Elizabeth are your children, and Letty your viscountess."

"My wife. My goodness." Fairly came to a halt before the tray Alice had sitting on the kitchen counter. "I had better be hungry."

"No," Alice said, "you had better be fast, or Nick will eat all of this before you can finish a proper grace. How is Joshua?"

"He's a very interesting case study," Fairly replied. "He will be fine, in my opinion, but he's likely to be tired for weeks yet, if not months."

Nick looked up from where he was slicing cheese at the long wooden counter. "Glandular fever? I didn't know it afflicted children."

"It isn't supposed to," Fairly said. "We know it as a young person's disease, and being young people, those who fall ill try to bounce back too quickly and end up right back in bed. It will be interesting to see how Joshua recovers, but by all means, encourage him to rest at every opportunity."

"We can do that," Alice said, her gaze glancing off Ethan's.

"And we can feed our guests," Ethan said, "if you'll stop slicing that entire wheel of cheese, Nicholas, and put that knife to use on the beef roast."

"I've put on a pot of tea," Alice said, "but I'm thinking you gentleman might want something stronger."

Nick beamed his approval. "Excellent thought,

lamby-pie. My tender parts were in the saddle too long, and I am in need of something medicinal."

"You are in need of a spanking," Alice said, "as usual. Ethan, if you will fetch some brandy, I will find us some plates."

Lord Fairly and Nick exchanged bemused smiles as Ethan meekly left to do his governess's bidding.

❧

Ethan hadn't meant to bother Alice, but the silky curve of her bottom snuggled against his groin bore predictable results. He was half-asleep when he realized he was already shifting his hips lazily against her, seeking entrance, seeking the comfort and joy of intimate union with her. He gathered Alice in his arms and adjusted the angle of her hips, nuzzling her sex with his cock even as he buried his lips against her neck.

It was relaxing in a way he hadn't experienced before, to join like this, letting arousal seep into all the tired and worried parts of him. He tried to find the same pleasure for Alice, stroking her back and arm and shoulders and hips with his hand, keeping his rhythm lazy and peaceful. After long, sweet minutes of that, she put his hand on her breast and began to shift with him.

"Easy," Ethan whispered. "Let it steal up on you, like sleep." Her grip on his hand loosened, her hips became less urgent, and she brought his hand to her mouth to kiss his palm. A few minutes later, Ethan felt her sex drawing on him in long, intensely pleasurable pulls. When he was sure she'd had her satisfaction of him, he let himself go in a similarly gratifying yet oddly peaceful orgasm.

He lay with her in his arms, gratitude nearly making

him weep. Alice tucked his hand around her breast and squeezed his fingers gently. *Hold me.*

He'd like nothing better, for the rest of his life. He untangled his fingers from hers and patted her behind gently.

"I'll be right back."

As he tended to their ablutions, Ethan considered what lay between him and taking Alice as his wife. It was true he was illegitimate, but he was also the son of an earl, and wealthy. The stigma of his bastardy hardly seemed to matter, at least to those whose opinion mattered to him.

It was also true, though, Alice didn't entirely trust him. He'd offered to listen to whatever scandal haunted her past, and she had declined to tell him. Scandals that sent a woman hundreds of miles from home, drove her from her only sister, and made her seek obscurity for the rest of her days were serious business. Ethan sensed without being told Alice would not marry anybody without confiding the details of her past. She would be honest both to assure herself her prospective spouse could weather the consequences, but also to give that man the last chance to betray her trust.

Ethan would not betray her trust. She could have ten children out of wedlock or have attempted to assassinate Wellington, and he would not betray her trust. Barbara had betrayed his trust as intimately and permanently as a wife could, and still, Ethan had understood, eventually, what she'd done and why.

He was already back in bed, arms around his prize, when he realized, in the twilight between sleeping and waking, the greatest barrier between him and a future with Alice was his trust of her.

Before he proposed in earnest—again in earnest—he'd have to tell her exactly what went on with Hart Collins all those years ago. Heathgate's lectures to the contrary, reality to the contrary, Ethan still felt in his weaker moments responsible for what had happened to him and shamed by it. He should have been more careful; he should have never antagonized such a petty bully; he should have fought all six of them off.

He should have killed himself rather than live with the shame of surviving.

Old, hopeless thoughts, but they were losing their power over him. He breathed in lemon verbena and hope, and let sleep claim him.

❧

At breakfast, Fairly had confirmed a diagnosis consistent with a version of glandular fever, and prescribed unlimited rest and comfort nursing. Jeremiah had towed Alice out to the stables to tell the ponies this good news, leaving Ethan to regard his brother.

The brother whom he had never been so glad to see as he had the previous night.

"Come with me, Nicholas. There are some things I want to show you, and I think I left them in the corner parlor."

Still munching on a piece of buttered toast, Nick ambled along at Ethan's side. "When are you going to marry Alice?"

"When she'll have me," Ethan said. "One doesn't want a woman to get notions about repairing to the North because her employer can't stop proposing to her."

"Have you tried proposing to her? I don't think many have."

"Have you?" The question was out of Ethan's mouth before he could stop it, and he really did not want to know the answer.

"I have not. She's far too managing for me, meaning no disrespect to my countess, who had to sneak up on me from behind, so to speak. I would not have married Leah, either, had I been of sound mind."

"Let's be grateful she did sneak up on you." Ethan opened the door, went to the middle of a small parlor finished in green décor and slightly musty with disuse, and swung his gaze in a circle. "I want you to have these." He collected the miniatures from a quarter shelf and held them out to Nick, but Nick's attention was riveted on the portrait hanging over the fireplace.

Nick cocked his head to study the portrait. "Is this your late wife? She was very attractive, but I have to admit she looks more than passingly familiar."

Seeing the shrewd light of curiosity in Nick's eyes, the strength of the intelligence with which he studied Barbara's portrait, Ethan felt despair flooding all the relief and pleasure the day—the season, his life—had held.

How could he have been so stupid? He'd kept that portrait for his sons, and to remind himself of his own folly, but he'd come haring up here, intent only on giving Nick some symbol of his unconditional welcome into Ethan's family.

And one brief moment of thoughtlessness was going to cost him most of what mattered to him—Nick, their siblings at Belle Maison, and possibly the son who even now battled to overcome a frightening illness.

How could he have been so damnably, utterly, unforgivably stupid?

Nineteen

"SHE HAS THE LOOK OF THE BOYS ABOUT HER." NICK went on peering at Barbara's image, ignorant of Ethan's world crashing to pieces. "I'm sure I was introduced to her, wasn't I? Did she mention it?"

Ethan could say nothing, could do nothing save stand there with two little portraits clutched in his hands.

"Ethan?" Nick took a step toward him. "Are you all right?"

Ethan shook his head, his eyes on the portrait of his late wife. He'd paid well for it, and it was a good likeness, the lady's gaze conveying a kind of brittle, mocking gaiety. At one side of the portrait a blond man stood, his back to the viewer, only a portion of his head and shoulder visible. The lady smiled at him, but also at the viewer, and the overall impression was one of irony, despite the subject's compelling blond beauty.

The design had been Barbara's. When Ethan had seen the completed image, he'd wanted to burn it on the spot.

"I assume that fellow on the left is you?" Nick asked, frowning.

Ethan considered lying then considered that Nick would figure out the lie sooner or later.

"It isn't me," Ethan said on a heavy sigh. He returned the miniatures to the quarter shelves, feeling moments trickle by like the sands in a glass.

Nick crossed the room to stand behind Ethan. "What aren't you telling me?" He sounded wary and puzzled, not yet furious. He would be furious and likely stay that way.

Ethan would not turn and face him. "You don't want to know, Nick."

Behind him, Ethan felt Nick pull himself up to his full height. "I do want to know. Tell me, Ethan. What fellow is the lady regarding with such mocking irony?"

Ethan put his hand out and steadied himself on the wall, feeling winded or aggrieved and barely able to keep to his feet.

"She's looking at you, Nick," Ethan said, turning to behold the portrait. "My wife is looking at her lover, and that man is you."

Nick backed away, expression horrified. "I did not dally with your wife, Ethan. I would have known… I didn't…" He scrubbed a hand over his face, and Ethan watched as Nick's nimble mind started sorting and comparing, recalling and rejecting.

Ethan could at least spare his brother the uncertainty.

"You didn't even know I had a wife until this spring," Ethan said. "You didn't know I had sons or a wife."

"But she was your *wife*," Nick protested. "I have not slept with females named Grey. I haven't, Ethan. I wouldn't."

"And how would you know what a woman's last

name was, Nick?" While Nick looked to be reeling with shock, all Ethan could muster was sadness. He dropped onto the couch, feeling as tired as Joshua had been acting. "You take their word for who they are, you take their bodies for what they want to share with you, or you did until you married."

"Christ…" Nick eyed the portrait with what looked like loathing. "I slept with your wife. You're sure?"

"She told you her name was Barbara Fitzherbert, thinking it a great jest to poke fun at Prinny's old amour," Ethan said. "She was angry at me, Nick, angry at her life. She'd had my child, and I remained unwilling to squire her about in society or admit her back to my bed. When I departed for business in Copenhagen, she went prowling, with revenge on her mind."

Nick eyed Ethan with the same expression he'd turned on the portrait. "I cannot believe you haven't killed me or at the least called me out. How long have you known about this?"

"Oh, let's see." Ethan closed his eyes, the better to toss all hope, all caution, and all sense to the wind. "Joshua is going on six, so nearly seven years."

Nick's eyes narrowed. "What has my nephew to do with this?"

Ethan said nothing, feeling pity for his brother, for himself, and even for the departed Barbara.

"Ethan…" Nick began to pace, a big, caged animal in the grip of more emotion than even his grand body could hold. "Please tell me I did not plant a cuckoo in your nest… I could not live… Ethan?"

Ethan could not give his brother those words.

Nick turned toward the door, and rather than let

his brother bolt out of his life, Ethan was on his feet in an instant.

"Don't leave." Ethan was at the door, blocking Nick's exit bodily. "It's as much my fault as anyone's, Nick." It being Barbara's scheming—not the child it had produced. Never Joshua.

"It can't be your fault, damn it." Nick backed away, looking like he wanted to destroy something, someone, anything. "How can you stand to look at me? I swived your wife, got her pregnant, and you're my brother, Ethan."

Ethan advanced on him, glad they were in a closed room where they were free to shout and worse. "That is the first sensible thing you've said: you're my brother. So sit your bony arse down and listen to me."

Nick closed his eyes, his big hands fisting. Ethan knew him and knew what he was thinking: *I've betrayed the one person I never wanted to hurt, and we are supposed to solve it with talk?*

Ethan shoved him down into a chair, taking the decision from him.

"Barbara was a kind of predator," Ethan said, keeping his voice even with effort. "She spied me, staked out with new wealth and no masculine confidence, and trained her crosshairs on me. Lady Warne nudged me to take her on as a mistress, and at first, I could not believe my good fortune. She was skilled."

Nick winced, nodded, and kept his silence.

"Too skilled," Ethan went on. "Even I could discern in a short time Barbara was tolerating my attentions, even as she pretended to encourage them. I began to see her less and less, but she'd made her plans for me, and I was as doomed as you were."

"I had choices, Ethan," Nick protested softly. "I always had choices."

"So did I," Ethan shot back. "Barbara conceived Jeremiah with all the forethought and planning in the world. She knew I would not *choose* to allow my son to be born a bastard, and she knew I'd capitulate to whatever she demanded to make it so. We married, and she immediately began taking other lovers, though she was at least amenable to discretion."

"Ethan, you don't have to tell me this."

"Yes, I do, so you will not blame yourself unnecessarily, Nick. You were stalked like prey, and I did not see it coming and did nothing to warn you. She went after me the same way and was still coming after me when she dragged you into her machinations."

"I had a choice," Nick repeated numbly.

"Nicholas!" Ethan glared at him, the urge to slap sense into the man nigh overwhelming. "Will you listen to me? When Barbara took up with her lovers, I warned her that our marriage was over. I would not escort her in public. I would not grant her marital favors. I traveled as much as I could. The more she begged and bargained and promised, the more excuses I found to leave her to her own devices. She told me she'd met you, and as much as threatened to have an affair with you. I didn't think even she would go that far, but she delighted—*delighted*—in announcing she had conceived your child. She said it was a belated Christmas present."

Nick stared at his hands in misery. "You're sure? Sure Joshua is my son?"

"I made sure there was at least a scintilla of doubt, and realized that I'd been a fool. Had I continued paying my wife even the casual attention of a normal husband, she likely would not have strayed, or at least not as wildly."

"I am going to be sick," Nick said on a sigh. "You're right. She was Barbara Fitzherbert to me. There weren't many people in Town, because it was the winter holidays, and she'd been cast into my path for the month or so before. She was pretty, charming, available, and amenable. I still recall some relief when she told me she was leaving for the country after Twelfth Night. She watched me... It wasn't a hungry gaze, but it made me uncomfortable."

"I saw you on the first day of the New Year," Ethan said. "Barbara's mood had shifted, from wronged and bitter to gleeful, as if she had a wonderful secret. I decided to follow her, and she met you in the park."

Nick nodded, though clearly details yet eluded his memory.

"Ethan, I am sorry. For whatever it's worth, I am so bloody sorry I could shoot myself."

Fortunately, he sounded as if the threat were rhetorical.

"I am sorry too, Nick." To say that felt astoundingly good. "I should have told you I was getting married, should have told you when Jeremiah was born. I should have told you the truth of my marriage. I should not have let it become one more thing separating me from you and from my family."

"Don't be so bloody noble," Nick said bitterly. "I was a stupid, heedless billy goat, and my weakness was used to hurt you. I hate that, and now we have a child conceived in the midst of this deceit and stupidity, and I don't know how you can stand the sight of him, much less me."

The answer to that was so simple Ethan should have seen it years ago. "Even if he's your son, I had no choice but to love him."

"My son." Nick turned away, his voice dripping with self-loathing. "God help me, I will have to tell Leah this. Short of that, I will honor your wishes, provided no harm comes to Joshua."

As an earl, Nick had influence that far exceeded Ethan's, and maybe this was why the truth had remained Ethan's secret for so long. That Nick would not wield his power unfairly came as a relief and brought with it a burden of compassion. "If you were his father, Nicholas, what would you wish for Joshua now?"

"Love him," Nick said, voice breaking. "Love him like he was your own, because as far as I'm concerned, he is your own. He's such a busy little man, all smiles and energy and galloping everywhere... Jesus."

He dropped onto the sofa like a stone, looking bewildered and uncertain for all his size and muscle. "Can't you at least call me out?"

Ethan knew the exact contour of his brother's sorrow: for the little boy created so carelessly, for the brother betrayed, for the stupid young man who might have sired a child without thought, and for the father who hadn't known his own son.

And Ethan could not allow Nicholas to hold that sorrow too closely. "We'll manage. I didn't want this to hurt you, too."

"How could it not?" Nick pressed the heels of his hands to his eyes. "You can't tell him, Ethan. I won't have the child suffer what you went through because I couldn't keep my damned pants on."

Ethan sat beside his brother. Any closer than that, and Nick would likely have tossed him through the window. "You and I are the only people who know the shadow on Joshua's paternity. Alice knows I may not be his father, but she will take that knowledge to her grave."

"You never told anyone?" Nick rose and went to stare out the window. "No one at all? Not in a bitter, drunken moment, not when you wanted to fling it in Papa's face, not when a sympathetic mistress tried to pry it out of you?"

"I've had no mistress since I married," Ethan said. "The whole business was too much bother, and it would have made me a little too much like my wife."

"Like me, you mean. You've been a damned monk, just as I suspected."

"Not a monk, Nick." Ethan sighed, sensing they were going to plow through more rough ground. "I had experiences at Stoneham—one experience, really—that rendered me all but indifferent to the pursuits you found so enjoyable before your marriage."

Nick's gaze shifted from the grounds beyond the window to his brother.

"What sort of experience?"

"One Hart Collins, now Baron Collins," Ethan said, and it was no relief, no relief at all to embark on this recounting—though neither did it engender the kind of choking shame it might have even a year ago.

"Collins rounded up his cronies, assaulted me in the stables my first week at school, and while they held me over a pickle barrel, raped me in the only manner one male can rape another. Heathgate came upon the situation while Collins was goading one of his minions to further violate me, and between us, we managed to break a number of bones." Ethan fell silent for a thoughtful moment. "I understand the term 'killing rage.'"

The words had come, Ethan marveled. They hadn't been delicate words, but saying them, saying them to Nick, had left him lighter, not heavier, in his heart.

"You were…" Nick sucked in a breath. "Buggered. Raped."

"Not a pretty word and not a pretty deed." And thank a merciful God, Nick wasn't scoffing at "school boy nonsense" or otherwise trying to diminish the vileness of the act. If he had, Ethan would have tossed *him* through the window. "It happened half a lifetime ago, Nick. I try not to dwell on it."

"You never said." Nick tone was accusing, quietly furious. "You never said a word, Ethan. You would not accept my letters. You would not see me. You shut me out, completely."

"This is why. It's hard to explain, Nick, what that kind of experience does to a young man. Ladies can be raped, and as gentlemen we protect them because they are vulnerable. A man does not conceive of himself being vulnerable in the same fashion. He just… does not conceive of it."

"You were raped at the school our father sent you to. Surely, somebody told him?"

"I assume they did, and he did nothing. I can hope he didn't know, but Heathgate's parents got involved, and the other boys were quietly sent home to recover. I haven't seen them since, nor have I wanted to."

"Hart Collins is a dead man."

Oh, Nicholas. He sounded every bit as fierce as Joshua or Jeremiah, and yet Ethan could not indulge him.

"No. You cannot kill him out of guilt over what he did to me, Nick. And I will not take justice into my own hands. If I accused him publicly, he'd be tried in the Lords, and I am, after all, merely an earl's by-blow. Then too, for all I know, the statute of limitations has run. If he keeps a wide berth from me, I'll let it lie."

The ire in Nick's gaze did not diminish, and that was good to see, too. Misguided, but good to see. "That is not right, and you know it. You have been wronged—by me, but apparently by others as well—and Collins should at the least be gelded for what he did."

"He should, for he left me all but gelded in spirit. It was part of the reason I was so willing to enjoy what Barbara offered."

"And what was my excuse?" Nick said, self-disgust resurging. "I went larking and swiving on my merry way, content to leave you to your suffering."

"That is your heartbreak talking," Ethan said gently. "You were the one who arranged for us to meet at Lady Warne's after so many years of silence. That... was timely. I was done with university, and I still hadn't been able to regain my balance in certain areas." The word for it was impotence. Ethan had read the medical treatises, hoping desperately it was a medical problem, knowing it was not. "I was on the verge of"—he looked for another delicate phrase, and abandoned the search—"making a permanent mistake. I felt hopelessly dirty, unlovable, useless, and ugly. It was five years later, and I still felt... Then I got your note, and you said you had to see me again, that my siblings worried for me and asked for word of me. It was more timely than you will ever know."

Silence stretched, while Ethan's gaze sought the miniatures of his sons. A man could not promise to keep his loved ones safe from all harm, else Joshua would not have fallen ill. If any son of Ethan's had endured what transpired at Stoneham, then Ethan could only hope he'd be the sort of father to know about it and take appropriate measures.

Somewhere in that sentiment lurked forgiveness for the old earl—an astonishing notion, and welcome. While a weight rose from Ethan's heart, Nick remained by the window, staring down at the Tydings park. "Ethan, what is that pony doing without its rider?"

Ethan was at the window in two steps, a father's dread congealing in his gut.

"That is Jeremiah's pony," Ethan said, "and he said nothing about riding out this morning, Nick. I don't think he'd leave the stables while his brother lies ill, not without a gun to his stubborn little head."

"Let's go." Nick beat Ethan to the door. "Alice went down to the stables with him, and I doubt she'd get on a horse without you there to supervise."

"For God's sake, make haste. We've trouble afoot."

❧

"Why in the hell did you turn the damned pony loose?" While Alice watched in horror, Hart Collins turned his gun barrel on his own minion.

"Begging your lordship's pardon," Thatcher drawled back. "You were going to shoot the pony, and that would have brought half the shire down on us in a heartbeat, since Grey is known not to hunt game. The little beast will stop and graze hisself into a colic as soon as he's over the rise. Now, we'd best stop arguing and get moving, or your little plan to hold the brat for ransom will be over before it starts. With these two"—he gestured to Alice and Jeremiah doubled up on Waltzer—"we're not going to move quickly."

"Oh, yes, we are." Collins's eyes gleamed with malice. "Grey's mounts are prime flesh, and we've got three of his best horses here. If anyone slows us down, it will be you, and if you're caught, you'll hang for horse thievery."

Alice knew not how it was possible, but in twelve years, Hart Collins had become uglier, meaner, and stupider. She sent up a prayer that Jeremiah at least came through this debacle safely.

"Let's go." Collins kneed Argus sharply, as Thatcher kept a sullen silence. "And you." He turned an evil smile on Alice. "Keep the boy quiet, or it will be a well-used body Ethan Grey ransoms—or two."

Alice nodded, but inside, her guts were churning as the horses cantered off at Collins's direction. Twelve years without laying eyes on Collins, and still, she became a terrified fourteen-year-old at the mere sight of him. He'd gained weight, and his hair was thinning, and the air of pure evil was thick around him, like a stench.

His plan was clear: hold Jeremiah for money, lots and lots of money. Ethan had the money and would turn it over along with both of his arms, his eyes, and his very life if it meant Jeremiah would be safe.

When Collins sent them pelting off through the woods, she clung to that thought, even as Jeremiah clung to her, his arms locked around her waist. He managed to whisper the occasional word of advice to her regarding control of the horse, but mostly, Alice sought not to fall off. She held the reins, but her control was limited by the lead rope kept in Thatcher's gloved hands and by the skirts she'd had to bunch awkwardly in order to sit astride the horse. Thatcher was mounted on Bishop, the gray nervous but still sane. Collins had appropriated Argus for himself and was apparently enjoying the horse's fights for control—enjoying the excuse to use crop and spurs on a high-strung animal.

"How much farther are we going?" Thatcher shouted to Collins. "Ye can't run the horses like this much longer."

A quarter mile later, Collins halted Argus with a jerk on the curb and led the way through a break in the trees lining the bridle path. Thatcher followed, with Waltzer on the lead rope bringing up the rear.

"Don't go inside the building," Jeremiah whispered. "I'll say I have to use the bushes."

Alice nodded, keeping her eyes forward. Her hip hurt like blazes from riding astride at breakneck speed, her hands ached from gripping the reins, and her head pounded with fear.

And anger.

She knew Hart Collins, knew him and hated him. She owed him two years of barely being able to walk, ten years of recurring pain in her hip, twelve years of not being able to look her only sister in the eye, and a lifetime of never feeling quite safe.

But Ethan would come. She'd stake her life on it. The question was, would he come in time?

❧

"Miller!" Ethan's bellow elicited a groan from an empty stall. Nick, Fairly, and Davey crowded on Ethan's heels.

"I'm a'right," Miller muttered, but he needed Ethan's assistance even to sit up.

"Fairly, you'd best have a look at him. Nick, help me saddle whatever's in here of the riding stock."

A big grey mare stood in her saddle and bridle in a loose box, her ears twitching in the direction of any sound.

"The bastards coldcocked me," Miller said as Fairly peered into his eyes. "I wasn't all the way gone. I heard 'em, and they got Miss Alice and Master Jeremiah. Damned if Thatcher didn't saddle the horses hisself."

"How many?" Ethan asked, barely able to keep from pounding something.

"Two, Thatcher and some nob." Miller winced as Fairly's fingers probed the back of his head. "Thatcher's on Bishop, Miss Alice was on Waltzer, the boy on his pony, and some fat, prancing ninny took Argus, gut rot him."

"Some fat, prancing ninny?" Ethan pressed. "Did you hear them address him? Did he have a name?"

"His lordship." Miller squinted, as if trying to force memory into the light. "Collard? Collar? No, Lord Collins. And baron. Thatcher called him baron. His lordship was not getting along with Argus."

Fairly glanced up from his patient. "Miller will be fine, eventually. If you're prudent, you'll wait for me and Nick to find mounts. If you're going to go off like a one-man column of dragoons, you'll take my mare and follow the pony's back trail."

Ethan nodded his thanks. "I'll need weapons."

"Pistols are in the coaches," Miller reminded him. "You can have my knife." He extracted a wicked-looking bone-handled weapon, provoking raised eyebrows from the other men. "You can't always shoot a horse what needs it, which means you have to cut the poor bastard's throat."

"Take mine as well." Nick held out a more delicate weapon, while Davey loped off in the direction of the coach house.

"Take mine too." Fairly's knife was plain, conveying its deadliness all the more effectively for the lack of ornamentation. "And the lady's name is Honey. Don't argue with her, ask. She'll take care of you if you're deserving."

"Honey." Ethan stuffed knives in his boots and at the small of his back. "Don't argue." He speared Nick with a look. "Heathgate's often out hacking at this hour. If you fired a shot, you might rouse him. I'll leave as much of a trail as I can, but they can't have gone far. Alice will slow them down if at all possible."

Nick led the mare from her stall. "I know this mare. You let harm befall her, Fairly will call you out."

"I'll send her home when I've found my quarry," Ethan replied, swinging up onto the horse right there in the barn aisle.

"Godspeed," Nick said, stepping back.

The mare trotted out into the brisk, early morning sunshine, responding to the tension around her despite the previous day's long journey. Ethan saw when he gained the lane that luck was with him. A layer of hoarfrost lay on the grass, the pony's little hooves leaving a clear trail to where a bridle path emerged from the trees. In the woods, the size of the group made the trail equally easy to follow. They'd been heedless of their trail, traveling two and three across, snapping branches, shuffling through fallen leaves, and stomping through damp ground at every turn.

At one point, Ethan thought he heard a twig snap behind him, but he wasn't about to pull the mare up and investigate. Collins had forced his party to move through the woods at a brisk canter, then stopped, paused, and turned the pony loose. He should have at least kept the pony with them, unless he wanted to invite pursuit.

But Collins was evil, and according to Heathgate, in need of coin—not brilliant. Ethan pressed on, one eye on the trail, one eye looking ahead for sign of the kidnappers. He wasn't even off his own property when he heard voices up ahead and brought his mare to an abrupt halt.

❧

"For God's sake, we're not even off Tydings land, Baron. Ye cannot stop here." Thatcher's tone was equal parts pleading and exasperation.

"He won't look in his own backyard," Collins retorted from atop a dancing Argus. "They never do, and there's no point haring all over the countryside when we can spend the morning in more enjoyable pursuits. Come nightfall, we'll meet up with my coach." His eyes landed on Alice, still glued to Waltzer's back, then his gaze narrowed, some of the avarice receding.

"I know you," he said. "I don't like you, but I know you."

"That be the governess, ye fool," Thatcher said. "Not somebody ye'd know."

"Baron Collins to you." Collins regarded Alice steadily. "Take off your glasses, governess, and be quick about it, or you'll regret it."

Her hands being tied at the wrists, Alice pulled her glasses off and handed them awkwardly over her shoulder to Jeremiah, whose hands were not bound.

"By God." Collins's face broke into a parody of a smile. "If it isn't little Lady Alexandra, slumming in the schoolroom. I knew her sister," he informed Thatcher. "In the biblical sense. Bitch threw me over just as we were about to cry the banns, if you can credit such a thing."

His jocular tone made Alice's flesh crawl, as did the surge of lust in his eye. Fortunately, he was enjoying his boasting and very likely enjoying the fear he saw in Alice's eyes as he nudged Argus over to stand next to Waltzer.

Collins used the butt of his crop to raise Alice's chin. "This one could have sworn out information against me, but she didn't. Probably hoping I'd be grateful, weren't you?"

"You are vile, and I should have laid information."

"You still could, but you won't, because there won't be enough left of you to speak coherently when I'm through with you. We'll let the lad watch, so he'll learn early the true purpose of a female."

"Not so fast, my lord." Ethan stepped out of the surrounding woods. "She might not be willing to swear charges against you, but I certainly am, now that you've been foolish enough to return to English soil."

Twenty

"WELL, IF IT ISN'T BELLEFONTE'S BY-BLOW, ALL GROWN up and calling me foolish." Collins sneered, dropping his crop. "I'm armed, I have the child, and I've reinforcements available. You're one man—half a man, if memory serves—and I've your son quite literally in my crosshairs."

Collins raised a pistol and cocked the hammer, the barrel aimed directly at Jeremiah. Alice succeeded in shifting Waltzer so her body was between the gun and the child, but Collins only grinned.

"Oh, well done." He leered at her over the gun, and Alice felt her gorge rise. She did not, however, feel her breathing hitch—not in the slightest. "You won't do the boy any more good than you did your sister, *your ladyship*. At this range, the bullet will pass through you and make quite a mess of him as well."

"Shoot them both," Ethan said, sauntering forward. "She's a governess, and he's a brat. Why on earth would you trouble yourself to make off with a little pismire pony like him anyway? It's my horseflesh I object to parting with."

It was an odd way to refer to one's firstborn son, but Jeremiah was small, if not quite ant-like. He was also paying attention; behind Alice's back, she felt him tense, as if readying for something.

"His pismire pony of a brother is just as bad." Ethan's tone was bored, while Alice felt the child's arms tighten around her waist and wondered what had just passed between father and son. If somebody yelled that particular phrase, there was a good chance…

Ethan arched an arrogant eyebrow. "So what do you want, Collins? You expect me to pay money for this folly? And you, Thatcher. Perhaps you're another one of Collins's reluctant conquests. Welcome to the club, I understand there are more like us. Phillip Edmonton, Beauvais Morton, Henry Fentress, and many others."

"Buggery?" Thatcher's brows drew down in horror. Alice gathered that in Thatcher's personal hierarchy of felons, the baron's predilections placed him well below a mere kidnapper of children, horse thief, or raper of women.

And there Ethan stood, facing the one who'd done him such violence.

Behind her, Jeremiah tightened his arms more, as if he were tensing—

When Collins swung to face Thatcher, Ethan threw up both arms and charged Argus, bellowing at the top of his lungs. Jeremiah added to the commotion by similarly hollering at the top of his lungs then wrenching himself over Waltzer's side, dragging Alice off the horse with him. Bishop, apparently at his wits' end with the morning's doings, reared until his burden fell from his back. As Argus shied violently, the baron toppled from the saddle then rose to his feet, aiming his pistol directly at Ethan.

"Get back, Grey, or I'll shoot!"

Ethan charged him, grabbing the gun barrel and forcing it aside. Ethan was larger than Collins and likely in better condition, but Alice suspected meanness also gave a man strength. They grappled over the gun while Jeremiah struggled to undo Alice's bonds.

As the binding on Alice's wrists gave way, Ethan's knee came up into Collins's groin with savage force. Collins dropped like a stone into the dirt while Ethan held the gun on him.

"Heathgate," Ethan called. "Show yourself."

The marquess emerged from the trees, leading both his chestnut and a gray mare Alice did not recognize. He tied up the mares and headed for Collins's prone form as Jeremiah pelted across the clearing into his father's body.

"We did it!" Jeremiah crowed. "We sent the bloody blighters packing! Wait 'til I tell Joshua. Papa, you were wonderful, and I got it, didn't I? I'm a pismire pony!"

"You are brilliant." Ethan picked his son up and hugged the child tightly. "You saved the day, and likely Miss Alice as well."

Both of them turned radiant smiles on Alice where she reclined with no dignity whatsoever on the hard ground.

"Alice?" Ethan knelt beside her, Jeremiah standing at her shoulder. "Sweetheart, is something amiss?"

Now he called her sweetheart, before the child and with the marquess hovering nearby. Alice closed her eyes and swallowed. "Something's wrong with my back or my shoulder."

Or both and everything in between. She did not want to cry before Jeremiah, did not want to diminish the heroics of the moment, but she could hardly draw breath for the pain.

"Hurts?" Ethan asked quietly.

"Hurts badly." Alice tried to nod but abandoned the movement. Even swallowing somehow hurt her shoulder, and now—how marvelous!—the marquess was glowering down at her too.

"It's probably dislocated," Ethan hazarded. "We'll fetch Fairly, and he can have a look at you. Can you sit up?" She did, but only with Ethan's assistance, and she felt a cold sweat on her forehead before they were finished.

"Is Miss Alice going to die?" Jeremiah asked quietly.

"I am not." Alice winced as Ethan set her on her feet. "Though you are growing rather substantial, Jeremiah, and I don't think my shoulder was quite up to breaking your fall and mine."

"Sorry." Jeremiah looked distressed. "That man was going to shoot you to shoot me."

"He was," Ethan said, expression grave, "and Miss Alice was willing to protect you at the cost of her own life. You did the right thing, Jeremiah, and we'll soon put Miss Alice to rights. Fetch the mare for me, lad."

Before Jeremiah had taken a step, Alice saw that Collins had managed to drag himself to his feet.

"Ethan, he's getting away!"

Heathgate moved first, while Ethan put himself between Alice and Collins. The marquess was lethally quick for such a big man, but Collins was desperate. He caught up Argus's reins and grunted his way into the saddle. With a vicious jab of his spurs into the gelding's sides, Collins took off at a gallop for the woods.

"Horse thievery," Heathgate spat over the sound of retreating hooves. "As the local magistrate, I am happy to report this is a hanging felony."

"Papa," Jeremiah said worriedly, "Argus is bolting."

Jeremiah had the right of it. While Alice watched, Argus flattened from a gallop into a dead run. The horse's ears were plastered to his head, and Collins was sawing frantically at the reins.

Ethan shifted so Jeremiah's face was hidden against his father's side, but over Ethan's shoulder, Alice saw Argus thunder beneath a low-hanging branch, the rider flopping to the ground like a rag doll.

Justice, Alice thought without a shred of remorse. She'd been dragged and lamed by a horse, thanks to Collins, her sister had been emotionally lamed, and apparently others—Ethan included—had suffered at the man's vile hands as well. The pain of that knowledge rivaled the throbbing in her shoulder.

"I'll see to him," Heathgate said, striding off in the direction of the fallen baron.

How long Alice stood there in Ethan's embrace, her hand on Jeremiah's shoulder, she did not know. The morning was crisp and sunny, the birds were singing, and nothing but the hurt felt real.

"Neck broken," Heathgate reported when he returned. "He didn't suffer, which is a great injustice, though the Crown might get its hands on his private holdings. I suppose that's something."

Because Alice was leaning directly against Ethan, she watched his expression shift from consternation to, not resignation, exactly, but acceptance.

"Ethan!" Nick's call was followed by his appearance through the trees with Fairly at his side. They were riding bareback, mounted on matching chestnut draft horses. "All's well?"

"Hullo, Uncle Nick," Jeremiah called. "Hullo, Doctor Lordship. Miss Alice is hurt, but she's not crying."

"Always a good sign," Fairly said as he slid off his horse. "Any bleeding?" he asked as he approached Alice.

"I'm not bleeding," Alice said. "It's my shoulder." Fairly did not reach out and touch her shoulder, he walked around her, gesturing to Ethan to drop the arm he had around her waist.

"Dislocated," Fairly said briskly. "Easily fixed, but more than a bit uncomfortable."

"Will she cry?" Jeremiah asked.

Fairly smiled slightly at the child. "I might cry. Grey, take the lady in your arms as if you've the honor of a very friendly dance. Miss Alice, let Mr. Grey support you, and close your eyes." Alice obeyed, letting Ethan's embrace and the warmth and scent of him sink past the pain. She felt Fairly's hands on her back, then on her neck, finally on her shoulder.

"We're going to do this on the count of five," Fairly said, taking a firmer hold of Alice's shoulder. "Deep breath, Miss Alice, then let it out and hold onto Mr. Grey tightly. One, two, three, four, five."

Except on "three," Fairly had deftly wrenched her shoulder, putting it back in place with an audible click. Alice saw stars and would literally have been felled by the pain except for Ethan's hold on her.

"Catch your breath." Fairly's gaze was sympathetic. "When you can see straight, have a nip of this." He tucked a silver flask into Ethan's pocket. "You'll be sore for a few days, and you shouldn't lift anything substantial until the soreness passes."

"My marchioness would be more than willing to have you recover with us," Heathgate said. He'd bound Thatcher's hands and left the man sitting on the ground. "Fairly will be in residence at Willowdale, if he knows what's good for him," Heathgate added with a sardonic smile. "You could be spoiled and attended by your personal physician."

When Alice might have demurred, might have expected Ethan to intercede, Nick came stomping over.

"Ethan?" Nick called. "Argus won't let me near him. We've too damned many horses, and something will have to be done with Collins."

❧

The next few minutes were spent organizing the ride back to Tydings, and all the while, Ethan wanted to tell his friends, his neighbor, his brother, and even his son to take themselves off so he could speak with Alice.

And yet, he dreaded what they might say to each other.

When all was sorted out, Collins's body was draped over the back of one draft horse, Thatcher sat bound on the other, Nick was up on Bishop, Fairly on Waltzer, each towing a draft horse. Heathgate had Alice up before him, while Ethan put Jeremiah up before him on a perfectly composed Argus and gave Jeremiah the reins to Fairly's mare.

"Argus was a good boy." Jeremiah thumped the gelding on his golden neck. "He remembered the falling-off game even when the baron was riding him."

"He did." Ethan sneaked a kiss to his son's crown. "And so did you."

"I'm glad Collins is dead," Jeremiah said on a sigh. "I'm glad Argus killed him. He was mean and nasty to everybody. Worse than a bad dragon."

"Much worse." Ethan glanced over at Alice where she rode on Constantina. He'd overheard what Collins had said to her, about knowing her sister and Alice being unable to help her sister. And Alice had overheard *him*, admitting he'd been one of Collins's victims too.

Was that why she wouldn't look at him now?

Even had he the courage, Ethan didn't have the opportunity to confront her. Collins's body had to be dealt with, Heathgate as local magistrate had to take statements, and Thatcher needed to be dispatched to the back room of the local tavern, which served as a makeshift gaol.

When Ethan saw Alice put into the most comfortable coach he had for the trip to Willowdale, it was close to noon.

"So, now what?" Nick asked as they trudged through the gardens.

"I want to see Joshua," Ethan said. "I expect you do too."

Nick turned his head to regard Ethan levelly. "You don't have to be that generous, Ethan. I'm a big boy. When you swive another man's wife, you don't have a claim on the progeny, particularly if your brother is generous enough to obscure the issue of paternity."

"Don't be an ass. You didn't intend to swive my wife, as you so vulgarly insist on putting it, and the progeny you refer to is a little boy who thinks his uncle is—God help you—capital."

"I may not be his bloody uncle, and if you weren't so busy trying to out-decent the Pope over having my bas—"

He never finished the word, because Ethan tackled him from the side and sent them rolling across the back gardens. They wrestled, as they hadn't since boyhood, elbows, knees, arms, and legs tussling, first this one in a hold, then that one, until they were both panting with the exertion.

"Joshua Nicholas Grey is not a bastard," Ethan hissed, his arm around Nick's thick throat. He hauled up, the result intended to be brutally uncomfortable but not quite dangerous.

"Joshua *Nicholas* Grey is not a bastard," Nick grunted. When Ethan relented, and the fight should have been over, Nick moved, quick as lightning, to reverse their positions, putting Ethan's arm behind his back and kneeling over him.

"Ethan Grey is not a bastard," Nick rasped in his brother's ear. "Say it, you stubborn ass." He tugged up for good measure. Ethan struggled fiercely beneath him, but Nick wouldn't give quarter.

"Ethan Grey is not a bastard," Nick insisted, voice hoarse. "Say it, or I'll break both your arms, Ethan. I swear I will."

Ethan renewed his efforts to break Nick's hold, but Nick had several inches and two stone on him.

"Ethan! You are not a bastard. Say it!"

Ethan went still, Nick's point finally becoming clear. "Ethan Grey," he said softly, firmly, "is no longer a victim."

"No." Nick shifted off of him. "He's not. You're not." He regarded Ethan, who'd pushed up on all fours and then sat back on his haunches, lungs heaving. "You're not. Come here. God, you're stubborn." Nick draped an arm across Ethan's shoulders and gave his brother one hell of a squeeze. "I have missed you until I'm crazy with it, and all this time, you were just ashamed, Ethan?"

Nick withdrew his arm, and Ethan could breathe again.

"Just ashamed." Ethan said the words as one might say, "mere plague."

"I could kill Papa," Nick whispered. "How could he leave you at Stoneham? How could he have sent you there?"

"I don't think he knew anything, Nick." Ethan sighed, settling in the grass beside his brother. "And I don't care. It's over. Now it's well and truly over."

Nick slugged Ethan on the shoulder. "Call me blood-thirsty, but like Jeremiah, I'm glad Collins is dead."

"So am I," Ethan admitted, because to Nick, he could admit such a thing. "Now will you come see the boys with me?"

"How can I face them, Ethan?" Nick plucked at the grass idly. "I am a disgrace. In their eyes, I will be a disgrace, and I can only imagine what Leah will think of this."

Ethan found a long blade of grass and split it with his thumbnail. "Firstly, children do not uniformly approve of their parents, nor we of them. This is not in the contract, so to speak. We love each other, and that suffices. Secondly, Leah knew you were a tomcat and will not hold this against you. Thirdly, you need to know these children. They will fall to your care should anything happen to me."

"That's right. You did that even before Papa died, didn't you?" Nick pounced on this realization with palpable relish as he pushed to his feet.

"I did it the day I knew Barbara had conceived,"

Ethan said, accepting a hand up. "Joshua's situation only makes it all the more imperative you make his acquaintance."

"But, Ethan, do we have to tell him?" Nick sounded so uncertain, it nearly broke Ethan's heart.

"Not now, Nick," Ethan said gently as they moved off toward the house. "Soon, so it doesn't strike them as a big, dirty secret rife with sexual connotations an adolescent blows out of all proportion. You and I are half brothers. Joshua and Jeremiah can adjust to being possible half brothers too."

"You're so matter-of-fact about this," Nick said as they gained the back hallway.

"I've had seven years to adjust to it, and you've had less than a few hours."

"True, and in all this commotion, I've not told you Hazlit's latest information."

"Which would be?" Ethan led them in through the kitchen, then to the back stairs.

"You are not a bastard," Nick said, humor lacing his voice. "He's confirmed your mother was still married to Colonel Markham when you were born, but the story is almost sweet."

Ethan paused on the narrow stairs to peer down at Nick on the step behind him. "*Almost* sweet?"

"They were lifelong friends," Nick said, "and he wanted his commission. She wanted to leave her parents' house and was good friends with his sisters. They married, and he used her dowry to buy his commission. She went to live with his sisters, and she kept up a lively correspondence with him, though they were never intimate. Your mother was faithful to my father once she met him, though they weren't fated to have much time together. She was married at the time of your birth, though, so technically, you are not a bastard."

"And she couldn't marry the earl, lest bigamy rear its head. *Almost* sweet."

"The earl paid a great deal of money to the solicitors to keep her adultery quiet," Nick went on as they gained the stairs. "Damned silly of him, if you ask me, but he was protective of her memory."

Ethan shrugged. "I wish he'd protected me more and her memory less." It felt odd to say such a thing out loud, except Nick was the one person to whom he could make such a disclosure.

"You and me both." Nick huffed out his disgust. "We're not sending our sons anywhere but Eton, are we?"

"And maybe not even there," Ethan said. He tapped once on the door to the nursery and opened it, finding both boys wreathed in smiles, sitting side by side on Joshua's bed.

❧

"You need to rest." Felicity, Marchioness of Heathgate, frowned at Alice with maternal concern. "You are pale, you have shadows under your eyes, and you aren't using your right hand to lift even a teacup."

Alice reminded herself that this soft-spoken, pretty redhead held the keys to the marquess's kingdom, and to his heart as well. Formidable was a polite term for the lady's determination when a guest's welfare was at stake.

"I will rest." Alice sipped her tea, an excellent hearty black that should have been fortifying. "It's difficult when every time you move, the pain jars you awake."

Her ladyship's eyes filled with sympathy. "I am so thoughtless. Of course your shoulder hurts. You're sure you don't want some laudanum? You don't want me to fetch Fairly?"

As if a physician or the poppy would cure what truly ailed Alice.

She set her teacup down. "I think I'll go upstairs now, if you don't mind."

"I'll walk you to your room. Once Heathgate and Fairly start talking commerce, you'd think there were no other acceptable topics. Lord and Lady Greymoor will come for dinner, because it's been an age since we've seen Fairly."

"He's a very kind man," Alice said as they made their way up the steps.

"Too kind, sometimes," Felicity said with a sister's asperity, for the physician was brother to her and Lady Greymoor. "He and Letty are perfect for each other. I suspect she inveigled him into traveling with Nick, knowing that would earn us a visit with him as well."

"You are fortunate in your family." Even coming up with clichés was an effort.

"As are you. I've met your brother Benjamin, you know. Heathgate respects him, and his lordship's respect is not easily given."

"Benjamin would be complimented, my lady." They neared the door to Alice's guest room, her sanctuary, her prison. Lady Heathgate was a dear, but Alice could not stand the weight of the woman's gaze boring into her soul with more insight than Alice's sore heart could tolerate.

"You'll want a tray for dinner, won't you?" Lady Heathgate followed Alice into the bedroom. "Your shoulder is injured, but that's not the worst of it, is it?"

Alice sat on the bed, dignity deserting her. She nodded dumbly at her hostess as the marchioness pulled draperies over the windows.

Her ladyship sat on the bed beside her guest. "Heathgate said Baron Collins was a bully and a parasite. He put Thatcher up to kidnapping Master Jeremiah because his own funds were gone, and he had unnatural relationships with any number of men, not all of them willing."

Alice nodded, feeling tears threaten. Collins was a bully and a rapist. Had been for years.

"I would hug you, but I'd hurt your shoulder. Is there anything I can do?"

Alice shook her head, wondering if there were any way to erase the morning from her life. Except that would mean Collins still roamed the earth, free to visit his violence on any unsuspecting victim.

"I'll leave you in peace, then." Lady Heathgate rose and brushed a kiss across Alice's cheek. "Whatever it is, when you're rested and feeling better, it won't be so bad. And if we can help, you must not hesitate to let us know. Benjamin would insist, and so do I."

Alice nodded, staring at her lap.

There was nothing anybody could do, and the ache in her shoulder was a twinge compared to the ache in her heart. Ethan had heard of her disgrace, heard how she'd been unable to help her sister, heard she'd not brought Collins to justice when she'd had the chance.

Ethan was a brave man, the bravest she'd ever met. He'd waded into Collins's pistol sights, orchestrated a rescue, and seen justice done. There was no way on earth a man like Ethan Grey deserved a woman in his life who'd failed miserably to keep her sister safe from the menace that had been Hart Collins.

Twenty-one

"SHE ASKED ABOUT YOU," HEATHGATE SAID, APROPOS of nothing. His mare walked along the bridle path beside Ethan's golden gelding, the leaves crunching underfoot in a sound characteristic of the woods in autumn.

"And what did you tell her?" Ethan had no dignity where Alice was concerned, hadn't had any for weeks.

"I told her a pack of lies," Heathgate said. "You're hiring trollops from London, becoming a drunken sot, carrying on with the tweenie."

"That is not humorous."

"The two of you aren't humorous." Heathgate brought his horse to a halt. "Talk to the woman. She mopes around Willowdale like a ghost, smiling only at the children. Lady Heathgate is concerned she's going into a decline, and she catches your Alice crying at odd moments. She doesn't eat much, save her desserts, and she spends a prodigious amount of time in bed."

"She's had a blow," Ethan said. "Seeing Collins, much less being taken by him at gunpoint, will put her off her feed." Finding out that the man she'd taken to her bed had been intimate with Hart Collins was more than a blow.

"She isn't a damned broodmare. At least call upon her, wish her well before she departs for London."

Ethan sustained a blow, another blow, at that pronouncement. "She's going to London? To live with her brother?"

"She does not confide in me, but she did speak of traveling to London tomorrow, and thanked me for my hospitality."

Ethan nudged his horse back to a walk. "Give her my... best."

⁂

Gareth Alexander, Marquess of Heathgate, held his tongue when he wanted to shout that Alice Portman was likely already carrying the consequences of being given Ethan Grey's *best*. But then he caught sight of Grey's sons, regarding him solemnly from the backs of their ponies.

"Did you say Miss Alice was leaving tomorrow?" Joshua spoke up, his tone oddly adult.

"I did," Heathgate replied, feeling strangely on trial.

Jeremiah scowled, looking very like his father. "And Papa didn't say *anything*?"

"Nothing of consequence."

"That's stupid." Joshua glanced over at his brother, who nodded. "Really stupid."

Heathgate glared down at them. "If it's so stupid, why don't you prodigies do something about it? God knows I've tried and gotten no damned where at all."

He twirled his horse in a walk pirouette and trotted

off, only a little chagrined that he'd spoken thusly to
mere children.

꙳

"You have callers." The marchioness's gaze traveled
over the possessions Alice had spread out on her bed,
then went to the two portmanteaus already waiting
beside the door.

Alice paused while folding up a green-and-blue
cashmere shawl. "Callers?" The vicar and his wife,
maybe? Lord and Lady Greymoor?

"They're waiting in the family parlor, and I've
ordered tea."

"Thank you." Alice ceased her packing—she still
hated to pack but doubted it would ever inspire her to
panic again—and took in her ladyship's guarded expression. The marchioness wasn't offering to chaperone in
the parlor, so it couldn't be Ethan and Nick waiting for
her, and besides, Nick was in Kent with his wife where
he belonged. Would Reese and Matthew have come to
fetch her? Might Nick have sent for them?

Mind whirling, Alice took herself to the family
parlor, glancing around for her visitors.

Joshua grinned at her bashfully. "Hullo, Miss Alice."

"Oh, Joshua." Alice went to her knees and held
out her arms. "Jeremiah, my favorite gentlemen, it is
so good to see you." They burrowed against her, all
elbows and chins and cold, fresh air. Tears sprang to
Alice's eyes as she hugged them to her, and only by
force of will did she let them go. "You both look so
very well." She rose to her feet and waved a hand at
the sofa. "Won't you join me for tea, gentlemen?"

"Told you she'd cry," Joshua muttered at his

brother. "There are chocolates too. Lady Heathgate said to tell you. She's nice."

"She is." Alice swiped at her eyes with her knuckles. "You boys are nice too, to come calling like this. I hope you brought a groom."

"We told Davey where we were going, because he likes to visit his brother," Jeremiah said, "but after we have some tea and chocolates, we're not calling on you."

"You're not?" Alice set down the teapot, her governess instincts picking up on little-boy mischief in the making. "What are you about?"

"We're kidnapping you," Jeremiah said. "We thought about kidnapping Papa, but he's bigger than you, and he's already home. You're not home."

"I don't have a home." This was one of the more painful realizations she'd come to in recent days.

"Yes, you do," Jeremiah insisted as he helped himself to three chocolates then obligingly held the box for his brother to plunder similarly. "Tydings is your home. We talked about it."

"Who is this 'we'?" Alice asked, thinking in some corner of her mind her charges needed to learn proper tea etiquette. Her former charges.

"Both of us," Joshua chimed in, helping himself to more chocolate. "We love you, so you have to come home with us."

"Davey isn't with you, is he?" She did love them—them too.

"We told him we were going to kidnap you," Jeremiah replied. "He probably followed us."

"You're going to get in such trouble," Alice warned them. "Your father will be beside himself."

Jeremiah paused between chocolates to spear her with a look. "He doesn't know we're gone. He rides with us, and he comes to the table, but he's in his stupid library all day, and when we tickle him, he only pretends to laugh. It's stupid."

"Really stupid." Joshua sighed dramatically and took yet another chocolate.

"That's enough, Josh. Miss Alice is getting peevish."

"Peevish." Alice rose and wanted to be peevish, but mostly, she was touched and uncertain and worried—worried about Ethan, who needed very much to laugh when he was tickled, and worried she ought to at least say her good-byes to him in person.

She owed him that much.

"Well, then." Alice held out her hands. "I give up. Kidnap me, gentlemen, or you'll make that poor box of chocolates walk the plank, right?"

"Right into Davy Jones's locker!" Joshua crowed, thumping his tummy. He eyed the chocolates, met Alice's frown, and took one of her outstretched hands. Jeremiah took the other, and when they passed Lord Heathgate on the front stairs, his lordship arched a fine dark eyebrow.

"Going somewhere with my guest, gentlemen?"

"Nope," Joshua said. "We're kidnapping her."

Heathgate nodded his approval. "That's all right, then. Have a pleasant crime, Miss Portman."

She managed a weak smile and let the boys tow her right out the door. Waltzer stood solid and handsome at the lady's mounting block. Alice climbed aboard, arranging her skirts in a semblance of modesty.

"This kidnapping will take place at a dignified walk," Alice warned her escorts.

"Alice!" The marchioness hurried down the steps to the front terrace. "Take your shawl, my dear. When the clouds cover the sun, it isn't the least warm today."

"You are abetting a pair of felons, you know," Alice said, taking the shawl and wrapping it around her shoulders.

"And such handsome felons, too." Lady Heathgate beamed a smile at each of the boys where they sat on their ponies. "Come again soon, gentlemen, and perhaps I can talk you into kidnapping Joyce."

"No, thank you, Lady Heathgate," Jeremiah managed. "Joshua?"

"I'm ready." His brother waved to the marchioness. "Thanks for the chocolates!"

Her ladyship waved them cheerily on their way, while Alice felt as if she were riding to the gallows. She wanted to see Ethan again, wanted it desperately, but she did not want to see cool tolerance in his blue eyes, or worse—pity.

Still, she needed to thank him. If nothing else, she needed to thank him for bringing about the death of the man who'd destroyed her sister's life and a fair portion of Alice's own health and happiness. Ethan would not want her gratitude; he'd probably not want anything from her ever again.

Inevitably the little cavalcade of two ponies and the captive on her gelding made its way to Tydings. Alice caught a glimpse of Davey following at a discreet distance, and he too waved at her with great good cheer.

They were daft, the cheerful, waving lot of them.

"We're here!" Joshua announced to the stables at large. Miller appeared and took Waltzer's reins.

"If it isn't Miss Alice, come back to us after all the

commotion last week. Well done, lads. Down you go, Miss, and I'll see to his nibs here."

"You have to come," Joshua reminded her. "You're kidnapped now." He grabbed her hand again, while Jeremiah was content to skip along beside them.

"Your brig can be the library," Jeremiah decided. "It has lots of books, and you like books, right?"

"I do like books," Alice said, feeling doom settle around her heart. She was going to see Ethan, after days of not seeing him, but it would be for the last time. Her heart was going to break, and then she honestly did not know how she'd go on, much less why she'd try to.

In no time, she was marched to the library and thrust inside by a pair of self-satisfied, giggling little boys. They banged the door shut behind her and ran off, squealing with laughter.

"I did not ring for tea." Ethan was at his desk, shirtsleeves rolled up, one finger running down a list of figures, the other hand holding a pen. He did not look up, which gave Alice a moment to study him.

He was gaunt. The bones of his handsome face were more prominent, the lines at the corners of his eyes deeper, and there was a tension in his big frame Alice hadn't seen since she'd first met him—fatigue, she guessed. A succession of bad nights.

"Ethan?"

He glanced up sharply and was on his feet in an instant.

"Alice?" He came around the desk, gaze fixed on her as if he were afraid she'd disappear. A large, elegant hand reached out toward her, then dropped. "May I take your shawl?"

She said nothing, merely stood there, drinking in

the dear, handsome, hopelessly unavailable sight of him. Gently, he eased her shawl from her shoulders, folded it neatly, and offered it back to her.

He'd done this once before, after one of their walks, a small intimate consideration so characteristic of him it had melted her heart. She burst into tears and stood there like a complete fool, clutching her shawl to her middle.

"Don't cry." Ethan stepped closer. "Alice, please don't cry. I didn't mean to upset you. Alice?"

He did not want to touch her, Alice concluded miserably. He was such a gentleman, but he could not stand to touch her now, knowing what he did about her.

"Come sit." He steered her by the shoulders to the sofa. "I'll ring for tea, and you can tell me what has you so upset."

"No tea," Alice choked out. "I don't want another blessed cup of blessed tea."

Gingerly, Ethan sat beside her, taking one of her hands in his. "No tea then." All it took was the touch of his hand on hers, and Alice lost any pretense of composure. She went from an inconvenient case of the sniffles to full out sobbing, clutching his hand to her with desperate strength.

"I miss you," she managed. "Ethan, I'm sorry, but I miss you so. I ache with it. I don't want to go."

"Go?" Ethan edged closer. "You just got here." Her nails were digging into his hand, gripping him for dear life. "No one will make you go anywhere." He tucked a lock of her hair back around her ear, and it was all the invitation she needed to pitch herself hard against his chest.

"I just won't go." She clamped her arms around him. "It wasn't my fault, what I saw. I tried to get help, Ethan. That's how I got hurt, and it was too late, anyway, and he had a knife, and I was too scared to think."

Slowly, Ethan's arms closed around her. Alice inhaled his evergreen scent, and she felt a wave of calm envelop her. Whether he was merely being gentlemanly or not, she was in his arms again, and it felt right.

Absolutely right.

"Tell me," Ethan murmured, his lips close to her ear. "Tell me what you want me to know, Alice."

"I don't want to tell you." Alice gulped and accepted his handkerchief. "It's awful."

"It might be awful"—Ethan kissed her cheek—"but you are not awful. Tell me."

Alice closed her eyes, tears leaking from the corners, while she tried to find words for something she hadn't mentioned to anybody in twelve years.

"Hart Collins was engaged to my sister." She tucked her face to Ethan's neck and would have climbed inside him if she'd been able. "He put on the pretty for her. Then we began to hear rumors. I barely understood them, but Avis is a little older than me, and she was much more worldly, not buried in books. Hart was always getting sent down and into trouble. His papa was a baron, though, so the trouble was kept quiet. Still, Avis had second thoughts and decided to break the engagement. There was another fellow who caught her eye—a worthy fellow. The day before our papa was to call on the baron to explain Avis's change of heart, Collins and his friends snatched her from her horse and made off with her. I was so foolish…"

"You were fourteen," Ethan said gently. "Fourteen is still a child."

"I should have gotten help right then," Alice said miserably. "We were on our own property, and Papa never made us take a groom if we were riding on Blessings land. I trailed after them and rode right into a trap, with Hart's cronies pulling me off my horse as easily as Hart had taken Avis. They'd been drinking, and when Hart dragged Avie, screaming, into a game-keeper's cottage, they cheered and tossed me in after."

"Go on."

"He cut her clothes right off her, laughing all the while," Alice went on, her voice dropping to a near whisper. "When Avie screamed at me to get out, he noticed I was there and held the knife to her throat."

"I'm listening." Ethan's hand went to her hair. "I'm right here."

"She stopped struggling," Alice said, voice catching. "She motioned for me to leave, and I knew she was trading her virtue for mine. When he started rutting on her, I bolted. I jumped on the first horse at the hitching rail and took off at a gallop."

"You did the right thing," Ethan said swiftly, before she could say another word. "You tried to go for help and made your sister's sacrifice worth something."

"He hurt her," Alice wailed softly. "He hurt her terribly, Ethan, and all I did was run, and even then, I couldn't control the horse. I ended up coming off, getting dragged, and taking forever to get her help. When the neighbors found her, Collins was long gone, and Avie was a wreck. He assumed no other man would have her, and he'd get her and her dowry despite her change of heart."

In the safety of Ethan's arms, Alice realized something else: Collins had hurt Avis, abominably, terribly, unforgivably, but he'd hurt Alice too.

"Avis couldn't contemplate marriage to anyone, and you could no longer walk," Ethan concluded. "Alice, you did the best you could, and you have to forgive yourself for not being older, wiser, stronger, and meaner. You have to. You were just a girl, a child, just... Good God, you were just fourteen..."

Ethan fell silent, and Alice let him hold her in that silence for a small, fraught eternity. At that moment, she didn't care why he was holding her; she only knew she needed his arms around her for as long as he would spare her an embrace. She needed that gentle caress of his hand in her hair, needed the scent and heat and strength of him.

And then his hand stilled, and the silence shifted.

"I was fourteen," Ethan said, surprising her enough that she pulled back to see his face. His voice was calm, almost meditative. "Collins's modus operandi was already established. He gathered his little mob, plied them with liquor, ambushed me, and had his pleasure violating me. Because Heathgate came upon the scene, we were able to do some damage to Collins and his thugs, but nothing permanent. He went on to rape others, including your sister, and for that, I will always, always be sorry."

Alice wrapped her arms around him. "You were only a boy, and so far from home, and it was just wrong."

"It was wrong." Ethan repeated her words quietly. "What happened to you and your sister was wrong too, Alice. I let Collins's brutality limit who I was and whom I allowed to love me for a long, long time. I am unwilling to give him that control any longer."

She blinked up at him, but burrowed back into his embrace without saying a word. As her mind calmed and she absorbed the quality of his embrace—sure, uncompromising, and snug—she realized something else: Ethan wasn't disappointed in her. His words assured her of it, but more fundamentally, so did the quality of his touch.

"Why did you stay away, Ethan? I waited for you to fetch me home, and you didn't." She'd been waiting years for somebody to fetch her home, in fact.   .

He brought her knuckles to his lips for a lingering kiss. "Why didn't you come home? I waited for you to come to me, and you didn't."

Alice nodded, accepting the validity of his point.

"Heathgate asked me if I'd heard what Collins said," she offered. "I did, but it hardly registered. You seem so… in charge of your own life, not knocking about from one obscure post to another just to hide from your past."

"Sometimes, we need privacy to get our bearings. We each hid differently, but I was as determined to have my obscurity as you were."

"Thank goodness for little boys and their games," Alice said. "They consumed more chocolate in five minutes than I've had since leaving Sussex."

Ethan brushed a kiss to her temple. "They play kidnapping a lot. I've decided, because they always vanquish their foes, not to forbid it."

"They've gotten good at it," Alice observed wryly. "I sit before you, thoroughly kidnapped."

"And it must be a tiring experience," Ethan countered, running a finger down her cheek. "Are you resting, Alice?"

"Not well. You?"

He shook his head, his expression grave.

Alice had already, with no dignity whatsoever, told him she missed him, and she didn't want to leave. Her recent confessions notwithstanding, his recent confessions notwithstanding, she still didn't know where she stood with him.

Ethan rose and went to the window. "I want to put a question to you."

"Ask me anything." She didn't like that he'd moved away, but framed by the window light, she could see he'd dropped some weight too, and there hadn't been any fat on him to lose.

"It's uncomfortable to ask this," Ethan said, glancing over his shoulder at her. "I'd rather put it off."

"Ask, Ethan. You put Hart Collins where I needed him to be, and for that, I would grant you any request."

He turned and frowned at her in earnest.

"That won't do," he murmured. "You see, I want to ask you to marry me, and I am not jesting, Alice. I cannot have you marrying me out of some misplaced gratitude, or you'd be better off accepting Argus's hoof in marriage. He's the one who sent Collins to his Maker."

"You want me to marry your horse?" Alice sat on the couch, trying to understand what he was asking, but a buzzing had started up in her ears.

Ethan shook his head. "No, love. I want you to marry me. I want you to belong to me and to the boys and to Tydings. I want…" He sighed and offered her a crooked smile. "I want children with you, little girls who look like you and peer down their noses at all things male and silly. I want babies, and great strapping lads who tease their sisters and drive us to distraction with their noise and ruckus. I want to someday drag my family off to Belle Maison in a parade of carriages and take over every inn we stay at along the way. I want you in my bed every night for the rest of our lives. I want you…"

She still said nothing but watched his mouth as if she could see his words.

"But most of all, Alexandra, I want you to be happy." Ethan paused and swallowed. "I stayed away because I thought that's what would make you happy. But you're here now, and I don't… I can't… Don't go, Alice. I'll never bother you again. Please, just… don't go."

He turned his back, leaving Alice bereft of the truths in his eyes. He'd no sooner braced his hands on the windowsill than a missile pounded into his back in the form of a silent, fierce Alice, intent on getting her arms around him.

"I won't go," she said, holding him tightly. "And you won't send me away."

"Never." Ethan turned and caught her to him. "Not ever. You belong to us, Alice, and I desperately want us to belong to you."

"You do." Alice laughed a little through her tears. "Oh, Ethan, you do. You and Joshua and Jeremiah and their ponies and Waltzer and Argus and Tydings and all of it. You're mine, and I will never let you go."

His chin came to rest on her crown, and they stood there, holding each other, until a solid knock on the door disturbed them.

∼≫

She was going to stay. This fact alone allowed Ethan to step back when some fool who did not value his wages knocked on the library door.

"I did not ring for tea." Ethan kissed Alice's nose before he let her go. "Come in."

Joshua barreled in. Jeremiah followed more cautiously.

"You found our prisoner." Joshua beamed. "Hullo, Miss Alice."

Jeremiah frowned up at his papa. "You made her cry. She won't like us if you do that."

Ethan's instinct was to sweep both children up in a hug and not let them go until Christmas.

And yet, being a father called for discipline of one's impulses.

"I do not like little boys who ride off without supervision," Ethan said in his most imposing-papa tone. "I do not like little boys who turn a game into more than it should be. I do not like little boys who make hogs of themselves at the neighbor's tea table."

He stared down at his sons, who looked abruptly shy and uncertain, but then Jeremiah's jaw set, and he put his hands on his hips.

"I do not like papas who mope around all day," Jeremiah announced, "and Miss Alice was moping too—Heathgate said, and he wouldn't lie. I do not like that you were going to get us a different governess, and you didn't even ask us. I do not like that you were packing up to go to London, and you didn't even give us your 'behave while I'm gone' lecture."

Ethan's brows rose, and from the corner of his eye, he saw Alice was just as surprised as he.

And that—the wonderful, unthinking, reflexive gift of being able to measure this moment with a woman who cared as much for his children as he did—warmed his heart beyond words.

"Apologize to Miss Alice for kidnapping her."

"You apologize to her for making her cry."

Ethan took Alice's hand and discarded the notion of going down on one knee before his children, lest there be weeks of imitation. "I am humbly and sincerely sorry for making you cry. For any time I've made you cry. Hurting you is the last thing I want to do, ever."

"Apology accepted," Alice said softly, leaning in to kiss his cheek.

Ethan quirked a brow at his sons. "Jeremiah?"

"I'm sorry we kidnapped you," Jeremiah said, his gaze on Alice's face in exact imitation of his father. "But you were going away, and Papa was going away, and Heathgate said we should do something, so we did. And Davey went to visit his brother, so we were supervised, and Lady Heathgate offered the chocolates, and we said please and thank you."

"We'll have a word with the marquess," Ethan said. "And his lady."

"Apology accepted." Alice spoke over him, suppressing a smile.

"I'm sorry too," Joshua said.

"So you'll stay?" Jeremiah asked, bravado gone. "Even if Papa made you cry?"

"Sometimes a lady cries not because her heart is broken, but because it's mending." The look she sent Ethan would have illuminated the dimmest corners of the coldest heart—and his was by no means cold. "I will stay, and I will marry your papa, if I have permission from my favorite gentlemen."

Jeremiah sent his father a very stern look. "You won't make her cry?"

"Never on purpose."

"You'll read us stories?" Joshua asked Alice, his tone wistful. "Papa tries, but he just can't get the wolf quite right."

"I will read you stories."

The boys exchanged brother-looks, and Jeremiah spoke for the pair of them. "That's all right, then. You marry Papa, but Joshua and I aren't wearing any stupid Sunday clothes and carrying around flowers and nonsense like that."

"I believe we have an agreement." Ethan's eyes lit with humor as he gazed at his prospective wife. "And we also have at least one little kidnapper who's overdue for his nap."

"C'mon, Joshua." Jeremiah pulled his brother by the arm. "They're going to kiss and carry on. Aunt Leah explained it to me when we visited Belle Maison."

Joshua let himself be pulled from the room, and Ethan and his bride did, indeed, kiss and carry on, every day and night for the rest of their lives.

Lonely Lords Family Tree

EDWARD LINDSEY m. **CAROLINE PIERCE**
- TRENTON LINDSEY — Book Ten, *Trenton* — m. ELEGY HAMPTON
- DARIUS LINDSEY — Book One, *Darius* — m. VIVIAN LONGSTREET
- LEAH LINDSEY — m. NICHOLAS HADDONFIELD

HARLAN HADDONFIELD, EARL OF BELLEFONTE m. **DARLA DANAHER**
(NAOMI GREY — - - - — connection)
- NICHOLAS HADDONFIELD — Book Two, *Nicholas* — m. LEAH LINDSEY
- ETHAN GREY — Book Three, *Ethan* — m. ALEXANDRA PORTMAINE
- NITA
- SUSANNAH
- DELLA
- KIRSTEN
- GEORGE
- ADOLPHUS
- BECKMAN HADDONFIELD — Book Four, *Beckman* — m. SARA HUNT

ANDERSON HUNT m. **ALMA SHAY**
- SARA HUNT
- POLONAISE HUNT — m. GABRIEL NORTH — Book Five, *Gabriel*
- GAVOTTE HUNT (deceased)

Acknowledgments

Thanks go, as always, to my editor, Deb Werksman, for being willing to publish this tale of a less traditional hero and heroine, and for juggling more plates than is humanly possible to see it done as part of a suite. To Skye, Cat, Susie, and Danielle, the same thanks apply. There ought to be a shortage of plates somewhere at the rate these ladies can keep them aloft.

Thanks go as well to Emily, Abby, Max, Leah, and the other ladies at Wax Creative, Inc. They are the talent behind my beautiful (if I do say so myself) website, and their know-how and guidance have also kept my nose above water in the social media sphere. As each book has hit the shelves, the Wax Creative team has been just out of the readers' view, yelling encouragement, good ideas, and commonsense advice to me far above and beyond the call of duty.

With people like this to work with, being an author is the best, most enjoyable job in the world.

Read on for an excerpt of

Beckman

the next book in the Lonely Lords
series by Grace Burrowes

"HE INSISTED ON SEEING YOU OFF."

Beckman Haddonfield heard his sister Nita clearly,
though she'd whispered. The Earl of Bellefonte,
glowering at his grown children from the foot of Belle
Maison's front steps likely heard her too.

"Your lordship." Beck stepped away from his
gelding and sketched a bow to his father. Even at this
early hour, the earl was attired in morning dress that
hung loosely on his stooped frame. His valet and the
underbutler were flanking him, each holding a bony
arm and trying to look as if they weren't touching
their employer.

"Leave us." His lordship didn't look at his servants
as he gave that command. "You too, Nita. I won't
perish from the cold, though it might be a welcome
relief all around if I did."

Nita's blue eyes turned mutinous, though she
gathered her shawl more tightly around herself and
ascended to the wide front porch.

The earl watched her go then turned to regard
his son.

He stabbed his cane in the general direction of the mounting block where Beck's horse waited. "Get me to the damned mounting block before I fall over."

Beck took his father's arm and assisted him to shuffle along until the earl was propped against the top step of the ladies' mounting block.

His lordship rested both gnarled hands on the top of his cane. "No dignity left whatsoever. Soon I won't be able to wipe my own arse."

The truth of this brought a lump to Beck's throat. "One shudders to consider the fuss you'll make then. If you're about to tell me how to find Three Springs, save your breath. I have directions."

"I'm about to tell you I love you," the earl groused. "Though such maudlin tripe hardly makes a difference."

Beck went still, hearing a death knell in his father's blessing. "One has suspected this is the case," Beck said slowly. "One hopes the suspicions have been mutual."

The earl's slight grin appeared. "Couldn't have danced around a tender sentiment better myself. You really should have been my heir."

"Stop disrespecting my brother," Beck retorted, but inside, oh, inside, he was feeling as decrepit and tired as the earl looked. His father loved him, something he had known without realizing it, but his father had also said the words aloud. More than the earl's frail appearance, this indicated the man was indeed making his final arrangements.

"I've said my piece, now get you off to Three Springs and put the place to rights. I've every confidence the solicitors have let it go to wrack and ruin." The earl made as if to rise, something Beck suspected he couldn't accomplish on his own. Beck drew him up, but not just to his feet. With Nita trying not to cry on the porch, the underbutler blinking furiously, and the footman staring resolutely down the drive, Beck gently hugged his father.

"Papa." He barely whispered his words past his father's shoulder. "I don't want to leave you."

He had never wanted to be sent away, but each time, he'd known his banishments were earned. This time, try as he might, the only fault he could find with himself was that he loved his father.

The earl said nothing for a moment then patted his son's back. "You'll be fine, Beckman. I've always been proud of you, you know."

"Proud of me?" Beck stepped back, depositing his father gently on the mounting block. "I'm nothing more than a frivolous younger son, and that is the plain truth."

A flattering version of the plain truth, too.

"Bah. You should have gone to London with Nicholas and selected yourself another bride, though I suppose you've been trailing him long enough to be ready for a change in scenery."

He's sending me away, Beck thought, his self-discipline barely equal to the task of maintaining his composure. *He's sending me away, and we're discussing my possible marriage to some twit hungering for Nick's title.*

"When Nick is in the room, the ladies do not see me."

The earl thumped his cane weakly. "Balderdash! Nick is a good time. You are a good man."

"Nick is a good man," Beck said, a note of steel creeping into his voice.

"He'll be a better man and a happier man for finding the right countess. It is the besetting sorrow of my dotage that my sons have not provided me with grandchildren to dandle upon my knee."

His lordship loved a good scrap. Heart breaking, Beck obliged.

"You would not know how to dandle if the regent commanded it of you."

"That prancing idiot." The earl snorted. "I am glad I will be dead before the full extent of his silly imitation of a monarch can damage the country further than it has."

"It's too cold to be discussing politics in the drive," Beck said, ready to have this most painful parting over. "Particularly when you've had nothing different to say since the man had his father's kingdom imposed on him several years ago."

"You're right. It's been the same damned nonsense all along. Pavilions and parks, while the working man can't afford his bread, and the yeoman's pasture is fenced away from him at the whim and pleasure of the local baron. Pathetic. Absolutely damned pathetic."

Utterly. "Good-bye, Papa."

The earl leaned forward again, signaling Beck to get him on his feet. "You will be fine, Beckman. Keep an eye on Nick for me, as you always have, and think again of remarrying. Good wives have their endearing qualities."

"Yes, Papa." Beck mustered a smile, hugged his father again, and waved the underbutler and the footmen down the stairs. "God keep you, sir." He resisted the urge to cling to his father, knowing he'd embarrass them both if he stayed one moment longer.

"I wish to hell the Lord would see fit to take me rather than keep me," the earl muttered. "Perhaps patience is the last lesson He has reserved for me. Safe journeys, Beckman. You are a son to make a father proud."

"My thanks." Beck swung up, nodded to his sister where she stood clutching her handkerchief at the top of the stairs. He touched his crop to his hat brim then nudged his horse into a rocking canter.

He did not look back. It was all he could do to see the road for the chill wind making his eyes water.

⁂

Sara Hunt took a final swallow of weak, unsweetened, tepid tea, looked out at the miserable day, and decided before the last of the light faded, she'd poke through the contents of Mr. Haddonfield's enormous wagon.

Lady Warne had written instructing the household to make her grandson welcome as he came to "take Three Springs in hand," but she hadn't said exactly when he'd arrive. If Sara was to make a proper inventory of the goods sent ahead of their guest, she'd best do it before the mincing Honorable was underfoot making a nuisance of himself.

She grabbed her heavy wool cloak, traded her house mules for a pair of wooden sabots, took up a lantern, and slipped out the back door. On the stoop she paused, listening to the peculiar sibilance of sleet changing to snow as darkness fell. If the sun came out in the morning, they'd have a fairy-tale landscape of sparkling ice and snow, the last of the season if they were lucky.

The barn bore the comforting scent of horses and

hay on a raw day. The four great beasts that had pulled the loaded wagon into the yard the previous day contentedly inhaled great piles of fodder, while the wagon stood in the barn's high, arching center aisle.

Sara had just hung up the lantern when she realized something wasn't right. A shuffling sound came from the far side of the wagon where little light penetrated. The sound was too big to be Heifer investigating under the tarps, not big enough to be a horse shifting in its stall.

She shrank into the shadows. Damn and blast if a vagrant hadn't spotted the laden wagon and decided to follow it to its destination in hopes of some lucrative larceny. The country roads were not heavily traveled, and such a load would be easily remarked. Silently, Sara directed her footsteps to the saddle room, sending up a prayer for Polly and Allie—may her sister and daughter remain in the house, or anywhere but this barn.

She chose a long-handled training whip from the saddle room wall, then retraced her steps and heard muttering from the far side of the wagon.

"And what in blazes is this doing here?" a man asked no one in particular. "As if one needs to fiddle while rusticating. Spices, too, so we might not want for fashionable cuisine in the hinterlands."

A daft vagrant, then. Sara paused in her slow, silent progress around the wagon. Maybe he was harmless, and simply brandishing the whip would suffice to chase him off, but in this weather… She considered putting the whip down.

A man could catch his death in this miserable wet and cold. Times were hard and getting harder, and there were so many veterans of the Corsican's foolishness still wandering the land, many of them ailing in both body and spirit. Shouldn't she offer the man a little Christian charity before she attacked him for merely being curious?

An arm clamped around her neck; another snaked around her waist.

"One move," said a voice directly behind her, "and you will be the first thing planted this spring."

About the Author

New York Times and *USA Today* bestselling author Grace Burrowes hit the bestseller lists with both her debut, *The Heir*, and her second book in The Duke's Obsession trilogy, *The Soldier*. Both books received extensive praise and starred reviews from *Publishers Weekly* and *Booklist*. *The Heir* was also named a *Publishers Weekly* Best Book of The Year, and *The Soldier* was named a *Publishers Weekly* Best Spring Romance. Her first story in the Windham sisters' series—*Lady Sophie's Christmas Wish*—received the *RT* Reviewer's Choice award for historical romance, was nominated for a RITA in the Regency category, and was a *New York Times* bestseller. She is hard at work on more stories for the Windham sisters, and has started a trilogy of Scottish Victorian romances, the first of which, *The Bridegroom Wore Plaid,* was a *Publishers Weekly* Best Book of 2012.

Grace lives in rural Maryland and is a practicing attorney. She loves to hear from her readers and can be reached through her website at graceburrowes.com.